THE SACRED CITY

A NOVEL BY

DAMIAN LAWRENCE

PENTELICUS PRESS

Princeton • Athens

<u>The Sacred City</u>
Copyright © 2011 by Damian Lawrence

Pentelicus Press
P.O. Box 682
Princeton, NJ 08542-0682

The Pentelicus Press name and logo are trademarks of Epignosis Publishing in the United States of America. For international rights inquiries, contact: publisher@pentelicuspress.com.

First edition: May 2011
20 19 18 17 16 15 14 13 12 11   1 2 3 4 5
ISBN: 978-0-9831721-1-6

Library of Congress Control Number: 2011926277

To the eternal memory of those who have loved the true freedom of the human soul more than their own lives, wherever and whenever they have lived and died—and been made free. They are indeed citizens of the Sacred City.

Book II

<u>THE SACRED CITY</u>

A man who was completely innocent offered himself as a sacrifice for the good of others, including his enemies, and became the ransom of the world. It was a perfect act.

—MOHANDAS K. GANDHI

Hence we will not say that Greeks fight like heroes, but we will say that heroes fight like Greeks.

—SIR WINSTON CHURCHILL

PROLOGUE

Standing high above the cavernous operations area, where the engineering crews were putting the final touches on the new particle accelerator assembly and the massive magnetic field generators below, Mark Lawson looked out through the thick safety-glass enclosure of the control room and felt a twinge of regret.

It had been nearly seven long years since his arrival, and now after innumerable trials and hardships, it was almost time to go home. The construction teams would be finishing their work in a couple of days, and then would come the first of a series of operational and safety tests before they would finally be able to fire up the accelerator to full power. Assuming all went well, he should be home by Easter.

The Resurrection—how fitting, he thought full of hope, yet not without feeling a vague sense of inchoate melancholy.

It was not that he did not want to go back—far from it. God only knew how much he had been yearning to return to his own life for a very long time. His mind turned immediately to his parents, who would now be in their late seventies. Remembering how he had suddenly disappeared without telling them anything, he experienced that same flutter of anxiety he always felt whenever he thought about what he might find upon his homecoming.

At the same time, after seven years and all he had been through, it was also not so easy to leave. He had made some good friends and grown to care about people here almost as much as he cared for those of his own home. In fact, the two places were not completely dissimilar—both fraught with so many challenges and so much uncertainty; both standing at the very edge of a steep precipice without a full comprehension of the gravity of their respective situations.

The stakes here were incalculably high, and there was so much that remained undone—so much, he worried, that could still go wrong once he was no longer there to help guide them through it all. And yet he must leave. It was absolutely necessary. He had accomplished a great deal, but his presence there had also done more damage already than anyone had anticipated.

As he stood looking through the glass in somber contemplation, he saw the reflection of a familiar figure coming up behind him, and heard a hearty yet mellow voice calling out to him:

"There you are, old man! Things are really taking shape down there—looking quite good, I must say."

Turning around, Lawson warmly greeted his friend of the last six years, and his partner in this daunting challenge they had undertaken, Sir Richard Vanderberg.

"Hello, Richard! Just couldn't keep away, could you?" he smiled. "You're like a bad penny, you know?"

"You don't say!" Sir Richard chuckled. "Mind you, I don't believe there is any such thing as a 'bad' penny. If I thought that way, I'd never have amassed the means to be able to finance this little project of ours."

He was right. If not for the vast personal wealth, the commercial resources and the access to the right people which the sandy-haired and idealistic British entrepreneur had so generously provided, Lawson never would have been able to achieve what he had come here to do—and he knew it.

LAWSON HAD ARRIVED in Egypt in April of the year 2000, alone and with only the basic resources he needed to get through the first few weeks: a respectable sum of money in a variety of major currencies, some forged identity documents, and a list of potential contacts at various governmental agencies and academic institutions. Somewhere among them, it was hoped he would find the backing for what needed to be done.

Of course, he also had with him the most precious piece of cargo of all—the digital archive containing plans and technical specifications for what would become the basis for an entirely new way of life. It was the foundation for a whole new global energy and industrial infrastructure, and it was the only thing that could save the future of civilization as he knew it. Now he just had to get them to listen.

After a few prayerful days at his beloved monastery of St. Catherine's, high on the rocky mountaintop where it was said that the great Moses had once beheld the burning bush, he had set out on his mission, determined to succeed. Istanbul, Rome, Geneva, London, New York, Washington, DC and even Kyoto, Japan—he had tried to contact influential environmental advocates, policymakers and academics in major centers around the world, and had gone through a good portion of his funds flying to various meetings, conferences and appointments. But after more than six frustrating months, he was beginning to despair.

For one thing, he realized that there were just too many entrenched interests. Those environmental advocates, and the activists and academicians who were most receptive to his message, were actually in no position to do much about it from outside of the system. It seemed to him that all they could really accomplish was to try and raise awareness, while tinkering around at the political margins. Indeed, even to him, his was beginning to sound like just another voice in an already large chorus of backup singers, whose refrain was hauntingly familiar yet easily overlooked.

Meanwhile, the so-called 'establishment' politicians and policymakers who perhaps *could* do something to change things were often among the very same people benefitting from the status quo—or at least so inextricably linked to it as to render them almost incapable of making truly transformational decisions. That certain international protocols had been agreed to, and that government agencies had been established in various countries for the purpose of protecting the environment, was, as he now understood it, something of a *façade*.

The protocols and the agencies themselves were real enough, but they had no inherent authority or mandate to actually protect the environment. In reality, all they could do was to regulate according to agreed-upon standards—measures which had never been formulated to be radically transformational in the first place—and attempt to monitor and enforce compliance with them on a case-by-case basis. It was hardly the kind of fundamental change that was needed now.

For another thing, he was in a place where he had absolutely no credentials. He could not substantiate his affiliation with any university or think tank or research institute, and had no published papers or research results to which he could refer. In fact, despite being considered a brilliant and ground-breaking scientist back home, he was not even in possession of a simple high school diploma that would be recognized here. The bitter irony of the situation had been brought home to him all too clearly one overcast and blustery October day in New York, several months into his trip.

He was returning, rather dejected, from a fruitless meeting that he had at long last managed to secure with some mid-level officer at the United Nations Environment Programme, and had caught a yellow cab heading back downtown towards his cheap hotel in Chelsea. It had just begun to rain, and as they sat in traffic near the Midtown Tunnel, the Russian cab driver had struck up a conversation with him.

It turned out that he, too, had been a PhD physicist in his own country; but lacking the right credentials, connections and resources in America, he had ended up driving a taxi for the last six years just to earn his daily bread.

For Lawson, that chance meeting had been a defining moment. Having made agonizingly little progress and rapidly running out of time, money and options, he finally decided that, for the sake of his mission, he was going to have to risk everything and go public. He was going to have to reveal the truth of his origins.

He had been looking through a major New York newspaper one day, preparing to do just that—skimming the articles in search of the name of a reporter whom he thought would be best placed to break the story—when he saw it. It was just a small piece in the paper's regular Tuesday 'Science and Technology' section, but he was immediately riveted.

According to the article, it seemed that the famed British industrialist, sportsman and aviation enthusiast, Sir Richard Vanderberg—who just a year before had founded a company aimed at commercializing space flight—had announced an open international design competition. The objective was to develop a radically new, environmentally friendly propulsion system for his planned experimental low-earth-orbit spacecraft; and the prize money—not to mention the international recognition that would go along with it—was substantial.

Lawson had wasted no time. Within a month, he was back in London and had been invited to meet with the panel of scientists and engineers responsible for evaluating the design submissions. The competition's deadline was not for another several months, but the judges had been so captivated by his advanced design concept and the astounding level of expertise he had demonstrated that they later arranged for him to meet unofficially with Vanderberg himself.

It was not a moment too soon. By that time, he was low on money and realized that this was probably his very last and best chance to accomplish that which had come for—and he did not intend to fail.

That first encounter with Vanderberg had been brief. Sir Richard was due to travel to South Africa in a few days for a board meeting of an economic development foundation he chaired, and had very little time to spare. But what the meeting lacked in its duration, it more than made up for in its intensity.

The two men had an instant personal chemistry and hit it off extremely well from the start. Far from being the egg-headed and self-absorbed scientist that Vanderberg had expected, he found Lawson to be visionary yet focused, and able to break down highly complex ideas into simple terms that were fairly easy for a layperson to understand. Indeed, he was a man after his own heart—passionate about his work, with a clear goal and the drive never to give up until he had attained it.

For his part moreover, Sir Richard was an astute businessman, if nothing else. He immediately saw the wider potential of Lawson's revolutionary design concept across a range of industries and applications, and was determined not to let it slip through his fingers. Within a few days, the physicist had received an invitation for a follow-up meeting over lunch at the wealthy industrialist's country estate. The wheels had been set in motion, and Lawson could finally breathe a sigh of relief. There was yet hope.

Over the subsequent months, the two men met several more times—along with an entourage of the entrepreneur's scientific and engineering experts and ubiquitous businesspeople—to discuss a variety of potential commercial ventures based on Lawson's technology, and their acquaintance gradually blossomed into a genuine friendship.

It was after one of those meetings, late on a clear afternoon in March of 2001, when the others had already left and Vanderberg and Lawson were alone together having a beer on the terrace of the industrialist's plush office tower, watching the sun set over the city of London, when the Englishman had asked him a point-blank question. Why had no one ever developed such technological applications before?

Startled at first, Lawson had finally decided to take his chances and tell Sir Richard the truth. No one had ever developed the technology before because, in the year 2001, it did not yet exist. Lawson had brought it with him from thirty years in the future.

Expecting Vanderberg to think that he was joking—or worse yet, that he was delusional—Lawson was completely unprepared for the other man's response. For instead of laughter or outrage or some other such predictable reaction, he saw something akin to a look of genuine realization wash over his face. Then Sir Richard had looked him straight in the eyes in all seriousness and said:

"I always knew there was something very different about you. Now it's all beginning to make sense."

Thanking God for his good fortune, Lawson had told Vanderberg everything. The real reason for his mission, he disclosed with an intensity bordering on desperation, was to share important breakthroughs in advanced clean-energy technology with the people of this time, so that an ecological cataclysm of unthinkable proportions some twenty-eight years hence could be prevented—or at least diminished in magnitude.

Much to Lawson's relief, Sir Richard had immediately taken the message to heart. Within weeks, he arranged a secretive meeting with a half dozen of the world's wealthiest and most influential men and women—those who, like himself, considered themselves to be not only entrepreneurs, but philanthropists and agents of change. Together with a few highly placed and discreet political figures who shared their trust, this small group—which, for lack of a better name, informally referred to itself as 'The Vanderberg Club', or 'the VC'—set out to formulate a strategy by which to carry out Lawson's vision.

By early that summer, the VC had developed its detailed plan—the Vanderberg Club Future Initiative, as they called it. Its stated aim was to seed and support both the public and private-enterprise development of clean and environmentally friendly energy technologies globally. Its true intention, however, was rather different.

In reality, it was designed to become a powerful behind-the-scenes clearinghouse—a secret multinational regulator of sorts—for clean-energy research and development. Thus the VC would ensure that academic, business and governmental resources were all constantly monitored and diverted as necessary to projects utilizing Lawson's technology, thereby preventing precious time from being wasted. And of course, the opportunity to make money from the industries that would be spawned while helping to save the world was not lost on any of them.

To spearhead the execution of their initiative, the billionaire participants in the unprecedented undertaking created and funded an international philanthropic institution known as the VCFI Foundation. Naturally, the Vanderberg Club members themselves served as the organization's very first board of trustees. Over time, however, as the foundation grew and new people were brought onboard, the old awkward moniker of 'VC' was destined to fall into increasing disuse among all but the original core group of participants. Instead, those at the helm of the secretive organization would eventually come to be known simply as 'the Trustees'.

IN THE SUMMER of 2001, things seemed to have been going as well as could have been expected. The VCFI Foundation was staffing up and offices had already been opened in New York, London, and Singapore. However, Mark Lawson's euphoria over the seeming success of his mission was short-lived. On the eleventh day of September, the unthinkable had happened and the entire world had been changed forever.

The horrific events of that clear and fateful Tuesday—the terrorist attacks on New York's Twin Towers and the Pentagon in Washington, DC, and the destruction of Flight 93 over a field in western Pennsylvania—caused universal shock and unspeakable grief the world over. They were also the beginning of a period of global turmoil and insecurity that would have lasting repercussions. For Lawson, however, in addition to the horror of the events themselves, there was a secondary source of distress.

It was a feeling somewhere between disbelief and despair; for he was cursed with the inescapable knowledge that, in the history of his own time period, those terrible events had never even occurred. Somehow, as an unintentional result of his having opened the gateway to the past, history had already begun to change.

The implications were devastatingly clear. Each and every minute he spent in that time period carried with it the risk that he might unknowingly trigger another change event. It was a risk that had to be mitigated as soon as possible.

Thus, as he worked feverishly to ensure that the primary goal of his mission was accomplished, he tried his best to isolate himself from all but the most essential of human contacts. At the same time, the secondary objective that had always been in the back of his mind took on an even greater sense of urgency. He had to leave as soon as possible; and in order for that to happen, a new dive facility had to be built.

Now five and a half years later, standing in the newly completed control room of the secret installation deep below the surface of the Sinai Desert and talking to his friend and financier partner, Mark Lawson suddenly felt a lump rising in his throat and struggled to maintain his composure.

"Richard, I just want you to know—," he started to say to the older man, his voice cracking slightly before he cleared his throat and continued. "I just want you to know how grateful I am for all you've done...and most of all for your friendship. It's been a difficult seven years for me in ways I can't even begin to describe, and aside from all this," he said, sweeping his arm around the control room, "I don't know if personally I could have handled it without the support of a friend like you."

"Come on now, old man," Vanderberg replied, smiling ruefully and giving him a rough slap on the shoulder. "You're not going to go all '*crackers and cheese*' on us now, are you? There are several more weeks yet before the good-byes. If you become like this now, what are you going to do for an encore?"

The two friends laughed and then immediately turned the conversation to a discussion of some outstanding technical issues. The moment had passed, and it was one that had meant a great deal to both of them. But for now there was still much work ahead of them, and neither man was the type to stand idly by when there was a job to be done.

CHAPTER 1

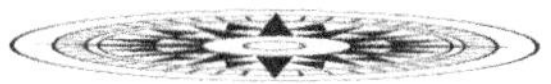

It was the second morning since the squadron of Egyptian cavalrymen had marched their Tsitzinan captives into Ibrahim Pasha's vast army camp in the plain between ancient Sparta and the medieval fortress-town of Mystras, and Paladin Vice Admiral Alexandros Ephraimoglou felt like death warmed over.

He had been tied up—more or less tightly, depending on the hour of the day—for roughly three days, and was experiencing the ill effects of his confinement. His arms and legs were stiff and cramped, and there were painful sores around his wrists from the chafing of the ropes.

He had eaten little, since the small supply of dry provisions he had brought with him—and which had originally been meant to sustain only him after his former colleague, and now captor, Commodore Mina Ghabry's planned infiltration of the Egyptian camp—now had to suffice for both of them. His head had been pounding constantly since the previous day, and he felt weak and feverish.

Even worse than his physical ailments, however, was the onset of a creeping sense of despair. He had tried to fight it off for a couple of days already and had held his ground bravely—even after Ghabry had suddenly and inexplicably destroyed his dive computer and other equipment, in a sure sign that he did not intend for them to go back to their own century. But ever since the previous evening, when he had seen the yellow glow of the flames devouring what remained of the lofty spires of medieval

Mystras in the distance, his spirits had flagged and hope seemed more elusive with each passing hour.

As for Ghabry, from the time of the hasty memorial service the two Paladins had held for the victims of the Tsitzina massacre three days before, he had spoken very little. He seemed to be distracted and irritable one moment, and withdrawn and sullen the next. Even his physical appearance had changed. He had become pale and wan, with a waxy pallor, and often seemed to be sweating profusely, which was unusual for him.

But even if he had been willing to talk, what could he possibly have said? '*I'm sorry, Alex, for betraying you and committing high treason; for ambushing you and tying you up like an animal*'? No, it was unlikely. Besides, they had already discussed everything, and there was nothing left to say. Their already divergent views, which had been a source of disagreement between them over the last years, had all at once become absolutely irreconcilable at the point of a gun.

And so in silence they had wandered about for the last couple of days, almost aimlessly it seemed to the vice admiral—out of the foothills of the Parnonas range and into those of the Taygetos range—making a great loop around the northern part of the plain between Sparta and Mystras. For a time Ephraimoglou wondered if Ghabry, having already accomplished his purpose of disrupting their mission, actually even had a plan.

Perhaps, he thought, his erstwhile friend was trying to make up his mind what to do with him. Or worse yet, he might already have decided and was only trying to work up the nerve to kill him. But then, seeing the concentration with which the Copt kept watch over the Egyptian camp day and night, sleeping very little, he abandoned that notion. Indeed, it seemed increasingly clear that Ghabry was waiting for something—but for what?

Then early that morning, in the bright rays of the rising sun, the rogue Paladin had brusquely awakened the sleeping Ephraimoglou and resolutely set out from their position high up in the hills towards the direction of Ibrahim's army. After covering about half the distance that separated them from the camp, they had settled down again for another vigil—closer this time, on the craggy slopes just a few kilometers to the northwest of their destination.

Ill as he was, the vice admiral spent the next few hours drifting in and out of consciousness, his mind being tossed by turbulent and vaguely remembered dreams. Before he knew it, the morning sun was already high and well on the way toward its meridian. Ghabry's concentration on the Egyptian campsite was now total. He seemed to be looking for something specific, though what it might be, Ephraimoglou could not tell.

At last, some time before noon, he abruptly broke off his surveillance and got up. Roughly tying a gag around the other Paladin's mouth, he only said with an uncharacteristic hoarseness to his voice:

"It's time. Let's go."

Perhaps it was due to the strange preoccupation that distracted him, but as they mounted their animals and Ghabry bent to give the still-bound Ephraimoglou a boost onto the back of his mule, he stooped a little lower than on previous occasions. As coincidence would have it, at that very moment, he suddenly went into a coughing spasm and appeared to lose his balance slightly. It was just for an instant, but it was long enough for the Paladin vice admiral to seize his first and only opportunity.

Acting almost out of reflex, he swung out hard with his right foot and caught a surprised Ghabry on the side of his jaw, knocking him down and drawing a flow of bright red blood from the corner of his mouth. Immediately Ephraimoglou realized the futility of his action. He was in an extremely weakened condition, his hands were tied behind his back and he was gagged. Even if he had managed to escape, where would he have been able to run?

He was kilometers away from the nearest inhabited village, with the entire Egyptian army just a short distance away; and dressed as he was, he would easily have been taken for a Greek Orthodox monk—under constant suspicion by the Ottomans for aiding and abetting the revolutionaries—and would most probably have been summarily executed. Still, that small spontaneous act of defiance did more to shake him out of his malaise and shore up his courage than anything he could have planned.

As Ghabry rose from the ground, his fingers pressed against his bloodied mouth, Ephraimoglou mentally prepared himself for the worst, expecting him to be enraged and retaliate in anger. But instead, the former Paladin simply snorted as if amused, coughed and spat out a mouthful of blood. He then pulled the antique pistol out of its holster on his belt and cocked it, and before cautiously helping Ephraimoglou mount his mule, said to him almost matter-of-factly: "If you try that again, I will be forced to kill you, Alex."

Having worked their way down the steep southward facing slope, the two men began a brisk canter across dry fields of mixed wheat and thistle—evidence of the sad neglect with which the once fertile land was treated during those harrowing wartime years—in the direction of the Egyptian camp. Unable to fathom what his former friend and comrade could be planning, Ephraimoglou murmured through his gag as they rode, looking for some kind of explanation. But Ghabry only replied:

"Just keep quiet and don't do anything foolish, Alex, and you may yet live to see another day."

As they neared the perimeter of the Egyptian camp, Ephraimoglou noticed for the first time the extensive double-ringed structure of earthen bulwarks. The outer line of defense was a long embankment over a meter high, composed of a combination of loose dirt and stones. Apparently this obstacle was not intended to stop potential attackers, but to slow them down enough so as to make them easier targets for Ibrahim's gunners.

Some fifty meters beyond this first barrier, there was a second rampart—higher still, and with a deep trench immediately in front of it—consisting of packed earth and stone, with niches mounted with heavy cannons every several meters. The encampment may have been only a temporary one, but it was clearly meant to be well defended nonetheless.

Under normal circumstances, the sight of the antique network of fortifications would have been of great historical interest to the vice admiral—but his situation was anything but routine. Instead, his mind raced, trying to figure out what was going on and looking for even the smallest opportunity to escape. As bewildered as he already was, however, once the two men reached the entrance gate on the camp's western flank, something happened that confounded him even more.

Disguised as an Ottoman cavalry officer, Ghabry had easily made it through the outer perimeter without incident, leading the bound and gagged Ephraimoglou behind him. Once they arrived at the gated sentry post, however, the story changed. The guards eyed Ghabry and his prisoner suspiciously and demanded to see his orders. It was then that the former Paladin commodore began to act aggressively, feigning impatience and insisting on being let into the camp, replying to the sentries in a loud and excited tone.

"Listen, I'm on urgent business from Reshid Pasha," he lied, referring to the commander of the Ottoman Turkish forces fighting in central Greece almost two hundred kilometers away. "My captain had the orders, but we were attacked by rebels several days ago and he and the rest of the squadron were killed. Only I made it through, *n'shallah*, with this prisoner. You must let us through to see His Excellency, Ibrahim Pasha. It's an emergency I tell you!"

"Nevertheless, I tell you," said one of the guards firmly, "no one gets in or out of the camp without orders. No orders, no entry."

"Look, there's no time for that—it's a matter of life or death!" Ghabry nearly shouted. "A plot has been uncovered against the life of His Excellency! We were sure that this monk had detailed information about it, but we weren't able to get it out of him. That's why we were attacked—so his compatriots could rescue him and prevent us from learning their plans! He must be interrogated by His Excellency!"

The words left Ephraimoglou thunderstruck. Exhausted and weakened, his head pounding and beginning to spin, he struggled to put the strands together and to figure out what it was that Ghabry was trying to accomplish. Then all at once it came to him. He was planning to kill Ibrahim Pasha.

His reaction was immediate. Realizing the incalculable effects such a second-order historical change event could have on the future, he pulled violently against his restraints and desperately tried to shout through the gag: *It's a trap, don't believe him!* But his muffled voice could not be understood, and Ghabry quickly snatched his carbine out of its saddle holster and struck him hard in the gut with its butt end, causing him to double over in pain. The Copt then continued haranguing the sentries threateningly, berating them for their stupidity.

"Fine! Have it your way! But as *Allah* is my witness, if anything should happen to His Excellency, I will make sure it is known as far as *Topkapi*," he shouted, referring to Sultan Mahmud II's palace in Constantinople, "that it could have been prevented except for two imbecilic soldiers who kept one of *Papaflessas's* closest co-conspirators from being interrogated!"

Ghabry immediately fell silent. A satisfied and cunning glint shone in his eyes as he watched the two sentries look at each other uneasily, already knowing that his ploy had worked. The name of Papaflessas—the Greek Orthodox priest turned freedom-fighter—was almost legendary among the Ottoman troops, as much for his passion in stoking the flames of revolution as for his famed physical strength and the gallantry and fearlessness of his recent death in battle. What was more, it was well known that he had been highly respected by Ibrahim Pasha.

In fact, so much had the supreme commander of the Egyptian army revered him that, it was said, he had ordered the deceased hero's body—freshly recovered from the battlefield—to be washed and dressed, and fastened to a tree in a lifelike standing position. After gazing at him for some time in silent contemplation, Ibrahim had then approached Papaflessas's corpse, kissed him on both cheeks in a sign of admiration, and declared: "If the Greeks had just ten more like him, I would never be able to take the Morea!"

On hearing of the supposed association between the captive monk and the fallen war hero of legend, the two sentries reluctantly relented and, calling over a cavalryman, allowed Ghabry and his charge to be escorted through to the camp. The men trotted through a labyrinth of tents, open squares and parade grounds, and after several minutes ended up in front of a large pavilion deep inside the encampment. It was Ibrahim Pasha's headquarters.

Ghabry and the cavalryman dismounted their chargers, and as a couple of young grooms—mere boys in worn-out uniforms that were much too big for them—ran up to take care of the animals, the Copt ordered Ephraimoglou down from his mule. Rather than cooperate, however, the vice admiral once again began to shout through his gag, trying to warn the guards around the pavilion that it was a plot. Immediately, Ghabry pulled out his flintlock pistol and pointed it at Ephraimoglou, dragging him roughly down from his mount.

"Do you want to die now, monk?" he snarled with exaggerated vehemence.

The cavalryman then went over to the soldiers standing guard at the entrance to Ibrahim's outer tent and relayed the information Ghabry had given at the gate. Coming back over to the two Paladins, he said:

"They say you'll have to wait. His Excellency is not seeing anyone right now, and he has quite a number of appointments scheduled."

"Wait?" snapped Ghabry irritably. "Don't they understand the urgency?"

Storming over to the guards, he tried to force his way past them into the pavilion, but the two massive sentries blocked the entrance and threatened to have him thrown into prison. Meanwhile, a number of other soldiers, who appeared to belong to some sort of honor guard, and who had been standing idly by, rushed over to see what the commotion was all about.

Surrounded by six or seven men, Ghabry suddenly looked uncharacteristically weak and tired, and was seized by another strange coughing fit. Deciding that it was not worth the risk of trying to fight through the crowd, he stood down and came back over towards Ephraimoglou. When he arrived, the Egyptian cavalryman spoke to him, nodding towards the Paladin vice admiral and saying:

"The priest here has been causing a ruckus the whole time you were over there. Why don't we have him taken to the detention area, and you and I can have some tea while you're waiting? It'll be good for that nasty cough of yours. Besides, I wouldn't mind hearing about what's going on up north."

Then, before Ghabry had a chance to respond, the man clapped his hands together twice, calling over one of the guards.

"Soldier," he commanded, "we don't want this prisoner causing any problems for His Excellency's visitors. Take him over to the detention area and make sure he is properly secured and kept alive. He is needed for questioning."

Ghabry tried to protest, but the cavalryman, anxious to hear about the progress of the war in Central Greece, would have nothing of it. As the guard seized Ephraimoglou by the upper arm to take him away, the Copt looked at his former friend with something resembling remorse and said:

"Yes, it's probably much better this way, after all. We don't need him here causing problems."

As he was being dragged away, Ephraimoglou turned and looked back at Ghabry with a pained expression. He once again tried to protest through his gag, but the guard roughly yanked him back around and pushed him onward, nearly causing him to stumble.

Ghabry watched him go in silence, embittered that, after a lifetime of friendship, their last good-bye should take place under such circumstances. It pained him to know that Alex would never be able to understand or to forgive him, but it was too late. The time was now at hand, and no matter what the cost, he had to carry through with what he had already made up his mind to do.

He had not intended for it to end this way of course, but the unfortunate decision had been forced upon him. It was the only practical alternative that had been left to him, once he realized that—during his brief rendezvous with Crowe in the forest outside of Tsitzina, while he had supposedly been scouting for a way down the cliff—he had somehow been poisoned and was slowly dying.

Calling over one of the young grooms, the cavalryman sent the boy to fetch some tea from the mess tent. He then started peppering Ghabry with questions about Reshid Pasha's campaign against the town of Messolonghi, and about the quality of life in the Ottoman Turkish Army compared with that in the Egyptian Army. But the Copt answered evasively, waiting impatiently for his opportunity to get inside the command tent.

They had been standing thus for several minutes, talking and sipping tea, when the cavalryman smiled and gestured towards the direction from which they had ridden in a little while before.

"Ah, look, some more of your colleagues have arrived!"

Taken aback, Ghabry turned to look and froze in his tracks. The Egyptian was right. About seventy-five meters away and riding towards Ibrahim Pasha's command tent was a small group of Ottoman officers, a couple of whom wore cavalry uniforms identical to his own. It was a delegation from Reshid Pasha which, at the behest of the *sultan*, had come to entreat Ibrahim Pasha to march with his army up to Messolonghi and help the Turks with their protracted siege of that city.

Commodore Ghabry's heart began to race and a surge of near panic swept over him. Surely these officers would contradict his story and then all would be lost. As he racked his brain, looking for a way out of the seemingly intractable dilemma, his opportunity unexpectedly came.

The honor guard that had gathered earlier at the entrance to Ibrahim Pasha's outer tent moved out to flank the sides of the thoroughfare. They stood there at attention with a fanfare of drums and bugles, presenting the Ottoman colors in an official welcome of the arriving officers. And as they did so, the two sentries at the entrance to the pavilion were left alone and distracted.

Seizing his only chance, Ghabry pulled out his and Ephraimoglou's diving bells, which he had kept stashed inside his uniform, and made a sudden dash for the pavilion, arming the devices as he ran. He crippled one of the sentries with a powerful stomp to the kneecap as he pushed his way through the entrance, and then burst into the tent, surprising several officers who had been waiting inside for their turn to see the *pasha*.

Instantly, the second sentry rushed into the pavilion's antechamber behind him with his musket leveled, ready to fire. As he screamed at the intruder to halt, Ghabry quickly spun around on his heel.

The explosions were almost instantaneous. They ripped through the tent in a powerful blast with a radius of more than thirty meters, disintegrating everything in their path and sending a storm of earth and debris flying at high velocity a further sixty meters beyond that.

An avalanche of dirt and rocks, chunks of burning wood, fragments of bone and twisted pieces of hot metal came showering down for several seconds. When the deadly rain had stopped, there was nothing left except for a still-smoking crater almost two meters deep, in the center of a charred and flattened circle where the command tent of Ibrahim Pasha's fifteen-thousand-strong army of Egyptian regulars had previously stood.

CHAPTER 2

It took well over a second for the thunderous clap of the deadly explosions to reach the column of soldiers marching towards the Evrotas River. When it did, every man abruptly stopped in his tracks and turned around.

A little over one and a half kilometers behind them, in the center of the camp, they could see a large black mushroom-shaped cloud rising to over thirty meters in the air. A shocked murmur ran through the company as the men wondered aloud what had happened. Rumors instantly abounded: the Greeks had attacked; an artillery accident had occurred; all kinds of improbable scenarios were imagined and nervously debated.

John Crowe looked back at the Egyptian camp with a deep sense of suspicion and foreboding. There was nothing he knew of in that era which could have produced such a compact yet powerful explosion, and his mind immediately turned to the firepower of a Paladin diving bell triggered outside of a hot zone—and to Ghabry.

He was already behind schedule and could not afford a further delay, but he could not leave the area without finding out if the incident in the camp had the potential to derail his carefully planned mission. Speaking gruffly to the three lieutenants with him—two of whom thought that the entire expeditionary force should return to the encampment in case of an enemy attack—he prevailed upon them to agree that the company would stay put. Meanwhile, two of the fastest horsemen would ride back to find out what was going on and bring their report.

"Moroccan!" shouted Lieutenant Al-Haweeny, calling for Rashid. "You're with me—come on!" Then slapping his charger hard with his reins, he galloped off in the direction of the camp with the Paladin ensign close behind him.

Within minutes the two riders had reached the eastern edge of the camp and disappeared inside, while the rest of the company waited anxiously to hear the news. After about fifteen minutes they returned, approaching the column at a steady canter. Crowe and the other lieutenants rode out to meet them, and the small group of men stood on the plain, still astride their mounts, talking for several minutes. They soon rode back to the company's formation and the command was given to resume marching.

Still speculating as they marched, those at the back of the column began to demand the soldiers in front of them to inquire up the line for some word about what had happened. Eventually, the news began to spread: there had been an assassination attempt on His Excellency Ibrahim Pasha. Someone had set off a powerful bomb in the headquarters tent and there were several dead and many injured. But Ibrahim Pasha was alive!

He had been with Suleiman Pasha—the French colonel turned Muslim convert—on a surprise inspection of some new artillery pieces in another part of the camp when the explosion occurred, and had not even been near the command pavilion. It seemed that some Greeks had been implicated in the plot and, at that very moment, one of them—reportedly a co-conspirator of Papaflessas—was about to be interrogated. The other assassin, it was said, had even posed as a Turkish cavalryman, but he had been killed in the attempt.

As the men talked animatedly about the affair, the officers became annoyed at the breakdown of discipline in the ranks and began to berate them, stepping up the pace of the march to a jog that cut off all further conversation. Only Crowe stopped riding for a moment to look back towards the camp with his face set in an expression of mordant irritation. He was not one to believe in coincidence, and, with Ghabry out of the picture, the most important part of his plan was now in jeopardy.

Perhaps, he contemplated grimly, it was a good thing he had not acted hastily and given in to his temptation to finish off the young Moroccan the night before, when he had caught him peering into his tent. As much of a nuisance as his presence was sure to be, he might just come in handy after all.

The explosion still ringing in his ears, Lord Admiral Rizopoulos stared for several seconds, stunned, at the holographic overlay image from his dive computer, which floated in front of his field of vision. Not trusting the information that was being beamed wirelessly to the contact lens-like optical interfaces he wore, he yanked the device out of its holster and smacked it a couple of times, as if that would change the reading. Instantly, however, he realized the folly of his action. He could clearly see the signal of his ensign, Rashid—who even at that moment was a couple of kilometers away, outside of the eastern flank of the camp—and he could also make out the faint intermittent ghost signal belonging to the former Paladin, Crowe. There was nothing wrong with the instrument.

Taking a deep breath and shoring himself up, he decided that there was only one thing left to do. He had to steal his way into the camp and check for survivors. He could not leave his men for dead based only on the lack of an EDT signal.

Goading his large bay mule onward, he headed for the camp at a brisk canter, arriving at the outer embankment within a couple of minutes. He slowly walked the mule over the loose dirt and stones, and then trotted the remainder of the way to the western gate. The sentries were on full alert now, and despite the fact that he was invisibly shielded, he would have to be careful, as any number of things could still go wrong.

Due to a phenomenon related to Doppler shift, even an electromagnetically cloaked object created a small visible distortion when it moved—like heat waves rising through the air—and the effect applied to the audible spectrum as well. If the mule brayed or whinnied while they were moving, some muffled sound could still reach the guards' ears and—as nervous as they already were—cause them to react unexpectedly. And if the sentries moved suddenly, the animal might rear up or kick, setting off a chain reaction of uncontrollable events.

Moreover, with the effective range of his SHIELD device set to an area large enough to cover the mule, its signal strength—and therefore its cloaking capacity—was proportionally weaker. Thus he would have to move that much more slowly and quietly to avoid detection.

However that was not even Rizopoulos's primary concern. He knew from long experience that, when confronted with a shielded object in close proximity, sentient beings often had a very keen sixth sense of the invisible presence of another. In other words, they were sometimes able to *feel* the aura of someone shielded nearby, even when they could not see or hear the person, as had happened with the horses in the Egyptian cavalry squadron's camp a few nights before. And in the close quarters of a crowded and panic-stricken army camp on high alert, the last thing he could afford was for one of the guards to take a step towards that invisible presence and make physical contact with him or the mule.

Waiting for what seemed like an eternity for an opportunity to slip through the gate, the lord admiral soon saw a squadron of soldiers arrive at the guard post and relieve the sentries on duty in what appeared to be a rather unexpected and irregular procedure. Nevertheless, it was just the chance he needed. As the gate was closing, he slipped through and guided his animal into the camp as calmly and quietly as possible.

Once inside, he quickly moved off the main thoroughfare onto a smaller pathway, where he could travel with relatively less risk of someone running into him. He also wanted a quieter spot from which to scan for residual energy patterns. The plume of smoke from the explosion had already begun to dissipate and he needed a more precise reading from his dive computer in order to pinpoint the exact location of the event.

Removing the slender device from its holster, his eyes opened wide in amazement at what he saw. There on the screen was the EDT signal of Vice Admiral Ephraimoglou.

For a moment Rizopoulos stared at the marker incredulously, searching for an explanation, and then it came to him. More than likely, the powerful electromagnetic pulse from the diving bells' matter-antimatter explosion had temporarily overloaded the EDT, knocking out its ability to respond to his 'friendly challenge'. It must now have recovered and come back online.

The lord admiral was immediately overjoyed. That tiny signal meant there was hope that Ephraimoglou might yet be alive. At the same time, however, he was gripped with alarm; for if he were indeed still alive, even at that moment he would be in the gravest peril. The timing of the explosion, coincident with the arrival of the Paladins in the camp, would not have been lost on the Egyptians, and even now they might be preparing to execute his second-in-command.

Mentally calling up his holographic overlay, he put his dive computer into tracking mode. Then, moving just as quickly as he dared, he guided the electromagnetically shielded mule through the buzzing encampment's narrow and overcrowded byways, hastening to find his friend and colleague, Paladin Vice Admiral Alexandros Ephraimoglou.

✢ ✢ ✢

Egyptian Army Field Headquarters—Forty-Five Minutes Earlier

It was only eleven thirty, and Ibrahim Pasha had already grown weary of the steady stream of appointments he had to deal with all morning. He had always preferred the excitement of the charge into battle over the dull routine of sitting behind a desk, listening to reports and issuing orders from early morning until late at night. But he was the supreme commander of an army of over fifteen thousand infantry and six thousand cavalry; and much to his frustration it often seemed that he could not trust even the slightest move to be made properly without his personal supervision. He was therefore becoming irritated and was longing for a respite, when one of his top military advisers, Suleiman Pasha, quite suddenly barged into his inner tent between two appointments, unannounced.

If anyone else had dared interrupt him thus, he would have had the man flogged mercilessly in front of all the troops, no matter what his rank. But he had a special fondness for the convert colonel. Indeed, it was he who had helped him enormously in modernizing his country's military forces along the French model—thereby advancing the political agenda of his adoptive father, Mohammed Ali, the *Wali* of All Egypt, and helping to solidify his own position within the competitive Ottoman military hierarchy.

"Your Excellency," the Frenchman—a seasoned veteran of the Napoleonic wars, whose real name was Joseph Sève—exclaimed in his native tongue, "I *'ave* wonderful news!"

Pushing back from his desk inundated with piles of reports and maps, Ibrahim Pasha folded his arms across his expansive chest and replied with a slightly sarcastic tone: "Well, it's about time that I received good news from some quarter, *Mon Colonel*—what is it?"

"Ah, *zis* is *somesing* I *sink* Your Excellency will really enjoy!" Sève replied with a smile, clapping his hands and rubbing them together like a child in a toy shop. "*Zey 'ave* arrived—*ze* new field-artillery pieces we ordered from France! *Ze* new twelve- and six-pound cannons, ze five-inch mountain *'owitzers, ze* new carriage system—*zey 'ave* all been brought up early *zis* morning!"

"Now that is something to be excited about, indeed!" proclaimed Ibrahim with evident delight. "Have you inspected them yet?"

"I was just on my way to do it, when I *sought* you could also use a break," replied Sève. "You *'ave* been shut up in *'ere* for days, and even in *ze* wartime we must eventually take a break and *'ave* some diversion, or we run *ze* risk of exhausting ourselves—and *zat* cannot *'elp* to bring *ze* victory."

Ibrahim Pasha frowned and thought about it for a moment, looking at the pile of work on his desk and remembering the crowd of officers outside in the tent's antechamber waiting to see him for decisions large and small. He was about to order Sève to go on without him, but then, rubbing his eyes and suddenly feeling fatigued, he realized that a walk through the camp might do him some good after all.

"*Allah* be praised! I do believe you are right, *Mon Colonel.* As a matter of fact, I will go with you. But come—let's leave from the back exit. Not everyone needs to know when I decide to take a break, or for how long."

Motioning for his personal guard—a permanent fixture standing at silent attention wherever the *pasha* went—to follow, Ibrahim Pasha and Suleiman Pasha exited through a secret entrance concealed beneath the folds at the back of the pavilion. The two men walked through the camp chatting amiably about the various new, highly mobile field-artillery pieces and how and where they could be deployed, finally arriving at a parade ground where the equipment was being removed from the packing crates. They inspected the heavy guns carefully, and looked on as the artillery unit attached them to their carriages and prepared to hitch them to the horse train that would pull them for a test run.

As they waited for a demonstration, Ibrahim Pasha wiped his perspiring face with a handkerchief and, shielding his eyes with his hand, looked up at the midday sky. It was already near noon and he realized that he had been away from his desk for almost a half hour. He would watch the artillerymen do one test run of the carriage system around the parade ground, he thought, and then get back to his appointments. The men were just making some final adjustments to the harnesses, when a sudden deafening blast rang out, shaking the ground beneath them.

"*Mon Dieu!* What *wath zat?*" exclaimed Sève, as he and the *pasha* instantly turned in the direction of the noise.

Seeing a thick mushroom-like cloud rising into the air over the camp, Ibrahim immediately went into action.

"A horse!" he commanded the artillerymen. "Unhitch the horses!"

Within seconds the men had unhitched two of the horses and the supreme commander, with Colonel Sève at his side, was racing in the direction of the explosion. Meanwhile, the members of Ibrahim's personal guard ran behind in a vain effort to catch up to their master.

Ibrahim and Sève arrived back at the spot where the *pasha's* pavilion had stood to find a grisly scene of near chaos. A vast blackened ring showed where the blast had scorched the ground and everything around it—tents, men and animals included. Charred and smoking corpses and body parts lay all around, and it was almost impossible to distinguish man from beast in the aftermath of the inferno that had been unleashed.

Outside of the immediate blast radius, dozens of wounded men lay on the ground moaning in agony, while those able to walk limped around in a daze trying to help their fallen comrades, their uniforms torn and their faces and clothing covered in soot. In the meantime, those who had been too far from the center of the blast to be wounded ran around in panic, searching for buckets of water to put out a number of secondary fires that had started and shouting out conflicting orders.

Seeing the delegation of Reshid Pasha's officers, who had been on their way towards the headquarters pavilion when the explosion occurred, Ibrahim rushed over to them. One of their number had been struck by a sharp piece of flying wood and lay on the ground bleeding profusely, as the rest of the group crowded over him and called for medical attention. Pulling one of the men aside, Ibrahim and Sève demanded to know what had happened.

"In the name of *Allah* the All-Merciful," he replied in Turkish, his voice quivering, "no one knows. All I can say is that when we got to the camp's gate, the guards told us that another officer from His Excellency Reshid Pasha's cavalry had arrived shortly before us—although in truth, we knew nothing of another delegation and were surprised.

"Then, just as we were riding towards Your Excellency's pavilion and were still some distance away—just where we are standing now—we saw a man in a uniform like ours attack one of your guards and rush into the tent. The next thing we knew, all heaven and earth were turned upside down. We heard a sharp report and found ourselves on the ground. Praise be to *Allah* that the rest of us were not harmed, but our poor lieutenant here has suffered what I'm afraid is a mortal wound."

Even as the officer spoke, the man lying on the ground in a pool of his own blood began to cough violently, splattering blood all over the other men, and then convulsed in a terrible seizure. The officer tried to turn back to his dying comrade, but Ibrahim seized him by the arm.

"From which gate did you enter?" he demanded. But as the man, distracted by the scene a few steps away, turned his head towards his fellow Turk, Ibrahim grabbed him roughly by the collar and forced him around. "Which gate?" he shouted again.

"The western gate! We came in from the west!" the man nearly whimpered, still in shock.

Letting him go, Ibrahim immediately called over an infantry captain who was in the area and ordered him to gather a guard and go to the west gate. There he was to arrest the guards on duty and replace them with a new watch, and then bring the men to him. Meanwhile, he and Sève quickly began to organize a work detail to put out the secondary fires, clear the area, and set up an emergency shelter for the wounded and a temporary command tent.

Several minutes had passed, when the captain returned with a small group of men surrounding the guards who had let Ghabry and Ephraimoglou into the camp just over half an hour before.

Under heavy threats, they were questioned on the spot and explained what they had seen—a Turkish cavalry officer, speaking Arabic like an Egyptian and holding as a prisoner a Greek monk whom he claimed to be one of Papaflessas's men, going on about a plot on Ibrahim's own life.

The Turkish officer to whom Ibrahim had spoken earlier had by that time regained his composure, and unable to do anything now that his comrade was dead, had come over to stand near the small circle of men. On hearing the arrested guards speak of the Greek, he interjected:

"Excuse me, Your Excellency, but the man we saw dressed as one of our own cavalry officers was alone. We saw no Greeks or monks anywhere in the area."

"You are sure about *zis?*" demanded Sève.

"Yes," replied the Turk, "quite sure. He was standing some distance away from the pavilion, drinking tea with an Egyptian cavalryman, and then he suddenly threw down his cup and ran into the tent when he saw us."

"Captain," Ibrahim commanded the officer who had arrested the guards, "confine these men to their tents. I will decide later what punishment they are to receive. But first I want you to have some men search the camp and find the Greek monk. And for his sake, I hope he has even a fraction of the courage of his comrade Papaflessas. He's going to need it."

CHAPTER 3

When Vice Admiral Alexandros Ephraimoglou heard the sudden explosion, he knew instantly what it was. For him, it was as if the searing heat and the terrible percussion that tore apart everything in their path had been set off inside his very own chest. Despite what had happened over the last several days, he had been close friends with Mina Ghabry for almost two-thirds of his life, and the pain of that moment made everything else pale by comparison.

Indeed, he had known who Mina was when he was at his best, and in many ways Ephraimoglou himself had been made a better person through their friendship. But now he had seen the man he had known as a brother die—first spiritually, and now physically—while at his very worst, lost in a blinding vortex of hatred, and had been unable to do anything to prevent it.

In the condition he was in—weakened, dehydrated, exhausted and feverish—it was almost too much to bear. He found himself half wishing that the Egyptian guards who had taken him to the detention area, where hundreds of prisoners of war bound for a brutal life of slavery were being held, had killed him on the spot or left him to die in the matter-antimatter explosion, rather than leaving him as he was.

Just minutes before, they had dragged him roughly into the makeshift prison—an area of no more than five hundred square meters set apart from the rest of the camp by a number of sharply pointed *chevaux de frise* fencing barriers arranged between several rows of large old olive trees—and had strung him up from a sturdy branch by his now raw and bleeding wrists, like some paschal lamb waiting for the slaughter. He twisted lazily around in a tight circle for a while—his head pounding, feeling nauseated, and with flies buzzing around his face and the sores on his wrists—while the ropes bit into his flesh and made his bones feel like they would break at any moment.

Gradually and almost imperceptibly, however, a gentle and soothing rain had begun to fall upon the parched and cracked field of his heart, and it gave him a strength that he knew was not his own. He could not remember the specific citation, but of one thing he was certain—the familiar words were from the Book of Psalms:

> But Thou, O Lord, deal with me for Thy Name's sake, for
>   Thy mercy is good.
> Deliver me, for I am a poor man and a pauper, and my
>   heart is troubled within me.
> Like a shadow when it declineth, I am taken away; I am
>   shaken off as the locusts.
> My knees are grown weak through fasting, and my flesh,
>   it is changed for want of oil.
> I have become a reproach unto them; they saw me and
>   wagged their heads.
> Help me, O Lord my God, and save me according to Thy
>   mercy.
> Let them know that this is from Thy hand, O Lord, and
>   that Thou hast wrought it.
> They will curse, and Thou wilt bless; but let them that
>   rise up against me be shamed, and Thy servant shall
>   be glad.

As those prayerful words resonated deep in his heart, a peaceful certainty had filled him—a feeling that whatever befell him, he would endure to the end. Little did he imagine at that moment just how his resolve was about to be tested.

Gently rotating as he hung from the thick bough overhead, he had been listening to the soft but persistent crying of some of the women and children, and the occasional moans of the wounded prisoners not far away, when the blast—and the violent shudder that came with it—was felt. The few frightened screams that had immediately erupted with the detonations quickly gave way to an unnerving silence. It seemed as if time itself had stopped in anticipation of what would come next.

At first, the desperate captives had held onto a fleeting hope that the noise was the first salvo of an attack by the Greek partisans, who they briefly imagined would storm the camp and rescue them. But, surrounded as they were by the full strength of Ibrahim Pasha's considerable armed forces, it was a vain wish. In fact, it was worse than vain; because as soon as the prisoners slowly began to realize that no further bombardment was forthcoming, they fell into an even greater state of hopelessness than before.

Even Ephraimoglou, who just moments earlier had felt a tranquil strength filling him, began to waver in the face of a new sense of despair that mercilessly besieged him. For, in addition to the knowledge of the sudden and irrevocable loss of his lifelong friend, he was also faced with another chilling realization: the diving bell that was his only means of returning to his own century was gone.

Surely they will eventually send a search party, Ephraimoglou thought, trying with logical reasoning to fend off the gloomy thoughts that stole into his mind. In the process, however, he unwittingly entered into a silent dialogue with the powers of despondency that assailed him.

Provided that you survive that long, the suggestion infiltrated his mind. *And even if you do survive this predicament,* the thought came out of nowhere, *what if you are sent off into slavery in Egypt or some other godforsaken corner of the Ottoman realm? The Paladins will never find you there.*

He exhaled in a heavy, shuddering sigh. It seemed that it was a debate he was destined to lose. But then, somewhere in the darkening recesses of his mind, a bright and vivifying light began to rise over the horizon. And in its noetic rays, he suddenly caught sight of his hidden spiritual assailant and recognized the true nature of his struggle.

Gathering his *nous* into his heart, he cried out with a defiant inner prayer: *Lord, have mercy!* And once again his soul was filled with sweet comfort from the words which came flooding across the embattled plain of his mind and washed away the dark assault against hope:

> *Let them that slander me be cloaked with confusion, and*
>> *let them be covered with shame as with a mantle.*
> *I will greatly praise the Lord with my mouth, and in the*
>> *midst of many will I praise Him.*
> *For He hath stood at the right hand of the poor man, to*
>> *save my soul from them that persecuted me...*

IT WAS NOT long—no more than twenty minutes after the explosion—before they came looking for him, just as he knew they would. A couple of Egyptian infantrymen walked briskly towards the detention area, and as soon as they saw him—a lone, black-clad figure hanging forlornly from the branch of a massive old plane tree—they said to each other loudly:

"There he is!" and "I'll go and inform the captain!"

While one of the men ran off, the other spoke to the guard and accompanied him inside the enclosure, heading straight for him. In what seemed like a dream to Ephraimoglou—who was by then only semiconscious—one of the two grabbed him around the waist and supported his weight, as the other cut him down from the tree.

"Now you'll see what the Egyptian army is all about, monk!" the man who had held him up by his waist gloated into Ephraimoglou's ear with a tone of contempt, imagining that he who was about to suffer cruelly was one of those who had aided and abetted the revolt, and who had now conspired against the life of the *pasha*.

Dragging him closer to the base of the tree, they turned him around facing the trunk and one of the soldiers bound him there around his legs and waist. Meanwhile, pulling his arms around the girth of the tree as far as they would go, the other man completed the circle with a length of the rope they had cut and tied his almost numb hands tightly together. After that, one of the two men cut his clothing open, exposing his back. He remained like that for what seemed a long time, his right cheek pressed hard against the peeling bark of the plane tree, drifting in and out of consciousness and waiting for the inevitable.

Finding his way through the Egyptian army camp in pursuit of Ephraimoglou's EDT signal took Lord Admiral Rizopoulos longer than he had expected. The labyrinthine turns down little paths winding between haphazard rows of tents and small clearings—where the soldiers spent their evenings smoking *hookah* pipes and talking around campfires—led him more than once into areas that were impassable for the mule without too great a risk of detection.

Having to retrace his steps several times cost the Paladin leader valuable minutes, just when time was of the essence. At last, however, he reached his destination—the detention area where, about fifty meters away, Ephraimoglou was being held.

He was tied up against a large old plane tree, with a group of Ibrahim's soldiers standing around him menacingly; and his back was exposed and bleeding from what appeared to be numerous lashes from a bullwhip. Taking in the situation at a glance, Rizopoulos instantly realized that there was no time to lose. For having tired of their game with the whip, the soldiers were preparing to move on to something even more persuasive.

"So you won't talk, eh monk?" the Egyptian captain snarled at the limp Ephraimoglou. "What is your precious religion doing for you now?"

Then he continued: "Listen, I'm giving you one more chance. Say you'll become a Muslim, and tell us what we want to know— where the rebel leaders are hiding and what attacks they're planning—and everything will be fine. His Excellency is prepared to reward you handsomely with anything you want: estates, riches—," and then to the ribald laughter of his men, he concluded with: "Even a harem!"

As the Egyptians continued to harass the vice admiral, Rizopoulos dismounted and tethered the mule to a nearby tree trunk. He knew that as soon as he moved away from the animal it would no longer remain electromagnetically cloaked, but under the circumstances he had little choice. There was something he had to take care of first. In fact, he decided, he would even be able to turn the situation to his advantage.

In addition to the half dozen Egyptians standing around Ephraimoglou, there was a single guard at the detention area's entrance about fifteen meters away. While Rizopoulos was sure he could handle them all, he would have to be careful. The last thing he wanted was to create a disturbance that would raise a general alarm—or worse still, cause one of the soldiers to start shooting and risk that Ephraimoglou or some of the nearby captives might be injured or killed. Since the guard was some distance away from the others and would be the first to notice something amiss, the Lord Admiral decided to take him out of the equation before engaging the rest.

Mentally adjusting the range of his SHIELD's electromagnetic field into a tight circle around himself, Rizopoulos abruptly tugged hard on the mule's bridle, causing the animal to bray. The guard, who had been watching his fellow soldiers in amusement as they tormented Ephraimoglou, suddenly turned in his direction to see what the commotion was. Observing a mule hitched there, where no animal had been before, he took the bait and began walking over, full of curiosity.

As the man approached, the lord admiral heard the Egyptian captain who was tormenting Ephraimoglou bark out an ominous command to one of his men:

"It looks like he doesn't want to cooperate, boys. Let's see if we can't convince him otherwise. Safir, bring the torch!"

The detention area's guard was about eight meters away—still too close to the others for Rizopoulos to launch his attack without giving up the element of surprise. As the man slowly walked over, the Paladin lord admiral noticed another soldier—the one called Safir—who had been squatting down and stoking up a small campfire a few meters away from the tree where Ephraimoglou was being tortured. Hearing the captain's order, he had quickly stood up and was walking over to the others carrying a flaming wooden brand.

The lord admiral's heart raced in sudden apprehension. One of the soldiers cut loose the ropes that had secured his second-in-command's arms around the tree trunk, and as two of the men held the semiconscious Paladin fast, the soldier grabbed his right arm and stretched it out. Then, on the officer's command, Safir held the fiery torch directly under Vice Admiral Ephraimoglou's outstretched right hand.

The scream was terrible. Instantly, the approaching guard turned to look back in Ephraimoglou's direction and, without hesitating, Rizopoulos seized his opportunity. Bounding silently as a cat across the distance that separated him from the guard, he quickly rendered him unconscious with a powerful blow to the base of his skull. Then, his blood running cold at the sound of Ephraimoglou's continued screams, he stepped on the crumpled form of the fallen guard and, using his body as a springboard, leaped over the spiked wooden barrier and headed as fast as he could towards the vice admiral.

By the time Rizopoulos reached Ephraimoglou, he could already see that his fellow Paladin's hand was roasted beyond saving—but there was no time to consider that. Still invisibly shielded and leaping to the attack, he immediately disabled Safir with a sharp strike to the windpipe, causing him to drop the torch and suddenly fall to his knees.

It seemed to the other Egyptians that their comrade was clutching at his throat for no apparent reason, and as they stared at him in confusion and watched him beginning to turn red, Rizopoulos disabled them one by one in rapid succession. He then enveloped the vice admiral within the field of his electromagnetic SHIELD and quickly cut off a piece of Ephraimoglou's cassock, wrapping it gently around his charred hand to provide whatever protection he could. All the while he spoke reassuringly to his comrade, who had obviously gone into shock.

"Alex, it's me, Leonidas—it's okay, you're going to be all right. I'm taking you home," he spoke breathlessly as he worked.

"Mina, is that you?" murmured Ephraimoglou absently, his eyes glazed over and his face waxen. "Mina, I thought...you were dead. I thought I...was going to die, too."

"It's all right," Rizopoulos reassured him, as he cut the ropes that had secured Ephraimoglou to the tree. "Nobody else is going to die."

Then, struggling to hold him up, he dragged his burned and bleeding comrade staggering out of the detention area.

The two men finally arrived at the place where Rizopoulos had left the mule tethered, and hoisting Ephraimoglou up across its back with some difficulty, he untied it and tried to saddle up behind the injured Paladin. The animal, however, brayed and backed away uncooperatively, resisting the heavy load. In the end, with his SHIELD already pushed to its limit, he decided to walk alongside the beast, rather than risk making so much noise.

Thus leading the bay mule on foot, he slowly and cautiously retraced the path he had taken a short time before, towards the western gate of the camp. As they walked, he held tightly onto his friend and comrade, Vice Admiral Ephraimoglou, while the latter moaned softly in his shock and agony, and quietly muttered half-intelligible words about 'confusion' and 'shame' and being 'covered with a mantle'.

There was something about his words—as much as he could make out through Ephraimoglou's feverish murmuring, at any rate—that was familiar to Lord Rizopoulos; but at the moment he had far too much to contend with to try and figure out what his second-in-command was saying. There would be time enough for that later on—if he survived.

LACONIA, GREECE—WEDNESDAY, SEPTEMBER 2, 1825

The orange-red disc of the sun was low in the western sky, reflecting a rosy tint on the highest peaks of Mount Taygetos to the southwest, as the company of Egyptian regulars headed for the high rock formation known as Lykovouni—Wolf Mountain.

Having started their expedition in the early afternoon, they had only marched for a little more than five hours, which was much less than their commanders were wont to drive them on a normal occasion. But having borne the brunt of the day's heat and having scrambled over fractured and rocky ground the last couple of hours before sunset, both men and beasts had been tired and in need of rest and refreshment. Thus the officers planned to camp for the night, before setting off again just after daybreak to continue their expedition.

Initially, after the explosion in the camp, the men had been nervous and agitated, and the infantry officers—already somewhat leery of their *fustanella*-clad guide—were hesitant to follow Crowe's direction. They had demanded to wait and march along in the relative safety of the army's main body, which was preparing to quit their field camp near the smoldering remains of Mystras and to begin marching southwards towards the coast. They argued that once the rest of the army began heading west for the town of Kalamata, recaptured by Ibrahim earlier that spring, they could march along the coast eastwards towards their ultimate target.

Crowe, however, had remained adamant. Aside from the risk of being diverted to some other operation if they traveled with the rest of the army, waiting for such a large force to catch up would easily mean losing two days or more. Such a scenario was completely out of the question.

For one thing, it would have caused them to arrive at their final destination with an even less favorable phase of the moon for their planned night operation than they were already bound to have. For another thing, his was a complex mission involving numerous assets, and there was little room for deviation from the plan. He had already been delayed far too many times as it was. Further interruptions simply could not be tolerated.

As the officers had continued to resist, Crowe offered a simple solution: they could leave the men with him and join up with the main body of the army to petition His Excellency the *pasha* directly for a change in orders. It did not take the Egyptians long to consider their alternatives. Ibrahim did not brook insubordination and was known to have put men to death for less. They also did not dare to annoy the supreme commander with such a trivial matter—especially after the day's earlier assassination attempt. Thus they had quickly stifled their complaints and commanded the men to march in accordance with Crowe's directions.

Throughout the course of the afternoon, the Trustee operative had led the company on a southeasterly course through the plain between Mystras and the remains of ancient Sparta, bordered immediately on the west by the forbidding mountains of the Taygetos range, and several kilometers to the east by the high rocky foothills of the Parnonas range. After about two hours, they had arrived at the western bank of the Evrotas River, roughly ten kilometers to the southeast of their starting point, opposite the old Turkish guard post at Skoúra. From there, the waters flowed southeast through a lush and boulder-strewn valley, winding their way down towards the sea roughly forty kilometers away.

Following along the bank, they had crossed over a ford about a half kilometer north of the junction of the Evrotas with one of its larger tributaries—a swiftly flowing stream that came down the eastern slopes of the Taygetos range from the region of

Potamiá—and by four o'clock had found themselves traversing an area of low rugged heights, with the river to their right, running through a rocky gorge at the upper extremity of Lykovouni. Slowly marching up a narrow path which skirted the Wolf Mountain's eastern shoulder, they stopped there to rest and water their animals at the top of a ridge with a natural spring, not far from the ruins of an old roadside church.

From the spectacular vantage point of the ridge, the wide plain of Élos could be seen spread out before them in slowly descending, rolling hills which stretched down to the marshes and lagoons bordering the Laconic Gulf. Almost directly to their east, several kilometers away on the rise of a high hill, was the town of Geráki, with the ruins of its ancient fortress standing out on the acropolis behind it. And far in the distance to the southeast, even the rugged northwestern shores of the island of Kythira were visible, rising out of the sea in a glint of fiery sunlight at the wane of the day.

Bathed in the warm golden light of the afternoon sun, the entire scene took on a pleasant atmosphere of bucolic serenity—oddly out of place with the martial character of the expedition. But as hungry as the men were, and with the supply wagons still far behind, no view of the surrounding area—no matter how breathtaking—could satisfy them.

Spying several villages in the plain below, the soldiers began to murmur about the potential spoils to be found there—the tasty victuals and the tender young women—and made such demands as they could on their officers to allow them to go on a raid. But Crowe refused to allow it. He had a mission to accomplish and did not want to waste time on distractions. Besides, having been granted fewer troops by Ibrahim than he had originally wanted, he could not afford to provoke unnecessary confrontations that could result in casualties.

Instead, after a short rest, he insisted that they descend into the plain below and begin looking for a suitable campsite. Lykovouni's foothills were no place for them to pass the night, as their ample crevices, boulders and outcroppings could easily provide a tactical advantage to roving bands of Greek rebels and leave them vulnerable to a sneak attack. It would be better to bivouac on a hill in the open plain, he maintained, where there were fewer places for guerilla fighters to hide; and the numerous ruins of the formerly Turkish towns the men had seen scattered throughout the hills—devastated by four years of the Greek's war for independence—provided sufficient evidence to convince them of the wisdom of his words.

Thus, tired and jittery, the company of infantrymen and their flanking cavalry made their way down into the hilly and gently sloping plain, and traveled a further three kilometers south. There they made camp in a wide meadow dotted with tall eucalyptus trees, within sight of the hilltop town of Vrontamás to the northeast.

The evening passed uneventfully enough. The supply wagons had eventually caught up, and while the soldiers had at first grumbled over their meager rations and lamented the fact that their officers had not allowed them to go out foraging, little by little they gathered in groups of five or six to talk and pass the time for a couple of hours before getting some much-needed sleep. Smoking, singing folk songs and reminiscing about their villages and loved ones back home, they slowly settled down for the night.

Meanwhile, the cavalrymen, who were encamped near a stand of trees where they could hitch their animals some distance away from the foot soldiers—with whom, as their presumed inferiors, they refused to mingle—had already rubbed down their horses and were chatting amiably amongst themselves. It was then that Rashid saw Lieutenant Al-Haweeny approaching him.

"There you are, Moroccan! How's your cheek?" the officer inquired.

"It's fine, Sir Lieutenant," Rashid replied, casually brushing off the other man's insult from early that morning.

"Good, very good," continued Al-Haweeny, obviously trying to make amends but not deigning to apologize. "You know, I've been watching you, Moroccan. You're not like the other soldiers."

At those words, Rashid froze, fearing that somehow his cover had been exposed.

"You're an excellent horseman, and I can see you have a lot of self-discipline. Has anyone ever told you that you would make very good officer material?"

Lowering his head to conceal his expression of relief, Rashid replied simply: "Sir Lieutenant flatters a poor Berber shepherd."

"Listen," Al-Haweeny insisted, "I know what I'm talking about. I don't want to make any promises, but after this special mission is over, I'm thinking of putting in a request to have you assigned to my regular unit permanently."

Immediately, Rashid saw the opening he had been looking for. Doing his best to appear grateful for the lieutenant's compliment, he thanked him profusely and then asked:

"Forgive my curiosity, Sir Lieutenant," he inquired, "but if it is not too bold of me to ask, what exactly is this special mission that we are on?"

Al-Haweeny frowned for a moment and wrinkled his brow, as if considering whether or not to tell the young cavalryman. Then, drawing closer to him, he began whispering in an air of conspiratorial confidence.

"We're under orders not to say anything, so I can't tell you the details—and even what I'm about to tell you, you must swear it to secrecy. We're going to capture an important fortress on the coast! Believe me, whoever is involved in this mission will not regret it. If we are successful—and I'm sure we will be—there will be plenty of spoils to go around, and plenty of recognition from His Excellency, the *pasha*!"

"But how can a company as small as we are hope to take an entire fortress?" Rashid protested, trying to get the lieutenant to divulge more information.

"Don't worry about that, Moroccan. Our guide, *Kara...kara...karakas*—those bloody Greek names are always so difficult to pronounce! Anyway, he has already taken care of everything. We'll lay waste to the garrison stationed there before they even know we're upon them! And now I've already said too much. Just stay close to me, and we'll see some real adventure soon enough."

Then, as he turned to go, Lieutenant Al-Haweeny made one last comment to the young Moroccan: "By the way," he said, "starting tomorrow, you'll ride up at the head of the column with me."

As Al-Haweeny walked away, Rashid could not help but think that, despite all that morning's harshness and bluster, the lieutenant was probably not a bad sort after all. He found himself wondering what kind of man he might have been under different circumstances, but then his thoughts soon gave way to weightier matters. Brief as it had been, the conversation was his first real break. At least now he had some inkling of what he should be looking for.

He was hardly familiar with the history and geography of nineteenth-century Greece, but from what he did know, there were any number of old fortresses along the extensive coastline from the Mani peninsula all the way to the Argolic Gulf. Several of them might make attractive and strategically significant prizes for Ibrahim's forces. It was only a matter of figuring out which one was their ultimate target, planting his time capsule and getting the Guardians the information they needed in time for them to intercept the attack—that, and getting out alive, of course.

Watching the last of the evening's light fading over the rugged profile of the mountains to the west, the young Paladin thought: *How difficult a thing could that be?*

Yet somehow he already knew that the answer to his question was not the one he was hoping for.

CHAPTER 4

Twilight came quickly that morning. Rashid had barely finished his predawn prayers when he noticed the eastern sky bathed in a pale light that pulled away the night's thick blanket of darkness. Everywhere around him, soldiers were beginning to stir, rising from their rest—some issuing forth from tents, others stretching on the ground where they had slept all night under the canopy of stars.

The small group of men did not take long to complete their morning routine and assemble. Shortly after sunrise they were already on their way, with the young Paladin riding up at the head of the column near the officers, as Lieutenant Al-Haweeny had commanded.

Heading towards the west, the company retraced its steps of the evening before, climbing a low ascent up the eastern shoulder of the Lykovouni to rejoin the road that ran roughly parallel to the Evrotas. At that point, the river—the personification of which had been worshipped as a god by the ancient Spartans—had already disappeared from sight, as it wended its way for more than fifteen kilometers through a narrow gorge deep inside the Wolf Mountain. Issuing forth from the mountain's southeastern boundary, it then converged with the road again some eleven kilometers distant, near the town of Skála at the head of the plain of Élos, and flowed down from there to the sea.

They had regained most of the height leading up to the road when, seeing a momentary gleam—as of the glint of sunlight against steel—on the rocky heights above, Crowe motioned for the company to halt. Pulling out his computer-enhanced, period-looking field glasses, he scanned the face of the mountain opposite them for some time, and then called Al-Haweeny over and spoke to him quietly. Rashid saw the cavalry officer nod to the Trustee, after which he headed directly towards the Moroccan and motioned for him to approach.

"Come on, Moroccan," he said quietly to the young Paladin. "It looks as if we may have some unwanted company. There's a spot a little way back where we can circle around these heights from behind and do some scouting."

The lieutenant had just finished speaking and was beginning to trot his mount back toward the northwest, in the direction from which the company had marched down from Mystras the previous evening, when Rashid suddenly heard the sound of something fly swiftly by his ear. It had made a strange buzzing noise, almost like that of an extremely fast hornet, and he quickly looked down towards his shoulder to see what it was. Not seeing anything there, he turned to follow the lieutenant, only to watch in utter amazement as Al-Haweeny slumped forward in his saddle and then fell limply to the ground.

"Lieutenant!" Rashid cried out, and leaped down from his mount to attend to the fallen man. At the same moment, he heard a series of loud popping sounds coming from the northwest, now clearly discernable as musket shots being fired.

In an instant, the surprised company of enlisted men had broken ranks and soldiers were running for cover down the road towards the south, as Crowe wheeled around on his horse and shouted in Arabic:

"Hold your ground, you cowards! Hold your ground!"

Kneeling down at Al-Haweeny's side, Rashid grasped the fallen lieutenant by his shoulders and lifted him up, but he saw that it was too late. He was already dead, with his eyes still wide open, and a trickle of blood oozing out of a small hole punched above his left temple. He had just laid Al-Haweeny back down and closed the dead man's eyes, when Crowe came riding up to him and barked out:

"You, Moroccan! Saddle up! These fools are running straight into a trap!" he said, motioning to the fleeing soldiers.

Mustering about fifteen of the horsemen who had not taken flight, Crowe ordered three of them to go with Rashid.

"There can't be more than two of them up there firing at us!" he shouted, observing the timing of the shots. "They're driving us straight towards the main body of their band, I'm sure of it! Take these three and circle around behind them and cut them off. I'll take the rest with me and try to salvage whatever I can from this bloody mess!"

With that, he pulled his carbine out of its saddle holster and charged off at full gallop down the slope towards some heights about a kilometer away to the southeast, with a squadron of a dozen cavalrymen following behind and trying to keep up with him.

Rashid took a deep breath and exhaled heavily. He knew that he was not supposed to get involved in any military engagements while on this mission, but under the circumstances there was nothing else he could do without giving himself away. He would at least have to pretend to try and flush out the snipers, while at the same time doing his best not to alter anything in this time period. Immediately he summoned his courage and set out at a brisk canter over the rocky and sloping ground, calling to the three men that Crowe had assigned to him:

"Let's go men—and in the name of *Allah*, let's be careful!"

It took the four men only a couple of minutes to cover the distance of about half a kilometer to a spot where a narrow defile led due west, up a steep slope into the interior heights of the Wolf Mountain. Riding towards the ravine, they had heard the percussion of musket fire, but it seemed to be targeted far from them towards the southeast. Once they entered the narrow gorge, however, the situation changed immediately. The snipers above had apparently picked up on their maneuver and now began to target the four riders to prevent them from ascending the heights and engaging them.

As they picked their way up the slope, musket balls whizzed by them with alarming frequency, seeming to close in on their position with greater accuracy with each shot. They tried their best to use the scattered rock outcroppings and boulders for cover as they moved, but the natural disadvantage of their lower position afforded them little in the way of real protection. They had climbed approximately forty meters in elevation when they heard a shot ring out and one of the three men accompanying Rashid suddenly screamed in pain, falling from his horse.

"Take cover!" Rashid shouted to the other men as he grabbed his carbine and jumped off his mount, quickly reaching the fallen soldier and dragging him behind a large fig tree that was growing out of a tangle of nearby brush.

It was not good. Moaning in pain, the man was bleeding profusely from his chest and was already becoming pale. From the quantity of blood the injured rider was losing, it was clear he would not last long.

Doing his best to comfort the dying man, Rashid shouted over to the other two cavalrymen, crouched behind a nearby boulder:

"Do either of you know this man? What's his name?"

"I know him," called back one of the men. "His name is Rafiq. He comes from a village not far from mine."

"Come here then and stay with him," Rashid ordered. Then as the other man dashed over from behind his boulder and joined him, he told him in a low whisper: "Your friend doesn't have much time—only a few minutes at the most. Do what you can to comfort him."

Leaving the two men behind the relative safety of the fig tree, the young Paladin sprinted for the cover of the boulder, where the third soldier crouched, frightened and trembling.

"Soldier, what's your name?" he asked calmly.

"A-a-amir," replied the terrified young man, who could not have been much older than twenty.

"Listen to me carefully, Amir. It's too dangerous to ride in this terrain. We'll be too exposed. We're going to have to leave the horses here and go the rest of the way on foot. Can you manage it?"

The young man looked up at Rashid with a terrified expression and nodded unconvincingly with a slight, jittery movement of his head.

"Okay then, see that tree over there?" Rashid continued, trying to soothe the obviously distraught soldier with a calm voice. "We'll go on the count of three—one, two, three!"

As he finished counting, Rashid jumped up and ran towards a low but thick-trunked pine tree overhanging the path a little further up the ravine. The other man sprang up as well, but instead of running up the slope with Rashid, he turned and fled, scrambling down the rocky ravine as a series of shots rang out.

Left alone, Rashid was at a momentary loss as to what he should do. Surely the rest of the company must have been far enough away by now that the snipers would not be a danger to them, he thought. Perhaps rather than risking an encounter, he too should turn back and rejoin the rest of the men? But he immediately began to have doubts about the idea.

For one thing, there was a good chance he would not make it very far down the ravine before his pursuers would have him targeted. For another, if he left them alone, the shooters might follow the company and try to ambush them again, and it would be clear to Crowe that he had not done his job. He would then be seen as a coward, or his cover would become suspect. Either way, it would make it even harder for him to discover the true objective of their expedition than it already was.

He was still trying to make up his mind what to do, when the soldier he had left with his dying comrade came running over to join him behind the pine tree, erasing all thoughts of flight from his mind.

"He went quietly," he said, panting as he leaned back against the gnarled trunk. "His last words were for his mother. I will be sad to have to deliver the news to his village when I finally get to leave this accursed country and return to Egypt."

Over the next thirty minutes, the two men gradually worked their way up the remaining thirty meters of the ravine under a steady rain of musket fire. At length they reached the opening of a grassy area about twenty-five to thirty meters in length and just as wide, sloping gently upwards at its eastern end. Several large rock outcroppings were situated at various points around its perimeter, and it was apparently behind one of these—at the highest part of the plateau on the east, from which they could overlook the road some seventy-five meters below—that the snipers had ensconced themselves. For as soon as the two soldiers entered the place, a volley of shots rang out from behind the rocks and they were forced to take cover behind a low mound covered with thick brush.

"We can't stay here!" Rashid whispered to the other soldier, and then quickly surveying the area he pointed out a rock outcropping about fifteen paces away to their left, and another sizeable boulder an equal distance to their right. "It's better if we split up and divide their fire. We'll shoot first and then make a run for it."

Settling on their plan, they readied their carbine muskets and prepared themselves. At the agreed moment, Rashid quickly rose and fired his musket into the air over the rocks where the snipers were concealed, while the Egyptian ran for the cover of the rock outcropping. Once the other man was in position, he in turn gave Rashid a signal and fired at the rebel fighters' location, giving the Moroccan his chance to run to the shelter of the boulder.

Sprinting as quickly as he could, the young Paladin reached his destination within a few seconds, just as a musket ball went skipping dangerously close to him off the surface of the rock behind which he had taken cover. As the two cavalrymen crouched behind their respective defensive barriers and reloaded their weapons, one of the snipers suddenly began speaking to them, calling out casually as if to old acquaintances.

"Come on now, friends!" he shouted. "You know you can't win. We're nice and comfortable here. We've got plenty of food, ammunition, blankets. We can stay here as long as we have to. But what about you? Got anything to eat over there? What about your water? How long is that going to last in this heat? Why don't you just throw out your weapons, and we'll go easy on you. Besides, the rest of your comrades have already run off and left you two behind for dead! I promise, come out now and we won't kill you."

The Egyptian soldier could not understand what the Greek was saying, but as if in defiance of the latter's mocking tone, he suddenly stood up and fired a volley of musket shot, making what would prove to be a fatal mistake; for it was just such an opportunity the snipers had been expecting. As soon as the Egyptian crouched back down to reload, one of the partisans suddenly sprang out from behind the rocks and charged his position, yelling wildly with two pistols at the ready, as the other one fired several musket volleys in rapid succession in Rashid's direction to keep him pinned down.

Too late, the Egyptian realized his mistake and immediately drew his sword, but he was no match for the burly Greek's frenzied attack. Within a few seconds the skirmish was over and the Egyptian lay dead, felled by two musket balls and then gutted by the Greek's *yataghan* sword. The *klepht* then took the dead man's place behind the rock outcropping, clearly intending a two-pronged attack, in concert with his compatriot, which would finish off their last opponent. Rashid was alone and outnumbered two to one.

Crouching behind his boulder, Rashid witnessed the clever coordination and the savage power of the *klephts'* attack on the Egyptian soldier. Instantly he realized that he would never be able to fend off two such attackers if he allowed them the chance to regroup, and his survival instinct immediately kicked in. Without a moment's hesitation—before he even knew what he was doing—he sprang out from behind the boulder and ran at full speed for the rock outcropping where the slain Egyptian lay drenched in his own blood, yelling and firing his carbine in the general direction of the other sniper as he went.

The sniper who had killed the Egyptian was just opening his powder box to reload his pistols when he heard Rashid's shots ring out. Seeing that he would not have time to carry out his purpose, he dropped his ammunition kit, swiftly took up his *yataghan* and began his own countercharge straight at the young Paladin.

Charging each other atop the high plateau like a pair of rival mountain goats about to butt heads, the two men were only a couple of meters apart when the Greek suddenly stretched out his *yataghan* to lunge at his opponent. Rashid reacted instantly, violently swinging his now empty carbine around like a club and painfully knocking the sword out of the *klepht's* hand with a resounding whack. The angular momentum from the swinging motion was too much for the Moroccan to recover from, however. Thrown off balance as he ran forward, he went careening into the sniper, sending them both sprawling onto the ground in a tangled and frenzied scrum.

As the two desperate men rolled on the rocky ground, wrestling for their lives, the Greek sniper chanced upon his discarded *yataghan*. Seizing it with his uninjured hand, he tried to run Rashid through, but the Paladin valiantly held him off. Finally, after a short struggle that seemed to last an eternity, the young Berber managed to twist the *klepht's* arm painfully around behind him and gain control of the situation.

Rising with some difficulty, Rashid was forcing the Greek up by his twisted arm and holding the captured sword close between the man's shoulder blades, when the other sniper emerged from behind the rocks. Evidently he had realized what was happening as the two men wrestled on the ground and, having reloaded his musket, had intended to charge into the melee to help his compatriot.

Upon seeing him, Rashid was stunned. The sniper was hardly more than a child—a young boy about the age of fifteen or sixteen. With a courage belying his youth, the boy now stood out in the open in the middle of the grassy plateau and leveled the musket, carefully aiming it in the direction of the two men in a daring stand-off.

"Let him go!" he shouted out.

"I don't want...I hurt nobody," Rashid called back in broken Greek, nervously trying to make himself understood. "Leave the...weapon...down and nothing...nobody...will hurt!"

But instead of backing down, the young man took a couple of steps forward. Holding the musket steadily, he began to speak to the other *klepht* so quickly in their local dialect that the young Moroccan could not pick up a single word he said.

"Papa, you remember that other time?" he said cryptically, slowly inching forward. As he did so, Rashid tightened his grip on the older man and forced his arm up painfully higher towards his shoulders, pressing the tip of the *yataghan* against the nape of his neck.

"You are not doing nothing...silly!" shouted an increasingly alarmed Rashid in broken Greek, as the boy kept on slowly creeping forward, coming to within seven or eight meters of the pair.

Suddenly, the young Paladin felt the *klepht* he was holding subtly shift his weight. Before he was able to do anything to prevent it, the man had leaned forward and pivoted, nearly sweeping Rashid off balance and forcing him around with his back fully exposed to the young sniper. At the same time, the older man shouted: "Now!"

Horrified, Rashid instantly realized that he had fallen into a trap from which it was already too late to recover. In what was sure to be his last act, he gritted his teeth and prayed for courage, expecting at any moment to hear the blast of the musket and to feel the hot searing pain of the bullet ripping somewhere through his back. But instead, nothing happened.

A chilling few seconds passed in silence and then Rashid—full of terror, and with his heart still pounding in his dry mouth—came to his senses. Using all the strength that his adrenalin and his pent-up fear gave him, he forced the kneeling Greek back around to face the second partisan. However, both men were caught by complete surprise at what they saw before them.

The *klepht's* young son, who only a moment earlier had been resolutely standing his ground with his deadly musket raised, lay sprawled out face down in the dirt with the weapon discarded in the dry grass several meters away. For a moment both men simply stared in shocked silence, and then the *klepht* suddenly cried out in a loud voice:

"My child! My child!"

Heedless of the *yataghan* at his back, he struggled against Rashid's grip and with one wrenching movement broke free and began running to his fallen son. Bending over him, he cried out again: "My boy!" Then, turning to face Rashid with a look of hateful vengeance, he shouted at him: "What did you do to my child, you Egyptian devil? What kind of black magic did you use?"

Rashid stood wide-eyed and speechless, staring at the scene uncomprehendingly. But then the same thought occurred to both men simultaneously. The loaded musket lay on the ground only a few meters away, equidistant between them.

Looking each other in the eye for an instant as the realization of their inevitable one-on-one struggle dawned on them, Rashid and the Greek broke out in a desperate race for the weapon. Before they had taken more than a couple of steps, however, the most astonishing thing happened.

Right before Rashid's very eyes, the *klepht's* legs flew out from under him and he came crashing limply down on his back, unconscious. The young Paladin had broken his stride and was standing still, staring at the supine Greek fighter in utter amazement, when he saw a faint flicker in the air just above the sniper. Suddenly out of nowhere, Lord Admiral Rizopoulos was standing there before him.

"My lord!" Rashid shouted out, filled with relief and at the same time falling to his knees from sheer exhaustion.

"Are you hurt?" Rizopoulos asked him tersely.

"No, my lord, I don't think so," replied the young ensign, whose sense of relief was beginning to give way to a state of keen embarrassment.

"Your orders were to gather intelligence, Ensign, not to engage in combat," the lord admiral continued reprovingly. Then as Rashid cast his head down in shame and began to apologize, he held up his hand and stopped the young man, saying: "But we Paladins must always be resourceful and think quickly. Under the circumstances, you handled yourself admirably. Just remember that, next time, you may not be so fortunate as to have a shielded comrade in the area to come to your assistance."

"Thank you, my lord," Rashid answered gratefully, reassured by his mentor's encouragement and rising to his feet.

"Now listen to me quickly," Rizopoulos spoke gravely and with a sense of urgency. "I don't have much time. An emergency has arisen. Commodore Ghabry has been killed and Vice Admiral Ephraimoglou has been seriously wounded. I have to get him back to Camp Monemvasia for medical attention or he will die. That means that I will have to leave you alone for the time being."

Looking at him in disbelief and thinking out loud, the young man replied half under his breath: "So that explains the explosion back at the camp."

"Yes, I'm afraid so," Rizopoulos affirmed. "But there is something else. The Trustee operative—do you think he suspects you?"

"I...I don't think so," the ensign replied hesitantly. "He told me that I looked familiar, but I'm sure it's because he saw me on the road when the Egyptians first picked me up."

"Hm," the lord admiral murmured. "I'm not so certain. I know who he is, and he is a very experienced and extremely dangerous agent. His name is John Crowe—and, Rashid, he is a former Paladin."

Rashid was shocked. He had never even considered the notion that a Paladin could turn bad, and the idea shook him to his core. He was still trying to wrap his mind around the concept, when Rizopoulos continued, asking him: "Have you managed to learn anything about the operative's mission yet?"

"Only this, my lord—apparently there is a plan to seize a coastal fortress by surprise. But I have not yet been able to ascertain which fortress it is, or how they intend to capture it with such a small contingent of men. There was an officer who was beginning to take me into his confidence, and I think I might have been able to get him to tell me, but unfortunately he was killed a little while ago by these very snipers that you have just disabled."

Rizopoulos closed his eyes for a moment and took a deep breath with his lips pressed tightly together.

"I see," he replied thoughtfully. "I wish it were not the case, but at this point it seems we have little other choice. You must continue on with your mission. But be on your guard with Crowe at all times and if anything seems the slightest bit out of the ordinary, do not hesitate to get out. The moment you find out what the objective is and plant your time capsule—or if the danger becomes too great before then—you must make your way back to Monemvasia and resurface. And Rashid," he paused weightily, "this time you will have to make the dive on your own."

He then reached under the folds of his cassock and brought out Rashid's crystalline diving bell, handing it to him carefully and saying: "Take this, and keep it well hidden until it's time for you to use it."

Remembering the near disaster of his first attempt at relativistic diving just a few days before, Rashid felt a surge of anxiety creep over him and was silent for a moment. He then looked at the lord admiral intently and said: "I just don't know if I can do it alone, my lord."

"Don't worry, Ensign, I have every confidence that you can," Rizopoulos responded in a calm but firm voice. "It's much easier to resurface than it is to make the initial descent. You don't have to do any navigation on the way back up. All you have to worry about is entering into the light—the rest happens practically of its own accord. You just ride the wave to the end and you will find yourself coming up at the initial dive date, plus whatever incremental amount of time has elapsed while you've been here at this depth."

Listening to Rizopoulos, Rashid nodded affirmatively and tried to push aside his fears. It sounded simple enough, but he knew that the part about entering into the light was not as easy for a novice as it might seem to an experienced diver such as the lord admiral. Nevertheless, he replied solemnly: "I understand, my lord. I will do my best."

"I know you will," smiled Rizopoulos reassuringly. "And now I must go. I have left Vice Admiral Ephraimoglou for far too long already. By the way, I don't suppose you're going to need all those horses you have back there on the trail." Then motioning towards the slain Egyptian several meters away, he quipped: "You don't think he'll mind if I borrow his, do you?"

With that, the lord admiral reactivated his SHIELD and disappeared as abruptly as he had first appeared.

After he had gone, Rashid carefully stowed his diving bell and tied up the two unconscious snipers with their weapons sashes and the cords of their scabbards. Eventually they would work themselves free, he knew, but it would take a while. By that time he would be far away from the area. He then began gathering the weapons that belonged to them: two exquisitely decorated muskets, assorted pistols, several boxes of powder and musket balls, and two *yataghan* swords.

When he was done, he descended the rocky path in the direction from which he had come, secured the weapons and ammunition in his saddle bags and mounted his charger. Leading the remaining two horses behind him, he began riding back down to the plain to rejoin the Trustee operative and the rest of the company. Somehow, though, he felt that things were very different than they had been before.

Previously, although he had essentially been operating independently, he had been aware that Lord Admiral Rizopoulos was always somewhere nearby watching over him. In a way, his mentor had represented the only point of contact—and a sense of continuity—with his own time and his real life. Now, he suddenly felt that he was completely alone. Not only was he a stranger in a foreign land, but he was indeed an alien in an unknown era.

This new experience was unexpectedly frightening, and Rashid felt a hitherto unknown anxiety bubbling up within him. At the same time, however, as he carefully made his way down the ravine and took in the breathtaking scenery all around him, he realized that the feeling was also oddly liberating and even...exhilarating.

CHAPTER 5

By the time Paladin Ensign Rashid Ibn Taleb Al-Noury reached the road and set out to catch up with the rest of the company, a little over an hour had passed since the first shots had rung out. His Egyptian Army–issue field glasses were nowhere near as powerful as anything from his own time, but over the relatively short distance of a few kilometers they would be adequate. He now looked through them to locate the rest of the men and saw that, about a kilometer to the south, a fierce engagement was in its final stages.

It appeared that Crowe had managed to rally the fleeing men and had launched a counteroffensive, closing in from three sides on a body of Greek guerilla fighters. The latter had been waiting in ambush near the top of a high hill on the shoulder of the Lykovouni, overlooking the road where the snipers had planned to herd the Egyptians.

With the advantage of their superior elevation, the Greeks—numbering fewer than a dozen men, as near as Rashid could tell—had held off the much larger force of Egyptians for a long while. Indeed, as the Paladin ensign could see from the scattered corpses littering the hillside, they had even managed to inflict a number of casualties on the so-called *'braimi*. By now, however, the Egyptians were closing in on their position, and it was only a matter of minutes before the battle would be decided.

Preferring not to watch the grisly scene that was unfolding, Rashid lowered his glasses. Instead, he walked the horses slowly down the road, confident that by the time he got there, the fighting would be over. His expectations were not to be disappointed.

Even before he arrived at the base of the hill about fifteen minutes later, loud cheering had erupted from the Egyptians' side. The battle had been won, but at no small cost. At least ten infantrymen and two or three cavalry were dead or severely wounded.

Not long afterwards, he saw Crowe riding his charger down the hillside towards the road with a grim expression set on his pale face. As soon as the Trustee noticed him trotting over and leading two riderless horses, he headed straight for him.

"What happened up there?" he called out to Rashid once he was within earshot. "How many did you lose?"

"Two of our men were killed," replied the Moroccan. "The third ran off. I don't know what happened to him."

"And what of the Greeks?" Crowe continued, riding up close to Rashid.

"There were two, just as you said—a father and his young son," Rashid reported. He then continued to elaborate, choosing his words carefully: "They put up a brave fight and perhaps might have won. But luckily when the son fell, it took the legs out from under the father and he did not last very long after that. Here are their weapons."

Crowe quickly surveyed the small cache of arms and then remarked wryly: "Well, Moroccan, it seems you're quite the fighter after all. Or perhaps you have a very active *guardian angel*?"

"*N'shallah*—according to *Allah's* will," was all Rashid answered impassively.

"In any case," the Trustee continued, "with Al-Haweeny dead, we'll need a new leader for the cavalry squadron, and it looks like you're the best of the lot, so you're it. The last thing I wanted was further delays, but I don't suppose after the battle the men have just been through that we can deprive them of their right to a little pillage, or it will be even harder to keep some kind of discipline in the ranks.

"But we need to impose some limits or we'll never complete our mission. See to it that the horsemen stay within a radius of five kilometers. There are three or four towns in the area that they can have their sport with. I'll inform the infantry lieutenants. I want to move out in no more than three hours."

Then, nodding back up the hill from which he had just descended, he remarked before riding off: "This is turning into a sorry spectacle. The Greeks from several of the villages around here have barricaded themselves up in an old monastery in the gorge up there, and some of those damned-fool Egyptians have taken it into their heads to waste our time trying to break in. They're convinced there is treasure in there."

It was not much later that a large cohort from the main body of Ibrahim's army, having been on raids in the area, caught up with the small company a little south of Vrontamás. Finding out about the attempted ambush, they took their revenge by laying waste to everything in sight, burning as many towns and villages as they entered.

At length, some of the officers learned of the action going on at the ancient monastery built into the rock face of the gorge overlooking the Evrotas River. It was supposedly dedicated to the Virgin Mary and to a fourth-century martyr—one Nikitas, a Goth who had been burned alive for the sake of his Christian faith.

Bringing in reinforcements, they too joined in the siege. Try as they might, however, they were unsuccessful in breaking through the stronghold's defenses, so they eventually decided to lay out explosive charges on the crest of the hill in which the monastery was located.

Blasting through the top, they then proceeded to fire their muskets into the opening. When they had had enough of that, they threw down barrels of gunpowder, smashing them open on impact, and tossed a flaming brand onto the exposed contents. By the time the Egyptians were done, nearly five hundred men, women and children from the surrounding area had perished in the flames that engulfed the centuries-old cloister, in macabre imitation of the martyrdom of its patron saint.

It was nearly noon by the time the men had finally been rounded up and were ready to continue on their expedition. The various delays had cost the company half a day's march, and Crowe seemed to have become increasingly irritable. By alternate threats and promises of spoils, he pushed the infantrymen hard to make up some of the lost time; but aware of their growing resentment, he was also careful to avoid provoking them too much, lest they rebel and he be left without a fighting force with which to carry out his purpose.

Heading east once they reached Skála, they covered almost thirty kilometers by the end of the day, with the soldiers grumbling all the way. That night they made camp south of Agios Ioannis, a small hamlet at the easternmost end of the plain of Élos, several kilometers northwest of the ancient town of Moláoi. From that location, the imposing summit of Kaloyerovouni—or Monk Mountain—could be seen not far to the northeast, catching the last rays of the day's setting sun.

As the soldiers began setting up their camp, a certain young cavalryman stared at the mountains with special interest. They were not quite as lofty, yet something in the jagged profile of those peaks, illuminated by the rosy light of the dusk sky, jarred

Rashid Al-Noury's memory and reminded him of the mountains of his youth in Morocco. But there was more to it than that.

Throughout the day, as the number of gulls wheeling raucously overhead proved that they were approaching the seacoast, the young Paladin had become increasingly concerned. He realized that the closer they came to their destination, the less time he had to discover the expedition's target and alert the Guardians.

Before their company had left the larger cohort they had fallen in with at Vrontamás and had begun to advance southward into the plain of Élos, he had caught wind of some of the soldiers talking about a plan to seize the Greek-held defenses at Trinisa. He had become excited at first, thinking that the towers there—situated just a few kilometers up the coast from ancient Gytheion—might be their goal. But once they had broken off from the rest of the troops and had begun marching eastward, he knew that he would have to keep searching.

As they had continued traveling eastward, however, something had tugged persistently at the back of his mind—a growing feeling of familiarity that he could not yet place, but which increased with each passing hour. Now, looking up at the western-facing ridges of the lower Parnonas range from the company's makeshift campsite, it began to dawn on him. These were indeed mountains he recognized. Perhaps he had seen them from a different perspective before, but there was no mistaking it.

Tracing the outline of the rugged peaks with his mind, Rashid closed his eyes and envisioned rotating the pattern they made, as if observing it from the other side. Suddenly everything became clear. They were the very same mountains he had gazed at while meditating when he had first arrived at the Guardian Institute, a few days before the new employees' orientation. He was headed back to his own starting point, almost two hundred and fifty years before that late-August day in the year 2074, when he had left the famed 'Gibraltar of the East'—the Rock of Monemvasia.

Rashid was immediately elated by his realization; but he still had to find a way to confirm that the Rock was their destination. After all, it was possible that they were headed towards some other stronghold, such as the fortress at Neapolis further down the peninsula near Cape Maleas. But how could he obtain the necessary proof without giving away his cover? He was in the midst of contemplating what to do, when Crowe came walking over and addressed him.

"I see that you appreciate the mountains," he observed nonchalantly, as if their presence there was due more to a simple nature walk than to a military expedition.

"Yes," murmured Rashid, gazing at the craggy heights. "They are very beautiful. They remind me a little of home."

Then, sensing an opportunity to test his hypothesis, he ventured to say:

"My country is not far from Gibraltar, and they say there is another Gibraltar of the East on the other side of those mountains. I am looking forward to seeing it. But some of the men are nervous about going there, especially after this morning's ambush."

Crowe glared at him intensely for a moment as if trying to read his thoughts, and then relaxing his stare, said matter-of-factly: "Then we had all better be on our guard, hadn't we?"

Before Rashid had a chance to decide whether or not Crowe's remark was a tacit confirmation of his suspicion or a veiled threat, the Trustee suddenly changed the subject. In a tone that was friendlier than any he had used before, but which somehow rang of insincerity to the young Paladin's ears, he casually asked:

"How is it that a young man from Morocco came to be in His Excellency's army?"

Rashid was momentarily caught off guard; but thinking quickly he said the first thing that came to his mind.

"My father is a merchant and was once quite wealthy. But a series of misfortunes at sea left him unable to pay his creditors. One of them was an Egyptian whose own son was being forced into the military. And so here I am—ransom for my father's debt," he said nervously, unaccustomed as he was to lying.

"Ah, what a shame," exclaimed Crowe sympathetically, pursing his lips and kicking the ground between them absentmindedly. "One hears these sorts of stories all the time."

Then suddenly staring at the young Moroccan with penetrating eyes, he demanded in what felt more like a first strike than a question:

"And what is your father's name? Perhaps I know of him."

Rashid hesitated for a split second, then rattled off the first name that came to mind—that of a distant relative from the coast near Rabat, an old scholar and poet by the name of Tariq Al-Jazuli.

"Mm," replied Crowe, "I see—and what about the Egyptian merchant whose son's place you have taken here? Surely I must know him," he continued, pressing Rashid, as if the two were locked in a silent but fierce mental wrestling match.

Feeling trapped, Rashid's mind raced and his heart began to beat more rapidly, as he struggled to come up with a name. He had just started to squirm uncomfortably, when it suddenly occurred to him that this was exactly what the Trustee was after. He was trying to provoke a reaction in order to gauge whether or not the young Moroccan was lying.

Realizing the danger he was in, he instantly took a deep breath. Using all the experience of his years of prayer and meditation as a shield, he tried to calm his mind and body, and to enter as quickly as possible into a state of complete relaxation. It was at that moment, however, that Crowe did the unexpected.

Reaching out swiftly, he grabbed the young Paladin by the wrist and squeezed it tightly for a second, surreptitiously feeling for his pulse. Rashid was panic-stricken. He had been caught—or so it seemed at first. But then the moment passed and the Trustee let go of his wrist, grasping him instead by the hand in a firm shake as if nothing out of the ordinary had happened.

"That's quite all right," he said as if unconcerned. "Not to worry. One can hardly be expected to remember everything."

Withdrawing his hand as he spoke, the corner of Crowe's mustached lips then turned upward in what was evidently intended to be a friendly expression. Rashid, however, could not help but think that it resembled more of a mocking sneer than a sympathetic grin, and that his cold, dagger-like eyes were far from smiling.

"Besides, how thoughtless of me!" he continued speaking casually. "I just remembered that you've been suffering from amnesia, haven't you then? I'm sure it will all come back to you in good time."

Then, addressing the Moroccan sarcastically by his hastily cobbled-together, fictitious patronymic, he concluded with:

"It's been very informative talking to you, Rashid *ibn Tariq*. I'm sure we'll have occasion to become better acquainted before this expedition is over. Poor Lieutenant Al-Haweeny seemed to have taken a great deal of interest in you before he was so unfortunately cut down. And now, be assured—so have I.

"By the way, before I forget, make sure the cavalrymen get to sleep early tonight. We have a long day's ride and a long night ahead of us tomorrow, and I want them all ready for action."

As he watched Crowe walk away, Rashid breathed a heavy sigh of relief. For a moment he had been certain that the Trustee was on to him, but the man's behavior was so oddly inconsistent and confusing that now he was not completely sure what was going on. Still, there was a strange pressure inside of his chest that made it hard to breathe, and his intuition told him that he was in more danger than ever.

Indeed, there was no doubt in his mind that, if his adversary had wanted to, he could easily have killed him in an instant. For some reason, however, he had let him go instead; and that thought alone gave Rashid sufficient cause to worry that something was not what it appeared to be.

The crescent moon had long since set, and the stars were shining brilliantly in the unfathomable abyss of the clear night sky, when Rashid rose from his pallet.

All around him soldiers were sprawled on blankets, sleeping on the open ground. A dozen or so meters away, he could just make out three officer's tents, one of which was illuminated from within by a dim flickering light—perhaps that of a candle, from the look of it. Silhouetted against the background of the tents, the young Paladin could see a figure moving slowly back and forth in the darkness. It was the sentry, who must have been on guard duty for more than an hour already, judging from the listlessness of his steps. He would have to be careful not to attract the soldier's attention.

After his conversation with Crowe earlier that evening, Rashid knew that he could no longer risk staying with the company. He had been warned by Rizopoulos about how dangerous the former Paladin was, and while he could not be completely sure that the Trustee was on to him, it was clear that he was suspicious at the very least.

Under the circumstances, he had to assume the worst and not take any chances—especially after hearing about what had happened to Commodore Ghabry and Vice Admiral Ephraimoglou. This was not a game to be taken lightly, and he was only a novice after all—woefully unprepared to face off against such an experienced and deadly adversary.

Besides, after having thought about it carefully, he was more convinced than ever that they must be headed for Monemvasia. The way Crowe had reacted to his mention of the Rock, and his remark that they would start out in the morning on a long day's ride, followed by a night of action, was as much of a confirmation as he could hope to get.

Given their present location, it would be impossible for the expeditionary force to reach any other major fortress within that time frame. Therefore, all he had to do now in order to complete his mission was to record the information, find a suitable spot to plant his marker beacon, and then get out while he still had the chance. That, however, would be easier said than done.

Looking around to ensure he was not being observed, Rashid quietly rose and made his way through the maze of sleeping soldiers, careful to avoid being seen by the yawning guard as he headed for a small hillock a short distance away. His first thought had been to unhitch his horse and flee from the camp, leaving his marker beacon somewhere along the way; but that would have been a much riskier move.

If he had been spotted untying his mount in the middle of the night, it would immediately have been clear that he was either a deserter or a spy. At least this way, he reasoned, he would accomplish his primary objective first. Then, if all went well, he would decide how and when to try and make his escape.

Climbing to the crest of the hill in the darkness, he looked around and, satisfied that he was unobserved, descended a little way behind its far slope, out of sight of the sleeping camp. It was far enough away, he thought, that he would not be heard by the others, but close enough that he would still be able to explain his movements if caught. Facing the southeast, roughly in the direction of the Muslim holy city of Mecca, he got down on his knees. But rather than beginning to recite his usual predawn prayers, he had something else in mind.

Drawing the dagger out of his belt, he bent over as if praying. Then, holding the instrument close, he touched the hidden controls on its handle as he had been instructed and began to talk quietly. After a minute, he straightened up, looked around again, and then began working the blade into the hard ground little by little, rocking it back and forth until it was embedded up to the hilt. He then grabbed the handle tightly, holding it exactly as he had been shown, and gave a sharp twist.

Instantly he heard a dull report, as of gas being expelled under extremely high pressure, and the dagger recoiled sharply. Afraid that someone might have heard the sound, which at that moment seemed much louder than it actually was, he quickly pulled the blade out of the soil, wiped it off and placed it back into its sheath. He then resumed his prayerful posture, feeling a wave of relief wash over him. His job was done.

Having remained on his knees, prostrating himself and praying earnestly for several minutes, Rashid gradually became aware of a disquieting premonition. It was as if he were being overshadowed by some kind of oppressive presence. Calling to mind his unnerving conversation with the Trustee operative earlier, he decided then and there what he had to do.

He was just getting up to go back to the camp, intending to try and saddle up his horse and disappear under the cover of darkness, when he was startled to see that he was not alone. Standing less than ten meters away and staring at him silently and menacingly was a tall figure wrapped in a black cloak. Obscured in the darkness and covered by a hood, the face was not discernable; but Rashid immediately knew who it was. It could be none other than the self-styled *Ioannis Karakorakas*—John Crowe.

Without a word, he faced his adversary, his heart beginning to race and the adrenalin coursing through his tense frame. At the same time, the hooded figure ominously took a silent step forward. As if in reply, Rashid took a matching step backwards, looking around nervously for an escape route and putting his hand on the pistol at his waist.

He tried to speak, imagining that the sound of his voice might break the intense and hostile focus with which Crowe now regarded him, but suddenly he felt as if a hand were gripped tightly around his throat and no words would come out. Instead he began to feel light-headed and dizzy, disoriented and more anxious than ever, as if some dark and hidden force were pressing upon him and trying to penetrate into his soul.

The more anxious he became, the more intently Crowe seemed to focus his unseen gaze—like a beast of prey smelling the fear of its quarry—until without warning he started to take several rapid steps in Rashid's direction. Seeing the agility of the Trustee's movements, the young Paladin immediately understood that there was no point in trying to get away. His only choice was to make his stand and defend himself as best he could. Novice or not, he was not yet ready to die and he would fight back with everything he had, win or lose. Losing, however, was not an option he favored.

Locked into an intense unseen stare with the approaching cloaked figure and bracing himself for the attack, Rashid was just about to pull his flintlock pistol out of its holster, when suddenly a jarring voice from behind Crowe caught both men off guard and froze them in their tracks.

"Am I interrupting?" called out the youthful voice. "I thought I might find you here, Rashid, and I wanted to come and pray with you—is that all right?"

It was Munir Abbas—the young Egyptian Sufi whom Rashid had befriended a few nights before in the Egyptian camp outside of Mystras.

Instantly the spell was broken and Rashid felt the invisible grip on his throat disappear. Coughing, he blurted out between gasps: "Why of course, Munir—come and pray with me!"

Lowering his hood, Crowe was completely transformed. He no longer appeared threatening, and even looked slightly smaller than he had just a moment before. He then spoke in a delighted tone, which nevertheless sounded forced to Rashid.

"Oh, it's only you Moroccan! I heard noises up here and thought there must be a spy scouting out our position. How fortunate this young man appeared when he did. Who knows what could have happened? Well, I'll leave you to your prayers—but remember, don't be late. We march at first light."

As he turned to go, however, Crowe spoke once again, his voice this time betraying a hint of the animal-like rage that had possessed him a moment before.

"And Moroccan," he said—a guttural, almost growling sound emanating from the depths of his throat—"pray well. You never know what tomorrow will bring."

Once the two young men were alone, Munir Abbas looked at Rashid questioningly and declared: "What a strange fellow! What do you suppose he meant by that?"

"I think," said Rashid somberly, "that we are going to face a difficult battle soon, and there is a good chance that some of us will not survive it."

At those words, both of them remained quiet for a moment, deep in thought. Munir Abbas was the first to break the silence, speaking gently to Rashid:

"So then, my brother, let us pray together and prepare ourselves for whatever it is that *Allah* has ordained for us."

"Indeed, Munir, *n'shallah*, let it be as you have said. You can't imagine how glad I am to see you, and how grateful I am that you came out to pray with me."

CHAPTER 6

In the dim light of the early morning hours, the Dive Control Center at Camp Monemvasia was quiet and nearly empty. Except for the two mid-level dive engineers quietly working at their stations, the only sign of activity was the occasional blinking of lights on various instrument panels or the subtly shifting, soft white light of a computer screen being scrolled.

"I'm going to make some tea," one of the men remarked, pushing back his chair and getting up from his workstation. "You want some?"

His colleague had not yet managed to answer when an alarm signal went off and the room's lights automatically brightened, as instrument panels sprang to life all around.

"Looks like tea's *gonna* have to wait," the other engineer exclaimed. "We've got incoming!"

While the two Paladins monitored the readings on their control panels, the lights in one of the receiving chambers at the far end of the room began to glow brightly in preparation for the diver's arrival, and its protective shield darkened in an almost instantaneous photochemical reaction.

Suddenly there was a blinding flash of white light within the chamber, causing the two Paladin engineers to turn away for an instant, followed a split second later by a sharp cracking sound. They turned back just in time to see the black-robed figure of the Paladin who had materialized in the chamber fall down limply in a heap on the floor.

Immediately the two men ran and bent over the fallen diver, whose cassock was ripped wide open at the back exposing a series of terrible-looking slash marks. Turning him slightly to see his face, the Paladins looked at each other aghast. It was Vice Admiral Alexandros Ephraimoglou.

"Get the medical team in here fast!" cried the more senior of the two engineers, as he began to check the pale and barely conscious vice admiral for signs of other wounds.

Instantly, the other engineer rose and shouted out: "Dive Control Voice Command on! Medical Emergency! We have an injured diver and need paramedics in here stat!"

He then ran to his work station to make two calls. He was still waiting for the first one to be answered when, fewer than thirty seconds after the medical alert was sounded, the wide double doors between Dive Control and the Medical Center burst open and two Paladin paramedics rushed in, guiding a magnetically levitating crash gurney between them.

"Over here!" called out the dive engineer who was still crouched on the floor next to Ephraimoglou. "He's breathing, but it's shallow and his pulse is rapid."

"What happened?" barked out one of the paramedics, as they ran over. "Is he bleeding?"

"I don't think so," answered the dive engineer nervously. "He just resurfaced and collapsed like this. I don't know how he even managed to make the dive in this condition."

"Okay, clear out and give us some room here," ordered the paramedic, tapping a control on the side of the stretcher and lowering it gently from where it had been levitating about a meter above the floor down to the ground next to the patient.

From the bottom portion of the gurney, which contained an array of storage compartments and instruments serving as an emergency crash cart, he grabbed a handheld CT scanner out of its holder and passed it slowly over Ephraimoglou's head, neck and back.

"No sign of trauma to the brain or spinal column," he reported to his colleague. "No visual indication of significant external bleeding."

"What happened to his hand here?" the second paramedic demanded of the engineer, noticing that Ephraimoglou's right hand, which had been obscured underneath him, was wrapped up and tied off with a swatch of uneven black cloth that seemed to have been cut from his cassock. "And look at the other wrist. Severe dermal abrasion—possibly rope burns—and there's definitely major sepsis."

"Oh, my God! I didn't see that before," exclaimed the dive engineer, standing well back and recoiling at the sight.

Taking a pair of sterile surgical scissors from a supply drawer below the cart, the technician cut open the wrapping around Ephraimoglou's right hand and slowly began to peel away the cloth; but as he did, he saw large chunks of charred flesh adhering to the material and coming off the remnants of the hand.

Wincing, the paramedic quickly returned the wrapping to its place and secured it with a spray-on medical adhesive. It was obvious just from looking at it that the hand was in awful condition; but the fact that the semiconscious Paladin did not seem to register any pain from the medic's handling of it was an even worse indicator.

"That's really bad," he pronounced glumly. "Definitely third-degree, possibly fourth-degree burns. There's massive charring and necrosis, possible infection. There's no way this hand is going to make it."

"All right, let's get him up on the cart," commanded the first paramedic.

Together the two Paladin emergency workers carefully lifted the vice admiral onto the gurney, whose illuminated side panels almost immediately displayed his elevated body temperature and heart rate. Once he was situated on the cart, the first paramedic locked down a set of padded restraints over the patient's ankles and forearms, while the second man prepared a cannula to be inserted for an intravenous drip.

"Use the cubital," commented the first paramedic gravely, referring to the median cubital vein in the hollow of his elbow. "I'm worried about the other hand too, and that way at least the IV won't have to be relocated if he has to lose both."

"You read my mind," replied the other EMT as he cut open the sleeve of Ephraimoglou's cassock with the surgical scissors and inserted the catheter. He then drew some blood for diagnostic testing, fitted the cannula's hub with a saline drip line, and after a few seconds reported: "Ready here."

"Okay, let's go," responded the first paramedic, and immediately he hit a button causing the stretcher to rise, magnetically levitating smoothly into the air about a meter above the floor.

Without a word to the dive engineers, the two men hurried for the exit, guiding the crash gurney which transported the vice admiral noiselessly above the floor between them, and disappearing through the double doors into the Medical Center. As soon as they had gone, the Paladin who had been speaking on the videophone walked over to join his colleague.

"I've alerted the Dive Master and Rear Admiral Petrovich. They should be here shortly," he reported.

"I hope they've both got strong stomachs," the other engineer exhaled deeply. "This isn't good at all."

✧ ✧ ✧

Georges Pelegris cursed as he stubbed his toe against a chair leg, groggily making his way out of his bedroom in the darkness. He had no idea how long the insistent ringing of the telephone on his desk console had been going on, but it had finally roused him from a deep sleep and beckoned him to his screen. Fumbling for his glasses in the pocket of his bathrobe, he put them on and glanced at the clock. *3:17AM.*

This had better be important, he thought, as he touched the screen controls to accept the video call. Immediately the image of one of the senior Paladin officers appeared before him.

"Director Pelegris, I regret the intrusion at this hour," the Paladin spoke in his lightly Russian-accented English. "However, protocol requires you to be informed..."

"Yes, what is it Rear Admiral Petrovich?" Pelegris interjected somewhat testily.

"Protocol requires me to inform you," he continued heedlessly, "of an emergency situation with regard to the current mission. One of the dive team members has resurfaced a short time ago. It is Vice Admiral Ephraimoglou."

Before Petrovich could continue, Pelegris again interrupted: "Yes, and does he have anything significant to report?"

"Unfortunately, Director, the Vice Admiral is in no shape to report anything. He is in critical medical condition. Our physicians are working on him now even as we speak, but it is too early for a prognosis. We should know more in a few hours."

Pelegris sat back in his chair and exhaled deeply. This was disturbing news.

"I see, Rear Admiral," said Pelegris, seemingly concerned. "What happened to him?"

"We do not have any details yet, but it appears he may have been tortured," Petrovich proclaimed gravely.

"Tortured? By whom?" Pelegris fired back, alarmed and sitting bolt upright in his chair.

"We do not have any information yet, Director Pelegris. And at this point, no one can tell us except for the Vice Admiral—if he makes it, that is."

"Of course, of course," replied Pelegris. "Let's hope for the best. And what about the other diver, Commodore Ghabry? Is there any word about him?"

"No, nothing yet. We are prepping a rescue team just in case, but for now they will remain on standby," replied the Russian. "Hopefully we will have more information by the time of the midday briefing."

"*D'accord*, Rear Admiral," Pelegris said. "I suppose you'll wake me again if there is anything urgent," he continued with an air of gravity. "Otherwise, we'll talk again at the twelve o'clock meeting. Thank you for the call."

Switching off the video call, Pelegris rose yawning from his desk. He would have to inform Station Chief Rigas of what he had learned, but it could wait until first thing in the morning, he thought as he headed back to bed. There was something about Petrovich's call, however, that made him feel uneasy.

Of course the news that Ephraimoglou was in bad shape was not comforting, but it was more than that—something he could not quite put his finger on. It almost seemed as if there was something the Paladin was not telling him. Tired as he was, that troubling thought prevented the director of operations from going back to sleep for a long while.

It was shortly before 12:00PM, and Director Pelegris was sitting at the large circular conference table in the Situation Room on Five-Indigo-One-North, sipping a double espresso and going over some operational issues with his interlocutors on the room's wall screens, when the door slid silently open. Rear Admiral Petrovich entered, flanked by two junior Paladins, one of whom Pelegris immediately recognized as Lord Admiral Rizopoulos's adjutant.

Petrovich's icy blue eyes were bloodshot and tired-looking, as though he had not slept all night, and he strode briskly into the room with a look of grim preoccupation.

"Gentlemen, let's try to make this brief," he commenced speaking without the customary formalities, as the Paladins took their seats at the table.

"As you know, Vice Admiral Ephraimoglou resurfaced early this morning in critical medical condition. Dr. Mariatos is standing by to give us an update. Director Pelegris, would you please do the honors?"

"Of course," said Pelegris, reaching for the nearby remote control and pressing the button to accept the pending holo-call. There was an immediate flicker in the air above one of the chairs, and the holographic image of the Paladin's chief medical officer appeared as though he were seated at the table.

"Doctor," Petrovich addressed the image, "would you kindly fill our colleagues in on the Vice Admiral's condition."

"Certainly. At this moment, the Vice Admiral is in stable, but critical condition. He arrived in the Paladin Medical Center a little after two thirty this morning in shock and severely dehydrated, with life-threatening burn trauma to his right hand below the wrist, as well as a number of other severe but non-life-threatening wounds. Unfortunately, the hand could not be saved and we were forced to remove it surgically. We're now treating him for septic shock. On the positive side, we were able to get to him in time. Another ten to twelve hours and things would have been much, much worse."

Pausing for a moment and rubbing his eyes, Dr. Mariatos, who had worked straight through the night, appeared to exhale heavily and then continued speaking:

"Uh, let's see. There is also specific infection of the left hand as a result of severe untreated skin abrasions. At this point we are hopeful that hand can be salvaged, but there is a thirty percent chance it too may have to be amputated. We'll know more in the next forty-eight hours as the antibiotics have a chance to kick in. It also appears that the Vice Admiral has been exposed to some sort of viral infection, although we're not yet sure what it is. I'll have to report back on that when the test results are in."

Mariatos had barely finished speaking when the room erupted in a cacophony of cross-talk, as several of the meeting's participants began firing questions at the doctor.

"Gentlemen, please, one at a time," demanded Petrovich. "Director Pelegris, would you like to start?"

"Thank you, Rear Admiral," Pelegris began. "Doctor Mariatos, I'm sure I speak for all of my colleagues on the Guardian side in saying that we are deeply saddened by Vice Admiral Ephraimoglou's misfortune and we all wish him a speedy recovery. But as Operations Director, my main concern right now has to be the mission. I would therefore like to know, first, if the Vice Admiral was able to say anything about what happened to him; and, second, when will we be in a position to debrief him?"

Mariatos shook his head as he replied: "Director, the Vice Admiral was barely conscious when he arrived at Dive Control. Due to the critical nature of his condition, we have had to sedate him heavily. If all goes well, I anticipate we should be able to bring him out of sedation in the next thirty-six to forty-eight hours—"

As the doctor spoke, the room once again broke out in a commotion, and he raised his voice in an effort to be heard over the noise: "—in the next thirty-six to forty-eight hours, and depending on his condition it might be possible—it might be possible to interview him twelve to twenty-four hours after that!"

"But that's outrageous, Doctor!" exclaimed Station Chief Rigas on the wall screen from which he had been following the briefing by videoconference. "We have a critical mission on the line here and we need intelligence about what's going on. We can't wait another two to three days before we talk to the only eyewitness to what happened—that's totally unacceptable!"

"Chief Rigas," replied Mariatos wearily, "I understand your concern. But my responsibility as the Paladin Chief Medical Officer is to protect the life of my patient. Now if there are any other medical questions, I'll be happy to address them. Otherwise, you'll need to excuse me, as I have work to do."

"Maybe you didn't understand me, Doctor," fumed Rigas over the screen. "We need information and we need it now, and if you're not willing to help us get it, I'll speak to someone who is! Where is Rizopoulos?"

At those words, Rear Admiral Petrovich interrupted with a cool and authoritative tone:

"Chief Rigas, Lord Admiral Rizopoulos is on urgent business and is unavailable. For the time being, I am the ranking Paladin officer to whom you should address any concerns. However I can tell you that until we are assured that the Vice Admiral's life is no longer in danger, I will not be authorizing any interviews without the formal written orders of the Lord Admiral or the Council of Peers."

For a moment, Rigas's image was so still and frozen on the video screen that there appeared to be some sort of technical glitch. But soon his face went from a tanned bronze color to a bright coppery red, although it was not clear whether the change was due to embarrassment or anger. It seemed as though he wanted to say something, but every time he opened his mouth to speak, a dumbfounded look came over him and he stopped abruptly.

After several attempts, he finally erupted:

"What kind of bullshit is this? I'm the bloody Chief of Station here for crying out loud, and I can't even get any information in my own goddamn base!"

The room was quiet for a moment as the station chief silently seethed and the rest of the participants, mortified over Rigas's outburst, avoided each others' glances. Just then, however, the Situation Room's door slid open and a young Paladin entered. As he quietly approached Petrovich and began whispering something into his ear, Intelligence Chief Brandauer took advantage of the momentary distraction to change the subject.

"Doctor Mariatos, I realize you need to get back to your duties, but before you go I would like to ask you one question."

"Go ahead, Chief Brandauer," Mariatos replied somewhat impatiently, eager to check on his patient and then get some much-needed rest.

"There has been some offline discussion around the fact that the Vice Admiral appears to have been tortured," the German inquired. "Is there any kind of time line—anything in his medical condition—that would allow you to pinpoint for us just when this might have occurred?"

"Well, as you can imagine, Chief, our primary concern since the Vice Admiral was brought in last night has been to stabilize his condition, so I can't say we have spent a lot of time on forensic analysis of his wounds. Of course, if that would help your intelligence work, we can certainly have a closer look. But my best guess from the look of the injuries—the degree of scabbing and infection on his left wrist—would be that he was in captivity for several days at least, perhaps even as much as a week. The wounds on his back and the burns appear to be significantly more recent—say, two to three days old."

"That's highly disturbing, Doctor," said Pelegris, frowning in consternation. "What you're saying suggests that he was captured soon after the initial dive. If that's the case, in the absence of any information about Commodore Ghabry's whereabouts, I'm afraid we have to presume that the worst may be possible—that the dive team may have been neutralized from the start and that the mission may already have failed."

A somber wave of silent tension swept across the room, as the implications of Pelegris's words sank in. But hardly a second passed before Rear Admiral Petrovich spoke up.

"No, we should not presume anything of the kind, Director Pelegris," he said in a dispassionate monotone. "In fact, I am quite positive the mission is still on track."

"And how can you be sure of that, Rear Admiral?" demanded Rigas, still smarting from his earlier rebuff.

"Because, gentleman," he continued pointedly, "early this morning, well after Vice Admiral Ephraimoglou resurfaced, we picked up a marker-beacon signal. The signal was very weak, so it took some time to verify and pinpoint its precise location. I have just been told, however, that a time capsule has been recovered from thirty-five kilometers outside of Monemvasia, near the town of Agios Ioannis in the vicinity of Moláoi."

The reverberation the news sent around the room was almost palpable. Immediately there was a murmur of low voices, as the participants began exchanging remarks and asking questions among themselves. It was Pelegris who first responded to Petrovich.

"Excuse me, Rear Admiral," he said with a tone of incredulity, "but could you please explain what you mean? If a marker-beacon signal has been detected and a time capsule recovered, how is it possible for the Paladins to know about it when our Cyber Security team has not informed us of anything of the kind? This is highly unusual."

"Actually, Director Pelegris, it's not," replied Petrovich bluntly. "The signal was sent on a specially encoded Paladin frequency."

Then, on seeing the lack of comprehension on the faces of the other participants, he continued:

"We Paladins have our own special transmission frequencies that are used for highly sensitive internal communications from divers, which are known only to us. Cyber Security did not know about it, Mr. Pelegris, because they were not meant to."

Pelegris became livid. In all the years he had been director of operations, he had often been frustrated by what he saw as the wasteful duplication of resources caused by the Paladins' parallel organization. However this was by far the most egregious example he had ever come across. It had simply never before occurred to him just how impenetrable the wall between the two divisions actually was, or that the Paladins might have capabilities of which the Guardians were not even aware.

Turning to the image of Rigas, who appeared flabbergasted on the wall screen opposite him, he raised his eyebrows and nodded in a knowing look which served to confirm everything they had spoken of several days before. He then replied to Petrovich coolly, with an uncharacteristic tone of barely disguised hostility, as if to remind the Paladin that the two branches were meant to be in collaboration with one another.

"I see. And when do you expect to provide the *rest of the mission team* with information about this highly sensitive communication?"

"That will depend on the specific contents of the time capsule—on a need-to-know basis, of course," Petrovich replied simply. "Now if you will all please excuse me, I am told that our technicians are in the process of decoding the message and my presence is required back in the Paladin Zone."

With that, Petrovich and the other Paladins got up from the table in unison and, without waiting for a reply, walked out of the conference room, their long black robes flowing behind them.

Georges Pelegris sat in stunned silence for a moment, as did the meeting's other participants, until Station Chief Rigas finally spoke over the video link.

"Director Pelegris, could I please see you in my office as soon as possible?"

"I'm on my way," Pelegris responded succinctly.

Without saying a word to the others, he got up to leave the room. The briefing was evidently, and quite abruptly, over.

CHAPTER 7

The late-afternoon sun threw its sparkling rays across the calm waters off the coast of Monemvasia's Lower Town, as Rear Admiral Petrovich and his two Paladin companions approached an antique-looking garden gate. Its long-faded green paint was still visible in the minute cracks and crevices of the wood, and the gate creaked as they pushed it open.

Entering the neatly kept courtyard, they began walking up the stone path towards the old villa. Before they had reached the stairs, however, the front door opened and an elderly white-haired man with a medium-length beard came out and stood on the veranda.

"Come in," he said as if he had been expecting them, and then he turned and went back into the house, leaving the door open behind him.

Once inside, Rear Admiral Petrovich—pale-looking, and with an austere expression on his tired face—bowed, while the two younger Paladins with him bent down on one knee before the Old Man.

"Enough, enough!" he snapped, irritated. "I never liked all that nonsense when I was a Paladin or an active Peer, and I like it even less now that I'm just a retired old pensioner. Get up!"

"By your leave, my lord," replied Petrovich solemnly. "But my lord knows that once a Paladin, always a Paladin."

"Are you so sure about that?" Sir Marcus muttered. "Anyway, whatever. Come, let's sit down. I thought you would have shown up here days ago—what's taken so long?"

Sitting down before a low table decked with a platter of fresh grapes and figs, a silver tray of sweet Turkish delight, glasses of water, small shot glasses of homemade *tsipouro* liqueur, and a large carafe of fresh-squeezed lemonade, the Paladin rear admiral briefed Lord Lawson on the events that had been discussed in Camp Monemvasia's Situation Room a few hours before. As Petrovich related the particulars of Ephraimoglou's condition, Lawson's normally relaxed face took on a worried expression.

The rear admiral then informed him of the time capsule that had been recovered and decoded, and nodded to one of the Paladins with him. The young man promptly reached into the folds of his cassock and set a small, round audio device, about the size of a large coin and with the appearance of polished obsidian, on the table before them.

"Before making his dive, Lord Admiral Rizopoulos instructed me to come straight to your lordship once the time capsule was retrieved," he explained. "Unfortunately, it seems that the capsule was somehow damaged. After a great deal of effort, our communications specialists were able to retrieve the voice recording and decode it. They've done as much as possible to clean it up and enhance it in a short time, but parts of the message are still badly garbled. It may take several more hours before we can decipher all of it, if that is even possible."

"Go ahead, Ensign," he said, nodding once again to the young Paladin, who touched the smooth black surface of the device, on which no controls of any type were apparent. Immediately they heard a low, soft voice speaking in English with a Moroccan accent.

"*September 4th, 1825, early ...rs ...fore dawn. Ensi... Rashid Al-Nou... reporting. With God's help, I have infiltrated the...,*' the voice said, after which several seconds of garbled sounds were heard. '*...pany of soldiers led by the Tr... operat... ...n Cr....*"

The playback broke up again for several seconds, before they could make out the soft voice saying: "*...sure he ... to ...spect me. It ... been diffic... to ...scertai... with ...ty the true purpose of ... ...dition, but there is talk of ... a seaside fortre... by stealth. I cannot be abso... sure of which f.... it is, bu... says we will reach our ...ation by ... ...vening.*"

Then, after another long interval of incomprehensible sounds, they heard the voice anew, this time almost in a whisper: "*can't ...gine how it wi... be possib... ...ture such a strongho... ...ewer than a hundr... men, ...lieve it is most like... ...vasia, repea... Mon...*"

At that point Petrovich motioned to the young Paladin, who touched the gleaming device again and paused the playback.

"It would seem," he said gravely to Lord Lawson, "that our young ensign is convinced the target is none other than our own Monemvasia. But if we have interpreted his message correctly, and the company he is with has fewer than a hundred men, I must also echo the doubt that even he seems to have expressed. How would it be possible to take such a fortress with such a small contingent? Unless—," he hesitated.

"Unless the attack comes from inside," Lawson finished the thought for him. "But how? That's the question. Is there any more to the message?"

"Yes, my lord," replied Petrovich with a tone of foreboding, "unfortunately there is more. The last thirty seconds are impossible to make out, but there is one small portion a little before the end that is audible—and rather troubling."

Nodding to his assistant, the rear admiral signaled for the playback to be resumed. The first few seconds were unintelligible, but then, just before the final garbled portion of the message started, they distinctly heard the chilling words: '...miral Rizop... ...y is dead, and I will have to act on my own now...'

Lawson froze. Then slowly, without betraying any emotion on his face tinged with the fatigue of the advancing years, he said only:

"Let me know if you succeed in cleaning that thing up any further, and let's pray that all our brothers return to us safely. And now, gentlemen, please leave me. I have some things to consider. Rear Admiral Petrovich, do an old man a favor and please stand by for an hour before you make any decisions. I will contact you within that time. Oh, and please advise me immediately if there is any change in Vice Admiral Ephraimoglou's condition."

"Of course, my lord—by your leave," replied Petrovich deferentially.

Watching the departing Paladins as they walked down the cobblestone path, he waited until they were out of sight. Then, grabbing his staff, his gardening bag and a wide-brimmed *petasos* hat from a peg on the coat rack, he stepped out onto the veranda and closed the front door behind him. He knew it was not good for him to go out in the midday heat, but these were exceptional circumstances. Lives depended on it.

As he ambled down the winding cobblestone lane past the church of the Panagia Chrysaphitissa, the only thing that distinguished Sir Marcus Lawson from the tourists—at least those few who were bold enough to venture out into the blistering heat of the summer's midafternoon sun—was the long staff topped by a double-headed golden phoenix which he used as a walking stick. Pulled down low over his brow, his headgear provided some measure of protection from the searing ultraviolet rays; but it also served another purpose. It obscured the Old Man's visage as he went along with lowered head, seeking to avoid being noticed—a hard-to-break habit acquired as a result of half a lifetime of relativistic diving.

Upon reaching the church, he quickly abandoned the walkway and made his way over the dry and unkempt grassy meadow behind it, in the direction of the Lower Town's eastern wall. Walking a short distance into the field, he began to examine the ground carefully, looking for something he suspected might be there. It had been many decades since he had roamed this piece of land and, as uncertain as he already was, the tall grass did not make it any easier to spot what he was looking for.

There ought to be some stones, he thought, looking around to be sure that no one was watching him. *I remember stones.*

After several minutes of searching, his eye was drawn to a rather large oregano bush, which was in roughly the same vicinity as the half-remembered object of his quest. On closer inspection, the plant turned out to be situated on top of a circular mound of earth—a bit too circular to be natural, it seemed.

Stepping up to it, Lawson placed the end of his staff on the ground beneath the bush and began to push it into the rocky soil as far as it would go. After several centimeters, he struck something hard which gave off a muffled metallic sound.

His heart raced. Perhaps he had found it. Perhaps it really was as he remembered it. His doubts beginning to recede, he probed again in another spot, producing the same effect. Something was definitely there.

This time Sir Marcus knelt down on the ground and, hastening to pull a spade out of his gardening bag, he began to work around the perimeter of the circular mound. Digging and brushing away the dirt, he at length found several large stones arranged in a barrier below the dry and rocky topsoil which formed the sides of the mound. Prying a few of them loose, the Old Man at last saw what he had come for.

It really was there after all, just below the layers of packed dirt and stone, and exactly as he remembered it—the grayish-white marble cistern head he and his cousin Dimitrios had found as children, six and a half decades earlier. He had no idea when or how the artifact had been covered up, but he was grateful nonetheless. Its concealment had kept it preserved for all those years without its having been placed under the control of the state archaeological authorities and closed off to the public.

Digging methodically, he cleared the space around the edges of the terribly rusted metal cover, leaving the mound of earth with the sweet-smelling oregano bush intact. Then, looking around one last time and reassuring himself that he was not being observed, he slid the cover to the side, exposing the cool musty darkness of the well shaft.

Lawson was filled with an inexpressible excitement. It was almost the same feeling he had experienced when he first saw the place as a child—a thrilling sense of wide-open possibility and imminent adventure. But this time, he realized as the gravity of the situation suddenly descended upon him, the life-and-death battle waiting below might not be just an imaginary one.

Retrieving a compact *Hydrofuse* flashlight out of his bag, he switched it on and looked down into the dark hole. He could see the iron rungs fixed into the stone wall and the dry floor of the room below, and he remembered clearly that first terrifying moment when—as a daring eight year-old—he had swung his legs over the edge and climbed down. This time was a little different, however. Instead of fear, it was pain that he felt. Wincing at the arthritis in his lower back and knees as he climbed in, he carefully made his descent, pulling the partially disintegrated cover back into place behind him.

He was not far from the bottom, when suddenly one of the rungs—rusted by time—gave way and his leg slipped out from under him, nearly causing him to lose his balance and fall. *That would be a fine predicament*, he thought, as he regained his footing and climbed down the remaining meter and a half to the chamber below.

The space inside the cistern was much stuffier and smaller than he remembered; but then again, he had been a child the last time he was inside. In fact, it was amazing that his vague memories of the place so closely resembled what he now found—a metal rung ladder leading down about five meters to the paved floor of a circular chamber littered with antique debris. Of course, in his child's imagination, the place had been a veritable palace, with all kinds of interesting treasures. Now, however, he saw it as it really was—not much more than a filthy hovel cluttered with stacks of old rotten wooden planks and beams, broken barrels covered with cobwebs, and dusty shelves containing a collection of antique and decaying books.

In the room's center, an old barrel with rusty nails protruding from a couple of wooden planks beside it, which had obviously once served as some kind of table, lay broken on its side—a testament to the fourth or fifth time he and Dimitrios had explored their secret 'pirate's cove'. On that occasion, he now remembered, they had climbed up on the makeshift table and tried to place candles—surreptitiously gathered from church the previous Sunday—into the antique iron candelabra hanging from the ceiling. Rather than lighting up the room, however, they had only succeeded in tipping the barrel over and nearly breaking their own heads in the process.

As he recalled, that had been their last visit to the cistern. The summer had soon come to an end, and he and his parents had gone back to America. Even though his family had moved to

Greece permanently the following year and he had spent several summers back in Monemvasia as he was growing up, for some reason he and Dimitrios had never again talked about, let alone visited, the secret chamber inside the cistern. It was as if the experience were something that had belonged exclusively to that particular and almost mystical moment in time.

Gradually, the reality of the whole adventure had begun to fade in his memory. Or rather, it had been embellished and replaced with all kinds of imaginary details—treasure chests, glittering amulets and magical swords, battles with Saracen pirates and the occasional dragon or two—so that by the time he had reached maturity, he had dismissed the very existence of the place as a childhood fantasy. That was at least until today.

Sweeping the light around, Sir Marcus headed across the room and picked up a book from one of the shelves on the nearby wall, in repetition of an act he had performed almost a lifetime before. Just as on that first occasion so many years ago, the brittle book nearly disintegrated in his hands. At that moment, his memory stirred and brought back a hazy recollection from his childhood—one whose reality he had long questioned, and the very reason for which he had come. It was time to prove or disprove, once and for all, that fleeting fragment of a memory that had stayed with him for so long, and which had always seemed so inconsequential before—but which was now infused with such vital import.

Walking deliberately, Lawson went over to the bookshelves on the south wall of the chamber, opposite the metal rung ladder by which he had descended, and began feeling around for some kind of latch. Despite his almost certain expectation, he was nevertheless startled when, leaning on one of the lower shelves, he heard a soft clicking sound and the entire section gave slightly beneath his weight.

His heart leaping, he quickly pushed against the wall. He expected it to swing inward easily at his touch, just as it had done before, when he and an astonished young Dimitrios had stood there sixty-five years earlier, gaping at their amazing discovery. But instead, the section of shelves moved only the slightest bit—no more than a centimeter or two—and then remained immobile. Something was blocking it.

Pushing the top part of the hidden door as far past its frame as he was able, Sir Marcus managed to peer in through the resulting gap. He could see that a portion of the wall just inside the doorway had collapsed, sending a pile of earth and rocks down behind the entrance. Immediately, he began working the door back and forth, noticing that each time he pushed, it moved a little further inward.

After several minutes of effort, he was eventually able to wedge his body into the opening, which afforded him even greater leverage. With one final, strenuous shove, the door gave way at last, swinging inward and banging hard against the opposite wall. Full of curiosity, he held up the light and stepped inside the low dank tunnel; but as soon as he entered, he was overcome by such an oppressive feeling of anxiety that he could go no further.

Lawson was completely surprised by his own reaction. He had never been particularly claustrophobic—a trait which his cousin Dimitrios had displayed for as long as he could remember. In fact, it was for that reason more than any other that the latter had so adamantly refused to join the organization when Mark had asked him to come and work with him decades before. Instead, he had ended up as a simple history professor in the northern city of Thessaloniki, precisely because he abhorred the Guardians' subterranean lifestyle.

For some reason, however, in this particular place Sir Marcus too was gripped by a sense of suffocation and fear. Taking a step back outside the tunnel's entrance, he wedged a rock against the door, testing it several times to make sure it would hold. He then forced himself to go onward, fighting against the rising tide of panic that welled up within him.

He had taken only a step or two inside, when a vivid childhood memory suddenly came crashing through a long-sealed barrier into his conscious mind. He recalled two terrified children—his cousin Dimitrios and himself—struggling in the dim light of a fading flashlight to find a way out of that fearsome place, which to them had become more like a tomb than an adventure-filled tunnel.

Of course!

He remembered everything now. That was the real reason they had never gone back down into the cistern, and had never talked about it again in subsequent years.

It was on their final visit to the 'pirate's cove' that they had decided—since it would be their last chance before leaving Monemvasia at the end of the summer—to explore the full length of the tunnel, which previously they had dared traverse for only a few meters' distance. But they had forgotten to secure the door.

They had gone a little way in—which at the time had seemed like some enormous distance to them, but which in reality was probably only eight or nine meters—when they heard a sudden slam. Moved by an invisible breeze coming from the open well head above, the door had closed behind them.

Running back in the impenetrable darkness and frightened out of their wits, they had tried in vain to find a way out. As the terrifying minutes passed, they screamed and shouted, banging on the door, but to no avail; deep under the surface of the earth there was no one to hear their cries.

Realizing that the batteries of their only flashlight were dying, they began to search desperately along the walls for some secret lever. It was only then that they saw it, high at the top of the door over one corner—a small latch fitted into a notch in the wall.

Too small to reach it, the boys tried jumping, but that was useless. They then tried lifting each other up, but they were too weak to support each other's weight for long enough to open the latch.

The light from the flashlight, which had been growing dimmer every minute, finally became so weak that they could barely see their own hands. They had all but given up hope, when suddenly Mark had an idea.

Remembering the small penknife he had in his pocket, he took it out and began scratching the hard earthen wall near the door, trying to dig a hole big enough to wedge his foot into. After a few minutes of frantic scraping, with Dimitrios fearfully pleading with him to hurry the whole time, he managed to carve a narrow groove in the wall about a meter above the floor. However the space was too small for his sneakered foot to fit, and by that time the light had gone out almost completely.

Frightened, frustrated and exhausted from his efforts, Mark suddenly began to cry. That was when Dimitrios came to the rescue.

"Take of your shoes, Mark!" he shouted, offering a simple solution which afterwards seemed so obvious, but which had never entered Mark's panicked young mind.

Thus, working together, the two boys extricated themselves from their dire situation. Mark, being the taller of the two, took off his sneaker and, with a boost from his cousin, managed to wedge his toes into the groove in the wall. With part of his weight thus supported, Dimitrios was able to hold him up long enough for him to reach the latch.

Lawson now remembered that never before in his young life had he heard a sound so welcome as that of the metallic click of that latch popping. And the rush of musty air that met them when the door swung open might just as well have been a fragrant breeze from paradise, as far as he and his terrified cousin were concerned. Slamming the secret door of the tunnel behind them and with their hearts still racing, the two boys had beaten a hasty retreat and climbed back up to the surface, covering up the cistern head with stones and earth and never daring to enter it again.

So that's what caused it, mused Sir Marcus, looking at the small pile of rubble at his feet beneath the partially collapsed wall. The groove he had dug with his penknife nearly sixty-five years before must have allowed the earth to shift, and over time a portion of the wall had fallen in and blocked the door.

Taking a deep breath, he began walking down the gently sloping path, bracing himself against the wall with one hand and holding onto his flashlight with the other. The further he went, the cooler the air was and the more slippery the surface became inside the narrow tunnel. In the bright natural light of his torch, he noticed some type of pale-purple lichen growing here and there on the rocky walls, and from time to time he could see the tangled ends of roots protruding through the beam-supported ceiling.

At last the path came to an abrupt end, roughly thirty-five meters from where it had started, in nothing but an apparent cul-de-sac. It seemed inconceivable to Lawson that a tunnel, which someone had obviously taken great pains to construct, could end with no way out. At the same time, the rock wall seemed to him too straight and symmetrical to be natural.

Remembering the hidden latch at the entrance, he began to look around for a similar mechanism on the nearby walls. At length he noticed a small crevice in the ceiling, in close proximity to the flat wall at the tunnel's end. Putting his finger inside, he felt something smooth—a small metal ring—and pulled it. Instantly, there was a clicking sound and the wall before him shifted slightly, exposing a shaft of light. He had found the exit.

Not knowing what he would find on the other side, Sir Marcus took a deep breath, crossed himself, and pulled the concealed door inward. He immediately found himself in front of a natural shelf which extended about a meter and a half over the jagged rocks forming the base of Monemvasia's seawall. Before him, calm and shimmering in the late-afternoon sun, was the wide expanse of the Gulf of Epidavros-Limiras.

So this is it, he thought. *This is how he plans to do it.*

It was through this hidden tunnel, prepared for the purpose long before, that the Trustee operative intended to gain access to Monemvasia and capture it with such a small contingent of men—most likely in the dead of night and by total surprise. It was a story as old as time itself. Like mighty fifth-century Rome, an unassailable fortress would be brought down by the tiniest of chinks in its almost impenetrable armor. It was to be betrayed by a single entrance opened in its massive city walls and taken from within.

Without pausing to appreciate the beauty of the spectacular sea view before him, Sir Marcus quickly went back inside and pushed the hidden door closed. He then touched a control on the side of his wristwatch, causing the clock face to give way to a small video screen. Sweeping through the contact list with a touch of his finger, he found the image he was looking for and tapped the screen to initiate the call. He needed to speak to Rear Admiral Petrovich and there was not a moment to lose.

CHAPTER 8

In spite of the relatively flat terrain, the marching was brutal that day. The company of weary and miserable men had set out from the hills near Agios Ioannis at sunrise, traveling due south and skirting along the seashore just west of the small mountain called Glykóvrysi. From there they had headed eastward across the wide flat plain that brought them to within a couple of kilometers north of the village of Sykiá.

Eventually they had turned into a valley that formed a natural pass between the high mountains of the Parnonas range and a chain of lesser, but nonetheless treacherous, foothills opposite Monemvasia to the south. At long last, just after two thirty in the afternoon—having traveled a good part of the day in the blazing heat and under the constant threat of ambush, with only a couple of short stops to rest—they had finally made the coast of the Gulf of Epidavros-Limiras and reached the small abandoned fishing hamlet of Old Monemvasia.

In plain sight of the fortress island, situated roughly eight kilometers down the coast and a half kilometer offshore from the mainland, the men had begun to rejoice, thinking that they had finally reached the end of their exhausting journey. It was no small wonder, therefore, that Crowe nearly had a mutiny on his hands, when after nine hours of walking the infantrymen learned they were continuing onward—and that the toughest part of their day's march was still ahead of them.

The low grumbling that had prevailed among the soldiers over the last several hours suddenly erupted into an outright clamor; and rather than discipline the ranks, the two infantry lieutenants joined them in protest, refusing to make the men march any further that day and heaping verbal abuse upon the man they knew only as their guide, Karakorakas. Witnessing the whole event, Rashid was surprised at how unruffled the Trustee operative remained. It seemed that he preferred to win the men over by promising a feast once they reached their stopping point, rather than by responding to the harangue with threats as he had done several times before.

Doing his best to pacify the troops, he told them that he had arranged for a ship to rendezvous with them at the large sheltered lagoon at Iérakos, about eleven kilometers further north. That vessel, he explained—a supposedly neutral Austro-Hungarian merchant freighter, which was secretly in the employ of some associates of his—was intended to transport the expedition force to their goal under cover of night. And in addition to carrying all the explosives and ammunition they would need for their raid, it was also laden with provisions for the hungry men—roast chicken, rice, mutton and any number of Viennese sweetmeats and pastries. They were to attack before dawn, and Crowe wanted the men to be rested and well fed, so as to have strength and inspiration for the fight.

By the time he had completed his mouth-watering description of the delicacies awaiting the soldiers, Crowe had them hanging on his every word, ready to follow him to the ends of the earth. All, that was, except for one. One of the infantry lieutenants—a tall burly man in his mid-thirties, who had resented Crowe's unspoken leadership of the company from the very beginning—refused to be assuaged by what he considered to be the *fustanella*-clad guide's empty words. Stepping up to confront Crowe in a bellicose manner, he began to rant.

"Do you really expect us to believe that rot, you offspring of a cur! A ship full of treats from Vienna, no less! Do you take us for children?" he shouted. "Where would you get the money for it, even if such a thing were possible? I'm sick and tired of your lies and of your lording over us, like you're in command here! Just who do you think you are? Why, I'm beginning to be convinced that all of this is just a clever trap, you—"

"Lieutenant," interrupted Crowe icily, "I suggest you stop right there and just get back on your horse. We have a mission to complete."

More flustered and enraged than before, the officer looked around at the gathering crowd, and feeling that he now had to prove his manliness, began to twitch as he took another step closer and shouted: "Stop right there? Why you little—! Of course I'll stop, right after I've wrung your puny little neck!"

It was then that he made his fatal mistake. Lunging towards Crowe, he reached out for the Trustee's throat with his large hands outstretched and his face contorted with anger. Instantly, in a move that was almost too quick to follow, Crowe grabbed his arm and pulled him forward, driving his knee hard into the man's solar plexus and knocking the wind out of him. As the Egyptian doubled over, the Trustee drove him down to his knees with a sharp and powerful blow to the back of the neck with the point of his elbow.

Stunned and gasping for breath, the lieutenant remained on his knees as Crowe turned and faced the other men, coolly panning the crowd to make sure they were all watching. Then without saying a word, he locked the lieutenant's head in the crook of his elbow, placing his other hand at the back of his head, and gave a sudden sharp twist that broke the man's neck in a sickening snap.

As he straightened up and smoothed down his clothes, Crowe looked around at the soldiers and said in a sardonic dead pan: "So much for neck-wringing. Now, does anyone else wish to discuss the plan?"

Met with utter silence from the horrified soldiers, Crowe continued: "I didn't think so. Now, someone give me a rope. We shouldn't leave our trash behind on someone else's beach."

Tying the length of rope around the Egyptian's feet, the Trustee operative secured the other end to the saddle horn of the lieutenant's now riderless horse. Leading the animal by its reins, he then gave the command to march, dragging the corpse behind him in a terrifying reminder to the troops of what was in store for anyone who objected to his decisions.

Practically starving and dreaming of roasted chicken and sweetmeats as the men were, it was a largely unnecessary display. They all fell into line and followed without complaint, hardly giving a second thought to the increasingly battered and disfigured corpse of the fallen officer bouncing along the rocky ground before them, whom no one had much liked anyway.

The company had traveled a little less than halfway up the coast towards Iérakos, reaching the barren promontory of Cape Kremmydi, when Crowe suddenly commanded the column to halt. Riding a little way out in front of the troops, he faced the sea to the northeast and, to the bewilderment of the men, held a small unidentifiable object over his head for a moment before stowing it back in the folds of his weapons sash. Only Rashid realized that it was a signaling device, though of what type—laser or radio-frequency—he could not discern.

Crowe then rode back to the cavalry unit, which was bringing up the rear. Informing them about a large depression at the top of the bluff a few hundred meters away, protected on three sides by a ridge and overlooking a narrow cove, he unexpectedly ordered them to make camp. The horse platoon would have to stay there, closer to the fortress, he explained, as it would not be possible to transport the animals by sea. Promising to send a dinghy with some food down to them from Iérakos in a couple of hours, he continued giving them instructions.

"We'll be sailing along the coast to our landing stage out on the southern side of the Rock. Look out for our signal, near the end of the second watch. Once you see it, make your way down to the hills opposite Monemvasia's causeway and wait there. When you see my signal coming from near the water on the south side, ride in for the attack. The Greeks will have two or three men on guard at each end of the causeway, and another two or three outside the citadel gate. If all goes according to plan, by the time you make it to the main gate, someone will have opened it for you from the inside."

The horsemen accepted Crowe's orders with bitter resignation. Every one of them was doubtful of ever partaking of the promised feast, but in the aftermath of the earlier incident with the infantry lieutenant, none of them dared protest.

Rashid, on the other hand, was ecstatic. Upon hearing the Trustees words, he immediately concluded that it would be the perfect opportunity for him to slip away in the middle of the night and reach the hot zone to resurface from his dive. But just as he and the rest of the cavalry squadron started to ride out across the rocky ground in the direction of the headland which Crowe had indicated, he heard a chilling voice stopping him in his tracks.

"Not you, Moroccan!" the Trustee operative called out behind him. "I want you with me."

The young Paladin stared back, perplexed, as did the rest of the cavalry unit. Crowe then explained:

"Now that we're short one infantry lieutenant," he said evenly, but with a sinister look in his eyes, "I need you to take his place. You'll ride with me."

"But...but, what about these men you put me in charge of just yesterday?" Rashid replied, unnerved and disappointed, as he tried his best to retain his composure.

"That's of no consequence," retorted Crowe. Then pointing at one of the other horsemen at random, he said: "You, what's your name? Hany? Very well, Hany, you're in charge now."

With that, he turned and slapped his mount's flank and trotted off again to the front of the column, shouting behind him to Rashid: "Let's go, Moroccan—these men are hungry!"

Crestfallen, Rashid glanced back at the high sloping profile of Monemvasia not far off in the distance and swallowed hard. Suddenly it seemed that his journey back home was not going to be as easy as he had imagined it would be just a moment before.

It was near six o'clock in the evening by the time the company of soldiers reached Iérakos, and although the sky was still light, the sun had already dipped below the towering mountains a short distance to their left. They had not traveled terribly far—a mere eleven kilometers from the point at which they had reached the coast. But the slippery footing along steep and uneven rocks which hung precariously over a churning sea had forced the troops to walk with an abundance of caution, making the relatively short distance the most torturous part of their journey thus far.

Exhausted from their long day's exertion, they at last found themselves descending a dry narrow path into the large basin that made up the salt-water lagoon of Iérakos; and as they made their way down, the view which met them was cause for great rejoicing. For sailing into the head of the wide and winding fjord-like cove which fed the lagoon, and escorted by two smaller *pinnaces* capable of carrying thirty-five to forty troops each, was a sleek two-masted brig of about a hundred and fifty tons, flying a red-white-red merchant ensign adorned with the double-headed eagle of the Austrian Empire. Their guide had made good on his word, and even the weakest of the men immediately felt their flagging strength revived.

Tired and hungry, the soldiers hastily made for the beach, where some of the younger ones among them dropped their heavy kit and stripped down to the waist, running into the gentle surf to await the brig's arrival. Turning almost in place with a grace and agility which so characterized the square-rigged ships of her kind—and which made them favorites of the period's naval captains, merchants and privateers—the larger vessel came to an abrupt halt with her bow facing seaward, lowered her sails and set anchor in the deep of the inlet.

Meanwhile, the flatter-keeled pinnaces continued into the shallow lagoon and, dropping their anchors as well, hoisted out four launches laden with baskets of food. A number of the infantrymen rushed into the salty water with shouts of joy to meet the rowboats and to help beach them, while others began eagerly grabbing at the victuals the crewmen were passing overboard.

Amidst the clamor of the provisions being unloaded, Rashid noticed a fierce-looking blond man—for whom he had an immediate and inexplicable feeling of revulsion—disembark from one of the beached launches and head straight for Crowe.

"You are late!" the man shouted in German-accented English. "You *vere zupposed* to *heff* been here already yesterday *evenink!*"

"Hello to you, too, Juergen," replied Crowe, unfazed.

"Do you realize how hard it *vas* to keep *ze* captain *efen vone exshtra* day in *zese vawters?*" the man demanded angrily. "You know *vhat vould heff heppened* if *ve'd* been caught carrying *munizhions—und ze* Greeks are already *zuspicious* enough of Austrian *wessels. Zey* know *ze Hepsburgs heff* not been keeping *zeir noytrality und heff zecretly* been *zupporting ze* Turkish fleet *viss zeir* merchant ships.

"As it *iss*, I *hed* to agree to unload *everysing* onto *zome* wretched *vindy* little rock *und* sleep *zere* all night, *vhile ze* brig anchored off Falconera. *Und* now *ze* captain *vants zat* I should pay him *tvice vhat vas* agreed."

"So what's the problem, Juergen? Give it to him," Crowe shrugged unconcerned. "You know as well as I do that the money is not an issue. Besides, it's not like it's coming out of your own pocket—or is it?"

Insulted by his colleague's remark, the German straightened up to his full height, towering over Crowe by several centimeters, and with a cold fire emanating from his icy blue eyes, replied:

"It's lucky for you *zat ve're* on a job, Crowe. *Ozervize* I *vouldn't akzept zuch inzinuations* from an *Arschloch* like you. *Anyvay, vhy* am I *vasting* my time here? I *heff* more important *sings* to *vorry* about *zan* keeping you in line. *Zere* are still arrangements to be made for Phase Two. My job here *iss* done. Just make *zhure zat* you do yours. I'll *zettle* my *perzonal* score *viss* you *zome ozer* time."

With that, he turned and climbed back into the empty ten-man launch, which a couple of crewmen pushed into the surf and ferried back out to the waiting brig.

According to the plan, the pinnaces—divested of their Austrian colors in the event they were intercepted by the fledgling Greek navy—would transport the expeditionary force to their destination later that night, and then rejoin the brig further down the coast. From there, the reunited convoy would set sail with the legitimate portion of its cargo for Crete, some hundred nautical miles to the south. It was from his temporary headquarters in the island's capital, Candia—that well-garrisoned port town still safely in the hands of the Ottomans—that Juergen would coordinate the other part of the Trustees' mission. And thankfully, thought Crowe, it was a part which did not involve him. At least not officially.

A little while after Juergen had boarded, the merchant ship weighed anchor and hoisted her sails, retracing her path out of the inlet to the open water of the Argolic Gulf. Seeing her leave, Crowe turned back to the beach and noticed Rashid quietly sitting on his own and eating a modest portion of the food the Austrian vessel had brought.

"Is that all you're having, Moroccan?" he queried. Then, walking away, he said in a cryptic tone that left the young Paladin feeling unsettled: "You'd better eat up. You're going to need all of your strength very soon."

MONEMVASIA, GREECE—SUNDAY, SEPTEMBER 2, 2074

"This is incredible," Paladin Rear Admiral Petrovich murmured to Sir Marcus as they looked around, moving slowly through the darkness of the rocky subterranean tunnel and finally emerging into the circular chamber beneath the cistern.

"To think that the answer has been sitting right under our noses all this time, undetected for so many years," he continued. "If it were not purely for the fact that your lordship happened to spend the summers here in Monemvasia as a child and stumbled on this secret passage, the Trustees certainly would have gotten away with their plan."

Switching off the holographic projector, the two men returned with a brief flicker to the reality of the brightly lit conference room in the Paladin Zone of Camp Monemvasia, where they sat discussing the footage the Paladin engineers had recorded just a little while before.

"That's just what worries me," replied the Old Man pensively. "One thing I have learned in my time as a Guardian is that, in this game, there is no such thing as luck."

Then, as if thinking out loud, he continued speaking in a near whisper: "What could motivate the enemy to make such a brazen move? Something just doesn't add up."

"Perhaps they're just trying to rattle us—throw us off guard, in order to pull off something else? Lord Rizopoulos implied something along those lines before he left," commented Petrovich, fishing for an answer.

"Perhaps," said Lawson. "In any case, it doesn't do us any good to sit here speculating. We have to take action, which is what I've come to talk to you about. Lord Admiral Rizopoulos seems to think very highly of you and to have the utmost trust in your loyalty and discretion. Can I count on you to keep what I'm about to say in the strictest confidence?"

"Certainly, my lord," replied Petrovich, "what is it?"

Lost in thought and staring into the distance, Lawson spoke distractedly: "I think we need to let these Trustees succeed with their plan."

"My Lord?" Petrovich reacted with surprise. "How...how could we possibly do such a thing?"

Smiling vaguely, Lawson shook his head.

"Don't worry, Rear Admiral, I may be old, but I haven't taken leave of my senses just yet. I don't really intend to let the Trustees' plan succeed. Obviously we must fulfill our directive and ensure that no changes are made to the past. But I think we should let everyone else believe they have succeeded—at least for the time being.

"This is a rare opportunity to intercept and capture one of their agents, and I don't think we should take a chance that information may somehow leak out. As much as I hate to encourage this sort of thing, I'm inclined to believe that this particular operation needs to be a Paladin-only affair. Not a soul outside of the Paladin Zone should know about this, or about what we are planning. There's just too much at stake this time."

"Of course, my lord," Petrovich replied earnestly. "It will be kept completely on our side of the house. You have my word on it. I'll start putting together the dive team right away."

"Very good," Lawson said. Then as he got up to leave, he added: "And let's not forget one other thing, Rear Admiral. We have a very young and inexperienced diver out there that we still need to bring back in one piece. From the look of things, this is already shaping up to be a very costly mission for us. Let's try and make sure we don't lose any more Paladins on this one."

"Aye, aye, my lord," responded Petrovich, bowing crisply. "My sentiments exactly."

CHAPTER 9

The weather was mild, with a light and steady northeasterly breeze—nearly ideal for the short voyage that would soon take Crowe's company of Egyptian infantrymen to their long-anticipated encounter with fate. After a hearty meal, accompanied by plenty of nervous joking and chatter, the spent soldiers had eventually settled down to sleep on the forested ground which gently descended to the beach of the lagoon at Iérakos.

It was in the deep of the night, at a little before two o'clock in the morning—as the middle of the second watch was approaching, and not long before the soldiers were due to be roused—that Paladin Ensign Rashid Al-Noury moaned softly under the drooping bows of a willow tree, and then awoke from his slumber with a start. Feeling a sharp pricking sensation on the back of his hand, he jumped up shouting:

"The devil!"

He was looking around on the ground in the dim starlight, trying to make out what had caused the sudden pain, when he noticed John Crowe standing behind him, holding up a small lantern and seeming to have appeared out of nowhere. He looked perfectly at ease, as if he had been standing next to Rashid the whole time.

"What's happening, Moroccan?" he inquired innocently. "I was just coming over to wake you and suddenly I heard you cry out. Is everything all right?"

"Yes...yes," replied Rashid hesitantly, slightly disoriented and drowsy, and thinking it odd that he should find the Trustee inexplicably standing there at that very moment. "I think something must have stung me."

"Really? Well, let's see," said Crowe with uncharacteristic solicitude, shining the light on the younger man's hand. "Hm, it does look a little red," he commented. Examining the ground near Rashid, he suddenly stomped down hard—almost exaggeratedly—with his boot heel and exclaimed: "Got you, little bastard!"

He then bent down and made a motion as if to pick something up, although Rashid could see nothing in the diffuse yellowish glow that fell around their feet. Straightening up, he held out his hand, causing the young Paladin to recoil in horror; for in the flickering lamplight, he could see curled up in the middle of Crowe's upturned palm the crushed remains of a yellow-brown scorpion, about seven centimeters long.

"In the name of *Allah!*" Rashid gasped, his mind immediately turning to the highly venomous and potentially deadly variety of scorpions of similar appearance, *Buthus occitanus*, found in his native Morocco.

Seeing the young man's shocked reaction, the Trustee operative suppressed an ironic smile and spoke reassuringly:

"Don't worry. They're not as bad as the ones from your part of the world. These little nasties hurt like the devil when they sting, but unless you're allergic they're not known to be especially harmful. You'll get over it."

Throwing the mutilated specimen down onto the dark ground, he glared at the young Paladin and continued speaking, this time in an eerily menacing tone:

"Believe me, you have a much better chance of dying in battle tonight than you do of anything happening to you from this little creature. Now let's go and wake the troops. It's time to get underway."

As Crowe walked away, Rashid looked after him suspiciously and rubbed his sore hand. He could not be sure exactly what it was, but something seemed very odd to him about the entire incident. Waiting a moment for Crowe to walk further ahead, he stooped down and found the discarded scorpion carcass on the ground. Surreptitiously, he slipped it into his pocket before hastening to follow after the Trustee.

Amidst the low sound of footsteps on rocky soil, the occasional soft clinking of metal on metal, the gentle splashing of oars, and the throaty warbling of disturbed waterfowl taking flight from the rushes, the company of Egyptian soldiers slowly began to move out. Embarking into the waiting launches, they were ferried by turns to the two sleeping pinnaces anchored in the deeper end of the lagoon. After a little more than a half hour the ships were ready to sail, and, weighing anchor, they let out their gaffsails and slowly navigated through the fjord-like channel towards the open sea.

Once they had left the narrow inlet behind and hoisted their mainsails, they kept close to the coastline and set their course for the ancient fortress island of Monemvasia, some seven and a half nautical miles away. For many of the men—largely conscripts from the numerous small agricultural villages that dotted the Nile valley—it was their third or fourth sea voyage since having left Egypt for the Morea by way of Ottoman Crete, and their reactions were as diverse as their personalities.

A few huddled near some barrels stowed on deck, talking animatedly over a hookah pipe as if unconcerned about the whole affair, until a Dalmatian crewman spotted them and chased them away, loudly cursing them in his native tongue for smoking so dangerously close to kegs of gunpowder. Others, still unaccustomed to the rocking motion of a sailing ship, felt ill and tried their best—with varying degrees of success—to keep their evening meal from making an unwelcome reappearance.

Most sat quietly on deck, their backs against the gunwales, silently contemplating the adventure they were about to experience. For his part, however, Paladin Ensign Rashid Al-Noury felt the excitement building in his chest for another reason. With each passing minute, he was coming closer to the hot zone that was his pathway back home to Camp Monemvasia and the year 2074.

As they sailed along, the calm seas and favorable winds blowing steadily from the northeast at about ten knots allowed the vessels to make excellent time. They had traveled for only about a half hour, when the high bluffs of Cape Kremmydi approached on their right. As they rounded the headland, Crowe flashed the signal lanterns to the cavalry unit bivouacked there and soon a small light could be seen swinging back and forth in answer from the rocky shore a half kilometer away. The horsemen had seen the signal and would now begin to mobilize.

By Crowe's estimate, however, it was highly doubtful that they would ever be able to get into position in the hills opposite Monemvasia's causeway on time. Taking the rough coastal terrain and the darkness into consideration, the riders would need about two hours to cover the roughly twelve kilometers of shoreline and make it to the Rock in time for a coordinated attack. But at the speed the pinnaces were currently making, they would have no more than ninety minutes.

No matter, the Trustee mused. It really was irrelevant at this point. He had done his job, and the events that had been set in motion were already unfolding as planned. Whatever the results of tonight's raid against the Greek garrison at Monemvasia were, they would do little to alter the overall outcome of Phase One.

Scanning the deck as if looking for someone in particular among the group of thirty-five soldiers being ferried on his ship, the Trustee operative's eyes came to rest on the young Moroccan Paladin. He was standing near the bow and looking out at the dark and mysterious waters of the Argolic Gulf. It was so brief as to be barely perceptible in the dusky starlight of the moonless September night; but for an instant, as his eyes locked onto his unsuspecting young adversary's shadow-ensconced figure, a smile of cruel satisfaction twisted John Crowe's mustached lips.

After leaving Cape Kremmydi behind in the enveloping darkness, the vessels carrying Crowe and his company of Egyptians traveled downwind for another twenty minutes before the men could finally begin to make out the massive rock of Monemvasia in the distance. Their attention was first drawn to it by several faint points of light which seemed to hang like dim yellowish stars suspended over the murky surface of the waves. Those lights, they would later discover, were the blazing torches illuminating the watchtowers of the seaborne citadel.

Once a focal point was established, however, their eyes began to perceive the obscure silhouette of the Rock itself—an impenetrable mass standing out in meager contrast against the darkness of the sea and the night sky. Soon the command was given to lower the sails and cut speed, and little by little the pinnaces came to a slow drift before their anchors were dropped and they were brought to rest about one nautical mile northeast of the Gibraltar of the East.

As the soldiers began to realize that the hour of their advance against the enemy garrison was at hand, a few of them fell down on their knees on the ship's deck and began to pray. Others, resigned to whatever their fate might be, simply gathered up their weapons and checked them over as they listened for the order to debark. They did not have long to wait.

Once the sails had been lowered, the crewmen began hoisting out the ships' eight launches one by one, as sailors clambered down the lines and jumped in, two to a boat, to load the munitions and man the oars. Taking on eight or nine soldiers per launch, the small flotilla of rowboats managed to carry all sixty-three infantrymen who had made it to the coast, in addition to Crowe, the surviving lieutenant, and Rashid.

When everything was ready, the convoy set out slowly and—aided by the currents and guided by the distant torch lights—silently cut its way through the gentle waves in the direction of Monemvasia. Heavily laden as they were, and manned by only two oarsmen each, the rowboats' progress was slow; but after about half an hour, the flotilla of launches found itself at its rendezvous point two hundred meters off the southeast coast of the ancient rock.

It was the most dangerous phase of the landing. Their ultimate success depended upon the element of surprise, and time was of the essence. Every minute they lingered offshore, within range of the lookout at the Lower Town's East Gate, their chances of being spotted and fired upon before they ever made landfall increased significantly.

Crowe's launch quickly took the lead and began to row at top speed towards the coastline. Once each launch came alongside the base of the seawall, another was to set out from the rendezvous point on the three- to four-minute dash to the landing site, giving the disembarking infantrymen enough time to scramble onto the rocky ledge before the next boat arrived. It was a daring plan, and fortunately for them the sea that night was calm and cooperative. Indeed, the Trustee agent had calculated each detail painstakingly—even down to the lunar phase, which ensured a cover of near-total darkness and a reduced gravitational influence on the tides.

As soon as the first launch came to within a couple of meters of the disembarkation point, the men hoisted out a long gangplank stowed in the bottom for that very purpose. With the two oarsmen working to keep the boat steady against the light waves slapping against the rocks, Crowe nimbly clambered over the side carrying an unlit lantern. Rushing to the seawall, he leaned against it and seemed to feel along its surface for something. Suddenly he froze and remained motionless for a few seconds.

To Rashid and the other men in the boat, tense with apprehension about being caught by the sentries, or alternatively being dashed against the craggy black rocks by the crosscurrents, the moment was interminable. Much to their relief, however, they finally saw a yawning black maw open in the side of the rock wall. Turning to face them, Crowe motioned impatiently for the men to follow, and one by one they made their way across the gangplank and into the dark mouth of the tunnel.

One of the last men off the launch, the young Paladin patiently waited for his turn to disembark, feeling the gentle rocking of the boat beneath him and wondering anxiously how long the oarsmen would be able to keep her steady. Looking at the dark wet rocks nearby and the black surface of the sea around him, his mind began to wander and he found himself imagining with dread what it would be like to fall in—the cold churning water, the probable undertow, the battering by the launch's wooden hull and the tearing of flesh against sharp rock. Shuddering, he shook off his distracting thoughts and inhaled deeply, bringing himself back to the reality of the moment with a small prayer. His turn had finally come.

Holding tightly onto his carbine and setting his boot firmly on the rough wooden plank, Rashid stepped up and out of the boat. He had just made it fully onto the narrow gangplank, when the surge of a wave larger than the previous ones suddenly swept in and jostled the craft, causing the gangplank to bump up and shift abruptly to one side.

Immediately the young Paladin, his legs drenched up to his knees in the cold salt water, lost his footing and was nearly thrown headlong into the surf; but at the last second, one of the soldiers already standing on the rock shelf reached out and grabbed him by the arm, steadying him and keeping him from falling into the inky swell below. It was Munir Abbas.

Rashid's heart pounded and he felt fear course through him as he realized how close he had come to experiencing one of his worst nightmares. As grateful as he was to the young Egyptian, however, he was also instantly overcome by a crushing feeling of guilt and shame. It was the second time Munir had saved his life, and yet not only was he unable to repay him, but he had actually helped lead him to certain disaster.

The young Paladin felt a strange anguish he had never known before begin to churn his stomach and cause an intense pressure to build inside him. He tried desperately to block it out, but an almost overpowering voice inside his mind began to drown out all else, shouting to his young friend to run and hide from the coming catastrophe. But then, closing his eyes tightly and swallowing hard, he slowly mastered his emotions. There was nothing else he could do except to finish what he had started; and so resigned to what must be, he thanked his friend, looking at him wide-eyed and grasping him by the shoulder in mingled gratitude and sorrow.

For a sudden realization had hit him like a cold hard tidal wave of reality, mystically transporting him to a previously unfamiliar plane. Despite all the wonder, excitement and adventure inextricably bound up with the experience of relativistic diving and the encounter with other worlds in time, one thing was now as clear to him as the crystalline diving bell neatly stowed in his pocket. By its very nature, the life of a Paladin must ultimately be a hard and a solitary one. It was a path whose truly ascetical and sacrificial character—not only in regard to himself, but also in regard to every personal attachment he might form—he was only just beginning to glimpse.

He instantly thought of Lord Admiral Rizopoulos, and felt a strange new kinship with him—a combination of admiration and pity for his mentor, whom he now began to understand in a way he never could have done before. But then, just as quickly, his mind was inundated with a flood of doubts. Sacrifice and asceticism were ideals with which he had been intimately familiar since his youth—but to what end?

It was one thing to exercise one's spiritual powers and to practice self-control and mental discipline for the sake of inner peace and the vision of God; but what did it really mean in the context of the Paladin Order and the Guardians' directive? Supposedly it was all in the name of preserving a way of life— ensuring peace, security and stability on a global scale unparalleled in the course of human history—and of safeguarding the advancements of modern civilization from the threat of temporal terrorism.

Even so, did that unquestionably noble purpose obliterate any moral obligation to those who were not fortunate enough to share in the benefits of such an era of progress? Did it render acts of kindness and cruelty, apathy and compassion any less real, any less existentially significant because they happened to involve those who were far beyond the sphere of influence—or even the awareness and understanding—of that way of life?

Rashid certainly had no qualms about sacrificing himself for a higher purpose—for honor and duty, and for the cause of virtue. But now he began to wonder for the first time what could possibly justify the knowing sacrifice of others—of those who were innocent bystanders on the periphery of a life-and-death struggle about which they were completely ignorant, and whose only connection to the enemies of the way of life he was pledged to protect was a happenstance of time and place.

All the usual logical arguments—that they had already ceased to exist hundreds of years before that undeclared war in which he was a combatant had even taken shape, for example—suddenly sounded hollow to his grasping mind. His head spinning far beyond the familiar territory of his normal emotional austerity and his thoughts becoming too alien for him, Rashid shook himself out of his momentary quandary and tried to focus once again on the task at hand. There were still two more soldiers about to disembark from the launch, and the least he could do was to help them onto shore.

Giving the infantrymen a hand, the young Paladin watched the oarsmen pull the empty rowboat away from the rocky base of the seawall and noticed uneasily that it seemed to disappear into the darkness a little too quickly. He then followed the other members of the landing party into the subterranean passageway, looking over his shoulder once more with an unsettled feeling as he unsuccessfully tried to catch a glimpse of the departing launch in the nearby waters.

By the time he got inside, Crowe and another soldier had lit their lamps, revealing the damp and rough-hewn rock walls of the tunnel. As soon as all the men from their launch were finally present, the Trustee operative tersely began whispering commands.

"Moroccan, you stay here and guard the entrance. When the next boat gets here, help them up and show them the way in. The rest of you, follow me!" he barked and instantly started moving up the gentle incline towards the underground chamber.

As the fading lantern light and the quiet rustle of the first Egyptian troops making their way up the tunnel's narrow slope gave way to darkness and the echo of waves slapping against the rocks below, Rashid found himself alone for the first time in days. His heart beat quickly and his mind raced as he felt for his diving bell and tried to decide what to do. Soon the moment would be gone. The next launch would arrive, and he would miss his chance to resurface without having any way of knowing when— or even if ever—his next opportunity would arise.

Inexperienced as he was, however, he was also uncertain whether or not his current position was far enough inside the perimeter of Monemvasia's hot zone for him to attempt the dive successfully. With something as potentially deadly as the matter-antimatter-powered diving bell in his possession, a process of trial and error would surely be a risky way to find out.

And then there was the problem of Munir Abbas. The young Egyptian had already saved his life on two occasions, and he was at that very moment walking into the proverbial lion's den. Although Rashid knew that, realistically speaking, there was little he could do to protect him, he felt a moral responsibility to stay and watch over the young man for a while longer.

Hesitating, he rested his finger on the diving bell's safety lock as he pondered his choices—whether to attempt to make the dive here and now, or to wait until he could be more certain of the outcome. It was a torturous moment, to be sure, and he was more torn than at any other time during his entire mission; but then a calming sense of firm resolve suddenly descended upon him and he knew what he must do. With a heavy sigh from the depths of his heart, he slowly returned the device back to its place. It was not yet time for him to leave.

If he had any doubts about his decision, there was little time for Rashid to weigh them. Although he could not see anything on the darkness of the water's surface, a moment after slipping the diving bell back into its hiding place he could hear the muffled whisking splash of oars upon the waves. Then suddenly, appearing as if out of nowhere, the second launch came gliding into view as it arrived at the landing stage.

For the next twenty minutes, a steady yet eerily silent bustle ensued, until the last of the eight vessels was successfully discharged of its passengers and cargo. Soldiers nervously disembarked from one launch after another; munitions crates full of powder, shot and a couple of large bore mortar cannons were offloaded; and a stream of troops plied their way through the secret tunnel to join the rest of their comrades in the underground chamber.

When the last few infantrymen had finally entered the tunnel, Rashid found himself alone with Crowe on the rock shelf above the sea. As the latter stared at him intently, the young Paladin averted his eyes uncomfortably and turned to follow the Egyptian soldiers. It was then that the Trustee operative stopped him with a sharp command.

"Not that way, Moroccan," he spoke ominously. "You and I have some business to take care of."

Perplexed and anxious, Rashid looked back at the launch, which had mysteriously remained near the rocks.

"Get in," Crowe commanded roughly.

Silently, the young Paladin obeyed, looking back over his shoulder nervously as he crossed the small wooden gangplank and stepped down into the waiting craft. Immediately, Crowe closed the tunnel entrance and stepped nimbly into the rowboat, pulling the plank in behind him. Without a word, the oarsmen guided the small vessel about sixty or seventy meters out to sea, and then turned westward, slowly and silently sculling in parallel to Monemvasia's rocky shoreline.

Growing more anxious by the second, Rashid discreetly reached for his dagger, feeling the bleakness the situation with an overwhelming intensity. If it came down to a fight against an experienced professional assassin like Crowe—and in a small boat with two less-than-sympathetic crewmen as companions, no less—it was not difficult to imagine what his chances would be.

His hand poised over the hilt of his blade, the young Berber felt his body tense in readiness. His heart rate increased, his breathing became rapid and shallow, and each of his senses tingled in keen anticipation as he watched catlike over Crowe's every move. As unprepared as he felt for such an encounter, he waited with doubled resolve for the faintest signal that would start the terrible and inevitable final confrontation.

Abruptly, however, and much to the young Paladin's bewilderment, the two sailors changed course and began steering the boat northward, back in the direction of the rocky shore. In the last thirty meters before reaching the base of the seawall, they gave several great pulls on their oars before letting the boat drift in silently with the waves; and as they approached the rocks, Rashid realized with alarm that they were heading straight for the small ancient *Portello* gate. It was the only entrance to the citadel that was accessible directly from the water, and one that was sure to be guarded by the Greeks.

Astounded, Rashid took everything in silently, almost unable to believe what was happening as the boat drifted towards the small jetty. First he saw Crowe move into position, crouching down near the edge of the launch as if ready to spring and drawing a long dagger out from under his cloak. Then he looked on in utter amazement as two tough-looking *evzonos* sentries clad in *fustanellas* peered out from the archway of the *Portello* and seemed to look straight through them without even the slightest flicker of recognition.

Suddenly it hit him. Looking back at the two expressionless oarsmen, who appeared completely unconcerned about being seen, he realized that they too were Trustee operatives, and that the entire boat was shielded.

Immediately his mind turned to the whole of the earlier debarkation process, and it dawned on him that it had all been one great deception from the start. There had never been even the slightest danger of them being seen from Monemvasia's watchtowers, because up until the very moment of their arrival at the landing, the launches and everyone in them had been invisible.

Rashid's momentary epiphany was short-lived, however. The instant the thought entered his mind, the drifting vessel gently bumped against the jetty and Crowe sprang into action.

Leaping from the boat, he moved out of range of the shielded launch and suddenly appeared before the two guards like a wild demon. Before they even had a chance to cry out in terror, he had slaughtered them both like animals and disappeared inside the arched gate in a ghostly silence. A minute later, he reappeared in the opening of the ancient stone portico, his face spattered with blood, and motioned in the unseen launch's direction.

"Come on, Moroccan—it's all clear!" he whispered. Then, speaking to his fellow operatives, he called out in a low voice: "Thanks, lads! See you sometime back on the other side."

"Right!" one of the men called back, knowing all the while that his voice would be inaudible outside of the SHIELD. "Watch yourself!"

For a moment Rashid hesitated to follow Crowe into the citadel, but then realizing there was nowhere left for him to go, he stepped out of the boat onto the shore. At first he could still see the launch and the two agents; but as soon as he was clear of the vessel, they pushed off from the jetty with an oar and disappeared within a couple of seconds into the darkness, leaving nothing but an eerie ripple on the troubled and murky waves.

After watching the boat disappear, the young Paladin stepped into the dark entrance of the *Portello*. Running his hand along the massive time-worn stonework as a guide, he cautiously mounted the stairway, which formed a narrow hairpin turn called a *volte*, in the ancient fortification wall.

He had climbed only a few steps when a large object in his path nearly caused him to trip. Stooping down, he peered through the darkness trying to make out what it was and abruptly stood up in horror. Splayed out across the stone stairwell in a slick pool of blood was another *fustanella*-clad sentry, whose throat had been slashed from ear to ear.

Rashid gingerly stepped over the body and continued onward, fighting back his growing sense of terror. His only thought was to make it up the narrow staircase and advance the few dozen meters into the open spaces of Monemvasia's Lower Town at all costs. Once there, he would be home free, able to use his diving bell in the certain knowledge that he was located within the perimeter of the hot zone.

As he rounded the corner, however, the Paladin ensign soon realized that he had completely lost sight of Crowe. Momentarily freezing in place, he listened for any sound that would betray the enemy's presence; but hearing nothing for several seconds, except for the splash of the waves from the jetty below, he decided to move on again. He had just taken his first step, when he suddenly felt a distinct presence behind him and heard the metallic click of a flintlock pistol being cocked.

"Nothing personal, Moroccan," growled a low familiar voice, "but, after you."

Chapter 10

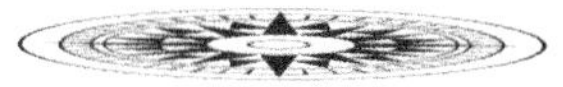

Forcibly wrenching himself from the blissful white light that enveloped him, the Paladin diver broke through the surface of the turbulent temporal waves and landed with a sudden jolt on the paved stone floor of a gloomy subterranean chamber. He involuntarily shook himself, as if waking from a dream, and stood up. Nearby, his dive buddy was leaning against a wall, similarly recovering from the effects of the temporal translocation, and appeared slightly nauseated.

"About time you showed up," they heard a familiar voice remark.

As they switched on their night vision and looked around the chamber, they noticed two Paladins in dive suits several meters away. They had been sitting on a stack of old wooden planks while they waited, but now they stood up and bowed slightly to greet their newly-arrived colleague and team leader.

"We ran into traffic," replied the first man wryly. "How long have you guys been waiting?"

"Only about four hours," the other quipped with a sarcastic smile. "We had just about written you off, but then we figured you must have taken the officers' tour and you'd show up once all the work was done."

"Ah, well," the team leader smirked, "better late than never, as they say. So, you *gonna* give me a status report or something, or are you *gonna* just keep busting my chops?"

"Sure, take the easy way out and pull rank! Anyway, everything's quiet around here," the other Paladin reported. "We've pinpointed our coordinates at September 16, 1825—that's Gregorian. The locals are still on the old Julian calendar, so for them it's only September fourth. Right now it's about...nine-seventeen in the evening local time."

Then turning to his colleague, he requested: "Ensign Zeffers, would you please synchronize the dive computers so Captain Dovas and Lieutenant Sisko here can take a look at the readings we've taken?"

"Right away, Lieutenant Demetriades!" responded the younger man, immediately taking out his dive computer and touching some controls on the screen. "There, you should be receiving the synch-request now, sirs."

While the two men completed the synchronization procedure, Demetriades continued his report:

"From this position we've encountered a lot of interference, and our ability to monitor any sound waves coming from the main fortress has been limited. We have managed to pick up some conversations among the sentries at the East Gate and also from the *Portello* down at the South Wall. There's absolutely no indication they are concerned about an attack.

"In fact, it seems to be just the opposite. Apparently they're expecting *Kolokotronis* and a band of his men to show up for a visit to the garrison here any day now, and they're all excited about that. There's a lot of chatter and not so much guarding going on, from the sound of it. Anyway, you'd think that with over eight hundred soldiers in the place, they could spare a few more to watch the doors, wouldn't you?"

"Mm," murmured Dovas, looking at the data which had appeared on his dive computer. "You're right. Looks like only four men at the East Gate and three down at the *Portello*. They must be relying on the watchtowers in the Upper Town to provide them with sufficient advance warning of any enemy movements—and the Trustees are no doubt planning to exploit that weakness."

Then changing the subject, he asked: "What about the countermeasures? Have you done anything yet?"

Demetriades stared at his friend incredulously, raising his eyebrows and retorting:

"In four hours? Are you kidding? If you'd taken another half hour to show up, we could have installed a sauna and a barbecue pit by now! Anyway, we've put hidden sensors in place in the seawall near the entrance and installed wireless cameras in strategic spots throughout the tunnel. Even if the attackers are shielded, they won't be able to open the door without our knowing about it; and if they're not, we'll even have a head count before they make it in here."

"Good," replied Dovas. "What about sweeping for surveillance devices?"

"Done—everything's clear. We've also rigged the charges in the tunnel. The detonation code is on your dive computers along with all the other info. We figured it would be a good idea for everyone to have it—you know, just in case. Anyway, once they're all inside the chamber here, we'll be able to fire the tunnel from safety to prevent anyone from slipping out the back door."

"Well then," Dovas commented, "looks like we're in good shape. Now we just have to wait. In the mean time, let's get the rest of these charges rigged up."

"Do you really think we need more explosives in the tunnel?" Demetriades asked. "We followed the engineers' instructions to a tee. There should be more than enough firepower in there already to bring down a good portion of the ceiling and completely block it off."

"The charges I'm talking about are not for the tunnel," Dovas answered, looking somberly at his fellow Paladins and speaking with a tone of finality. "Gentlemen, just in case anything goes wrong, we need to rig this whole chamber to blow."

All was ready and the Paladins inside the underground chamber below the cistern head had been waiting for hours when the signal finally came. At just about 4:22AM, the screens on their dive computers flashed in unison and the devices began to vibrate gently, alerting the divers that the tunnel's hidden entrance down at the seawall had been opened. The four men instantly sprang to their feet and activated their SHIELD devices.

"Well, boys and girls, looks like it's finally show time," Dovas stated calmly.

Watching the live video feed from the cameras installed in the tunnel on his dive computer, Demetriades murmured: "I don't see anybody yet—they must be shielded."

Indeed, as the first group of Egyptians gathered at the tunnel's entrance, they unwittingly remained cloaked by the Trustee operative's SHIELD. As soon as they began to traverse the length of the narrow tunnel in single file, however, Crowe switched off his device and the column suddenly materialized, suffused by the flickering light of their lanterns.

"Look—there they are now!" Lieutenant Sisko exclaimed. "One, two, three...eight of them."

"Okay, boys, take a good look—does anyone see Al-Noury in that bunch?"

No one could see the Moroccan, but after a moment Zeffers spoke up: "Wait, I see something here! His EDT signal just showed up out of nowhere. He's outside the entrance on the rocks."

"What's he doing out there?" wondered Demetriades. "Why doesn't he come in with the rest?"

"I don't know," Dovas replied, "but we're not to do anything until he's in a safe position."

Then, suddenly catching a glimpse of Crowe as he passed in front of one of the cameras, a surprised Dovas blurted out:

"Hang on a second, I know this guy—son of a blip! He looks really familiar—just like a Clandestine Ops instructor I had in England when I did my training years ago. What the heck was his name?"

"You mean he's a Paladin?" asked Sisko in utter disbelief.

"If it's the same guy, yes—or at least he was once upon a time. He's definitely not one of ours now," Dovas replied, still trying to remember Crowe's name. "I can't believe it. Anyway, I could be wrong. It was a long time ago. Besides it doesn't matter—we still have a job to do. STRATCOM wants him alive, whoever he is. Let's be extra careful with him, though, just in case."

Then pulling Demetriades to one side, he confided in a low whisper:

"Terry, when the time comes, I'll take the Trustee, but I want you to keep a close eye on Al-Noury. I don't want to believe it, but if that is a rogue Paladin, there's a chance Al-Noury could be in on this thing with him, too."

After a couple of minutes, the Paladins heard the faint click of a latch being opened and a section of the wall at the far end of the room swung out. The chamber was filled with dim lamplight as Crowe stepped into view and looked around, carefully surveying the space and finding everything as he had left it. Just as he was turning to usher in the seven infantrymen behind him, however, he mysteriously stopped as if suddenly on the alert.

Turning back to face the empty room, he slowly eyed the chamber as if looking for something. Finally his gaze rested for a moment on a spot just a short distance away from the group of shielded Paladins, and he gave a snort and a mocking chuckle. Clearly something had amused him, though it was not evident exactly what it was. He then turned back towards the tunnel and motioned for the Egyptians to enter.

Disquieted though they were by the Trustee's odd behavior, the Paladins nevertheless stood poised for action as Ibrahim's soldiers filed into the room. Once all of the men were inside, Crowe proceeded to speak to them gruffly in Arabic, issuing his final instructions. He then disappeared back into the tunnel, leaving the Egyptians to mill around the chamber, nervously talking to each other in hushed tones and examining the array of objects they found in varying states of decay for anything that might be of value.

As the remaining troops gathered over the next several minutes, the Paladins observed a number of crates and a couple of mortar cannons being transferred into the underground vault. The room gradually became more and more crowded with infantrymen and supplies, so that the dive team eventually found it necessary to split up in order to avoid being inadvertently jostled by the soldiers. Before they separated however, a tense Dovas gave the men their final orders:

"Remember our three objectives: stop the attack, bring Ensign Al-Noury back safely, and bring in the *perp*, alive if possible—in that order. And whatever happens, don't do anything until I fire the tunnel. That'll be the signal to start the operation. God be with you, Paladins!"

"And with you, Captain!" they called back in unison.

From that moment on, each member of the dive team watched in heightened anticipation of what would happen next. Crowe went in and out of the tunnel several more times. Munitions were brought in, and the Egyptians gathered in greater numbers until there were eventually more than sixty armed men assembled in the room. At no point, however, did the divers pick up any sign of Rashid entering the tunnel.

The tense minutes seemed to pass excruciatingly slowly, as they waited for their young colleague to join the company of 'braimi. However, as time went by and the Egyptians seemed ever closer to launching their attack, each of the Paladins became increasingly alarmed until Captain Dovas finally reached the limits of his patience. As the team leader, he could not afford to let the opportunity slip away, and he determined that, with or without Al-Noury, he would soon have no other choice but to make a move. The next time the Trustee entered the chamber, he decided, he would detonate the charges.

But as he watched the images from the tunnel cameras on his dive computer, the most astonishing thing happened. Instead of coming into the tunnel with the last few Egyptians to arrive, the Trustee apparently remained outside—and then closed the door! The Paladins had no visual contact with the rock shelf outside the tunnel entrance; but within a second or two, one thing became perfectly clear. Ensign Al-Noury's EDT signal had suddenly disappeared.

Moving through the darkness of the Lower Town with the muzzle of a flintlock pistol pressed between his shoulder blades, Rashid walked quietly, not daring to defy his captor.

"Just stay close to me," Crowe had told the young Paladin calmly, "and you won't have to die this instant."

The pair had skirted alongside of the southernmost fortification walls, heading westward for about seventy-five meters, when Crowe motioned for Rashid to turn right. They then traveled through a series of narrow twisting lanes, beneath archways and through a long gallery, so that the young Paladin soon became disoriented and marveled at how well the Trustee agent seemed to know the town's tiny paths and byways. After several minutes of walking, Rashid finally began to recognize some of the larger streets from his brief stay in the Lower Town before his orientation at the Institute—now a lifetime ago it seemed. They were coming closer to the citadel's main gate.

As they neared the gate, the gloomy darkness of the narrow pathways was cut by the flickering yellow glow of torchlight, and the low voices of a couple of sentries could be heard murmuring indistinctly. Rashid could not tell what they were saying, but it seemed to him that they sounded calm and unconcerned. He knew they would pay dearly for their lack of vigilance. Abruptly, Crowe roughly pushed the young Paladin into a shadowy recess in the wall of a building adjacent to the long gallery which led to the gate.

"Don't move!" he growled, and in an instant he was gone.

Left alone, Rashid was filled with relief; but it only lasted a second. After what he had witnessed on the beach at Old Monemvasia earlier the previous evening—and down at the *Portello* just a few minutes before—he knew what Crowe was capable of, and he realized that every moment he spent with him could very well be his last. At the same time, thinking about his friend Munir, who reminded him so much of his younger brother back home in Morocco, he was torn.

Should he stay and try to protect the young Egyptian Sufi, or should he just take out his diving bell and attempt to resurface right away? As he agonized over the decision, Lord Admiral

Rizopoulos's words at the beginning of the mission came to him and resounded forcefully in his mind:

"Your job is surveillance, not engagement...if your cover is in danger of being compromised, or your immediate safety is threatened, you are to get out. That's a direct order, Ensign."

So that was it, he thought. As difficult as it would be, not knowing what would become of the friend who had twice saved his life, he nevertheless had his answer.

He was just about to take out his diving bell, when seemingly out of nowhere Crowe reappeared, aiming the flintlock pistol straight at him. It was too late. In the few seconds it had taken Rashid to make his decision, the Trustee operative had killed three sentries, slid open the massive iron bolt of the main gate to make it ready for the cavalry unit, and returned for him.

"Come on, Moroccan," he said, wiping the glistening blood off his face with the back of his free hand. "Time to earn the wages of our sins."

Pushed along by the Trustee operative, the young Paladin headed back towards the east, behind the Lower Town's main square and along dark and narrow pathways. All the while he struggled to keep the fear and the darkness that were growing within him from spinning out of control. After several minutes, their walk led them to an open meadow behind a small white church building gleaming in the darkness, which he recognized from his tour of the Lower Town a few weeks before—or rather, two and a half centuries hence. It was the church of the Panagia Chrysaphitissa.

Not far from the church, and illuminated only by the faint glow of torchlight from the guard post at the East Gate some fifty or sixty meters away, Rashid saw the ghostly white marble reflection of a low cistern head protruding from the ground. Suddenly he realized just how intricate the Trustees' plan had been. Once the Egyptians had infiltrated the Lower Town from within, in the dead of night and with only a few guards awake, the great citadel of Monemvasia—the Gibraltar of the East—would fall to Ibrahim's men with the greatest of ease, and history would be changed forever.

His heart pumping with adrenalin, Rashid's eyes darted around quickly to find some means of preventing such a disaster—an event with the potential to alter the future, his future, in unknown ways. In the dim reflection of the torchlight, he saw the ruins of a low stone foundation wall rising from the ground about ten meters away. It was his only hope.

Just as Crowe stooped down to unlock the cistern cover with a small key he had drawn from his vest pocket, the young Paladin suddenly broke away and made a mad dash for the cover of the wall. As he ran, he shouted at the top of his lungs in his broken Greek:

"Egyptians here!"

Instantly, Crowe whirled around to face Rashid with his pistol raised, but realizing it was too late to stop him, turned back and threw open the cistern cover instead. He was just about to step down onto the rung ladder when the peaceful little meadow behind the church of the Panagia Chrysaphitissa erupted into chaos.

On hearing Rashid's cry, the four guards at the East Gate were roused from their torpor and, peering through the archway into the meadow, understood that something was amiss. Shouting for reinforcements, they picked up their muskets and *yataghan* swords and two of them came running down from the gate to have a closer look.

At that very moment, an earth-shattering blast rocked the meadow, throwing both the sentries and Crowe to the ground and sending a shower of loose rocks and soil into the air. From his position inside the cistern's underground chamber, Captain Dovas had seen Ensign Al-Noury's EDT signal suddenly appear within the citadel's walls, as the young Moroccan moved out of range of Crowe's SHIELD. He had immediately set off the charges rigged within the secret tunnel, collapsing it and causing a long narrow depression to form in the field above.

For the briefest of moments, the Egyptian soldiers sequestered underground were paralyzed with shock from the impact of the explosion. Surprise and fear quickly gave way to panic, however, as the sixty-four men moved in a crushing stampede towards the rung ladder leading up to the surface— their only escape from what seemed to be certain death in the inevitable collapse of the ready-made grave in which they found themselves. Fighting desperately to get out, the men began to trample one other, so that even before the shielded Paladins took action, several infantrymen had fallen at the hands of their own comrades.

Realizing that the Egyptians were no longer in any condition to carry out an attack on the citadel, Dovas left the other Paladins with the task of disabling as many men as possible, while he concentrated his efforts on clearing a path to the exit. The Trustee agent was still at large above ground, and there was not a moment to lose if he was going to bring him in alive. Invisibly fighting his way to the top of the cistern head, he emerged from underground just in time to witness a shocking scene.

Stepping out of the bedlam down below and into the mayhem on the surface, the Paladin captain saw that about a dozen Egyptian infantrymen had made it out of the cistern before him. Panicked, they were running around in every direction, looking for a way to make their escape from the cursed fortress. Scanning the area around him for the Trustee, Dovas caught a glimpse of the young ensign, Al-Noury, crouched down behind a partially collapsed stone wall about ten meters away.

He was about to run over to him when suddenly the Moroccan shouted and lunged in the direction of a very young-looking Egyptian infantryman, who was standing in a confused daze and was apparently unaware of the Greek *evzonos* bearing down on him with his musket raised. The young Paladin managed to step in front of the Egyptian just at the moment the *evzonos* fired and, to Dovas's horror, was violently knocked to the ground. He had been struck in the upper body by a musket ball at point-blank range.

Bleeding profusely from the right side of his chest, Rashid lay on the ground moaning in pain, and appeared to be reaching into his jacket for something. It was his diving bell. Unable to move his right arm, he clumsily tried taking off the safety lock with his left hand, but the crystalline bell—smeared slick with blood—slipped out of his grasp and fell to the ground.

Dovas immediately made for Al-Noury's position as fast as he could move, but the *evzonos*, his *yataghan* raised, was only a couple of steps away from leaping on the young Moroccan in a murderous rage. It was then that Captain Dovas saw something completely inexplicable happen.

Suddenly there was a muffled popping noise and the charging *evzonos* stopped dead in his tracks, as if he had slammed into an invisible wall. He immediately fell backwards with a gaping wound newly opened in his chest. Then came a momentary flicker, and standing over Ensign Al-Noury with a still-smoking flintlock pistol in his hand was the Trustee agent, John Crowe.

Bending down, Crowe picked up Rashid's diving bell, looked it over for a second and then deftly flicked the safety switch off. He then shoved the flintlock into his weapons sash, and dragging the young Paladin off the ground, stood him shakily on his feet. Placing the recovered diving bell into the wounded ensign's hand, he said to Rashid with a mysterious smirk and a deeply sarcastic tone:

"There you go, Moroccan—give my very best regards to Lord Admiral Rizopoulos!"

Before Rashid could react, Crowe suddenly whirled the young Paladin around forcefully, as he leaped away and disappeared again into thin air. The abrupt spinning motion was enough to set off the diving bell, and in a blinding flash, followed by a sharp crack, Paladin Ensign Rashid ibn Taleb Al-Noury vanished unprepared into the thundering rapids and the deep and treacherous currents of the swiftly flowing river of time.

CHAPTER 11

Perfect, he thought.

The thickening brown foam of boiling liquid having converged into a diamond-like eye in the center of the copper *briki* coffee pot, the Old Man had quickly whisked it away from the stove top. As he carefully poured it into the delicate bone-china *demitasse*, the steaming and frothy brew reached the very brim of the cup and hung there precariously, as if suspended in time, ready to spill over at any moment.

Balancing the cup and saucer in one hand, and a glass of pure spring water in the other, he inhaled deeply to smell the soothing fragrance of the dark, foamy liquid. He then walked carefully towards the open veranda doors, there to sip his Greek coffee in the golden light of a warm September afternoon. He had crossed halfway through the sitting room when he was startled by the sound of a pleasant computerized voice announcing an incoming video-call.

"Oh, bless it!" he grumbled, annoyed as his hand shook and hot coffee poured down around the rim of the cup onto the saucer.

Setting the cup down, he looked at the screen and immediately recognized the caller. It was his former secretary from Guardian headquarters in Geneva, Switzerland. Taking a seat at the antique writing desk in the sitting room, he voice-activated the call.

"Good afternoon, Vicky, how lovely to see you! What a pleasant surprise!" he answered.

"Good afternoon, my lord," the young woman smiled back. "It's been such a long time! You're looking well. Are you taking care of yourself?"

"Eh, you know how it is, Vicky. Once you get to be my age, there's only so much you can do. Parts break, and you don't worry so much about replacing them anymore," Lawson quipped back. "How are you, my dear? How is that little girl of yours? I'm sure she must be getting big by now. How old is she—four, four and a half?"

"She turned five last month, my lord."

"My goodness, how time flies! Well, what can I do for you, my dear?" replied Lawson amiably.

"My lord, the First Peer would like to speak with you—if you have some free time, that is," the young woman explained.

"What else have I got but free time, now that I'm retired? Go ahead, put him on!" exclaimed Sir Marcus.

"Right away, my lord. Please hold on just a moment while I connect you," she said, disappearing from the screen only to be replaced by a colorful and slowly morphing floral pattern, accompanied by soft music.

While he waited, Lawson retrieved his coffee and slowly sipped it until a familiar face filled the wall screen a moment later. It was the man who had succeeded him at the end of 2073, when he had formally retired as the presiding *first-among-peers* of the Guardian Council of Peers.

He was actually ten months older than Lawson, though he wore the years well. It never ceased to amaze the former *first peer* that, at the age of seventy-five, his successor still had a thick and wavy tussle of naturally black hair, sprinkled with the lightest touch of silvery gray. And just as impressive as his youthful appearance was the seemingly inexhaustible supply of vibrant energy and contagious good cheer he spread wherever he went.

The two men had known each other all their lives, and had worked together closely for decades. Sir Marcus was normally always glad to see him, but on this occasion he felt strangely awkward. It was the first time they had spoken since the Paladins' Monemvasia mission of a few days before, and Lawson knew that something had changed.

"What's happening, Mark, old man?" smiled the face, whose every change he had seen in detail over the more than seventy-three years they had known one another—that of his cousin, Lord Dimitrios Vasiliádes.

It was a hard thing for Lawson to accept; but once the time capsule implanted by the Paladins at the beginning of the Monemvasia mission had been recovered and decoded, he had no choice but to believe it. Apparently—as he had been confidentially informed by Petrovich—before the mission took place, his cousin Dimitrios had never even worked in the Guardian organization. Instead, he had been an ordinary civilian history professor. Something had occurred which changed all that and resulted in his becoming the current first-among-peers of the Guardian Council of Peers.

While Sir Marcus could not be sure exactly what had caused it, something told him that it had to do with the old abandoned cistern the two of them had discovered as children—the same chamber with the collapsed tunnel that had often been the subject of their childhood imaginings. As he now knew, the rubble that had always prevented them from getting into the tunnel had only been created a few days earlier, when Captain Dovas and his dive team had set off the explosion in the predawn hours of September 5, 1825. Perhaps, prior to the Paladins' mission, the tunnel had been accessible and he and Dimitrios had actually been able to get inside more than sixty-five years before.

All that was just a matter for conjecture, however. They would never know what had truly happened; and more to the point, it no longer really mattered. Like it or not, there was a new reality now. What concerned Sir Marcus the most was just how he was going to break the news to his cousin, and what its effect would be. Such a delicate subject would have to be handled judiciously and with extreme sensitivity, but eventually Dimitrios and the rest of the Council would have to be told about the temporal paradox. Now, however, was not the time.

"You made me spill my coffee, that's what happening!" Lawson shot back at his cousin's image on the wall screen, pretending to be annoyed in order to cover up the discomfort caused by his awareness of the truth. "Don't you know that it's indecent to call people at this time of the afternoon?"

"Oh, well, at least you'll finally have some good luck now," Sir Dimitrios retorted, referring to a traditional old wives' tale about spilled coffee.

"Oh, yeah? Does that mean you're finally going to retire, too, and leave me alone to finish my afternoon coffees in peace?" Lawson wisecracked, and the two chuckled with each other mirthfully as old cousins often do. "So what can a simple old pensioner do for you, my lord?"

"A simple pensioner can't do anything for me," remarked Vasiliádes. "You, on the other hand, can still do a lot. By the way, I hear that congratulations are in order to the Paladins there in Camp Monemvasia on their latest mission. The entire Council of Peers appreciates their efforts, if you could please let them know that."

"All right," replied Sir Marcus, taking a loud sip from his still scalding coffee, "I will. But come on, Jimmy," he admonished, calling him by the nickname he had used since they were children. "You didn't call me just to ask me to pass on your congratulations to the Paladins. What's really on your mind?"

Dimitrios snorted. "Always getting straight to the point, aren't you? How old were you when you moved from America—eight, nine? But you never got rid of that awful directness."

Then, sighing, he continued.

"All right, Mark, I'll tell you what's on my mind. There's been a lot of talk going on lately about waste reduction and cost cutting, and it just doesn't help matters for the Paladins when we have things come up like the other day—you know, that Rear Admiral of yours down there, what's his name? Pavlovich?"

"Petrovich," Sir Marcus corrected him.

"Right, Petrovich. I mean, what was he thinking by telling the Chief of Station that the Paladins have their own communications channels and he would get information only on a need-to-know basis? Do you realize the kinds of political problems that little episode has been causing up here in Geneva the last several days? Rigas may be a prick, but he's a prick with friends in high places. Those Paladins of yours have to stop being so self-righteous and learn to be a little more politically correct once in a while. I always thought Rizopoulos was more sophisticated than that—it's just not like him."

"Well, first of all, Jimmy," Lawson interrupted, "you know as well as I do that the Paladins are an autonomous Order. Of course they work in tandem with the Guardians, but let's not forget the reality. Historically speaking, they have always been self-supporting and self-financing. I suppose that's one of the advantages of being able to go back in time, knowing what the world's stock and bond markets are going to do at any given moment. In fact the Guardians grew up essentially as an administrative support structure just so the World Council would have some skin in the game."

"Come on, Mark," Dimitrios tried to dismiss his cousin's comments, "that's ancient history. The two organizations have been attached at the hip for decades—what's the point of bringing all that up now?"

"The point is, Jimmy, when push comes to shove, I don't think there's much you or the OHCP or even the World Council can do about the Paladins' organizational structure or their operational procedures, unless you want to find yourselves with a real problem on your hands. At the end of the day, the Paladins are the only ones who can translocate temporally—and that makes them a monopoly. You know it, I know it, and what's more important, *they* know it. So next time you start getting political pressure from the OHCP or the World Council, just remind them of that."

Dimitrios frowned and remained silent. He didn't like it at all, but he grudgingly had to accept the truth of what his cousin had said. Meanwhile, Lawson continued.

"Secondly, as for Rizopoulos, I agree with you one hundred percent—of all people, he generally appreciates the need to try and keep a smooth working relationship between the two lungs of the system, if you want to call them that. Unfortunately, he's...out of the picture right now."

Dimitrios looked up in surprise.

"What do you mean, 'he's out of the picture'? Where is he?" he demanded.

Lawson sighed heavily, then replied to his cousin reticently.

"He had asked me as a personal favor to hold off on informing the Council for a couple of weeks, in the event that he came back sooner than expected. But under the circumstances...," he said, pausing for a moment for effect. Then clearing his throat and taking another sip of coffee, he continued: "Lord Admiral Rizopoulos has taken an indefinite personal leave of absence. At this point, no one knows when—or even if—he's coming back."

Dimitrios was shocked. Straightening up behind his desk, he knitted his brow in obvious thought, and then began questioning his cousin Mark.

"Well, why? I mean, what did he say? This is very serious. Does anybody know where he is or what he's doing?"

"I wish I could say," said Sir Marcus, his heart heavy and his jaw clenched tight. He didn't like lying—least of all to his own cousin—but this time it was necessary. "All I know is that only a handful of Paladins, including the Chief Medical Officer, even know about it. I can't say any more than that."

"Oh, I see," replied Sir Dimitrios slowly, a look of comprehension coming over his face, "that's too bad. Well then who's running things on the Paladin side?"

The deception had worked. Dimitrios had been left with the impression that Rizopoulos was on some kind of serious medical leave.

"For now it's Petrovich," Lawson answered. "He's temporarily in command until Ephraimoglou is able to resume his duties. After that—well, I guess we'll see. The canons of the Paladin Order are very explicit. If Rizopoulos doesn't inform the Council within six months of his intention to return, a new leader will have to be chosen. But it's a long while before things get to that point."

Resting his face against his hand with his elbow on his desk, Dimitrios spoke again with a faraway sound to his voice.

"I understand. Well, look, as for this other issue, couldn't you just have a little talk with this Petrovich? There are too many things going on in the World Council right now for this to get thrown into the mix. Believe me—none of us needs that headache. We should at least try and give the appearance of a united front. In fact, I have a very good suggestion as to how we can smooth this thing over."

"Oh, really? What's that?" asked Lawson.

"That interview that we're supposed to have with Ephraimoglou tomorrow morning," Dimitrios began tentatively. "I think it would make a lot of sense for Petrovich to allow a couple of the top Guardian officers to participate."

Sir Marcus was silent for a moment. So that was what this was all about. Exhaling deeply, he raised his eyebrows and asked: "Well, who do you have in mind?"

"Oh, I don't know, Mark—let's say, for example, Brandauer up here in Geneva. And, of course, obviously Rigas, since he's the one making all the noise."

"Then I suppose you'd also have to have Pelegris there, since Rigas is helpless without him," Lawson remarked, as his cousin silently shrugged and nodded in agreement. Then after a deep sigh and a final long sip from his coffee cup, he said: "Okay, Jimmy, I'll see what I can do."

After a few minutes more of friendly conversation about family matters, the two men ended the call. As soon as it was over, Lord Dimitrios Vasiliádes immediately called his secretary on the videocom.

"Yes, my lord?" she replied with an efficient smile.

"Vicky, get me Ops Director Pelegris in Monemvasia on an encrypted line, would you please? Thanks."

As he waited for the call to come through, Dimitrios pondered his conversation with his cousin. Mark was a good man. Aside from being blood relatives, they had also been best friends their entire lives. He had been an outstanding leader of the Council for many years, but even he would be the first to admit that he sometimes failed to appreciate how drastically things were changing. New approaches had to be taken and new strategies considered; and part of the problem, as far as the first peer could see, was exactly what the Old Man had pointed out a few minutes before. The Paladins were a monopoly provider, and they knew it.

Well, he thought, *maybe that ought to change.*

After all, it had been proven time and again throughout modern industrial history—one of the best ways to improve the efficiency, product quality and customer service of any monopoly was to give it a little competition.

CAMP MONEMVASIA, GREECE—WEDNESDAY, SEPTEMBER 5, 2074

The soft, steady hissing sound of the ultra-purified air being circulated throughout the room was a constant reminder to Vice Admiral Ephraimoglou that he was still in intensive care.

He had awakened the previous afternoon to find himself in a MediCenter hospital bed, his hands and feet heavily bandaged and an array of tubes and needles stuck in him. It had taken him some time to become oriented and to realize where he was, though he still had no idea how he had gotten there. The last thing he remembered was being a prisoner in Ibrahim's camp and that awful explosion.

How could things have turned out this way? How could Mina...?

Even now, just thinking about it brought him to the edge of a dark yawning chasm of despair in his mind and heart.

As he lay in his hospital bed agonizing over the events that were still fresh in his mind, he was interrupted by a young Paladin physician and a nurse-technician who entered the room. The fact that their mouths and noses were covered with surgical masks was yet another reminder of what Dr. Mariatos had told him the previous afternoon. It seemed that his immune system was severely weakened and he was at high risk of secondary infection, which was one of the reasons he was being pumped full of antibiotics and antiviral drugs.

"Vice Admiral Ephraimoglou," the doctor spoke to him kindly, "I just want to have a quick look at your injuries to see how everything is healing up, before the technicians come in to get you set up for the videoconference. Dr. Mariatos will be here in a little while."

Oh, yes, there's that, he remembered wearily—his deposition before a select committee of the Council of Peers.

It was the very last thing he was looking forward to, as weak and heavily-medicated as he was. Still, he recognized the necessity of the task, especially given the significance of what he had learned while on his mission and the unimaginable consequences it could have for the Paladin Order and the entire Guardian organization. He would have liked to discuss everything with the lord admiral first, but under the circumstances there was no excuse for delaying things until his return, whenever that might be.

Turning him over on his side, the doctor examined the deep slash wounds on his back. Having been treated for infection and painted in several places with a coating of growth-factor-infused extra-cellular-matrix solution, they now seemed to be quickly on the mend.

"Mm-hm," murmured the physician, as the nurse-technician spritzed the injuries with an antibacterial spray and changed the bandages, "these are looking pretty good. I don't think we're going to have any problems here."

Turning Ephraimoglou back over, they raised the head of the bed until he was in a sitting position, and then carefully began to unwrap the bandages from around the stump of his right hand.

Mariatos had of course informed him of what had been done, but it was nevertheless a shock for which he could not have been adequately prepared. A heavy, oppressive feeling began to fill his chest as he looked at the site of the missing hand, amputated just below the wrist, with the healing wound still raw and the bandages spotted with dark traces of blood.

Seeing it for the first time, it was still hard for him to believe; for what his eyes assured him must be true was at once belied by his sense of touch. He could still feel the member as if it were there—could still wiggle his non-existent fingers and clench his absent fist, and was still bothered by a dull ache and an annoying itch that he could not scratch.

He understood that it was only temporary. The hand would eventually be replaced within a few months in a complex reconstructive procedure with a fully functioning new one, already being prepared for the purpose—using his own induced pluripotent stem cells—in a Guardian medical laboratory in England. Nevertheless, he experienced a pervasive sense of bereavement—although whether that feeling of loss was for his bodily appendage or for something far greater, he could not fathom.

His wounds having been examined and the dressings changed, the young doctor left. Two jump-suited technicians wearing surgical masks and gloves then entered the room to upgrade the audio-visual equipment, allowing the conference to be streamed with the highest level of security and encryption available. Having finished their work and performed the necessary sound, camera and monitor checks, they also took their leave.

Ephraimoglou was finally left alone to try and eat a light breakfast of toast and tea at the nurse's insistence, before he was joined at about 8:45AM by the Paladin's Chief Medical Officer, Dr.

Mariatos. Although the latter's presence was not required for the conference, Petrovich had insisted that he be seen in the room in order to lend greater emphasis to the seriousness of the Vice Admiral's condition and to help keep the proceedings brief and to the point.

Shortly before nine o'clock, the large flat-screen monitor the technicians had installed earlier suddenly flashed to life, showing an image of Ephraimoglou's hospital room. Immediately, an overhead camera suspended from the ceiling began to move silently, remotely controlled by the communications technicians, until Ephraimoglou—sitting upright in his bed, with Mariatos seated in a chair nearby—was positioned in the center of the screen. A moment later the screen split and, side by side with the feed from Ephraimoglou's room, an image from Camp Monemvasia's Situation Room appeared.

Ephraimoglou could see Rear Admiral Petrovich, along with an adjutant and a couple of other senior staff officers from STRATCOM, sitting at the familiar large conference table. But as he looked closer, he was taken by surprise; for also present in the Situation Room were Lord Lawson and two other participants he had not expected to see—Station Chief Thanassy Rigas and Operations Director Georges Pelegris. Cognizant of what he would have to report to the committee, Ephraimoglou was disturbed at the presence of the Guardian officers and would much rather have seen the attendance limited to Paladins only, but there was little he could do about it now.

At exactly eight o'clock Geneva time—nine o'clock in the morning local time—the image on the monitor changed yet again, this time to show the feed from the hospital room as a tiny window in a corner of the screen. In its place on one side of the main split-screen was the image of a well-lit formal conference room decorated with dark, imposing wood paneling, crystal wall sconces and chandeliers, and massive, forest-green velvet drapes hanging in deep folds from floor-to-ceiling window casings. The Vice Admiral immediately recognized it as the executive conference room of the OHCP's headquarters in Geneva, Switzerland.

Seated at a large antique burnished-mahogany table were three out of the twelve active *peers*. Ephraimoglou immediately recognized two of them—the first-among-peers, Lord Dimitrios Vasiliádes, and the chairwoman of the Guardian Intelligence and Security Committee, Lady Isabel Villaréz-Joya. Ephraimoglou had dealt with both of them on a number of past occasions, but he had never felt quite at ease with Lady Isabel and their working relationship remained formal at best. The vice admiral did not know the third peer personally, but surmised from his appearance that he must be Lord Niranjan Chandra, a relatively new member of the Council and chairman of the Guardians' Legal Affairs Committee.

In addition to the three peers, there were also a handful of senior Guardian officers, most of whom he knew. Among these were the Guardian's director of Intelligence Analysis, Martin Brandauer, as well as Paladin Commodore and Chief Legal Officer Wei Zhiqiang, who were both based in Geneva. And finally, much to his discomfort given the sensitivity of what he had to report, there were a couple of relatively junior-looking staff officers on the Guardian side, whom he had never met before. Unfortunately, he knew the type—young, brash and arrogant, they had obviously been identified as 'high performers' and were being groomed as future Guardian leaders.

Without wasting any time, the committee chairwoman—a severe-looking but attractive woman in her early sixties, who spoke with a very slight South American accent—immediately called the proceeding to order and introduced the participants for the record. She then began to address the assembly with the weighty and dignified air of a stateswoman.

"Vice Admiral Ephraimoglou," she said graciously, "on behalf of the Intelligence and Security Committee—and I think in this instance I can also speak for the entire Council of Peers—I would like to thank you for your service, your courage and your dedication. I would also particularly like to commend you for your willingness to give us testimony today concerning your recent mission, despite the inconceivable hardships you have faced in the last days. We wish you a speedy recovery and look forward to seeing you resume your full responsibilities as soon as possible.

"Now, it's a bit of a departure from normal procedure, but I have been informed that General Counsel Wei has a procedural motion he would like to put forth before this Chamber, before we begin our proceedings. Commodore Wei?"

"Yes, my lady," the Paladin's chief legal officer—a tall and lean Hong Kong native with a protruding Adam's apple, wearing a formal white magistrate's wig and black robes—replied in a deep voice that commanded attention. "In view of the Vice Admiral's serious medical condition and weakened state, I am petitioning the Committee on behalf of the Paladin Order that in lieu of his verbal testimony today, a written affidavit be entered into the record within the next seven days. I further move that the Committee proceed directly to the question and answer period, in order to help ensure that Your Honors' questions are all dealt with while we still have the benefit of Vice Admiral Ephraimoglou's full strength and attention. Thank you, my lady."

Lady Villaréz conferred with the other two peers briefly and then, switching back on the microphones, replied: "Let the record reflect that the motion is granted. Vice Admiral Ephraimoglou will have seven days from today to submit a detailed written affidavit to this Committee, which will appear in the record in lieu of his verbal testimony. With that, I will exercise the chair's privilege of opening the question period with my fifteen minutes. After that, Lord Vasiliádes and Lord Chandra will also each have fifteen minutes.

"Essentially I have one point of inquiry for the Vice Admiral," the chairwoman continued, "and that is, could you please describe to the Committee how you were taken prisoner by the enemy agent, and what, if any, intelligence you may have gathered on the Trustees' plans, their methods, or on the operative himself, which may be helpful to our security efforts going forward?"

Hesitating, Ephraimoglou coughed slightly and then took a sip of water, using his still-bandaged left hand. He then sighed heavily and began to speak laboriously, the fatigue and sorrow evident in his face.

"My lady, my lords, I will gladly supply the Intelligence Committee with whatever information I can about the Trustee operative in due course; but I regret that it may prove to be of limited value, since it was not the Trustee agent who captured me. Sadly, what I must tell you now—as difficult as it is for me to say—is of much greater significance, however, since it involves one of our own."

Then, as all eyes stared at him in silent consternation, he continued, forcing the words out with obvious strain: "Your Honors, I must ask that the information you are about to hear be kept at the highest level of secrecy, as the security implications are enormous. I was taken captive and the mission was sabotaged by...by a fellow Paladin—Commodore Mina Ghabry."

For an instant there was dead silence. Then Lord Vasiliádes interrupted Ephraimoglou, demanding: "Vice Admiral, do I understand you correctly? Are you saying that one of your fellow Paladins is a traitor?"

"Was a traitor, my lord," Ephraimoglou replied somberly, closing his eyes briefly and sighing. "Commodore Ghabry is dead. He died while attempting to assassinate the Ottoman general Ibrahim Pasha in a suicide bombing, using our own diving bells. And not only one of my fellow Paladins, my lord. As I have so terribly learned through this ordeal, there may be numerous traitors still active among us—"

A loud commotion instantly erupted in both the Council Chamber in Geneva and the Situation Room in Monemvasia, drowning out Ephraimoglou's emotion-filled near-whisper of a voice, as he tried to continue speaking.

"Order! Order!" shouted Lady Villaréz, banging a small gavel in front of her several times. And as she busied herself trying to restore calm to the proceedings, a surprised but not-displeased Georges Pelegris leaned over to Station Chief Rigas on one side of the conference table deep in Camp Monemvasia's Situation Room and softly whispered into his ear.

"Imagine that," he said with an air of quiet amusement, "out of chaos, opportunity."

CHAPTER 12

The glow of the soft white light seemed too harsh for Ensign Al-Noury when he first opened his eyes, and he involuntarily blinked and began to squint. Almost immediately he detected a faint antiseptic odor in the air, and he could also hear the soft, steady whooshing sound of centrally conditioned air being circulated.

As he slowly regained his awareness, he began to notice other familiar sounds which he had not heard in what seemed to have been an eternity—short, high-pitched electronic beeps, and the occasional mechanical whirring of a machine. He was home, he thought with a flood of relief tinged with excitement, back in his own time.

Raising his head, he realized that he was lying in a hospital bed with an intravenous drip attached to his left arm. A dull ache radiated from his right shoulder, which was heavily bandaged and had some sort of synthetic pins protruding from it. On seeing the sturdy but light-weight plastic frame that protected it, he suddenly remembered what had happened.

Munir, he thought, recalling the young Egyptian, whose life he had managed to save by stepping in front of the *evzonos*'s bullet.

He wondered for a moment about the young man's fate, but then realized just as quickly with a feeling of dismay that one thing was certain. Whatever might have transpired in the citadel after he was shot, Munir Abbas, along with all the other men he had sojourned with for days in that hot and terrible September of 1825, were long since dead. Indeed, they were mere footnotes on the pages of a history that would be read only for its major chronological events and its most dominant political themes.

The young Paladin tried to sit up, but with his shoulder immobilized, it was impossible. Noticing that his head hurt and that for some reason he felt weak and dizzy, he decided to lie back and wait for someone to come. From the next room, he could hear muffled voices, and after a moment the door briskly slid open and he saw a familiar face. It was Dr. Mariatos.

"Good morning, Ensign," he said flatly, entering the room with a Paladin nurse-technician. "Welcome back to the land of the living."

As he took note of Rashid's vital signs displayed on the side panel of the cot, the technician adjusted the IV-drip. The doctor then added:

"We were a bit worried about you there for a little while. You took a pretty nasty hit from a musket ball and lost a lot of blood. Another couple of centimeters and things would have turned out much differently. Anyway, thank God the surgery went well and we're glad to have you back."

Rashid cleared his throat and, speaking with a raspy voice, addressed the doctor, asking: "How long have I been here?"

"You came in the day before yesterday," Mariatos answered. "You've been sleeping the whole time since we operated on you. The pain-killers you're on have a sedative effect, but that doesn't really fully account for it. I suspect you were just plain exhausted from the mission."

"And what happened...back then?" the young ensign inquired hesitatingly. "Was the mission successful?"

"From what I hear it was mixed, but I don't really know the details. You'll have to ask the other divers about that," the doctor replied. "You'll get your chance pretty soon. But there are a lot of other folks who want to talk to you first, as soon as possible. From a medical point of view, there's no reason why you shouldn't be able to see them for a short debriefing later on today, but it's up to you. If you don't feel up to it, I can try to put them off a little longer."

"What does Lord Admiral Rizopoulos say?" Rashid asked, hesitant to make any decisions without the approval of his mentor.

"Well, he hasn't resurfaced yet," Mariatos informed him matter-of-factly. "But I'm sure I can get them to wait until tomorrow morning if you prefer."

Thinking about it for a moment, the young ensign decided: "No, I'm sure it will be all right, Doctor. I'll be fine."

"Very well, then. I'll let Rear Admiral Petrovich know that you'll be ready later this afternoon and we'll arrange for a meeting in our conference room. I'd prefer to keep you here at the MediCenter for at least another twenty-four hours before releasing you. That shoulder of yours is going to be in traction for a few weeks, and you'll need some time to get accustomed to the harness. The technicians can show you a few tips that'll make it easier for you to get around and perform everyday tasks. Eventually you'll need physical therapy for a couple of months or so, but we'll go over all the details before that happens."

"Yes, sir—thank you," replied Rashid, before suddenly erupting in a heavy coughing spasm, causing him to wince from the pain in his shoulder.

"That's a nasty cough you have there," commented Mariatos. "How long have you had that?"

"I don't know," the Moroccan answered, clearing his throat uncomfortably. "I don't remember it from before. I think it must have just started."

"Hm. Open up there and let me have a look," murmured the Paladin Medical Chief, pulling out a small light and stepping closer to the young ensign. "Well, your throat definitely looks a little red, but it could also just be irritated from the intubation."

Mariatos then instructed the nurse to give Rashid a throat culture, remarking before heading out to arrange the debriefing:

"Let's try to hit this thing early, whatever it is. The last thing the ensign needs with his shoulder in that condition is a respiratory infection."

Then, pausing in the open doorway, he suddenly remembered: "Oh, yes, there is one thing I wanted to ask you. When they first brought you in, the paramedics found this in your pocket," he said, fishing out a small transparent bag and holding it up.

It was quite a bit more shriveled than he remembered, and the yellowish-tan hue had given way to a darker brown, but Rashid recognized it instantly. It was the scorpion Crowe had crushed.

"Were you keeping this for some reason?"

A shiver went up the young Paladin's spine on seeing the creature again, and he explained: "I'm not sure, but it's possible that scorpion may have stung me just a few hours before I resurfaced. I thought I should bring it back with me, just in case."

Mariatos shook his head.

"It's very unlikely. I'm familiar with this type of scorpion— it's a *Mesobuthus gibbosus*. It's native to this part of the Mediterranean and it's not particularly aggressive. I can't recall any divers having been stung by one in all the years I've been here at Camp Monemvasia. Besides, you haven't presented any of the symptoms normally associated with it.

"Anyway, I'll have someone take another look at your blood work to see if there are any traces of residual neurotoxins, but I don't think there's anything to worry about." Then he smiled and, as he walked out of the room, said simply: "I think you'll live."

From the reddening hue and the shifting intensity of the *Hydrofuse* light panels embedded in the MediCenter's walls and ceiling, Rashid could tell that it was already late afternoon. A little while earlier, for the first time in a week of scanty and almost inedible food while on his dive, he had finally eaten a decent meal. Encouraged by the nurse-technicians, he had abandoned his characteristic self-restraint and, for the sake of his recovery, allowed himself a second helping and even dessert.

He was resting comfortably with his hospital bed partially raised, when the nurse entered and informed him that he had a visitor. For a second Rashid grew excited, thinking that it might be Lord Admiral Rizopoulos, but then a Paladin whom he did not recognize entered the room.

"Ensign Al-Noury," he greeted him, "I'm Captain Nick Dovas. It's okay, don't get up," he joked. "We haven't met before—at least not in person—but my team and I were there a few days ago at Monemvasia, back in 1825."

Realizing that Rashid did not really comprehend, he explained: "Our team deployed on the basis of the intelligence you sent back in the time capsule—to stop the attack at the fortress."

"Oh!" said the young ensign, surprised. "I didn't know that any Paladins were there. I wondered about that explosion."

"That was us, all right," Dovas grinned. "We're usually a bit more subtle, but sometimes—"

As the captain spoke, Rashid coughed heavily and cleared his throat, trying to disguise the pained look that shot across his face.

"Anyway, I know you need to get some rest, so I won't bother you," continued Dovas. "I just wanted to check in on you and welcome you to the team."

"Thank you, Captain," replied the ensign. "Actually, I'm glad you came. I was just wondering how the mission turned out? Did we stop the fortress from being taken?"

"Yes, we did, thanks to you. It was a little messier than we would have liked, but we got the job done. I checked the historical record once we got back, and everything squared up properly. Apparently Ibrahim Pasha came at Monemvasia with a column of men just a few days after we were there, and burned everything in the surrounding area. He must have prearranged it with the Trustee to rendezvous there, but when he found the Greek garrison still holding the citadel, he turned back and went up to Apidiá, a few kilometers north of Agios Ioannis.

"I guess he wasn't expecting to have to undertake a major siege, and he must not have considered it worthwhile. Unfortunately, though, we weren't able to apprehend the Trustee. But the good news is that we recognized him, and that helps. He's someone we all thought was dead; but now that we know better, it'll be harder for him to move around with impunity."

"That's very good to hear. Um, excuse me, Captain, but what about the Egyptians inside the citadel? Does anyone know what happened to them? I mean—," Rashid asked, hastily trying to think of a way to rephrase his question so as not to betray his interest.

"There's not much about it in the document archives, but from what we've been able to piece together, it seems that most of them were taken prisoner," Dovas answered. "Apparently a number of them were later traded in a prisoner exchange for some captured Greek fighters."

Then, pausing and looking at him intently for a moment, Dovas said: "I know what you did, Ensign. I saw you take a bullet to save that young Egyptian kid."

Rashid froze. He had been caught interfering in events between the locals, and he immediately thought that he would be suspended from diving duties, or perhaps even court-martialed for having violated one of the Guardians' highest principles. Not knowing what to say, he stammered, but the captain just raised his hand and stopped him.

"It's okay, Ensign," he said kindly. "Don't worry. There are a lot of Paladins who would have done the same thing. It's true we're not supposed to make any changes in the past, but when we're talking about events that weren't originally part of history anyway, let's just say we have a little more leeway."

Then lowering his voice to a near whisper, he continued with a wink and a smile: "And, frankly, if you hadn't done it, I wouldn't have thought very much of you. But not everybody around here thinks like that, so let's just keep it between you and me and the diving bell, shall we?"

Dovas was just about to leave, when a grateful Rashid suddenly asked him: "Captain, is there any news about Vice Admiral Ephraimoglou? Is he alive?"

"Yes, I hear he's recovering here in the MediCenter. They have him isolated in intensive care and he hasn't been able to receive visitors yet. Apparently his immune system is still very weak and they're worried about infection. But I hear he was interviewed by videoconference this morning by the top brass. I don't know any details, but rumors are that something big is happening. I suppose we'll find out eventually, but anyway, that's nothing for you to worry about. Just concentrate on getting well fast. There's always a lot to do and we need all hands on deck."

A LITTLE WHILE after Dovas had gone, the nurse-technician came back in to tell Rashid that the officers from STRATCOM were ready to interview him.

Touching a control on the side of the ensign's bed, he magnetically levitated it off its base and smoothly guided it to the center of the floor. He then pressed another control which slowly raised the head of the bed to an upright position and lowered the feet, transforming it into a floating chair, complete with arm- and footrests. Showing Rashid how to work the controls, he accompanied the young Paladin and directed him along the way as he navigated towards the conference room.

When Rashid entered the room, he found two mid-level Paladin officers sitting at a large conference table and awaiting his arrival. He recognized one of them as the same adjutant he had seen at the Dive Control Center the morning he and Lord Admiral Rizopoulos had made their tandem dive. Rashid tried awkwardly to get up from his chair to bow, but the harness on his shoulder prevented him.

"Please, Ensign," said the adjutant charitably, his vulpine face framed by a bushy reddish beard. "It's not necessary. Make yourself comfortable. We understand that you've been through quite a lot recently, and we'll try not to tire you out too much.

"Unfortunately this is one of the less glamorous aspects of life as a Paladin—the documentation. But in time you'll get used to it. Fortunately, on most missions the divers are able to record all their actions on their dive computers. On undercover assignments, however, we often have to rely on post-dive depositions, such as the one you are about to give."

He then introduced the other officer, a notary from the Paladin legal secretariat. The latter quickly explained to the ensign some arcane legalities concerning the deposition, which was to be recorded and would apparently be entered into his personnel file. He then required him to take a solemn oath before they started.

Once the recording began, the notary asked Rashid to recount in detail everything that had happened on the mission. The Paladins sat impassively, remaining silent throughout most of his narration; but they immediately showed interest when he started to talk about Crowe and the other suspected Trustee operatives he had encountered—Juergen, and the oarsmen who ferried the soldiers to the landing site outside of Monemvasia.

Interrupting several times, they asked detailed questions about the agents—their physical descriptions, the languages they spoke, what they talked about and a number of other points. They also showed great interest in Rashid's description of his encounter with the snipers at Lykovouni. In what seemed to the ensign to be more of an interrogation than a deposition, the lawyer probed him suspiciously. Why had he engaged the two Greeks in combat? And why had the Trustee placed him in charge of the cavalry unit afterwards?

More than an hour passed, and the more intense the interview became, the weaker and more light-headed Rashid felt. He began to cough more frequently than before, so that his testimony was interrupted several times. Soon the nurse-technician entered the room and informed the officers that the monitors showed the ensign had a slight fever, and that Dr. Mariatos was asking that they wrap things up as quickly as possible.

"Certainly—we're just about finished here anyway. Aren't we, Lieutenant?" replied the adjutant, addressing the notary in obvious annoyance over his caustic and even accusatory demeanor. "Unless you have any final questions for the Ensign?"

"Actually, just one," the lawyer responded, shrugging off the adjutant's disapproving tone.

Shooting Rashid his most intimidating look of the entire interview, he demanded in a loud voice: "Ensign Al-Noury, just what is your connection with this John Crowe, as you call him—and why do you suppose that instead of killing you, he actually helped you to resurface from your dive?"

Rashid was shocked. He had done his job to the best of his ability under circumstances of extreme danger, and he had also tried to be as helpful as possible throughout the entire interview process. But now it seemed that the lawyer was implying the unthinkable—that he had somehow collaborated with the enemy. He paused for a moment to clear his throat before answering, more saddened than outraged.

Then, before being shaken by another coughing fit and wincing from the pain in his shoulder, he furrowed his brow and moved his head from side to side.

"I don't have any connection with him at all, sir. I was sent by Lord Admiral Rizopoulos to infiltrate Ibrahim Pasha's camp and spy on him, and that's exactly what I tried to do. I really don't know why he helped me like that. In fact, I've been wondering the very same thing myself."

CAMP MONEMVASIA, GREECE—SATURDAY, SEPTEMBER 22, 2074

The intensive care ward of Camp Monemvasia's Paladin MediCenter buzzed with activity. Just a few weeks before, the unit had been occupied by a single patient—Vice Admiral Ephraimoglou. Now, however, all its rooms were filled and technicians had been called in to rig up temporary isolation tents in every bit of space that was available. Entering the ward wearing a surgical mask, a weary-looking Dr. Mariatos went over and spoke to one of the duty physicians, who stood near a row of monitor screens.

"What's happening, Paul?" he asked. "Any improvement?"

"I'm afraid not, Captain," the younger doctor replied, addressing Mariatos by his military rank. "Whatever we do, we just can't seem to get the fevers down, and a couple of them have gone into severe respiratory distress. We also have one case we're working on that is presenting symptoms of an acute hemolytic reaction, but we don't know yet if it's related to the same condition."

Pointing at one of the monitors, he continued: "Sub-lieutenant Phillips is the seventh case since yesterday morning, and—"

"What is it, Lieutenant?" Mariatos pressed.

"Well, sir, I'm really starting to worry that this is turning into something big. We've never had a situation like this before, and I don't know if we have the resources here to handle it."

Mariatos looked at his subordinate grimly for a moment and then said: "We'll just have to do the best we can, Paul. Unfortunately this is just the tip of the iceberg. I've just been on a call with Genetics over in the UK and it's not looking good."

"Why? What is it?" the young physician asked, his voice tense.

"They've done the sequencing and confirmed that it's definitely what we were afraid of," Mariatos sighed. "It's a Type A influenza—a strain that hasn't been seen before."

"Oh, my God," replied the duty physician in dismay. "Have they modeled it? Any idea about virulence and potential mortality?"

"High," said Mariatos, a frown framing his drawn mouth. "Both high. I think it's time to bring Sotiropoulou into the picture," he continued, referring to the medical officer in charge of the Guardian zones of Camp Monemvasia. "For one thing, we don't have enough beds here to handle what I'm afraid may become a local epidemic. For another thing...I think we're going to have to quarantine the whole damn base."

The young physician listened, staring off into the distance, imagining the frightful ramifications of what the chief medical officer had just told him. Shaking himself back to the present conversation, he suddenly asked: "Do we have any idea yet who Patient Alpha is?"

"I've had Arjuna and his team working on that," Mariatos answered, referring to one of the other physicians, "and I think we're just about certain that it's Ensign Al-Noury."

"Well, that's something positive!" Paul exclaimed. "You think he picked it up on his dive? If it originated back in 1825 and didn't cause a major outbreak then, maybe we can—" he began speaking excitedly; but seeing the look on the other man's face, he stopped abruptly.

"I see where you are going, but I don't think we can necessarily make that assumption," said Mariatos somberly. "For one thing, as you know, medical records from the nineteenth century are far from complete. It's certainly possible that specific strains of a virus existed locally that did not succeed in propagating, or which never achieved the critical mass to trigger a documented large-scale epidemic for some reason.

"Lack of sufficient population density, for example, particularly in a rural setting and in a time of war, when mortality rates were already high—that could be one explanation." The doctor hesitated for a moment and then, with a grave expression overshadowing his face, added: "And there could be others."

Looking intently into the younger doctor's eyes, as if trying to decide whether to divulge something significant to him, he motioned to him to step out of earshot of the nurses and technicians working in the vicinity. Once they were standing out of the way, he told him more of what he had learned.

"Unfortunately it's not that simple," he whispered. "Genetics are not a hundred percent sure yet and they've still got some analytical work to do, but there are some disturbing indications—some telltale markers, including residual proteins similar in structure to certain kinds of scorpion toxins used in many laboratories for protein scaffolds. Paul, it's beginning to look like this virus was engineered."

Seeing the young duty physician's eyes open wide in surprise, Mariatos put his finger to his lips and quickly silenced him.

"You cannot let anyone outside of our group know what I've just told you," he said sternly. "Even as we speak, there are teams in the UK, the US, Russia, Japan, China and Korea working on this thing. It's going to take time, but we *will* produce a vaccine. Until then, we are going to have to manage as best we can to avoid infections and to keep the numbers down. And the very last thing we need right now is a panic, or for rumors to start flying around that there is a designer virus on the loose, created to kill Paladins."

"But...but who would do such a thing?" Paul gasped, seemingly unable to take it all in.

"Who knows?" retorted Mariatos bitterly. "It's a dangerous world out there, and these kinds of things are not without precedent. There are documented cases from the early decades of this century where viruses were artificially created and spread just so the big pharmaceutical companies of the time could profit from the vaccines they sold. Obviously nothing like that could ever happen in this day and age—at least not for the same purpose. All I'm saying is, it's not beyond the realm of possibility that there are still those out there—terrorists or what have you—who would do something like this for their own reasons."

"Now listen," the Medical Chief continued, "I'm about to go and have a call with the senior commanders. In the meantime, I want you to quietly arrange for all the team leaders to meet me in the conference room in, say, forty-five minutes. The next several weeks are going to be long ones and we need to get everyone up to speed. We have a lot of organizing to do."

"Yes, sir," replied the young physician, aghast at what his commanding officer had told him. "I'll get on it right away."

"Good, Paul—I knew I could count on you," Mariatos said, pressing his lips together and trying in vain to summon a smile of encouragement.

What he had told his colleague was bad enough, but he had not disclosed everything. The latest information Mariatos had received from Genetics had put an even more sinister blush on the whole affair; but before saying anything to his team, he first needed to discuss the situation with Petrovich. For the truth of the matter was that, while the virus had the potential to affect a significant percentage of the population within Camp Monemvasia, it was beginning to look like it was aimed at a more specific target.

The initial results of the genetic analysis that had just been completed implied that some patients—those of certain blood antigen groups—were at far greater risk of mortality than others. But that was not all. Some indications had even emerged that the virus might have been designed to have its most deadly effects on those with specific genetic markers—markers that were oddly consistent with those in the genetic profile of one Lord Admiral Leonidas Rizopoulos. As much as he did not want to believe that such a thing was possible, the doctor found himself wondering if this was actually a perverse and hellishly conceived plot to assassinate the Paladin leader.

Turning and walking out of the intensive care ward to head for his office, Dr. Mariatos experienced a brief moment of wooziness and began to cough. Thank God for Rizopoulos's sake that he was not around to be exposed, he thought, but there were still so many others who would be affected. He only hoped his colleagues in Genetics were working round the clock, because at the rate the infection was spreading, there would be very little time left to spare.

CHAPTER 13

The sun was high overhead as the small bark, heavily laden with its cargo of corn, dry biscuit, and artillery shells, approached the narrow channel marking the entrance to the shallow lagoon. Yet the cheerful brightness of the blue and cloudless winter sky was in no way reflected on the tense and anxious faces of the dozen men on board.

At daybreak five and a half hours before, when they had first set sail from the British protectorate of Zante—the old Venetian name for the Ionian island of Zakynthos—a stiff and bitter wind had blown at their backs from the south, driving them easily forward on a choppy sea. The captain and his three mates had been engaged in lively chatter to ward off the cold; but as they made their way around the horn of Cape Klarenza and bore northeastward towards the Gulf of Patras, the sailors fell ever more silent, even as the winds calmed and the waves abated. Once having entered the gulf, moreover, every tongue was completely stilled and each eye grew watchful for the sight of the red flags of the Ottoman fleet.

Fortunately for the crew and eight passengers, it was the third day in a row in which the Turkish sail had remained inactive. Several Zantian vessels had already made the crossing to deliver much-needed provisions to their desperate comrades-in-arms and to ferry the few travelers desirous of making such a perilous journey, and had returned safely to their port of origin. Still, these were treacherous waters and dangerous times, and there was no way of knowing when, after a brief respite, the Ottomans would once again set out to intercept any ships caught in their path.

Only a few days before, eight seamen from the island of Hydra had been killed in a skirmish off the nearby coast of the tiny island of Dragomestre, and a resumption of hostilities was to be expected at any moment. Thus, even as they neared their destination, all on board the craft remained silent, their firearms locked and loaded and their two small eight-pound guns ready for action at the slightest provocation.

Despite the blustery chill of the early morning breeze, the day had proven to be rather mild for early December. One of the eight passengers on board had long since removed the heavy woolen mantle he had purchased in Zante almost a fortnight before, while awaiting his earliest opportunity to embark on the dangerous sea journey to the besieged town of Messolonghi. He was a large bearded man, quiet and solemn, and almost regal in his bearing. He spoke little with his fellow passengers, who for their part seemed content to leave the black-robed figure they assumed to be a monk to pray in peace.

As they sailed along, beating against the wind on their starboard side, it occurred to him how inconceivable it would have been to his fellow voyagers to discover that one of the men in their midst was not only a naval officer, but one with the lofty rank of lord high admiral of the fleet. His, however, was a navy that plied a different kind of sea—one whose buffeting waves stretched across the vast expanse and unfathomable depths of time.

Lord Admiral Leonidas Rizopoulos's stay in Zante had been much longer than he had intended—more than twelve days in all, ever since he had broken off from shadowing the movements of

Ibrahim Pasha and his army in the latter part of November. Almost three months before that, after a long and difficult journey, he had succeeded in carrying Vice Admiral Ephraimoglou to the hot zone at Monemvasia. Sending his critically wounded colleague back with his own diving bell had been a huge risk in his barely conscious state; but there had been very little choice. If he had not done it, Ephraimoglou surely would have died. He only hoped he had made it through.

After a much-needed rest, he had then doubled back in the direction of Mystras in order to track down his apprentice, Rashid. Riding through the foothills that would give way to the broad plain of Elaía, he had been greatly relieved to pick up not only the signal from the ensign's EDT, but another one as well—that of the marker beacon which the young Paladin had evidently succeeded in deploying.

He had eventually caught up with Crowe and his company of soldiers somewhere near Sykiá, and, following at a distance, had traveled behind them all the way to the lagoon at Iérakos. All the while, he had sought an opportunity to make his presence known to Rashid, but it was not as easy as he had hoped.

Crowe had been watching Rashid like a hawk—a sure sign that he either suspected, or had already identified the young Moroccan as a Paladin. Either way, Rizopoulos knew that his protégé was in danger and had decided that he would have to find a way to get him out as soon as possible. He was still working out a plan of attack, when the situation had become even more complex.

Arriving at the bay of Iérakos behind Crowe and his men, Rizopoulos had seen the Austrian-flagged brig enter the harbor and observed the altercation between the two Trustee operatives. Immediately his suspicion was confirmed. Whatever the Trustees were up to was far more involved than just Crowe's part of the operation, and the lord admiral had to find out what it was.

The choice had been an agonizing one. Rizopoulos knew that Rashid was in danger, but he also knew the young ensign was very capable and had already proven his resourcefulness. Besides, his marker beacon had been deployed, which meant that a Paladin dive team would soon be on its way and he would not be without backup for very long. It was also apparent that Crowe had some use for him—otherwise he would have gotten rid of him long before, and certainly would not have gone through the trouble of keeping the Moroccan by his side. At the same time, letting the other Trustee agent go with no idea of what he was planning was out of the question.

Weighing the risks, Rizopoulos had made his decision. Looking anxiously back at Rashid one last time, he had invisibly slipped into the empty launch that ferried the German back to the waiting brig, from there to sail with him down the coast and onward to the southern island of Crete.

Confident that his Paladins would prevent any significant changes from being made to the time period's sequence of events, Rizopoulos had a clear idea of what to expect. In a few days, after discovering that the fortress at Monemvasia was still in the hands of the Greek garrison, Ibrahim and his column would begin their long slow march back across the Peloponnese, slaughtering, burning and looting all the way. Stopping briefly at Kalamata, they would then move on to the Ottoman stronghold at Methoni. There, in early November, they would be refreshed with provisions and reinforcements brought up from Alexandria via Crete—and the lord admiral planned on being with them.

From Methoni, Ibrahim would send most of his army ahead by sea to Patras. In total, the small fleet of Egyptian ships would carry more than eight thousand disciplined Arabs, eight hundred

Turkish irregulars and twelve hundred mounted cavalry—along with yet again as many grooms, artisans and servants, and all their train of supplies and equipment—to the Peloponnese's northwestern coast. Meanwhile, the commander himself would continue to march northward by land at the head of a four-thousand-strong detachment, making for the old coastal castle at Rio, on the westernmost extreme of the Gulf of Corinth.

In the end, Rizopoulos's instincts had been correct—going to Crete had been the right decision after all. Although the picture that emerged was not as complete as he would have liked it to be, the information about the Trustees' plans that he gathered there was crucial. It seemed that Chief Brindakis's theory had been very near the mark indeed, and at least he now knew what he had to do.

Rejoining Ibrahim's army at Methoni, the lord admiral trailed the Egyptian commander along his entire inland march. He watched with incredulity as the would-be supreme commander of the Peloponnese had almost been killed leading a senseless skirmish in the swamps of Agoulinitsa, on the southern bank of the Alpheios River. Almost comically, it seemed that the Egyptian satrap had become mired in the thick silt and, having been thrown from his horse, barely managed to be dragged to safety by his men through the muddy water and under heavy musket fire.

Perhaps it was in revenge for this humiliation at the hands of a small company of ragged canoe-paddling insurgents, who had taken refuge with their families in the lagoon's low-lying islets, that the *pasha* had crossed the Alpheios on the twenty-first of November in a murderous rage. By fire and the sword, he laid waste to towns throughout the province of Ileía: Pyrgos, Gastouni, Andravida and Lykania, to name but a few.

Meanwhile, the inhabitants were driven before him through the now-desolate region, taking refuge in such places as the distant mountains of Arcadia, or the old Venetian coastal forts of Castel Tornese and Pontikocastro, or the fortified monastery at Skaphidia. Some, however, refused to flee, preferring to die proudly defending their villages, as at Vartholomaíon. It was there that the masses of the marauding Egyptian army were held off for an entire day by a paltry but intrepid two hundred fifty armed residents, until all but forty-five of the valiant defenders—mainly women and children—had been slain.

With Ibrahim's destructive progress through the western side of the peninsula corresponding to the documented historical accounts with uncanny precision, the Egyptian army's objective was clear. Knowing the difficulties he would encounter attempting to cross over the Gulf of Corinth from the Ottoman-controlled northern coast of Achaïa, Rizopoulos decided to break off from pursuing his quarry for a time and make for Zante, where he hoped to find transport to his final destination. Thus it was that, after nearly two weeks of suspenseful waiting, he now found himself entering the broad and shallow lagoon in plain sight of that long-contested and desperately besieged town—that which future generations would come to call the 'Sacred City'—the Aetolo-Akarnanian capital of Messolonghi.

Situated strategically at the southeastern edge of the vast and bountiful Aetolo-Akarnanian lagoon ecosystem, that quondam fishing village—known to the once-occupying Venetians as 'mezzo laghi', or 'amidst the lakes'—was both blessed and cursed by its location.

On the one hand, it had been abundantly provided for by nature with a bounty of fish and vast natural salt flats, which over time had transformed it into an important regional commercial and trading center. With the city's growing wealth and its picturesque setting among the lush green agricultural plains and the soaring purple mountains of the Arakynthos range, it had begun to attract a growing population of entrepreneurs and men of letters. It had even lately become the final resting place of the cenotaph-entombed heart of that renowned English poet and gentleman, George Lord Byron, who had so recently given up his very soul for the cause of liberty there.

On the other hand, its firm command over the entrance to the Gulf of Corinth and the access it provided to Epirus and the other regions of northern and western Greece had long made it a coveted prize, the capture of which was a military priority for the Ottomans. From early in the uprising, they had laid bitter siege to it with tiresome regularity—first by the agency of the Albanian *pasha*, Omer Vrioni, whose assault from November of 1822 until January of 1823 pitted a combined Ottoman army of more than ten thousand soldiers against a poorly equipped Greek force of a little over two thousand men.

Through a combination of subtle strategy, the diplomatic adroitness of the defending Greeks under their famed leader Mavrocordatos, and the besieged fighters' prowess in battle—as well as the ravages of disease and famine among the Ottoman troops—that first attempt had ended in abject failure. Thousands of Turkish and Albanian foot soldiers had perished senselessly, and the once-esteemed *pasha* was utterly disgraced.

Then, after a hiatus of more than two years, during which intermittent naval blockades and invasions of a number of fortified islets in the lagoon were unsuccessfully attempted by various Ottoman chieftains, the siege was once again prosecuted in earnest. This time, the military operations were led by the Ottoman army's recently named commander-in-chief of all Central Greece, the so-called *roumeli vasely*, Reshid Pasha.

A Georgian by birth, this unlikely son of an Orthodox Christian priest from the Caucasus mountains had been kidnapped as a child, forcibly converted to Islam and raised as an Ottoman *janissary*. And having once become a protégé of the naval commander Khosref Capitan Pasha, he had quickly risen through the military ranks.

As bloodthirsty as he was clever, Reshid occupied the plain in front of Messolonghi from late April of 1825 until the following October, at the head of an army of thirty thousand men. He nearly succeeded in taking the unfortunate town on several occasions; but being repulsed innumerable times by the uncommon valor and the brazen daring of the hard-pressed Greeks—and overcome by the vagaries of supply chain interruptions, inclement weather and the spread of disease and famine in his camp—he was finally forced temporarily to lift the siege in bitter frustration. And to add insult to injury, he was then ordered by none other than the *sultan* himself to await reinforcement by his powerful archrival, Ibrahim Pasha.

The Greeks and their handful of foreign *philhellene* allies were thus barricaded behind Messolonghi's poor mud walls and simple ditches in conditions of near starvation, with the full weight of the military resources of one of the world's mightiest empires about to bear down like the razor-sharp point of a bayonet on the nine thousand desperate but defiant souls there. It was at this most decisive hour that Sir Leonidas Rizopoulos, Paladin lord admiral and knight of the World Council, first set foot on the sacred ground of the city that was soon to become the sacrificial spring lamb for the hard-fought liberty of a nation.

BEFORE SO MUCH as stepping onshore, Lord Rizopoulos realized that even his detailed knowledge of the history of the time and the place could not adequately prepare him for the reality he was about to face. Spying the approaching Zantian bark as it navigated its way through the channel around the barrier islet of Vasiladi and entered the lagoon, a throng of people had gathered just outside the city and let off a volley of musketry in welcome. Others, meanwhile, had come out in small *monoxyla* canoes across a narrow channel to a nearby islet with a large windmill a little more than a hundred meters offshore, which served as a quay for vessels with larger drafts.

It was this same windmill—a building now being used as a munitions depot—that the Paladin lord admiral recognized as the place where, in just over four months' time, one of the most tragic scenes would occur in the drama that was about to unfold. In a final act of retribution, hundreds of those making their defiant last stand there would blow themselves up, along with scores of storming Ottoman troops, rather than fall into the hands of the enemy.

As the crew rowed nearer the landing site with sails lowered, the men aboard could see the haggard faces of the crowd. Beneath their expressions of obvious relief and joy at receiving another precious shipment of provisions from their ardent supporters in the Ionian islands, there were the unmistakable signs of the most extreme exhaustion mixed with despair. For, even before the goods were unloaded, they already knew that such meager supplies would do very little to alleviate the wretchedness of their condition.

Jumping out of the vessel as soon as it anchored, Rizopoulos and the other seven men—*pallikari* militiamen from the Morea who had come voluntarily to join in the defense of the town— although strangers, were greeted as heroes with warm hugs and kisses from everyone in the crowd. At the same time, the captain and crew of the boat, nervous lest they be caught out in the lagoon by a Turkish ship of war, clamored for the men to start unloading the supplies, so that they would lose no time in making their retreat.

Moving quickly despite their obvious fatigue, the group of armed men, together with a few women and boys, set up a human chain and began unloading the wooden barrels of foodstuffs and crates of supplies. Rizopoulos and his shipmates soon found themselves also pressed into service, engaged in their first collaborative efforts with the locals. By the time the supplies had been offloaded and the boat had pulled its way off into the lagoon amidst waves and cries of encouragement from both sides, many more people—some in flat-bottomed launches and others wading across up to their knees in water and thick mud— had crossed over to the islet to help.

Rizopoulos then noticed that his fellow shipmates had found acquaintances in the crowd and were being conducted towards a couple of small dinghies to be ferried the short distance to the city, where they would be attached to some military unit. Taking advantage of their departure, he left the crowd of people beginning to organize for the task of bringing the supplies up into town and hastened to fall in with his erstwhile travel companions. Once ashore, he began making his way through the city streets, and what he saw there shocked him.

The damage to houses and buildings—even those visible from the relatively sheltered part of town closest to the lagoon— was much more extensive than he had expected. As far as the eye could see, structures lay in rubble. Vast amounts of stone and charred, splintered wood had been laid up in great heaps along the roadsides in an apparent attempt to keep some order and to facilitate movement through the main thoroughfares. Many of the unpaved streets were still muddy from the recent rains, and everywhere the ground was marked with craters and potholes filled with turbid water—the result of months of incessant bombardment.

The relatively few people Rizopoulos saw out in the open were either soldiers briskly walking to or from some assignment, or artisans performing some job such as filling in potholes or repairing collapsed ditches. And then there were the shades: the gaunt and emaciated residents in little more than rags—women, a few children and the elderly—who meandered slowly through the streets in a daze, as if shell-shocked, heedless of where they were walking, and stepping equally in puddles of cold murky water as on solid ground. They could not yet know it, but they were already the living dead.

As he made his way towards the main administrative quarter, Lord Admiral Rizopoulos could not help but marvel, mentally contrasting the picture of the bustling and wealthy metropolis he knew from his own time with the shattered town that lay wounded and bleeding before him. Indeed, every place he looked, there was a stark presage of the fate that was soon to befall both the city and its residents.

On one street he passed stood the house where Lord Byron had lived during his stay in Messolonghi—and where he had died from pneumonia almost two years before. In a few months, the lord admiral mused grimly, nothing would remain of the structure except a huge crater. The home's owner—one of the city's leading men, Christos Kapsalis—together with dozens of the last-remaining residents, would detonate a massive amount of ordnance stockpiled there, as the Ottoman soldiers closed in all around them.

In another place was the printing press and office of the *Greek Chronicles*, a newspaper edited by a Swiss *philhellene* named J.J. Mayer, who also commanded a detachment of *pallikari* fighters. He would die that coming April, sword rather than pen in hand, cut to pieces by Reshid Pasha's cavalry on the night of the final battle, and his Greek wife and their child would be captured and sold into slavery. As Rizopoulos recalled, after the events that were soon to take place in the city, his last and most poignant letter—written shortly before his death and later published in numerous continental journals—would posthumously do more to help rouse the spirit of European outrage against the Ottomans than his newspaper had ever done.

Pausing for a moment to stand before the shop, the lord admiral looked through the window and saw Mayer inside, bent over his machines with his shirt-sleeves rolled up, setting blocks of type in the press. Seeing him there, the ominous words he would pen in several weeks' time began to intrude presciently upon the Paladin leader's mind.

'The labors which we have undergone,' he would soon write, *'and a wound which I have received in the shoulder, while I am in expectation of one which will be my passport to eternity, have prevented me till now from bidding you my last adieu. We are reduced to feed upon the filthiest of animals—we are suffering horribly with hunger and thirst. Sickness adds much to the calamities which overwhelm us. Seventeen hundred and forty of our brethren are dead. More than a hundred thousand bombs and balls, thrown by the enemy, have destroyed our bastions and our houses. We have been terribly distressed by the cold, for we have suffered great want of wood.*

'Notwithstanding so many privations, it is a great and noble spectacle to witness the ardor and devotedness of the garrison. A few days more, and these brave men will be angelic spirits, who will accuse before God the indifference of Christendom for a cause which is that of religion. All the Albanians who had deserted from the standard of Reshid Pasha, have now rallied under that of Ibrahim. In the name of all our brave men, among whom are Nothis Botsaris, Tzavellas, Papadiamantopoulos, and myself, whom the government has appointed

general to a body of its troops, I announce to you the resolution sworn to before heaven, to defend foot by foot the land of Messolonghi, and to bury ourselves, without listening to any capitulation, under the ruins of this city.

*'We are drawing near our final hour. History will render us justice—posterity will weep over our misfortunes. I am proud to think that the blood of a Swiss—of a son of William Tell—is about to mingle with that of the heroes of Greece.'**

THE SUDDEN SOUND of several concussions in the distance shook Rizopoulos out of his momentary contemplation. They were accompanied by high-pitched whistling sounds lasting about ten to fifteen seconds, and followed by a series of dull blasts from shells exploding somewhere near the fortifications.

Taking his leave from the printing press, he continued walking hurriedly through town. In order to succeed in his mission, it was not enough for him simply to show up in Messolonghi. He had to insinuate himself into that society—but he must manage to do so without being compelled to take up a weapon and potentially affect the past. And given his appearance, there was only one practical way to do it.

After a little while, having been directed by some artisans repairing the collapsed wall of a building, Rizopoulos found the place he was looking for. It was a modest house near a church dedicated to the fourth-century physician and martyr, Saint Panteleimon.

Inside the fenced-in garden, gathered around the entrance guarded by a single *evzonos* soldier, was a crowd of people—mostly older women and mothers with dirty, ragged children clinging to them—waiting for someone to leave so that they might push their way inside and make their petition for help. On seeing Rizopoulos in his long black cassock, the guard demanded that a path be cleared and motioned for him to come through. Speaking to him briefly and satisfied that he was not a threat, the sentry opened the door a crack and allowed the presumed monk to enter.

Once within, Rizopoulos saw that, although the *evzonos* was using his body to bar the way from the press of clamoring women who tried to take advantage of each momentary aperture, it was even more crowded inside the house than it was outside. For every person who left, two or three managed to force their way in past the guard and take their place. Squeezing his way through the packed foyer, the lord admiral eventually made his way into a sitting room, where he was immediately struck with unexpected awe upon seeing the man he had come to meet.

Seated on a plain cushioned chair, wearing a simple black cassock distinguished only by an ornate gold and enamel pectoral cross hanging over his breast, and surrounded by a multitude of piteous residents pleading for his assistance with various urgent needs, was the local church hierarch, Bishop Joseph of Rogon and Kozylis. Rizopoulos was immediately struck by his face, which was at once severe and compassionate, stern but also kind.

Despite the dire circumstances all around him, the prelate's presence strangely filled him with a sense of serenity and reassurance. At the same time, however, he could not escape the horrible picture that, like the crowd outside the house, pushed its way insistently into his mind. It was the image of how this austere-looking yet saintly paternal figure, with his flowing white beard, would soon be found amidst the rubble of the blast-torn windmill—badly burned and barely alive—only to face death a second time by hanging at the hands of the Ottoman Turks.

Flanked by a couple of priests and a deacon, the bishop patiently sought to comfort all those who had come to him for succor, taking note of their problems and their worries and offering whatever assistance he could. In some instances, the help came in the form of material aid, with the hierarch issuing instructions to his clerics to provide extra rations or a small amount of money. In other cases his support was purely spiritual—a confession heard, a warm smile and a hand held, a blessing and a word of encouragement in a time of great anxiety and emotional distress.

Rizopoulos waited a long while as the prelate greeted everyone who came to him, no matter what their rank or social standing, with the same unhurried warmth and affection, as if they were the only person in the room. Finally, the bishop took notice of the Paladin lord admiral standing in the crowd and smiled, calling out to him.

"And you, Father? You're not one of ours, are you? Come here so I can have a better look at you," he said cordially.

The people around him giving way a little, Rizopoulos managed to squeeze through the crush and make his way over to the hierarch, bowing before him and kissing his hand upon receiving his blessing.

"Yes, that's better—my eyes are not quite what they used to be," remarked the bishop. "Ah, I see, you're new among us. What's your name, Father, and how is it that you've come to join us here in Messolonghi in our final hours?"

"They call me Leonidas, your grace," answered Rizopoulos, feeling pleasantly strange—having become accustomed to the responsibilities of high titles and the privileges of rank—at the sudden lightness of being associated with such simplicity. "I've just arrived from the Peloponnese. I have this for you."

From the folds of his cassock, the Paladin leader drew out a letter with a wax seal, given to him a few months before by the abbot of the monastery of the Holy Forty Martyrs of Sebaste, Elder Aetios. Without having been informed of Rizopoulos's ultimate intentions, the holy old man had said to him simply: "Give this to the bishop of the place you are going."

Taking out his reading glasses, Bishop Joseph broke open the seal and began to read the letter, smiling at first when he recognized the handwriting and remarking: "Wonderful! It's from my old friend, Aetios. So you're one of his." But then as he read on, the hierarch appeared briefly shaken, and his face grew ashen and grave and he exhaled deeply.

When he had finished reading, he folded the letter neatly and made the sign of the cross over himself, and then speaking to his deacon, instructed him to throw it into the fire burning on the hearth. He sat for a moment with his brow knitted, but then his face brightened and he turned back to Rizopoulos with a gentle smile and said:

"The Elder speaks well of you. You are welcome here among us. The deacon here will help you get settled. I'm afraid, however, that there is little we can offer in the way of true hospitality. As you see, our conditions are becoming more primitive day by day."

"Never fear, Your Grace," answered Rizopoulos stalwartly. "I came not to accept hospitality, but to perform a duty for my fellow men. I am ready to do whatever work is needed—anything, that is, except for bearing arms."

"Of course," replied the bishop, "that goes without saying. As it happens, there is much more work of a non-combatant nature to be done here every day than able-bodied men we have to perform it, since all who can are defending the walls. May you be blessed for your service."

Thus Lord Admiral Rizopoulos entered into the community of the besieged, daily performing whatever tasks were required of him—from helping to repair the ramparts, to shoring up the ditches and digging new ones; from bringing rations to the soldiers and invalids, to assisting in the care of the sick and the wounded. At the same time, however, he also clandestinely carried out another duty—one known only to him, and the true reason for which he had come.

As the days wore on amidst the constant toil and incessant dangers of a life under siege and bombardment, he made careful observation and diligent investigation. Out of the town's population of nearly three thousand militia and six thousand civilians, there was one man in particular he had to find. And as abhorrent as the idea might be, the safety of that one man mattered more to him at that moment in time than that of any other person in the city of Messolonghi. For it was this one—a man whose very existence was to become synonymous with the perfidious treachery that would attend the final hours of that noble place—whom he was sworn to protect, even though he did not yet even know his name.

CHAPTER 14

The days passed quickly for Lord Admiral Rizopoulos in a swirl of events, with news from the outside world trickling in bit by bit.

After several days in the besieged town he learned that, just one day after his arrival by boat from Zante, the Turkish fleet had intercepted seven Zantian vessels ferrying Peloponnesian volunteers to Messolonghi. The engagement had drawn a nearby Greek patrol into a naval skirmish that resulted in the loss of one of their best *brûlotiers*—those daring fire-boat captains who risked their own lives to steer explosives-laden vessels into the enemy fleet, igniting them and attempting to escape in small getaway craft at the last minute.

After that, the weather had deteriorated rapidly. Due to a combination of storms and the increased activity of the Ottoman fleet inside the Gulf of Corinth, the meager flow of supplies into the city was choked off even further. Then, exactly two weeks after Rizopoulos's arrival, another event had occurred which chilled the blood of all those who witnessed it and contributed greatly to a sudden darkening of the mood within the city's walls.

Perhaps it was out of frustration over the recent stalemate between the belligerents, in which sickness and desertion were slowly wreaking havoc on the sustainability of his army; or perhaps it was due to a desperate attempt on the part of the *roumeli vasely* to force the defenders into a last-minute capitulation, before his archrival Ibrahim could take the field and claim the laurels of any eventual victory. Whatever the reasons, the Georgian-born Reshid Pasha—known among the Greeks and Albanians by the epithet '*Kioutahí*', which referred to a region he had once governed in Asia Minor—had shown the apparent limitlessness of his capacity for barbarity.

On the twentieth of December, less than a week before Ibrahim Pasha sent the first of his advanced troops to take up their positions on Reshid's flank, the *Kioutahí* had ordered a handful of Greek prisoners—a priest, two women and several teenage boys—to be impaled alive at the front of his camp, in full view of the Greek garrison.

The ramifications of this singular event were manifold and deep. For most of those defending the walls, the sight of the weakest and most innocent of their countrymen being butchered so savagely just a couple of hundred meters away, while they remained powerless to help, only served to magnify their hatred for an enemy that had oppressed them for so long, and stiffened their resolve.

Thus, a few weeks later, when Ibrahim Pasha sent a message to the leaders of the besieged city asking them to delegate Turkish-, Albanian- and French-speaking representatives to be escorted to his camp for negotiations before he initiated his siege operations in earnest, the Greeks answered laconically: '*We are poor and unlettered and do not know so many languages; but we do understand how to handle our guns and our swords.*'*

But for a few of those on the ramparts that day, physically and psychologically drained after months of hunger, privation and danger, the grisly scene had planted a different kind of seed—one of fear and revulsion at the thought of being slaughtered in the mud like animals. And among them, secretly beginning to nurture the corrupted and misshapen fruit born from a loathing of just such a death, was a certain Bulgarian *pallikari* militiaman.

Rizopoulos had been one of those present that day—working with a crew of artisans to help reinforce a section of the wall which had begun to collapse from the impact of an exploding mortar shell the night before—when the execution had taken place. Mesmerized by the gruesome spectacle along with everyone else, he had finally gone back to working on the wall.

While trying to overcome the feelings of bitter indignation that arose within him, he noticed a thin man with blue eyes and a look of deep anxiety etched on his Slavic features staring at him from his position by one of the loopholes. He had seen the fellow before and had been keeping an eye on him for several days, but he was not yet certain if he was the one he was looking for. Now, however, the man finally spoke to him of his own accord, as if unable to contain his apprehension.

"How can you just go back to work like that, Father?" he called over in his lightly accented but fluent Greek to the black-robed Rizopoulos, whom he supposed to be an Orthodox monk. "Didn't you see how they just killed that priest and the others with him? They just slaughtered them like lambs! And that's just what's going to happen to the rest of us when they finally get in here!"

Rizopoulos stood up from where he had been working and looked up at the man, seeing in his dilated pupils and flared nostrils the telltale signs of fear and desperation, as if he were struggling with a violent urge to flee. He was sure he had found his mark.

Saying nothing, he was about to return to his digging, when one of the Greek *pallikari* soldiers standing at the wall nearby—a wisecracking young man called Odysseus—remarked loudly, drawing a round of morbid and derisive laughter from his fellow soldiers:

"Come on now, Bulgarian, stop worrying! You're certainly no priest—but if you keep on whimpering like that, *Kioutahí* just might mistake you for a woman or a child and stick you on a spit, too!"

The reaction was swift. The Bulgarian immediately spat on the ground, cursing in his native language, and moved as if to go after Odysseus with his *mahaira* short-sword raised, ready to strike. The two men would have come to blows, if not for the intervention of several of their comrades-in-arms, who held them back and calmed the situation down. Even so, as they grudgingly returned to their posts, Rizopoulos noticed the cunning look that contorted the Bulgarian's angry face, as he muttered with contempt:

"We'll see who ends up with his head on a pike before this whole dirty business is over!"

From that moment on, the Paladin lord admiral kept a close watch on the Bulgarian, making every effort to arrange his work schedule to be near him when he was serving guard duty, and shadowing his every movement when he was off duty.

THE DREARY REMNANT of December's days passed in a collage of gray skies and cold winter rains, punctuated by intermittent periods of thunderous cannonades and flashing bombardments originating on both sides of Messolonghi's defensive walls. Occasionally a strike would hit its mark and a few citizens— civilians, more often than not—who happened to be in the wrong place at the wrong time would be severely injured or killed. However, the artillery fire did little to change the overall dynamics of the siege.

After a few weeks, Lord Admiral Rizopoulos had become so inured to the quotidian, almost routine sound of falling bombs and exploding shells that he no longer took particular notice of them. Indeed, in those relatively rare hours of quiet, when by some coincidence both sides relented from their noisemaking for a time, it seemed to him and everyone else that something was out of place. The exchange of fire would soon start up again, owing more to habit than to any realistic hope of a tactical advantage being gained on the part of either of the belligerents.

The year 1826 arrived to more of the same, except that during the first week of January, Ibrahim Pasha—newly arrived from the Morea—marched with his entire army to take up a position to the left of Reshid Pasha's troops before the pitiful mud walls and defensive ditches of Messolonghi. The assault force now stood at greater than forty thousand soldiers and cavalry, with nearly another ten thousand servants, artisans, grooms and slaves, spread out in the vast marshy plain before the city, and afflicted with nearly as many hardships as those suffered by the defenders barricaded within.

In the absence of suitable roads, the Egyptians had been forced to carry their equipment, supplies and ammunition up from the coastal magazines on foot, balancing their cargo on their heads for a distance of twenty kilometers over rough terrain, across the torrent of the icy Evinos River, and through tracts of muddy and frigid swampland. As a result, many in the Egyptian camp died from illness and exposure before they had ever seen a single battle. Still countless others met their end through the agency of the periodic blazes that swept through the rows of tents and huts, from campfires gone out of control.

Heedless of the calamities within his encampment, for six weeks the would-be viceroy of the Peloponnese concentrated his efforts on constructing a flotilla of flat-bottomed barges with which to effect an invasion from the lagoon. At the same time, he built up artillery batteries, completed networks of trenches and earthworks, and transported ordnance to the camp from his depot at Krioneri on the coast.

He also ordered a stop to the constant cannonade that his colleague, the *roumeli vasely*, had kept up for the better part of six months, judging it to be a useless waste of ammunition. In fact, more than anything else, it was this unaccustomed silence from the enemy camp which eventually led the Greeks to notice that the Turks and their paid Albanian mercenaries had been replaced at the front lines by the Egyptians.

But the defenders' initial lack of attentiveness regarding the enemy's change in command was not completely inexcusable. Hemmed in as they were on all sides, the garrison had been distracted by other pressing matters; for by the middle of January, at just about the same time that Ibrahim issued his invitation for negotiations, their scant provisions had begun to dwindle precariously. Bread was fast on its way to becoming a memory within the confines of the city, and all of the large animals had already been slaughtered and consumed.

If not for the few thousand armed defenders' sheer determination to hold out until the bitter end against an army more than ten times their number, the siege of Messolonghi might have ended then and there, a full three months sooner than it was ultimately to conclude. But hold out they did, and on the sixteenth day of the month, after a three hour naval battle against an Ottoman squadron of superior size, the intrepid Greek Admiral Miaoulis—a former merchant seaman from the island of Hydra—broke through the Turkish blockade for the last time and managed to throw two months' worth of basic provisions into the starving town.

Even as the gallant but desperate defense of Messolonghi was slowly and imperceptibly grinding to its inevitable halt, Rizopoulos was daily amazed by the acts of uncommon heroism—both great and small—to which he was witness. By the middle of February, Ibrahim Pasha had completed his preparations, establishing several heavily fortified artillery batteries within four hundred meters of the city walls. He then announced the commencement of the full force of his siege operations by unleashing a brutal three-day campaign of continuous bombardment on that unfortunate place.

In a period of seventy-two hours—from sunrise on the twelfth of the month until nightfall on the fourteenth—more than eight thousand bombs and shells were fired mercilessly into the city, destroying what little remained of the houses and infrastructure, but taking a surprisingly small toll in terms of the lives of the populace sheltered in ditches and underground bunkers. Then, immediately afterwards, at two o'clock in the morning of the fifteenth, Ibrahim ordered a general assault and the combined armies of the two *pashas* savagely stormed the town's fortifications under a barrage of covering artillery fire, capturing an important outwork and threatening to break through the main defenses.

Undaunted however by the display of superior firepower and the vastly greater number of their enemies, at first light the Greeks gave their daring and insolent answer. Rushing through the gates and the breaches in the walls caused by the Ottoman shells with little more than swords in hand, through their sheer ferocity and unbridled courage they drove the Egyptian forces back and reclaimed their fortifications.

Then, as if their spirited defense were not enough to show their true mettle, the garrison regrouped and sallied out at nightfall, counterattacking the enemy's trenches with such a punishing blow that they effectively put an end to Ibrahim's plans for a ground assault. From that moment on—although his troops continued in vain to carry out attacks and were repulsed on an almost daily basis—the *pasha* began to turn all his thoughts to the lagoon, which formed a natural barrier on Messolonghi's western and southern flanks, and on which the relatively weaker defenses on that side of the city depended.

The bold military exploits of the besieged, however, were by no means the only way in which Lord Admiral Rizopoulos discerned the genuine courage and stalwart resolve of the Greeks. About this time, as the beleaguered town was entering its darkest final weeks, one of its leading men, John Papadiamantopoulos—a wealthy merchant from Patras who had taken up the cause of national independence with fervor, and who had become one of the provisional government's leaders in western Greece—returned from Zante. He had gone there earlier in the year attempting to arrange for a delivery of desperately needed food, ammunition and other supplies; and, braving the dangers of the sea crossing under the threat of the Ottoman patrols, he had returned with what meager supplies he had been able to gather.

Although his numerous and influential friends had insisted that he remain on the Ionian island in safety, arguing that he was too old to fight and that he could do more for the cause of liberty there than by returning to almost certain death in Messolonghi, the sixty-year-old patrician had refused to listen. His only answer to their persistent entreaties was: "I invited my countrymen to take up arms against the Turks, and I swore to live and die with them. This is the hour to keep my pledge."*

The latter he would soon do with great valor—as Rizopoulos recalled with admiration upon seeing him once at Bishop Joseph's residence—fighting bravely in the final exodus, only to be wounded and captured, and ultimately beheaded by a Turkish scimitar.

THE MONTH OF MARCH finally approached, heralding with its advent the beginning of the end for the besieged city of Messolonghi. It also put Paladin Lord Admiral Leonidas Rizopoulos in a permanent state of high alert. But just when he needed to be at his most vigilant, he was distressed to find that— like the rest of the beleaguered town's faltering inhabitants—he was becoming weaker all the time.

Each day since his arrival in the town, he had diligently compared the events he witnessed or heard about with the detailed historical record programmed into his dive computer. Thus far the correlation had been perfect. While that knowledge had given him a certain amount of comfort, it also told him that the probability of a Trustee strike was increasing significantly with each passing day.

Therefore his sleep, which had never before been indulgent, was even more limited now—down to only two or three hours a night. And what little rest he did get was often interrupted, coming in short stints of fifteen to twenty minutes at a time. Struggling with ever-present fatigue, it was only through great mental and physical effort that he was able to remain continually watchful. But that was not all.

With the city's provisions already so perilously low, he had been loath to present himself as yet another hungry mouth to feed—something which, under the circumstances, might have led indirectly to the premature death of one of the locals. Therefore, he had all along avoided accepting any food rations from the town authorities. Instead, he had been subsisting on the remnant of a small supply of nourishing, high-energy protein pills he had brought with him from Camp Monemvasia.

However, these too were now beginning to run low, and he had been taking them only every other day of late, rather than the normally recommended twice daily. Thus it came to him as no surprise that he began to experience frequent piercing and distracting headaches, along with vague feelings of light-headedness and nausea; or that his movements were sometimes sluggish and seemed to lack their usual dexterity and coordination.

These were indeed troubling developments, especially considering the dangers of the environment and the magnitude of what was at stake. But there was nothing else to do except carry on as best he could, observing every event—looking out for any sign of potential divergence from the historical accounts, no matter how small—while all the time playing the role of undercover bodyguard to a skittish and increasingly paranoid Bulgarian.

Meanwhile, for Ibrahim Pasha and the combined Ottoman armies, this period also represented a significant turning point. Amidst the daily bombardment of the city, and the frequent skirmishes and raids outside the walls in which the Ottomans invariably came out the worse for wear, the Egyptian satrap devoted much of his time and energy to one unyielding occupation—the slow but relentless conquest of the small Greek outposts on the islets of Messolonghi's lagoon. It was this persistence more than anything else that would ultimately pay off, resulting in the delivery of the long-awaited and hard-fought Aetolian prize into his rapacious and blood-caked hands.

The first major break for the Ottoman assailants came with the conquest of Vasiladi, the largest of the small barrier islands at the head of the lagoon. Having constructed and fitted out several dozen flat-bottomed boats with light artillery pieces, and with his larger warships anchored in the Gulf as close to the island as possible, Ibrahim pounded the garrison there continuously for several hours on the twenty-fifth of February. The next morning, he ordered a general assault by forty flat-bottomed boats, each equipped with small cannon and carrying thirty Egyptian infantrymen.

The island's defenders—a sixty-two-man mixed company of artillerymen and irregular militia, captained by a battle-hardened Italian *philhellene* named Giaccomuzzi—responded bravely and inflicted material damage on the enemy's first waves. But in the end, there were simply too many of them. Overwhelmed by the vastly superior force of the one thousand two hundred soldiers thrown at them so violently, they retreated across the lagoon. Captain Giaccomuzzi and most of his men barely escaped with their lives, reaching Messolonghi half-frozen and exhausted after struggling for hours through the mud and the frigid waters.

Spurred on by his success at Vasiladi, Ibrahim wasted no time in sending his flotilla to attack the battery situated on a small mud bank called Dolma off the island of Aitoliko, which straddled the narrow straits separating the saltwater lagoon from its freshwater neighbor. For almost seven hours on February the twenty-eighth, the defenders' company of one hundred twenty *pallikari* fighters held out unflinchingly against the assaulting Ottoman forces, but were finally cut down to a man.

As a result, the three thousand men, women and children of Aitoliko—surrounded on all sides, without provisions or ammunition to withstand a siege, and driven to despair by the capture of Vasiladi and Dolma—capitulated to the Egyptians. The next day they were marched off in captivity to the Turkish garrison at distant Arta in exchange for their lives. Coincidentally, that first day of March was 'Kathará Deftera', or

Clean Monday—the first day of the Greek Orthodox Lent—and a hard Lent it was to be, indeed.

Ibrahim now controlled the two ends of the Messolonghi lagoon, and under the guidance of some European naval officers in his hire, arranged his flotilla in such a way as to block all transit between the besieged city and the outside world. With this stranglehold in place, he had effectively seized the town by its windpipe and, squeezing tightly, only had to wait long enough for his hapless victim to expire. Even to the last, however, the defenders were not to go down without a fight.

When on the twenty-fifth of March—a date which marked both the fifth anniversary since the start of the Greeks' war of independence, and their solemn celebration of the Annunciation of the Virgin Mary—the Ottomans tried to take the tiny islet of Kleisova, situated less than a kilometer from Messolonghi proper, they paid dearly for their miscalculation. Although the tower there was garrisoned by only a hundred and thirty fighters under the command of war hero Kitsos Tzavellas, by the end of that day the bodies of as many as a thousand Turks, Albanians and Egyptians lay floating in the blood-red waters of the lagoon.

Despite this last and encouraging victory for the Greek defenders, however, time was rapidly running out for the beleaguered inhabitants of Messolonghi. In early April of 1826, two developments in particular ominously signaled the point of no return.

First, there was the fact that, by the beginning of that month, the city's food rations were almost completely exhausted. For, aside from the Turkish naval blockade which had prevented any relief from reaching the town by way of the Gulf, the incessant firing and bombardment over a period of months had driven all the fish from the once teeming lagoon. The city that had made its fortune because of its abundant supply of seafood and agricultural produce was therefore now literally starving to death.

Thousands of sick and wounded inhabitants desperately tried living on anything they could attempt to digest—the bitterest of seaweeds, whatever raw animal hides they could get their hands on, and, when they were extremely lucky, even the few rats that could still be found within the city walls. Meanwhile, the last remaining rations were distributed only to the active-duty soldiers guarding the fortifications; but even those were so scanty that they were barely enough to keep the men on their feet.

Second was the fact that the last tenuous channel of communication with the outside world that had been left to the besieged residents was fatally cut off. For indeed, despite the Ottoman fleet's near-constant presence in the lagoon throughout the yearlong siege, one secret waterway hidden by dense reeds and known only to the Greeks had always remained open. By means of it, they were occasionally able to send and receive messengers and covertly obtain small quantities of supplies by canoe. Early in the month, however, the Turks discovered the conduit and intercepted the last of the Zantian boats trying to make their way through it, seizing the grain they were carrying and executing their pilots.

All contact with the town having thus been brought to an abrupt and absolute halt, any hope of succor from their comrades outside to which the defenders had so stubbornly clung was finally laid to rest. Messolonghi—that sacrificial city with nine thousand inhabitants, starving, wounded and under daily attack—was completely and irrevocably on its own.

CHAPTER 15

So began the final countdown. According to the historical record, Lord Admiral Rizopoulos knew that it was to culminate one week later in the last and most desperate act of the entire siege—and one that would have dramatic consequences for the remaining course of the war—the so-called 'Sortie of the Guard', or the famed 'Exodus of Messolonghi'.

During that final week, several more last-ditch attempts were made to rescue the perishing defenders. On the third of April, the hero of the Greek fleet, Admiral Miaoulis, engaged the Ottomans in a long and indecisive naval skirmish in the Gulf of Corinth; but despite gaining some tactical advantages, he was incapable of breaking through the blockade for long enough to throw supplies into the lagoon.

Although he was to try again, attacking the combined Turkish and Egyptian fleets twice more on April ninth and tenth, his little squadron of brigs—hopelessly outnumbered and outgunned by the Ottomans' six massive ships-of-the-line, nine frigates and as many as ninety other vessels of war—would be unable to assist his starving compatriots. Ultimately he would be forced to turn back and head for his home port of Hydra, steeped in grief and bitter disappointment.

Within the city itself, the situation grew increasingly dire by the hour. On the fifth of April, several women, children and elderly people finally died of starvation, and the same thing occurred again on the following day in even greater numbers.

Faced with such a grim reality and the hopeless realization that, after another few days without sustenance, the defenders would soon be too weak even to lift their weapons—and determined not to surrender, but to continue fighting to the very end—the military and civilian leaders of Messolonghi assembled on the evening of April sixth at the small chapel of Saint Paraskevi and made their fateful decision.

They would send out a handful of messengers in an attempt to reach the renowned *klepht* general, George Karaiskakis, whom they knew to be encamped with a small force somewhere in the hills behind the combined Ottoman armies. Their message to him was simple: be ready to attack the enemy from the rear—for on the night of April tenth, the besieged garrison would stage a massive sortie, attempting to break through the enemy lines with as many of Messolonghi's remaining inhabitants as were physically able to flee.

As messengers, several men from the garrison were to be chosen—those who were still strong enough to make the journey and who knew the area well; but those were not the only criteria. The best fighters could not be spared, as they were needed to defend the walls, and the men who were to make the attempt had to be fast. They also had to be able to speak and dress as Albanians—for slipping out of the city walls under the cover of darkness, they would split up and make their way through the enemy camp, posing as Albanian mercenaries under the *roumeli vasely's* command in the event they were intercepted. It was thought that this would increase the likelihood of at least one of them getting through and making it back again to confirm the delivery of the message.

But there was yet one more important criterion to be met. The men had to be willing to go. Many of those with families, who otherwise possessed all the requisite qualities, were not prepared to leave their loved ones behind undefended. In the end, out of the dozen or so who volunteered for the duty, eight good messengers were chosen, the other candidates having been rejected by the town leaders for one reason or another. In the case of one of the rejects, however, the committee's decision was not taken without significant rancor.

The would-be volunteer was originally from a part of Ottoman-occupied Macedonia that was a melting pot of many different nationalities, including Greeks, Albanians and Turks. He therefore spoke all three languages, as well as his own native tongue, with ease. He was fast and knew the hills; and what was more, he had no family to hold him back. In short, he fulfilled all the requirements for the assignment—but there was one damaging strike against him. The head of his own militia unit declined to recommend him, saying that his behavior during the past few months had been erratic and his comportment towards his fellow soldiers increasingly sullen and contentious. There were even doubts about his mental stability. It was the Bulgarian.

Enraged at the slight—which he convinced himself was due to his being an outsider—and desperate to quit the dying city, the Bulgarian slowly worked himself up into a fever pitch of contempt and hostility towards the Greeks with whom he had lived, fought and bled for so many months. He argued with the commanding officer who had informed him of the committee's decision, and then when he had gone back to his position at the fortifications, began to spit on the ground and mutter under his breath.

Two or three more times, he went back over to his unit head to argue, each time more angrily than the last, until finally he kicked dirt at his captain and stormed away from his post to sulk in some isolated place. A few of his fellow soldiers started to go after him, but the captain held them back.

"Let him go and calm down," he said dismissively. "He's no good to us here anyway—not in that kind of state."

Alone and wandering the muddy and broken streets in a rage, the sharp pain of hunger gnawing deep in the pit of his belly, the hopelessness of the entire situation suddenly seemed completely absurd to the Bulgarian. Why should he die here in the filth and the slime of Messolonghi, he began to wonder, alongside those who—he now imagined—did not even consider him to be one of their own? The very plan for a mass exodus became utterly ridiculous in his mind.

His paranoia growing by the minute, he began to conceive of it as nothing more than a conspiracy to drive him out of the city so that he could be impaled by the Turks, while the rest of the inhabitants would fall back and remain inside, laughing at him from behind the safety of the walls. But, he decided, they had chosen to ridicule the wrong man. He would show all of them—especially that odious Odysseus, who had called him a coward the day that priest and the others had been executed some months before. If they wanted him out, he decided, they would have their wish—but not in the way they imagined.

It was long past nightfall on old-calendar April sixth, and the messengers had already exited through the city's main gate, taking advantage of the brightness of the nearly full moon to head off on their uncertain quest in search of General Karaiskakis's camp. Whether they succeeded in reaching him or not, however, the die had already been cast. The city's leaders had decided that, help or no help, four nights hence—under the light of the full moon and on the eve of the Greek Orthodox Palm Sunday—they would carry out their plan.

The garrison's soldiers having already been made aware of their commanders' decision, all that remained was to inform the civilians of the details of the strategy, so that everyone would be prepared. That task they entrusted to one of the most respected men among them—none other than Bishop Joseph of Rogon.

Earlier that evening, during the council meeting held by Messolonghi's military and civilian leaders, the same Bishop Joseph had argued vehemently and persuasively against some of the military chieftains who suggested that the elderly and invalids of the city—essentially anyone who was too feeble or injured to participate in the proposed sortie—should be put to a merciful death rather than being allowed to fall into the hands of the Turks. But the venerable hierarch had refused to condone such an unthinkable act.

He determined, rather, that all who could not endure the physical hardship of the planned exodus would remain behind, shutting themselves up in buildings with gunpowder and explosives, and only after all hope was exhausted, depart for the other life by their own hand. And as if to cut off any further debate, and to render the matter inviolable with the pledge of his own soul, he announced that he too—although he was physically strong enough to leave with the rest—would be one of those to remain behind to minister to his flock to the very end. Thus, in sealing his own fate, he narrowly managed to avert an even worse tragedy on top of the already horrible calamity that was about to befall the doomed city.

Having dictated detailed instructions, the bishop arranged to dispatch a group of trusted men to go around town that evening and all the next day to inform the leading citizens about exactly what was to be done, and to spread the word quickly throughout the city. At nine o'clock in the evening on the night of old-calendar April tenth, the people were to gather outside the city walls in the companies to which they had been assigned to await the signal. For as soon as the garrison sallied out to the attack, driving a wedge through the flanks of the enemy's camp, they would follow them in a mad dash to reach the rendezvous point at the monastery of St. Symeon in the hills eight kilometers away.

One of those who had been present with Bishop Joseph at the council meeting earlier that evening—and whom the hierarch now wanted to send out with the others announcing the plan to the civilians—was the man who had been recommended to him by his old friend, Elder Aetios. Looking around among his priests and monks for the man he knew only as the monk Leonidas, the bishop noticed that Rizopoulos was not there and briefly wondered where he had disappeared to; but amidst the demands of the moment, he quickly became engrossed in other matters.

What he could not have realized was that, at that very hour, the Paladin lord admiral was engaged in averting yet another terrible tragedy—one that was being played out in the heart of the enemy encampment less than two kilometers away, and which had the potential to affect not only the lives of thousands in just a few days' time, but also those of billions in a future far too distant to be imagined by the heroic defenders of Messolonghi. Nor could he have realized that the chilling prophecy contained in Elder Aetios's letter, and known only to him, was about to be fulfilled.

'Crowns of martyrdom are being prepared for you and for many,' the saintly Abbot had written. 'Strangers from far away will seek to steal them from many in your flock—but have no fear. One like them, who is also one like us, will stand in their way. Prepare yourselves therefore. Good Friday, with the Passion of the Crucifixion, comes to the sacred city early this year. And once you have gone ahead, dear brother in the Lord, prepare a place for me, too. For I will come to you soon, and together we will exult in the unending paschal feast, which is that true Sacred City where there is no sorrow, but only the joy of the Resurrection!'

Meanwhile, for Rizopoulos, attending the gathering earlier in the evening and seeing some of the famed heroes of the war of independence in action—many of whom he knew would soon make the ultimate sacrifice for their country—was an incredibly moving experience. It stirred in his heart the embers of a national and cultural pride that had long been dormant, covered over by the cool ashes of international technocracy and leveling globalization. Weary and weakened as he had been when he first entered the little church, the passion for the cause of freedom that had radiated from those great men—incomparable giants of a bygone era—now kindled a flame in his breast that ignited within him an even greater sense of urgency than that which he had already felt, and which helped revive his flagging spirit.

Now, however, he had to channel that renewed energy to his own cause—one which he knew was fundamentally antithetical to the immediate plans being deliberated that night. Thus, as the tension between that which was in his heart and that which was in his mind grew ever stronger during the course of the council meeting, the Paladin lord admiral felt that he could no longer stand as proudly as he ought to in the presence of such noble men. As soon as an opportunity to slip unnoticed out of the assembly presented itself, he took it, stepping out of the fiery warmth of the chapel of St. Paraskevi and into the chill and obscure damp of Messolonghi's misty evening air.

After arguing bitterly with his captain about the decision that had been taken, the Bulgarian had wandered the desolate streets of Messolonghi for a long while, disregarding his good fortune that the shelling from the enemy camp had all but stopped for the night and sulking miserably in the bright moonlight. Thoughts assailed him from every direction, and in his anger and despair every little thing that he despised about the place—the dampness and the humidity, the mosquitoes, the incessant chirping and croaking of the frogs in the nearby marshes—became magnified enormously and drove him into an even greater rage. Eventually, without paying attention to the steadily northwestern direction in which he had been traveling, he found himself very close to the city's wall nearest the lagoon. And although he had not thought about it consciously, there was indeed only one reason why he had headed there.

It was a part of the fortifications that was among the town's least guarded, being covered by a single artillery battery on a mud bank at the shores of the lagoon, and situated in a swampy area that made it difficult for the enemy to penetrate in large numbers without becoming mired in the thick mud. However, as well-suited as the natural defenses of the place were to preventing a hostile army from getting into the city, they were not at all conducive to keeping a lone deserter from getting out.

Standing with his back against the wall and looking at the wretched town before him—shrouded in mist and moonlight, and looking to him more like a putrid cemetery than a glorious last stronghold of heroes—the Bulgarian suddenly felt light and unencumbered, even giddy. He could not imagine why he had not done a long time ago what he was about to do now.

Looking quickly around to ensure he was not being observed, he hoisted himself up over the low earthen wall and down the other side, crouching down behind it and trying his best to remain hidden in the shadows. For the first time in many long months of misery and suffering, he finally felt like a free man.

It was not very far—barely ten meters—before the earth under the Bulgarian's feet became soft and muddy. As he left the relative safety of the wall and quickly made his way towards the northeast, he knew that his trajectory would first take him through the marsh before he could reach solid ground, but he had little other choice. If he tried to skirt around it along the base of the fortifications, he would surely be been seen by the garrison's sentinels. Besides, going through the misty bogs would afford him plenty of tall reeds, rushes and swamp grass in which to hide.

Soon he felt his worn and flimsy shoes filling with cold water. Sinking in up to his ankles, it became impossible to keep them on his feet as one after the other was sucked into the deepening mud. Then after another ten meters, he found himself wading above his knees, as he slowly struggled through the marshy terrain on his way towards higher ground.

His progress was laborious, since the greater the distance he put between himself and the city, the deeper the mud and silt became. Moreover—constantly looking over his shoulder in fear of being caught—he had to move carefully to avoid making any loud splashing noises that might attract the attention of the Greeks guarding the fortifications behind him, or that of the Ottomans whose furthest outposts were just several hundred meters ahead. Finally however, a little less than half an hour after initially climbing over the wall, the fugitive reached the furthest extent of the marsh.

Spent from the strenuous effort of trudging through the morass, barefoot and shivering with cold, with his leggings and his embroidered greaves drenched and covered with slimy mud, he collapsed on the ground in a bank of tall reeds. After resting there for a little while, the Bulgarian forced himself to keep moving. Slowly raising himself up, he peeked furtively over the high vegetation and, imagining there was no one in sight, stepped into the open field and began trotting north in the direction of the road leading to distant Arta. But he was not to make it very far.

He had jogged along for less than five minutes when, suddenly and quite unexpectedly, behind a thicket of bushes he came upon an Albanian foot soldier who had wandered a short distance from a nearby Ottoman outpost to relieve himself in privacy. On seeing him, the startled Albanian instantly began shouting in alarm, sending the frightened Bulgarian running for his life.

He was remarkably fast, especially considering the weakened condition that all those from Messolonghi were in, but it was to no avail. Within a few seconds he was cut off on all sides by a group of nine Albanians that converged upon him with their muskets aimed. Stopping abruptly and dropping his own flintlock, he lifted his hands in the air and begged for mercy in the Albanians' language, and they quickly grabbed him and confiscated his weapons. They then began to harass him, pushing him around roughly for their own amusement and questioning who he was and where he was going.

The Bulgarian was in a precarious situation and he knew it. For one thing, even within the enemy camp, deserters were looked upon with contempt, and he knew his chances of survival would be minimal if his captors found out he was running away, regardless of which army he was fleeing. Moreover, the Albanians were mercenaries. Not only were they paid a salary to fight against the Greeks, but they were also paid a special bonus for each insurgent they killed—typically evidenced by bringing in the severed head, or a pair of the victim's severed ears.

The only thing that kept him alive for even a short time was the fact that there were so many Albanians in the party that detained him. It was not in anyone's interest to kill him just yet, since they would then have to split the prize several ways. Rather, each one hoped to find a way to get the Bulgarian alone and then kill him, claiming the full amount of the reward for himself.

Under the circumstances, he had to think quickly. His only chance for survival would be to increase his value to the Albanians if brought in to the commanding officers alive rather than dead, and he knew just how to do it. As soon as the men began to tease him, prodding him with the points of their daggers, and remarking that he was running away like a loose chicken trying to escape the slaughter, he answered defiantly, slyly pretending to let slip some valuable information.

"What kind of coward do you take me for?" he retorted to the Albanians. "I'm not running anywhere! I have a message to deli—"

At those words, the interest of the Albanians—ever motivated by anything that might result in a greater number of *piasters* in their purses—was piqued and they began to accost him aggressively, demanding more information.

Feigning despair at having given away his 'secret', the Bulgarian played his role to the hilt—as if his very life depended on it. It did.

No matter how violently the Albanians intimidated him, he pretended to resist their threats stoically, maintaining that he would rather die than divulge such important information to the enemy. At first the outcome was uncertain, as one or two of the Albanians became angry and wanted to kill him on the spot; but in the end, his risky tactic worked.

Imagining that they might be rewarded handsomely for turning someone with important information over to the *pashas*, the others convinced their friends to spare the Bulgarian's life. Another round of arguing soon erupted over who would deliver him up to the main camp, but the Albanians finally settled the matter by appointing a representative from each of their clans to escort him. Thus he was bound and marched off between three mercenaries, assured that he would be kept alive—at least for the time being.

Making their way across the fields towards the Ottoman encampment—pushing their captive ahead of them and talking loudly all along the way, lest they be mistaken for insurgent intruders—the Albanians were stopped several times at various checkpoints. More than once they had to prevent others in search of a reward from joining their party—or had to climb through muddy trenches or scramble across *fascines*—but after about forty minutes they at last arrived inside Reshid Pasha's main camp and began to search for an officer on duty.

Eventually they found a young Turkish lieutenant, who seemed rather annoyed at having his evening routine disturbed, as he distractedly listened to the Albanians presenting their case and describing the circumstances surrounding the Bulgarian's capture. Scowling at the prisoner and looking him up and down skeptically while the Albanians tried to convince him of their captive's value, the officer ignored their demands for payment and spoke directly to the Bulgarian, querying him in Turkish.

"These men seem to think you should be worth a lot of money," he remarked coolly. "Are you worth a lot of money?"

"Whether I am or not, let that be for your *pasha* to decide," the Bulgarian retorted in excellent Turkish, cleverly feigning defiance. "But I will never tell you or him what I know. And even if I did, it wouldn't stop what's going to happen. Do you think I'm the only messenger that's been sent?"

The lieutenant gazed at him for a moment with his eyebrows raised, as if estimating the truth of what the prisoner had said and the significance of what he might know, and then replied nonchalantly: "Well then, if there is no possibility of learning anything useful from you, what's the point of having you around disturbing my camp? Maybe I should just have you put to death right now."

The Bulgarian knew he was bluffing. First of all, he understood the Turks well and it was inconceivable that, in the midst of a large headquarters camp, such a junior officer would take the initiative and make any kind of decision on his own, rather than referring the matter up the line.

Secondly, the entire Ottoman system was built on bribery and patronage; and wherever the slightest possibility of a monetary reward existed, the officer—just like the Albanians who had captured him, and the Greeks he had deserted—would try to drag things out so that every last *piaster* of value could be extracted from him before he met his end. Still, he reasoned, it was a game that had to be played very carefully if he wanted to come out with his life. The last thing he wanted was for the officer to think that he too was bluffing.

Plucking up his courage, the Bulgarian cunningly opened his eyes wide and hesitated for an instant in a feigned show of fright, and then replied to the lieutenant in a voice that wavered enough to show he might yet be swayed:

"Do whatever you like," he said uneasily. "I am in your power. But what is my life compared to the lives of so many thousands?"

The lieutenant smirked and let out a snort. He then gave the prisoner a derisive look and, just before walking away, said:

"No, I don't suppose I'll have you killed now. We have plenty of time for that. Besides, we might as well have a little amusement first."

CHAPTER 16

As the Turk walked briskly away, a couple of the Albanians went after him, accosting him and demanding payment for the valuable prisoner they had brought. The Turk, however, waved them off contemptuously and told them to go over with the Bulgarian and wait for him to return.

After persisting for a while and seeing that they could not move him, and that some sentries were starting to take notice of the clamor, they relented and went back to where their fellow mercenary held the Bulgarian in a clearing under a gnarled and ancient-looking olive tree. There they squatted on the ground for what seemed like a long while, disappointed and blaming each other angrily for their misfortune and cursing foully at their captive. Eventually, the lieutenant returned with another man—a European wearing an unfamiliar uniform—who was evidently accompanied by his manservant.

This officer—seeming to be one of those many European advisors to Reshid Pasha, who could be found everywhere in the Ottoman camp—had previously made it known among the junior cadres that he was interested in interviewing any deserters from the besieged Greek garrison before they were turned over to the commanders for questioning, and that he would pay handsomely for the privilege. He was tall and blond—apparently a Prussian or an Austrian—with a fierce-looking face dominated by a high aquiline nose and cold blue-eyes that were now focused eagle-like and unflinchingly on the Bulgarian.

"*Iss zis ze vone?*" the German asked the lieutenant in heavily accented Turkish, before addressing the prisoner in Bulgarian, saying: "*Zo, mein Freund,* you've got yourself in *quvite* a *jem,* eh? *Perheps* I can be of *assistenz?*"

The Bulgarian was taken-aback on hearing his native tongue being spoken by the man with the heavy German accent, and suddenly felt very insecure. It was one thing dealing with Albanians and Greeks and Turks, with whom he had lived all his life and knew how to manipulate, but he now felt completely thrown off balance by the presence of this foreigner. Not knowing how to respond, he simply murmured back in his own language:

"How can you assist me, and why should you?"

A cruel smile touched the corner of the German's lips. So it was confirmed—the prisoner was indeed a Bulgarian.

"Oh, let's just say," he replied mysteriously, "I *heff* a *shtrong* interest in Bulgarian deserters from *Missolonghi.*"

Immediately the prisoner protested: "But I am not a deserter, I tell you! I am delivering an important message!"

"I *untershtand,*" said the German calmly, continuing with a strange smile and a macabre glint in his icy eyes. "But don't *vorry*—my role here *iss* not *ess* judge."

Then, turning to the lieutenant, the German asked: "And *vhat* about *zem? Heff zey* been paid?"

"No, *effendi,* they have not," the Turk replied. "Not yet, anyway. I am not authorized to pay the Albanians for prisoners. The Chief Bursar has that responsibility, and he will not be on duty again until the morning."

Ignoring the lieutenant's last remark, the man nodded to his servant, who promptly opened a large leather satchel he was carrying and took out a pouch. He handed it to his master, who opened it without saying a word. Taking a step towards the three

Albanians, the German turned it upside down and emptied a pile of Austrian *florins* out onto the ground in front of them.

The Albanians stared wide-eyed at the large quantity of silver coins—many times more than what they would normally have received for the Bulgarian's head, had they killed him—and hurried to pick up the treasure, knowing that they should have been satisfied. But when they saw the ease with which the foreigner had parted with the money, they were overcome with greed and exchanged a silent glance, signaling to each other that they should hold out for more.

After they had picked up all the coins and made a show of counting them out, the eldest among them complained to the Turk that it was not enough. But no sooner had the words come out of his mouth than the German—in a movement too quick for them to follow—whipped out his pistol and suddenly appeared behind the man who spoke, with the weapon cocked and pointed at his temple.

"*Loytenant*," he said, speaking to the Turk in a voice at once calm and deadly serious, "tell *zese* men *zat zey shoult consitter zemselves* fortunate to be able to leave *viss vhat* I *heff* already paid *zem—vich iss* more *zan adequvate*—along *viss zeir* miserable lives. But if *zey* insist on *bargainink, ozer* arrangements can be *easilly* made."

Astonished at the speed with which the large German had moved, the Turk was momentarily speechless; but then he began cursing the Albanians, who had already understood the foreigner's words. The two companions of the man being held at gunpoint slowly backed away and nodded their agreement, at which point the German released their comrade. Immediately the three Albanians gathered up their belongings and made their escape back in the direction of their outpost as quickly as they could manage.

As soon as they were gone, the foreign officer turned to the Turkish lieutenant and said: "Now, *zat* just leaves us to *zettle* our business."

Before the servant could take another pouch out of the satchel, however, the Turk interrupted him, saying: "Please, *effendi*, surely you can understand that as an officer of His Excellency's general staff, I—"

"Are you *zuggestink zat* you don't *vant ze* money, *Loytenant*?" the German asked dubiously.

Embarrassed, the Turk shrugged his shoulders and replied: "I only meant to say, *effendi*, that perhaps there is a more suitable place than out here in the open."

The foreigner suddenly made a strangled and sinister sound, which the Turk recognized with amazement as laughter.

"Of course, you are right, *Loytenant*. I *shoult heff sought* better! Come—let's go to my tent *und zettle sings*," he said cheerfully.

The lieutenant commanded a nearby soldier on guard duty to take custody of the Bulgarian and follow, and the small party walked for several minutes through the narrow streets of tents, separated by long rows of large old olive trees, until they arrived at the foreigner's quarters. Instructing the guard to wait outside with the prisoner, the Turk went into the tent with the other two men and reemerged a few minutes later with a broad smile painted across his previously somber face. He then grabbed the Bulgarian by the arm and pulled him roughly into the German's tent, and said before taking his leave: "I believe this is your prisoner now, *effendi*."

The Bulgarian, still anxious after seeing the foreign officer's handling of the Albanians a few minutes earlier, entered the tent as if going into a lion's den. It was a rather spacious affair for a field tent—neat and orderly, with a tall center pole and few possessions. There was a carefully made-up cot, a wooden writing desk, a large footlocker, and a small table with a couple of high-backed wooden chairs. It was at this table that the German was seated, and he looked at the Bulgarian almost invitingly.

"Come in—don't be *nervose*. Do *heff* a *zeat*," he said calmly. Then as the Bulgarian approached the table, he pulled out a large knife and said: "Please, allow me."

The Bulgarian immediately recoiled, shrinking back on seeing the blade, but the German quickly assuaged his fear.

"Oh, *zere, zere*—no need to *vorry*," he said, as if comforting a small child. "At least not yet."

Then, motioning to the Bulgarian to stretch out his hands, he placed the blade under the ropes the Albanians had bound him with and, with a quick upward thrust, sliced through them in one clean cut. Rubbing his sore wrists, the Bulgarian sat at the little table nervously, trying to fathom what was happening.

"*Vould* you like *zome* tea? Of course you *vould*—you must be *shtarfing viss everysing zat hess heppened zere* in *Missolonghi*." Then turning to his servant, he called out in Turkish: "Hakan, bring us *zome* tea please—*und zome* biscuits—*quvickly*!"

Instantly the servant fished a teapot and some supplies from the footlocker and went out, leaving the two men alone for the first time. But rather than making any sudden moves, Juergen seemed to be taking his time, wanting to ensure that the man across the table from him had the information he was looking for. Cordially he continued talking to the Bulgarian, who foolishly seemed to have relaxed a bit as a result of the foreigner's hospitality.

"Now," said the German, "*vhile ve vait* for our tea, *vhy* don't you tell me about *zis* message you are *carryink*?"

Instantly the Bulgarian tensed, suspecting a trap. Squirming nervously, he finally said: "And how do I know that I won't be killed once I've told you? I need a guarantee—my life for what I know."

"*Vhy* of course," the officer said, smiling. "*Zat iss a wery* reasonable *requvest*. But you see, I can't help you unless I know *vhat* you *heff* to offer His Excellency, *ze pasha*, can I? But I'll tell you *vhat*. If *ze informazhion* you *heff vill* be of any *walue*, I promise I *vill* do my utmost to make sure *ze* Ottomans do not kill you."

The Bulgarian seemed to relax a bit again, and remembering the ease with which the foreigner had paid the Albanians, another thought entered his mind.

"What about a reward?" he suddenly asked the German. "I'm sure the information I have will be very helpful to the *pasha*, so why shouldn't I get a reward as well?"

"I'm sure *zat* if *ze informazhion* you *heff vill* be of *walue*," the other man answered slyly, "you *vill* get your just *revard*."

Then getting up and walking over to the writing desk, he reached into the leather satchel the servant had left there and pulled out another pouch jingling with silver coins and brought it over. Putting it on the table in front of the Bulgarian, he said: "*Sink of zis* as just a small deposit on *vhat* you *heff comink* to you, if *ze informazhion* you *heff vill* be of interest."

The Bulgarian stared at the bag of coins on the table for a moment, and exhaled heavily as if in deep thought. Then, looking up at the foreigner, he slowly said: "What if I were to tell you that the Greeks are planning a massive sortie from the city in four days' time? Would that be of interest?"

The German smiled and, turning his back to the Bulgarian, calmly said: "Yes, it certainly *vould*. In fact, *zat iss pretzisely vhat* I *vas* hoping to hear."

Then without the slightest warning, in one swift and fluid motion, he pulled his Turkish-design *kilij* saber out of the scabbard at his waist and at the same instant began to spin around, swinging it with all his considerable strength at the other man's vulnerable and waiting neck.

The moment the Bulgarian realized what was happening, his eyes flew open wide and a look of horror masked his face, but it was too late for him to do anything about it. The German's furious and razor sharp blade was already in motion and would have connected within a fraction of a second, if the chair the deserter was seated on had not suddenly been yanked over as if by some invisible force, throwing him hard to the ground.

A look of utter consternation flashed over the foreigner's face for a brief second, only to be quickly replaced by an expression of sudden comprehension at what was happening. But there was little he could do. Before he had time to react, a bearded black-robed figure had materialized directly in front of him. Stepping in close, he deftly used the angular momentum of the German's swing to spin him around, and jerked the sword up over his head with a powerful grip. It was Rizopoulos.

Having left the council meeting in Messolonghi, the Paladin lord admiral had located the Bulgarian—in whose embroidered vest he had long ago managed to conceal a tiny low-frequency radio-tracking device—and had invisibly followed him out of the city and into the midst of the Ottoman camp. As sickened as he was by what the deserter was about to do, and knowing that the success of his mission would mean nothing less than the death of thousands of those who had already suffered the deprivations of a brutal siege for so long in the name of freedom, he was nevertheless duty-bound to save him.

Thus he entered into close-range mortal combat with the man who had been sent to kill his ward. It was indeed the same man he had followed from the beach at Iérakos in the Peloponnese all the way to Crete, and who had even then caused a feeling of intense revulsion within him—the Trustee operative known as Juergen.

With only the briefest of moments to take advantage of the element of surprise that was in his favor, Rizopoulos immediately went on the offensive. He stepped to the side and drove his knee hard into the big German's abdomen, intending to wrench the saber out of his hands. But although Juergen doubled over slightly and grimaced in pain, to Rizopoulos's surprise the blow did not have anything close to the intended effect. The German managed to hold on tightly to his weapon, and then straightened up in an instant.

He was a much younger man than Rizopoulos, and obviously quite strong; but the lord admiral had never had a problem fighting younger and stronger opponents before. The truth was, as he suddenly realized with alarm, that the last couple of months in Messolonghi had drained him much more than he had previously been willing to admit to himself, and he was just not physically up to such a contest.

Sensing the other man's weakness, Juergen curled his lip and sneered at the Paladin derisively as the two men grappled over the sword, snarling at him from between clenched teeth like a wild predator:

"*Iss zat* all you *heff*, old man? *Zat* idiot Crowe *vas suppost to heff killt* you, but as *zey* say—if you *vant zomesink* done, you *heff* to do it yourself!"

And with those words the German exploded in a powerful surge of strength. A look of hellish fury came over his reddening face and the veins on his neck and temple bulged, as he attempted to drive Rizopoulos to his knees.

At first he seemed to be succeeding. He arched his back and bent downward, pressing hard and dominating his struggling opponent little by little, and feeling the other man's legs slowly beginning to tremble. But then, after several tense seconds, as the Trustee stared fiercely into Rizopoulos's dark and intensely penetrating eyes, something changed.

It was almost imperceptible at first. As Juergen pushed harder on the grip of the saber, causing the blade to inch closer to the Paladin's neck, images began to flash through his mind of the moment the steel would enter smoothly into his flesh and let loose a river of the older man's dark-red blood. Initially he ignored the mental suggestions, as he had been trained to do. Nevertheless, they corresponded so well with what he was actually trying to achieve that they began to inspire him. Thus he began to take pleasure in them, and once he had accepted them—claiming them as his own thoughts and even beginning to elaborate on them of his own accord—he felt his mind wandering and becoming distracted.

In his mind's eye, without wishing it, he soon saw that the Paladin he was struggling with was wearing some sort of chain mail with a thick leather neck guard, and that the imaginary blow he was trying to deal from his saber was certain to be deflected. He then began to imagine that it was altogether a different weapon he was holding—no keen and finely crafted Turkish scimitar at all, but a rather dull, short dagger with a slippery handle. In an almost dreamlike torpor, he slowly began to notice that instead of vying against one old man, he was actually in a large open field, fighting single-handedly against an entire horde of armed men—and his previous confidence started to give way to small waves of anxiety.

It only took a moment before Juergen understood what was happening. The Paladin had been using hypnosis to mentally project thoughts into his mind—the suggestions of which he had foolishly accepted—allowing him to open a channel that could very well prove to be the German's undoing. It was almost too late, but he would not allow it.

Bracing himself in mind as well as in body, he gathered his own powers of mental concentration and tried with all his might to break the strong but silent grip in which Rizopoulos held him with his *nous*. The more he struggled, however, the tighter it seemed that the Paladin's probing eyes locked onto his own, and the deeper his thoughts penetrated into his mind. For the first time in as many years as he could remember, Juergen began to experience true fear.

He desperately tried to close the floodgates of his mind, but it was already too late. He suddenly saw himself standing at the head of a long dim corridor lined with numerous doorways, with the one directly in front of him being slightly ajar. Having carelessly opened that unfamiliar entrance a crack, he had unwittingly allowed a dangerously powerful force to begin squeezing its way in, beaming with a mesmerizing white light—and despite his strenuous efforts to resist it, it was almost inside.

Realizing that he could no longer hold it back and seized by dread, Juergen began running down the corridor in search of safe refuge. He quickly entered one of the most familiar doorways and, shutting the entrance fast behind him, he found with a momentary sense of relief that he was secluded in a dark room illuminated by flickering candlelight. It was replete with all the dark trappings of his Order of the Nemesins—the Trustee equivalent of the Paladins. Ritualistic symbols adorned the walls, floor and ceiling all around him, and at one end there was a massive stone altar, stained dark with the sacrilege of human blood. He had found his sanctuary.

Immediately on entering, he heard the familiar words of his cabalistic rites starting to flood the room, and as he intoned them, he felt their dark powers beginning to envelope him.

Putting on his hooded robe, he grabbed a long staff from its place on the wall and stood in the center of a large pentagram etched into the stone floor. He then began to trace out a circle of power around himself as he chanted the ancient and mystical words; but before he was able to complete it, entering fully into its protective sphere, something dreadful happened.

From the corridor outside, he began to hear the sounds of another prayer issuing forth and rising high above his own. It was a prayer using that despised name, which at once enraged and confused and terrified him, and to which he dare not even give voice—that of the Nazorean, the one whom *they* called the 'Christ'.

With each passing second, the excruciating words thundered louder and the room began to shake, as if suddenly seized by a violent earthquake. Then a blinding and caustic light began to penetrate the darkness of his refuge from the spaces all around the doorframe, and the door itself began to warp inward and buckle. Shouting out his incantations at the top of his lungs, the Nemesin used all his strength to barricade the door; but instead of succeeding in pushing the Paladin out of his mind, he only began to see intense, blinding flashes of light and to hear loud and disjointed voices echoing in strange *non sequiturs*.

Juergen soon began to feel dizzy, and as the spinning accelerated, he heard a violent crack and a heavy stone-like object seemed to come hurtling from the direction of his altar, smacking him hard on the side of his head. Instantly a jolt of searing pain ripped through his temple and left one side of his face feeling numb and drooping. It was becoming hard to breathe, and as a sensation of intense nausea began to overwhelm him, it suddenly dawned on the German—he was having a stroke.

Whether it was real or perceived, Juergen could not tell. He only knew that his right arm, which formerly had possessed such strength and dexterity, now felt heavy and limp. Through a window that suddenly opened in the recesses of his mind, he could see into a faraway and shadowy distance, where the arm that had once belonged to him still gripped the hilt of a sword.

Two vaguely familiar men seemed to be fighting for control over it inside a dimly lit tent, but the image had already lost all sense of reality, time and purpose, and he shifted his gaze away without any further interest. For in his mental world, he now sat in a wheelchair in an unfamiliar and brightly lit white room that smelled faintly of antiseptic spray. It was a long-term-care facility not far from the town where his parents lived, and he was paralyzed from the neck down and unable to speak.

After a short time, a pretty young nurse entered his room with a tray of food and, upon checking his vital signs, began carefully feeding him. A brief look of disgust showed on her smooth and milky white face as he drooled involuntarily, trying to speak to her; but his tongue was thick and unresponsive and she could not understand his plaintive moans and grunts. In his mind, however, the words he tried to say to her echoed clearly—louder and louder—as he contemplated the unbearable hopelessness of wasting away in a vegetative state for time without end.

Let me die! he silently cried out in the most absolute despair fathomable. *Please, let me die now!*

As his worst nightmare invisibly unfolded in Juergen's mind, about two meters away and still rooted to the spot on the tent floor where he had fallen, the terrified Bulgarian watched the bizarre scene that transpired before him in awe. As soon as he had hit the ground, he had looked up to see the German officer spin around and seemingly disappear in a hazy blur. He was sure the phenomenon was caused by the combination of the tent's dim lantern light, his own state of near panic and the sudden jolt he had received a second before—not to mention the role that his mental and physical exhaustion, and the delirium caused by his unbearable hunger, must have played.

Staring dumbfounded at the place where the German had been standing, his suspicions were soon confirmed. For after several seconds, the foreigner seemed to appear once more, but now he looked quite different. His face was red and strained and his back hunched over, while his knuckles had become white from gripping his sword so tightly, as if he had just been struggling mightily with some unseen foe. Then, as the Bulgarian started to scramble to his feet, something completely unexpected happened.

All at once, the foreigner seemed to reel backwards as if in some form of deep trance, with a vacant and desolate look of hopelessness on the face which only a minute before had appeared so confidently fierce and menacing. Next, murmuring unintelligibly in a pitiable voice in his native language, he took the glittering saber that was still clenched tightly in his hands and raised it high above his head.

Turning it so that the blade pointed downward, he emitted a long and forlorn moan, which rose from his chest as from an abyss of the most profound loneliness and despair. He then suddenly plunged the sword downward and inward, slicing it into the center of his own bowels and out through his back, twisting it and raking it violently upward in a sharp *hara-kiri* movement.

Instantly, an expression of horror came over the German's face, as if he were shocked by his own actions. He looked down for a second at his exposed entrails—his bloody hands still holding the hilt of the sword—and was clearly stunned at the sight.

He briefly glanced up in the Bulgarian's direction with a bewildered look on his face and seemed to try and mouth something, but could only gasp. Then a sudden shudder shook his entire frame in one last violent spasm and he collapsed in an inert heap on the floor. Silently—and marked only by the soft sound of his dying breath escaping—the Trustee operative known as Juergen exhaled and was no more.

A FEW METERS away from the Bulgarian, an unseen figure inaudibly breathed in gasps of air, invisibly leaning heavily against the writing desk. Although it had lasted less than a minute, the battle with Juergen had unexpectedly been one of the toughest Rizopoulos had faced in many years, and for the first time ever, the thought entered his mind that perhaps he was growing too old for such a life.

Still weak and trembling from the strain of the intense physical and mental combat, the Paladin lord admiral looked at his fallen opponent with a conflicting mixture of remorse and relief—remorse over the deplorable circumstances that, over something as imaginary and fleeting as earthly power, required men to kill or be killed; and relief that, at least this time, the verdict for him had been the former. Sighing heavily, Sir Leonidas raised his right arm and made the sign of the cross—first over himself, and then slowly and thoughtfully over the dead body of the man who only a few moments before had tried to kill him. It was the least he could do.

CHAPTER 17

On the other side of Juergen's body, the Bulgarian stared in disbelief. Having watched the foreign officer suddenly and inexplicably take his own life right before his very eyes, it took him a moment to recover his senses and decide what to do.

Cautiously, he stepped over to the body, under which a large pool of blood had already formed, and pushed it on to its side with his bare foot to see if the German was really dead. As luck would have it, at that very moment the officer's servant, Hakan, returned with the tea. Standing in horror in the entrance of the tent, he dropped the tray and ran out screaming.

"He's killed *effendi* Juergen!" the servant shouted. "He's killed my master!"

It was a disaster the Paladin lord admiral had not anticipated. Looking around in frantic desperation, the Bulgarian instantly seized the hilt of Juergen's *kilij* and yanked it out of the corpse. Then, grabbing the pouch of silver *florins* resting on the table, he fled for his life. Rizopoulos immediately went running after him, but, still winded from his fight with the Trustee operative, he was unable to keep up with the terrified fugitive as he disappeared through the labyrinth of tents.

Stopping after a brief chase, Rizopoulos mentally called up the holographic overlay screen of his dive computer to reacquire the signal from the tracking device he had planted on the Bulgarian. There was not much time. If he managed to slip out of the camp, it would be that much harder to deliver him back to the Ottomans, so that he might fulfill his despicable but necessary destiny.

At the same time, the servant's shouts had roused the sentries and the duty lieutenant, who even at that moment were gathering to find out what all the commotion was about. Soon the Turks would also be after the escaped prisoner, and the lord admiral had to make sure they did not reach him first, lest they kill him in hot pursuit.

His only choice was to get to the Bulgarian before he managed to get out of the camp and render him unconscious, so that he could be taken into custody by the Turks without incident. Thus he would once again be given the opportunity to bargain for his life—performing that wretched deed for which history had already anonymously vilified him, and for which he had earlier demonstrated such a willing propensity—by divulging the Greeks' plan to the Ottomans.

Overlaying the path the Bulgarian was taking onto his *GPSSI* mapping interface, Rizopoulos could see that the man appeared to be traveling through the camp on a winding route which trended northward, in the direction of the high foothills of the Arakynthos mountains a couple of kilometers away. He immediately plotted a course that, with a little luck, would allow him to intercept his quarry not far from the Ottomans' rear lines, and set out without delay.

As he made his way through the encampment, it did not take long to see why the fugitive seemed to be taking such a circuitous path; for although it was late and most of the soldiers were already asleep in their tents, every now and again Rizopoulos came upon a sentry making his rounds, or a small group of two or three infantrymen talking quietly around a still burning campfire. Shielded as he was, he easily passed by the soldiers undetected and continued along his way; but the Bulgarian would have had to make wide detours around such posts, giving the Paladin lord admiral a tactical advantage.

Trotting as fast as he dared through the encampment's muddy and improvised streets, it took Rizopoulos about ten minutes to finally reach the last rows of tents. Fifty meters beyond that, a series of low earthen embankments and several halfhearted ditches with a few sparsely manned guard posts began. Evidently the Turks did not expect any significant action to their rear, which made it even more bitterly apparent that, in the absence of the betrayal of their plan, the Greeks' chances for success would have been surprisingly high.

Having found a suitable spot from which to watch for the Bulgarian, the Paladin lord admiral waited; and as he followed his subject's progress on his dive computer, he saw that within minutes the fugitive would be in visual range. For some inexplicable reason, however, rather than feeling more confident as the deserter came closer, Rizopoulos became more anxious. He was gripped by an eerie sense of foreboding which he now realized had been with him—and which had been growing stronger with each passing minute—ever since he had left Juergen's tent.

Switching his optical interfaces into night-vision mode, he carefully began scanning the perimeter of the camp, looking for something that could explain his odd premonition. After a few minutes, he saw something moving stealthily in the shadows about a hundred meters away. Magnifying the image, he zeroed in on it and clearly saw that it was the Bulgarian.

He was moving quickly through an olive grove, heading north towards the mountains as the lord admiral had suspected, and running from tree to tree for cover along the way. Immediately, all other thoughts left Rizopoulos's mind, as the shielded Paladin leader began to jog briskly towards the deserter's skulking figure, intending to intercept him as near as possible to the last row of tents. The two men were only about ten meters apart, when suddenly something went horribly wrong.

As the Bulgarian ran out into the open space between two stands of olive trees, he abruptly stumbled forward and fell to the ground cursing. He was in the midst of picking himself up and was still on one knee when, without warning, his head snapped back as if pulled by the hair from behind. For an instant a hazy shadow passed in front of him, and when it was gone Rizopoulos was aghast to see the man he was meant to protect—his head still tilted backwards—with his throat cut from ear to ear.

The desperate fugitive dropped the saber he had taken from Juergen's body and grabbed at his neck, his eyes bulging wildly, but it was too late. There was nothing he could do but collapse on the ground in a sickening fit of gurgles and blood-spattering coughs, which became more violent by the second, and which lasted for almost two full agonizing minutes until the final moment of his miserable death.

Several meters away, Lord Rizopoulos stood thunderstruck. He instantly realized what had happened, and at last understood the source of his previous unease. But more significantly, his mind began to reel with the manifold ramifications of the Bulgarian's death. Without him, the Ottomans would not be apprised of the Greeks' strategy and a major turning point in the history of the current war would be altered. It was something that must not happen at any cost—and yet the very agent of what was supposed to transpire was dying right before his eyes, drowning in his own blood.

The Paladin lord admiral was seized with a sudden and inconsolable inner grief, unlike any feeling of remorse he had ever felt before. He had failed, and the resounding echo of his failure would reverberate throughout the ages. But the moment was short-lived. For even as he looked on in anguished disbelief, he saw a faint shadow disturb the air next to the dying Bulgarian, and then a dark-robed figure appeared standing before him. It was John Crowe.

The Trustee operative gazed down at the writhing Bulgarian pitilessly, and then looking up with a cruel smirk on his mustached lips, began calling out in a singsong voice:

"Come out, come out wherever you are!"

Seething with the righteous indignation that the sight of his traitorous enemy engendered within him, Rizopoulos switched off his SHIELD and stood face to face with the former Paladin without saying a word. For an instant, Crowe seemed disconcerted on seeing the lord admiral, but he quickly recovered and addressed him in an even, almost casual tone.

"I had a feeling things were about to get interesting," he observed with a touch of irony. "You know, I've been waiting for this chance for a very long time—but to be honest, I never thought it would actually come. Then when I saw what happened to Juergen, somehow I knew it had to be you."

"Then you should also know," replied Rizopoulos, his eyes narrowing intently and his solemn bass voice reverberating in something that very nearly resembled a growl, "that it is pointless to try and oppose me."

Crowe laughed.

"Ah, don't take yourself so seriously, my lord!" he admonished. "It's bad for your health. Juergen was an arrogant oaf who began to believe too much in his own legend. He deserved what he got. But I think you'll find that I am not quite so careless. It's too bad the same can't be said for all of your Paladins.

"Our man Ghabry didn't realize until it was too late that I had injected him with the virus that was meant to kill you. Too bad he went and killed himself when he realized what was happening to him. That young Moroccan of yours, though—just brought it straight back to the base like a good little pup. I wonder how many died?

"Agonizing death, I'm told. It seems that the virus turns the body's immune system against its own red blood cells. Yes, such a shame to see so many careless Paladins! But what about you, my lord, are you as careless as they were?"

As the significance of the Trustee operative's words sank in, a tornado of wild outrage began to rise up within Rizopoulos, threatening to distract him from his total concentration on the enemy before him. Indeed, while the Paladin knew his adversary was speaking the truth, he also knew that this was precisely Crowe's intent—merely one weapon in his well-equipped arsenal—and his opening salvo in the battle that was about to begin.

Mastering his thoughts and easily dodging the psychological attack, the lord admiral narrowed his eyes as he growled back in a rumbling bass voice:

"Let's find out, shall we?"

For what seemed like a moment suspended in eternity, the two warriors from nearly a quarter of a millennium in the future stared at each other in intense silence, their long black robes stirring in the evening's light breeze—a pair of deadly panthers measuring one another's will and facing off in the bright moonlight of an April 1826 night. Then, as if triggered by the sudden last gasp of the Bulgarian's dying breath, the two mortal enemies—Paladin and Nemesin—flung themselves at each other with a fury that could only be described as explosive.

Their first contact erupted in a blur of intense hand-to-hand combat, with one deadly blow after another being met with supple parries and dexterous counterstrikes at a speed that would have defied the ability of any interested observer to follow. With dance-like precision they moved around each other, as graceful as they were lethal, each looking for that one sought-for opening which would allow him to land the *coup de grâce* that would shatter his opponent's defenses.

Within seconds, both men instinctively knew that, were it not for his state of extreme fatigue and hunger, Rizopoulos would have easily dominated the battle; but in his weakened condition, the match was an even one. It was perhaps because of this knowledge that Crowe fought even harder, holding nothing back and realizing that there would never be a second chance—for this was a fight to the finish.

Like almost everything about them, the strategies of the two men were polar opposites. The Trustee operative knew that time was on his side. The longer he could defend himself and keep the Paladin fighting, the weaker and more fatigued the older man would become. For his part, Rizopoulos likewise knew that, in order to win, he would have to finish Crowe off quickly. And so the two struggled for several minutes—one man trying to prolong the encounter and the other trying to press his opponent hard and force him into making a fatal mistake—until the Paladin lord admiral finally found his mark.

Breaking through with a sharp open-hand jab to the base of the Englishman's throat, Rizopoulos stunned the Nemesin for a split-second—long enough to follow up with a powerful roundhouse kick to the side of the gasping man's head, knocking him off his feet. Crowe recovered in an instant, but he knew the blow had been costly. It had dazed him enough that he would be at a serious disadvantage. There was only one thing left to do, and that was to even the odds.

Rolling away from another of the Paladin's powerful thrusts, Crowe quickly stood up and swept his flowing cassock to the side, revealing the *yataghan* sword which hung at his belt. He then activated his SHIELD, invisibly fading into the darkness. It was a dastardly thing to do, he knew, but it was practical—and he had always considered himself to be a pragmatist. The tables were suddenly turned, and it was now Rizopoulos who was on the defensive.

Savagely, he lunged at the Paladin before he had a chance to engage his own SHIELD, intending to deal him a final deadly blow with the *yataghan*; but his reckoning was flawed. For on seeing Crowe disappear, Rizopoulos instantly turned inward, descending into the stillness of his own heart, to a place where the motion of the outside world seemed to slow to a crawl. All of his senses were heightened, and while he could not see his opponent with his eyes, nor hear him with his ears, he could sense the violent turbulence of his presence. He could feel the flow of the air around his outstretched arm and over the blade he held in his hand, and he could read the hidden but unmistakable signals of his lethal intent.

Trusting in his instincts, he sidestepped the sword stroke and reached out, making contact with Crowe's arm and using his adversary's own momentum to throw him off balance. Then catching sight of Juergen's discarded *kilij* saber lying a few meters away near the motionless body of the Bulgarian, the lord admiral dived after it, retrieving the weapon and mentally activating his own SHIELD.

Slowly, the two men invisibly approached each other, using every means in their mental arsenals to discern the other's position—a hazy and indistinct shadow rippling the air; the silent recoil of grass springing back to its original position after the passage of an unseen foot; and most importantly, the acuteness of a mind's eye that sensed the proximity of imminent danger. They were no more than a meter and a half apart when the final battle erupted, *yataghan* sword against *kilij* saber—steel against steel in an invisible and muffled clash which sounded through the barrier of the electromagnetic shielding like the distant clinking of glasses in some frenetic prelibation toast.

The speed and intensity of their fight absorbed both men so completely that their senses of touch and smell, their perceptions of the slightest alterations in the angular momentum of their clashing blades, and even of the infinitesimal changes in the currents of the wind—together with their subtle awareness of the shifting patterns of their opponent's body heat and aura—became a second vision. Thus, while they each 'saw' the other as clearly and unfailingly as clairvoyants looking into some arcane psychic mystery, all else in the world around them faded into oblivion.

When after a minute of blazing combat, they suddenly heard the shout of an Ottoman soldier who had come to investigate—one of a small group of infantrymen about thirty meters away, whose attention had been attracted either by the muffled sound of their swordplay or by a glimpse of the Bulgarian's body lying prone on the ground—both the Paladin and the Nemesin were yanked out of their absolute concentration for the tiniest fraction of a second. It was enough.

Seizing the minute opening, Lord Rizopoulos launched a powerful thrust at Crowe and drove the *kilij* deep into the man's upper chest, just below the shoulder, taking him down by the force of his lunge and pinning him to the ground with the blade. Shouting in pain and unable to wield his own sword, the Trustee operative tried to rise, but Rizopoulos planted his knee squarely on his chest and leaned on the saber and twisted it, causing his enemy to writhe in agony.

Perhaps any other opponent would have been finished at that point, but Crowe was not to be counted out so soon. In one final act of cunning, he mentally called up the controls of his SHIELD and, switching it off, became visible. Immediately he began to scream in perfect Turkish:

"Help! There's a demon attacking me! Shoot it quickly!"

The Ottoman soldiers nearby heard the screams and, noticing Crowe for the first time, ran over towards him with their muskets raised. Lord Admiral Rizopoulos suddenly found himself in a terrible predicament. He could not appear out of nowhere in front of the Turks, or superstitious as they were, they would most assuredly consider him to be some kind of evil spirit and try to shoot him on the spot. At the same time, he knew that Crowe would take advantage of the slightest shift in his position to wriggle free. He had only seconds to react.

"Who are you? What's going on?" one of the infantrymen—an Albanian from his accent—shouted in alarm. But as Crowe struggled desperately with the invisible Rizopoulos, he shouted out again.

"Shoot it! It's a demon! It's right above me!" he yelled.

Perplexed, the soldiers looked at each other and shrugged, thinking they would do no harm by firing into the air above the man—whom they took for a Turk from his speech—and that they might even render service to *Allah* by driving away the demon, if there actually were one attacking him. They therefore took aim and were about to shoot, when all at once two of their fellows went limp and collapsed on the ground at their feet.

Astounded, the other three infantrymen looked at them and then glanced up at each other, just in time for two more of them to fall unconscious. The last man instantly dropped his weapon and went running back towards the camp as fast as a frightened rabbit, but after about twenty meters he too fell tumbling in mid-stride and hit the dirt.

Motionlessly locked in their struggle, Rizopoulos and Crowe looked on in tense anticipation, preparing for the worst, as a dark hooded figure on horseback suddenly materialized a short distance away from them. An instant later he was joined by four more riders and then the last horseman, who had returned from chasing the Turkish soldier. Slowly the squadron walked their mounts towards the pair of fighters, still frozen in mid-battle, giving no clue as to their identity—whether Paladin or Nemesin, friend or foe.

Approaching wordlessly to within a few meters, the black-robed figures abruptly stopped and dismounted, and then removed their cowls. There in the illuminating rays of the nearly full April moonlight stood Vice Admiral Alexandros Ephraimoglou along with Ensign Rashid Al-Noury, and a search party of Paladin divers.

As soon as Crowe saw the Paladins, he desperately struggled to break free, cursing and twisting his body in spite of the terrible pain in his shoulder; but with a single mighty jab to the face, Rizopoulos knocked him unconscious. Rejoicing to find both Ephraimoglou and Al-Noury safe and well, the lord admiral then switched off his SHIELD and appeared before his comrades, with a look of evident relief and good cheer lightening his otherwise drawn and care-worn face.

"Well met, good Paladins!" he called out cordially. "You wouldn't happen to have a length of rope, would you?"

Immediately, two of the men ran over to secure Crowe with strong synthetic tethers and a delta-wave-inducing headband, temporarily placing him in a state of deep sleep. Meanwhile,

Ephraimoglou and the others bowed to the lord admiral and approached to help Rizopoulos to his feet for a joyful reunion.

"My lord, you're injured!" cried Ephraimoglou in alarm, seeing blood running from a slash mark on his commander's forehead. "Medic!" he shouted, calling one of the search and rescue team members over.

"Oh, it's nothing—barely even a scratch," said Rizopoulos, waving the man off dismissively. "But you'd better go and take care of him," he motioned towards Crowe, who was still skewered through the shoulder by Juergen's saber. "It's not fatal, but it's a serious wound. Mind that you control the bleeding when you remove the blade. We'll need him alive."

He then noticed Ephraimoglou's hand, which he still held in his own, and which had been nothing but a charred stump the last time he had seen it.

"Well," he proclaimed joyfully, "it certainly looks like they've done a decent job fixing you up!"

"Yes, it's not bad," the vice admiral replied, flexing his fingers. "It's almost completely healed from the attachment surgery now. Of course there's still a little weakness, even after all the physical therapy. But Mariatos says it'll keep getting stronger over time, and before too long I won't be able to tell the difference between this one and the original."

As two of the dive team members guarded Crowe, and another two positioned themselves several meters away on each flank to act as lookouts, the two senior Paladins and Rashid continued exchanging their greetings for a few minutes and then soon began to talk of weightier matters.

"We've been looking for you for more than two weeks, my lord," said Ephraimoglou, beaming with satisfaction at having found him. "When I learned from Ensign Al-Noury here that you had given up your diving bell for me, I was determined to come back for you myself. It's taken us quite a while to be able to make this dive—many things have happened that have delayed us until now. But that's a long story for another time. The main thing for now is that we have found you and that I can give you this."

Reaching into the folds of his cassock, Ephraimoglou drew out a crystalline diving bell which he presented to Rizopoulos, fully expecting the lord admiral to be pleased. But instead, both he and Rashid were surprised to see a troubled look immediately overshadow the Paladin leader's face. Rather than thanking them, he quickly turned away and, shaking his head, spoke to the two men gravely.

"No," he said mysteriously. "I appreciate what you have done, but I won't be needing this."

Ephraimoglou and Rashid looked at each other perplexed, wondering if perhaps the lord admiral already had another diving bell of which they were not aware; but this strange and sudden mood shift told them that something else was bothering him.

"I don't understand," murmured a stunned Vice Admiral Ephraimoglou.

After a brief pause and a heavy sigh, the lord admiral answered, motioning in Crowe's direction.

"As tempting as it would be to send him back to Ibrahim, who I'm sure has unfinished business with him," he said somberly, "it's important to get him back and have him interrogated. I'm sure there is much valuable information about the Trustees' organization and their plans that can be learned from him. He's about my size—use the bell for him. That will give our engineers a chance to examine the current state of the Trustees' technology. It's not often we get a chance to take apart one of their diving bells."

"Hm, of course," Ephraimoglou replied thoughtfully. "You're right. But I suppose we can plant an emergency beacon and send a message to have a diver waiting for us with another bell by the time we all get back to Monemvasia—"

But before he could finish, Rizopoulos stopped him with a wave of his hand, looked at his two Paladins and said plainly: "Gentlemen, I've made a decision. I am not going back to Camp Monemvasia with you."

The words hit Ephraimoglou and Rashid like a battering ram, confusing them and drawing an immediate protest from both.

"What do you mean, you're not going back?" cried Ephraimoglou. "How much longer are you going to stay here?"

"My lord, forgive me, but you're exhausted and half-starved! Surely you need some time back home to recuperate," pleaded Rashid.

Shaking his head, Rizopoulos looked at the two of them and said grimly: "I came here to do a job, and unfortunately I have...not succeeded. And now things have become complicated. I must do what I can to salvage the situation."

Then, taking out his dive computer, the lord admiral pulled up a draft of a memorandum he had composed while still in Messolonghi—an encrypted letter addressed to the Paladin Council of Peers.

"I have already been thinking about this for some time now anyway, and today's events have only served to make up my mind for me," he said, as he beamed the letter to Ephraimoglou's dive computer. "Alex, I want you to deliver this letter to the Old Man for me when you return."

Then, putting away the dive computer, he paused for a moment and reached under his robes. Pulling something out from around his neck, he reached out and handed it to Ephraimoglou. "And also give him this."

Looking at the object Lord Rizopoulos had just given his second-in-command, Ephraimoglou and Ensign Al-Noury were speechless. For in the vice admiral's open palm—the same hand that had been charred to ashes and replaced with a new and genetically identical one from the Paladin's own induced pluripotent stem cells—was the solid-gold pectoral pendant representing Rizopoulos's office as lord high admiral of the fleet. It was the emblem of the Paladin Order, the double-headed phoenix.

After a moment of stunned silence, Ephraimoglou stared at the pendant in his hand and finally blurted out: "What...what's the meaning of this? Surely you don't mean to tell me that you're resigning your commission?"

"My lord!" gasped Rashid, unable to believe what was happening after having just accomplished his long-awaited reunion with his mentor.

"It's all right, Ensign," responded Rizopoulos gently and simply. "It's all right, Alex. It's something I have to do. And where I'm going, this will be of no use to me."

The two began to assail him with questions, but bowing his head, he refused to answer and just said:

"Enough. I must ask you to respect my decision—which has not been an easy one for me—and leave it at that. And now it's time for you to take the prisoner and leave me before these Turks regain consciousness. I still have much work to do. All I ask, Alex," Rizopoulos entreated, "is a small personal favor. I would like you to take on the Ensign here as your apprentice. I'm afraid his former master has not had a chance to teach him very much."

He then turned to Rashid, who struggled to keep his already moist eyes from welling up with emotion, and said: "And you, my young Paladin, have made me proud in the short time I have known you. Stay close to your new mentor. He is a good soldier and there is much you can learn from him."

The two Paladins looked at one another in astonishment, and then Vice Admiral Ephraimoglou turned back to face his lord admiral. Whether it was through some sudden intuition, or due to seeing the body of the slain Bulgarian lying on the ground a short distance away, he suddenly began to put the pieces together and understood what Rizopoulos intended to do.

"My lord, don't tell me that you're going to—," he started to protest. But with a motion of his hand Rizopoulos silenced him.

"Please—don't try to stop me, Alex," he said gravely. "It has to be done. I wish it could be different, but there is no other way."

Churning inside with anguish, and struggling inwardly with the notion that one's duty as a Paladin demanded such an inconceivable act as that which he now knew Rizopoulos to be contemplating, he realized there was nothing he could do but to acquiesce to the lord admiral's demand. Drawing himself up to his full height, he made a deep bowing prostration before him and rose up again, with Rashid—who understood that something momentous was happening, but who was not yet able to fathom what it was—immediately following his example.

"By your will, my lord!" the two Paladins exclaimed in unison.

Then, in a gesture that surprised both men, Lord Admiral Leonidas Rizopoulos, knight of the World Council, humbly asked their forgiveness and bowed down before his two subordinates. Rising and saluting them, he then quickly turned away and resolutely walked off in the direction of the Ottoman camp without once looking back.

Still holding the golden phoenix in his hand, Vice Admiral Ephraimoglou stood silently watching as the Paladin leader moved across the field that separated them from the last line of Ottoman tents. All at once he felt heavily weighed down by a host of conflicting emotions and, having tremendous difficulty reconciling his thoughts, found himself at an unsettling mental impasse.

For one thing, it alarmed him to see his commander and longtime friend heading into grave danger, uncertain of whether or not he would ever return. At the same time, he understood the profound sense of duty and honor that motivated Sir Leonidas to do what he knew in his heart to be right, even at the cost of his own honor. It was that which he had sworn to do as a Paladin knight, even in the face of extreme adversity, and he admired his great courage and fortitude. Nevertheless, for perhaps the first time in his military career, Ephraimoglou also began to wonder whether or not the mission was worth such a price.

Turning his mind to another lost friend—who had likewise followed his conscience and done what he believed deep in his heart to be right, even though it must have been extraordinarily difficult for him—Ephraimoglou began to wonder what the essential difference between the two men truly was. During his long convalescence, the vice admiral had spent a great deal of time contemplating Mina Ghabry's unforgivable actions, and had still not come up with any satisfactory answers. But now he suddenly began to see things in a different and more diffuse light; a light in which the lines between right and wrong, trust and betrayal—previously so clear to him—seemed to shift and blur.

After all, both Rizopoulos and Ghabry were soldiers fighting for what each believed to be a righteous cause; but the similarity did not end there. For not only was each man willing to sacrifice himself for his cause, but both were also willing to do that which they believed was necessary, and that which would otherwise have been repugnant to them, in the name of preserving their way of life—even to the point of sacrificing others who were non-combatants on the battlefield of their undeclared and clandestine wars.

Perhaps the biggest difference between the two of them then, Ephraimoglou concluded, was the fact that one man's actions were officially sanctioned by the world's ruling elite, and therefore viewed as 'just', while those of the other were not. Perhaps.

Such reasoning, however, still did not satisfy the silent turmoil that had been going on in Ephraimoglou's soul for months, and which now, with Rizopoulos's departure, seemed to take on an even greater sense of urgency. The harsh reality was that—like it or not—there was a war going on; and, for the sake of the survival of the world as they knew it, losing was not an option.

In the end, he decided, there really were no clear answers. It all depended on which side of that blurred and shifting line of truth one stood on at any given moment in time. But the lack of certitude continued to leave him feeling disturbed and uneasy, and one thought kept insinuating itself insistently into his consciousness, over and over again. There had to be another way.

As these thoughts drifted through Ephraimoglou's troubled mind, he saw the Paladin lord admiral arrive at the opposite side of the field. Standing before the Ottoman camp, Rizopoulos slowly spread out his arms in a wide, stretching gesture and, lifting his palms, gazed up at the heavens as if in solemn prayer. He remained like that for a long moment, and then at last, crossing himself, he took the final few steps into the camp, activated his SHIELD and vanished from sight.

CHAPTER 18

The morning of old-calendar April 7, 1826 dawned chill and clear in the Egyptian army camp, spread out before the battered but unyielding walls of Messolonghi. As per his usual practice, Ibrahim Pasha rose early and, after his morning tea and daily medical checkup, spent a large part of the day in meetings to hear the latest reports and confer on strategy with his officers.

Aside from the routine intermittent bombardment of the town, there had been very little activity during the last couple of days on the land side. The Ottomans were aware of the dire conditions within the besieged city, and therefore could afford to be generous with their time. Meanwhile, by sea, after a protracted naval skirmish a few days before, the Greek squadron seemed to have pulled back into the open waters of the Gulf, although it was generally expected that they would attempt another run on the lagoon at any moment.

Being ruthless competitors for both the superiority of their military reputation and the favor of the Ottoman *sultan*, Ibrahim and his fellow *pasha*, Reshid, were by no means on friendly terms; and their troops—ever jealous of the spoils they would gain from a victory—were even less tolerant of one another. Because of their vicious mutual antipathy, the Egyptian and Turkish camps even had to be separated by more than half a kilometer, and the communication between the two was generally kept to the bare minimum necessary to facilitate the conduct of official business. Every once in a while, however, rumors would spread from one army to the other, usually by the agency of Albanian mercenaries, who had access to both camps and—holding both of their employers in equal contempt—showed no more partiality to one than to the other.

Thus it was the case that, early in the afternoon, the Egyptian satrap learned that a deserter from the Greek garrison had been captured late the previous evening and, once inside Reshid's camp, had managed to kill a foreign officer. Apparently he himself had been killed soon after, outside the camp while trying to escape; but as several soldiers were claiming to have been responsible for the deed, no one was really sure of what had actually happened.

Although the event was minor in itself, the news was of particular interest to Ibrahim for two reasons. First, because any misfortune that occurred to his rival *pasha* was a source of great entertainment for him; and second, because word of increased numbers of deserters from the garrison suggested that the situation inside the city was reaching that critical point of no return. It would not be long before the insurgents would either capitulate or die of starvation.

Seeing that the *pasha* seemed to take a great deal of interest in such a trivial report, one of his junior officers—ever keen to curry favor with him—was emboldened and went on to tell him of yet another deserter who had mysteriously appeared in their own camp earlier that day and given himself up. What made this case even more unusual, he recounted with evident delight, was that this man appeared to be some kind of a monk. On hearing this news, Ibrahim's interest was aroused, and he began to question the captain.

"One of their monks, you say? And he just walked into the camp and surrendered of his own free will? Rubbish!" he exclaimed, characteristically challenging the other man's words. "Why would someone take such a foolish risk? It can't be true!"

"By your words, my *pasha*, you must be correct," the officer excused himself before continuing to insist on his account. "Nevertheless, this is what my men have told me, useless liars that they are."

"And what have they learned from this deserter-monk? Anything of importance?" Ibrahim continued, as if he had never doubted the officer's story.

"Unfortunately, my *pasha*, we have not learned anything from him, as he refuses to speak, even under severe beatings."

Letting loose a peculiar shrill cry, the *pasha* marveled at the news.

"Now I am sure you are lying, Captain!" he exclaimed. "A Greek monk, you say, enters our camp as a deserter and surrenders—but then he refuses to speak, even when beaten! And what would you have me believe next? That he is Papaflessas come back from the dead? Nonsense!"

"Forgive me, my *pasha*," the officer squirmed uncomfortably. "You are wise beyond your years! I am a fool and only report what my useless men are saying. It seems that this slave of yours refuses to speak to anyone but Your Highness. In fact, he specifically requested to see you, my *pasha*. We beat him even more for suggesting such a ridiculous thing, and—"

As the officer spoke, a strange look came over Ibrahim's round, bearded face, and he said curtly: "Captain, I will see this man. Make sure he is well guarded until I call for him, and have him ready to be brought to my tent—well-secured, mind you— after the evening meal."

Taken aback, the officer bowed and, leaving the tent to make the arrangements, said: "Why, yes, of course, my *pasha*. It will be done according to your word."

The captain's words had inflamed Ibrahim's curiosity. It was highly unusual for a deserter to present himself in the enemy's camp voluntarily, though not completely unprecedented. Perhaps the man was starving and desperate for something to eat. But the fact that he was a monk—someone who would ordinarily be accustomed to living on comparatively little food— and that he even had the fortitude to withstand beatings, made that scenario more remote. No, it was much more likely that he had an entirely different motive for wanting to see the *pasha*.

Ibrahim might be taking a risk, but this could actually turn out to be a golden opportunity, he thought. He might finally be able to learn if the would-be assassins who had had the temerity to infiltrate his camp and try to kill him several months before in Mystras—one of whom had also been a monk—had acted alone, or if there were more like them skulking about. And as for the man's refusal to speak, he thought, that would not be an issue. If he continued to remain silent, there were certainly many ways to remedy the situation.

THE SUN HAD ALREADY sunk below the western horizon, and the evening prayer had long been completed, when the Egyptian supreme commander, drinking tea with two or three of his senior officers and military advisors, finally called for the deserter-monk to be brought to his pavilion. Accompanied by the same captain who had spoken to the *pasha* about him earlier that afternoon, and escorted in by no less than three soldiers, with his hands securely chained behind his back, he was brought in—a large and physically powerful man, as Ibrahim immediately saw.

He was also older than the *pasha* had imagined he would be— another reason to be suspicious of his motives for entering the camp. Those few deserting at this stage of the siege were typically younger men without the fortitude and commitment to see through what they had started, now that things looked desperate for the Greeks.

Despite the obvious punishment the man had endured, as evidenced by the multiple bruises and lacerations on his face, he nevertheless moved with the grace and self-assurance of one accustomed to being in command of others. But that would not have seemed at all surprising to the *pasha*, had he the means of knowing anything at all about the Paladin lord admiral who stood stalwartly before him.

As soon as the guards brought him in, they tried to force him to his knees before the *pasha*, but he defied their attempts to make him budge. The captain then motioned to one of the men, who prodded the captive on the right side of his rib cage with the point of his bayonet—but Ibrahim quickly put a stop to it, waving the soldier off.

"Never mind," he said, carefully observing the black-robed man, "let our guest be seated."

Then clapping his hands together sharply, he called for one of his servants to bring over a hard-backed chair, which was set down opposite the *pasha's* divan at a distance of about two meters. "Please, sit," Ibrahim said to the man, motioning to the chair. But seeing that the captive refused to sit, he asked: "Does he speak any Turkish, or perhaps Albanian?"

"I do not believe so, Your Highness," replied the captain. "He only seems to speak in Greek."

Although Ibrahim—born of a Greek mother—was well acquainted with the language, he did not deign to speak what was considered to be a slave's tongue in front of his subordinates. Clapping his hands together, he called for the *dragoman*, his official interpreter and diplomatic secretary, who had an excellent knowledge of several Middle Eastern and European languages, and who was himself an ethnic Greek. Thus he began to converse with the captive, who continued standing peacefully before him, with one guard on his right and another on his left.

"What is your name and why have you come here?" the *pasha* asked through his interpreter.

"My name is not important," replied Lord Rizopoulos through his swollen and bloodied lips, the tranquility of his voice belying the raging battle of emotions being waged within him. "What matters is that I have come as one seeking mercy."

"And how is it that you have come to me now, when less than one week ago I sent my embassy to your leaders to propose terms, which they flatly rejected? Do they now wish to reconsider my offer?"

"I do not come at the behest of the leaders of Messolonghi, who are ignorant of my presence here, Your Highness, but on my own initiative," Rizopoulos stated in his resounding bass voice.

On hearing those words, Ibrahim let out a shrill laugh and made a derisive gesture, before upbraiding the black-cassocked Paladin for his insolence.

"And who are you, pray tell, that I should hear the personal plea of a despicable deserter to save his own life?" the *pasha* asked, becoming annoyed with the audience. "If you have nothing of interest to say to me, then you have made a grave mistake in wasting my time begging for mercy!"

"Your Highness is mistaken," replied the Paladin lord admiral with perfect composure. "I have not come to beg for my own life, which was already mine to do with as I pleased before I entered your camp, and which has meant nothing to me ever since I renounced it on the day I joined my Order.

"Rather, I have come seeking mercy in regard to the lives of innumerable innocent people—women and children and elderly folk among them—who at this moment do not have a voice in the events about to take place in our sight—events about which even Your Highness is not aware."

"The man is mad!" exclaimed one of the *pasha's* officers. "Why do we even listen to him?"

But Ibrahim silenced him and continued speaking to the prisoner, asking with intense curiosity: "And which events might these be, of which you speak?"

Rizopoulos sighed heavily. In spite of his cool exterior, a stormy emotional dichotomy raged deep inside of him. He knew unequivocally what must be done, and there was no doubt in his mind that it was ultimately the right thing to do. Yet, at the same time, he could not escape being withered by the searing self-condemnation and shredded by the violent self-loathing which came from actually being the one to do it—to betray the very same people to whose needs he had helped minister in the preceding weeks and months, and to pronounce an irrevocable death sentence upon so many, in order that countless others might be saved.

"Tell the prisoner," Ibrahim snapped to the *dragoman*, "that I am waiting for his answer, and that he should not continue to try my patience if he does not wish to feel the difference between the wrath of a captain and that of a *pasha*!"

With his head pounding, and feeling slightly nauseated at what he was about to do, Rizopoulos took a deep breath, garnered his inner strength, and slowly began to speak.

"At this moment, there are nearly nine thousand souls inside Messolonghi," he said in a deep voice, husky with emotion. "Of these, as many as five thousand are women and children, and another thousand are non-combatant farmers and artisans from the surrounding area. All of the town's provisions have long been exhausted, and the residents have not tasted bread for more than forty days. Many of the weak have already died. Within a few days, even the garrison will no longer have the strength to defend the fortifications..."

Rizopoulos paused, his voice trembling, as he fought the sick, sinking feeling in the pit of his stomach and struggled to continue. He had never felt such absolute loneliness and emptiness in his life.

"Yes, go on," Ibrahim urged, listening with rapt attention.

"Therefore," the Paladin lord admiral continued, his words coming slowly and painfully, "the city's leaders...have taken the decision...rather than submit, to fight to the very end...and...to stage a...a mass exodus from Messolonghi these three days hence...on the night before Palm Sunday."

Hanging his head in exhaustion and shame, Rizopoulos exhaled deeply. It was done. Somewhere inside, he felt as if an invisible force had rent his soul in two, shaking him to his core, and that he was now shrouded in a deep and impenetrable darkness.

The conversation continued for a little while longer, as Ibrahim Pasha demanded to know more details about the planned sortie; but while he heard himself responding to the *pasha's* questions as if from afar, everything that transpired from then on was a mere blur to the Paladin lord admiral. Before the audience ended, one or two of the *pasha's* senior officers had voiced their concern that the information was not to be trusted, but the Egyptian commander remained silent and pensive for several minutes. Finally he made his decision and began to issue orders.

"Captain, keep this man in your custody and make sure he is well guarded at all times. We shall see in three days' time whether or not he speaks the truth," Ibrahim commanded. "If so, he may yet find mercy; but if not, he will pay for his foolishness with his life."

"Yes, my *pasha!*" cried the captain, and motioning to his soldiers, he exited the pavilion with Rizopoulos being pushed along between his guards.

When they were gone, the *pasha* next addressed the *dragoman*, saying: "Draft a letter for my signature to my brother *pasha* in the next camp, to be delivered within the hour. I want to arrange a war council with him tomorrow afternoon."

Then turning to his officers, he continued: "Gentlemen, I do not know if we can trust what this prisoner has told us; nevertheless, we must be prepared for every eventuality. He strikes me as a righteous man."

For the soldiers in the combined Ottoman camps, the next three days were full of the usual activities that occupied an army during a lull in the fighting—the continual drilling, the guard duty, the advancing of trenches and repairing of earthworks, the maintenance of weapons, and many other routine duties. But for Lord Admiral Rizopoulos—well aware of what was happening inside the besieged city of Messolonghi—they were days of dark mourning, as if he had been swallowed up by the very maw of Hades itself.

From the moment the erstwhile Paladin leader was led out of Ibrahim Pasha's pavilion, he slept very little and ate nothing at all, knowing that with each passing hour more and more citizens were dying of starvation and disease just a couple of kilometers away. Although he was already weakened from lack of food, he reasoned that his complete fast was necessary out of a feeling of solidarity with them. Nevertheless, deep down he knew that it was also a hopeless effort on his part to win some sort of redemption for the unforgivable act he had been forced to commit.

As the days passed and the fateful hour inevitably approached, a mental newsreel of the scenario then unfolding in the beleaguered town played over and over again in Rizopoulos's thoughts. He could see those still strong enough to continue working, as they prepared mines and laid up stores of munitions in a few key buildings where the remnant of the population—anyone too feeble to attempt the escape—would soon shut themselves up in anticipation of their final awful encounter with the enemy.

He imagined the artisans preparing the makeshift wooden bridges that would be thrown over the more than two-meter-wide moat outside the city walls, enabling the population to pour out from the breaches that would be made in the ramparts at key points. And he envisioned the throngs of the faithful who would attend a last mournful liturgy in Messolonghi's main cathedral, to be forgiven their sins and to receive holy communion from the hand of their beloved hierarch, Bishop Joseph, who had once so trustingly accepted the Paladin leader into their community.

Grieving ever more deeply in his soul, the lord admiral retreated inward into an intense state of prayer. After what he had done, he felt that it would have been better to go back and suffer with those whom he had condemned to certain death. But going back now was impossible, and he knew it.

He was a prisoner, held fast as much by the shackles of searing guilt as by the chains of iron which encircled him. All he could do now was to wait—and, waiting, to endure that unceasing mental anguish known to all prisoners who are unable to erase from their minds' eye the horrors of the crimes they have committed and the reproachful faces of their victims.

Thus it was almost a welcome relief to Rizopoulos when, shortly before sunset on the evening of the third day, the agonizing delay finally came to an end. At around half past six on

April 22, 1826—or April tenth, according to the ancient Julian calendar still then in use by the Greeks—a sudden fusillade of musket fire was heard from far behind the Ottoman camp, from the direction of the monastery of St. Symeon on the high ridges of Mount Zygos. It was the signal from Karaiskakis's men: they were in position, as the commanders at Messolonghi had requested by secret messenger several days before.

From the location in which he was being held—securely tethered to an ancient olive tree with a heavy chain fastened around his ankle, and his hands bound tightly in front of him—Lord Admiral Rizopoulos could just manage to catch a glimpse of a section of the distant walls of Messolonghi. Peering through the narrow spaces between the rows of canvas tents, it was not a view that allowed him to see anything of particular importance. Even so, he knew the history well enough to be painfully aware of everything happening there in minute detail.

To begin with, as dusk fell, amidst a highly charged atmosphere of anxiety and nervous tension, the Greek commanders mustered their troops and caused four wide plank footbridges to be carefully and silently lowered across the city's outer defensive ditch. At the same time, a patrol was sent around the walls to announce to all the defenders that, in two hours' time, their operation would begin. Except for the occasional firing of their muskets and the calling out of the sentries to one another, which they continued doing in order to keep up an appearance of normality, a profound hush fell over the rest of the garrison as each person prepared for what was about to come.

Inside the city, the women gave the youngest children water laced with opium to drink, causing them to be drowsy and preventing them from crying or making noise. They then donned men's clothing, attempting to appear less vulnerable, and, together with any boys who were strong enough to use them, took up swords and daggers so as to be able to protect themselves during the flight.

Meanwhile, the infirm and the seriously wounded—along with as many of the inhabitants who refused to leave their homes out of loyalty to their family members who could not flee—began barricading themselves in several defensible buildings which had earlier been prepared for that purpose. Among these were several of the city's leading men, including Joseph, Bishop of Rogon and Kozylis, who—true to his word—closed himself up with a company of several hundred citizens in the town's old windmill, there to await their fate.

When at last the time came, just before nine o'clock in the evening, a second patrol was dispatched around the walls, which little by little began siphoning off the troops from their posts and sending everyone to the ramparts' eastern flank. There, the whole population was to assemble beneath the artillery batteries and lie in quiet anticipation of a sign from General Karaiskakis and his men, who were to harass the enemy from the rear in a diversionary attack signaling the beginning of the exodus.

The plan was for the refugees from Messolonghi to split up into two columns. The first one, at more than six-thousand-strong, would consist principally of civilians spearheaded by a vanguard of militia. This massive body would attempt to storm through the Egyptian camp, where relatively less resistance was expected from Ibrahim's force made up largely of untested conscripts.

The second column was to be comprised of more than two thousand of the Greeks' most battle-hardened troops, who would try and drive a wedge through the Turkish camp, where it was anticipated that Reshid's Turkish regulars and Albanian mercenaries would put up more of a fight. Those who managed to get through were instructed to assemble at a certain vineyard, about seven kilometers outside the city, and from there to make their way up the steep slopes of Mount Zygos to the refuge of St. Symeon's monastery.

The strategy was perhaps the best one that could be devised under the circumstances, but unfortunately it was to be plagued from the outset by a number of costly miscalculations. First, many of the civilian residents of the besieged city—loath to abandon their homes and any loved ones remaining inside—lingered behind, saying their heartrending final farewells until long after the appointed time.

Thus instead of gathering *en masse* under the batteries as planned, small groups of inhabitants slowly trickled out of the breaches in the walls in a much-delayed and drawn-out affair. Eventually the garrison's frustrated soldiers, deciding they could wait no longer, crossed over the moat with their families and whomever else they found ready, leaving the largest part of the civilians on their own to use the last bridge—the one nearest the lagoon and least exposed to danger—without military supervision.

Second, and perhaps most significantly, the enemy—forewarned about a possible general sortie and hearing the noises from beneath the walls—soon began to direct a heavy and tenacious barrage of musket fire from the front line of their trenches against the section of the ramparts where the defenders were gathered. The number of casualties from the Ottoman fire was relatively minor, since the shot mainly buzzed harmlessly above the heads of the prostrate Greeks; but the overall effect of their blistering assault, combined with the nerve-racking delay in the anticipated signal from Karaiskakis, was dramatic. The morale and discipline among the ranks of the civilians deteriorated quickly, contributing greatly to the disaster which was to follow.

After being pinned down by enemy fire for more than an hour, and finally losing their patience for a sign that Karaiskakis had engaged the foe from the rear, the men of the garrison at long last rose up from their position and drove forward with a great shout, leading their families and anyone who followed in a massive shock wave against the opposing lines. Despite having reinforced their defenses with additional men and artillery batteries, the Egyptians were overwhelmed by the suddenness and the ferocity of the garrison's onslaught, and within minutes, their defenses were shattered and a wide swath had been cut through their broken lines.

Riding the back of such a valiant and defiant wave, perhaps most of the civilian population of Messolonghi could still have been saved that night. Sadly, however, it was not meant to be. For in the confusion and the heat of battle, one catastrophic mistake resulted in the failure of the largest part of the citizenry assembled outside the walls to follow the advance troops through the enemy camp.

Instead, still gathering on the bridges and the opposite bank of the outer ditch, and being pressed from behind by the swelling crowds, those in front began to admonish their fellow citizens behind them to stop pushing. And, as if in some tragic and nightmarish version of a child's game, those few hushed murmurs of "Get back!" became distorted as they were passed down the line, somehow instantaneously morphing into a panicked cry of "Back to the batteries!"

Believing that a general retreat had been called, the majority of the crowd surged back into the town, with many women and children being trampled underfoot or knocked into the murky waters of the moat to drown. Utterly defenseless now that the soldiers of the garrison were no longer there to protect them, those who made it back through the breaches abandoned all hope, as the hordes of the marauding enemy scaled the walls and poured into the city after them in hot pursuit.

Thus the brave Messolonghi—the final resting place of heroes, which had stubbornly withstood a bitter yearlong siege—fell into the merciless hands of the Ottomans. For the remainder of that long and savage night, and for several days after, the screams and cries of carnage and bedlam rang out and echoed over the plain and the lagoon. These were further punctuated by the continuous peals of gunfire and the frequent rumble of violent explosions that rocked the city whenever the enemy forced their way into a building and caused the desperate inhabitants within to set fire to their stockpiles of ammunition.

Among the structures so detonated that first night was the massive powder magazine under one of the fortifications' principal bastions, in which scores of Greeks along with hundreds of their Turkish and Egyptian attackers were obliterated. The great windmill by the lagoon—the last refuge of Bishop Joseph and hundreds of others—managed to hold out a little longer; but in the end, it too suffered a similar fate. For, after two days, Ibrahim's men finally succeeded in storming their way in, and it was the venerable old hierarch himself who put the torch to its store of gunpowder and leveled the entire edifice.

CHAPTER 19

For the Christian residents of Messolonghi, Palm Sunday was meant to be a celebration of victory—a participation in Jesus' triumphal entry into Jerusalem, riding on the back of a humble donkey as 'King of kings'. In the year 1826, however, it was anything but that. For as the armies of the two Ottoman commanders poured into the fallen city, slaughtering the civilian population indiscriminately, and even viciously turning upon each other in their jealous lust for plunder, those from the besieged garrison who had fled through the enemy camp soon faced their own deadly battlefront.

Carried forward by the tremendous inertia of their initial surge, the escaping defenders plowed through the Egyptian camp in one massive train, rather than dividing up into two separate columns as per their original plan. As fate would have it, this fortuitous arrangement actually helped save many of them in the end. For, although he was skeptical about the warning he had received, in addition to reinforcing his front lines, Ibrahim had taken the extra precaution of deploying his cavalry in the plain behind his camp.

He had also induced his fellow *pasha*, Reshid, to send a contingent of Albanian mercenaries to wait in ambush in the foothills of Mount Zygos. As soon as the Greeks made it through the enemy's encampment, they were set upon by a brigade of five hundred horsemen; but by the sheer size and momentum of their column they managed to cut their way through it, albeit at the dear price of more than a hundred of their company, including many women and children caught straggling at the rear.

As difficult as their flight across the plain had been, their next test proved even more costly. Having run the entire gauntlet of the enemy's artillery, infantry and cavalry, and believing themselves finally to be in the clear, the insurgents began the long climb up the foothills leading to the peak of Mount Zygos. As they ascended the forested and rocky ground in the bright moonlight, they saw a group of *fustanella*-clad men in the distance, who called out to them in Greek and waved them on, encouraging them to approach.

Assuming they were a band of General Karaiskakis's *pallikari* fighters, the column drew near. However, once they were in range, the treachery was revealed. Instead of greetings and protection, they were met by a hail of heavy musket fire from a large company of Reshid Pasha's Albanian mercenaries.

With no place to go, the Greeks rallied to the attack and fought for their lives, being joined by a brigade of three hundred of Karaiskakis's men coming down from the heights above. They managed to repulse the enemy at last, but the damage had already been done. By the end of the encounter, hundreds of men, women and children lay dead on the bloodied slopes of Mount Zygos.

Moreover, on marching more than forty kilometers to Karaiskakis's base camp, the remaining fugitives found the renowned *klepht* general seriously ill and his army with barely enough supplies to provide for their own needs, let alone to feed a crowd of more than two thousand starving refugees. Forced to march for days through difficult and desolate terrain—with many dying of hunger, exhaustion and exposure along the way—they finally found succor more than eighty kilometers from their point of origin, in the distant Greek-held town known to the Ottomans as Salona, and to the Greeks as Amfissa.

Of the roughly nine thousand souls that inhabited Messolonghi in the months before the exodus, barely one thousand eight hundred escaped with their lives. Another five hundred or more were killed in the sortie, between the action in the plain and that in the foothills; and as large a number again, having made it to the mountains, later died of hunger before finding refuge.

Of those who remained in the city, about two and a half thousand were killed during several days of mayhem, while as many as three and a half thousand women and children were captured by the Ottomans and enslaved. Meanwhile, the number of Ottomans who perished—many as a result of the fighting that broke out between Ibrahim's Egyptians and Reshid's Turks—was nearly as great as that of the Greeks killed.

It seemed, however, that the wholesale human slaughter that occurred during that tragic episode of history was not enough. When it was over, Ibrahim Pasha did something to crown his gruesome victory with the seal of even greater barbarism. In an act of desecration that made all the previous atrocities of a savage siege pale by comparison, he commanded his men to take off the heads of as many of the fallen defenders as possible. He then collected three thousand of the macabre trophies, and ordered them to be displayed on pikes or strung up around the walls of the vanquished city.

It was intended to be a grisly warning to the rebellious Greeks of the price of their obstinate defiance. In the end, however, it would turn out to be perhaps the Egyptian satrap's gravest miscalculation of the war. For it was largely due to the images of such brutality associated with the Sacred City's fall— broadcast throughout Europe in print, paintings and even song—

that the hitherto 'neutral' governments of the Great Powers would be forced by a growing tide of popular sentiment to intervene on behalf of the Greeks in their faltering struggle for national independence.

With the chaotic sounds of fighting and pandemonium raging all around him, Lord Admiral Rizopoulos spent almost the whole of the night of April tenth on his knees in deep and fervent prayer—first and foremost for the repose of the souls of those being killed in the nearby action, and secondly for divine forgiveness in regard to the role he had played in facilitating those savage events.

Initially, a terrible sense of guilt had pervaded his soul so thoroughly that even simple meditation—which usually came so naturally and easily to him—seemed entirely out of his reach and required an enormous struggle. At last, however, he found some small measure of consolation in the knowledge that what he had been forced to do would ultimately turn the tide of the war and ensure the continuity of history as he knew it. Thus he was able to still his turbulent thoughts and achieve a modicum of peace in his heart, so as to enter into a true state of mental prayer.

After a few hours, a little before dawn—being weakened by days without food or sleep, and exhausted from his mental anxiety—he collapsed unconscious near the foot of the olive tree to which he was chained. Thus it was late in the evening of Palm Sunday when he awoke to find himself on a pallet in a strange tent, his chains removed and with a damp cloth compress on his forehead.

Sitting up quickly, he felt a wave of dizziness come over him and realized that he was still quite weak. He therefore sat still for a moment to get his bearings and, having gathered his strength, was about to activate his SHIELD, when a man in European clothing entered the tent together with Ibrahim's *dragoman.*

"Ah, I see we *'ave-a* finally *awakened-a!*" said the mustachioed man, speaking in Italian. Then addressing the *dragoman,* he said: "*Tell-a de* friar *'oo* I *am-a.*"

Speaking to Rizopoulos in Greek, the *dragoman* informed him that the Italian was Ibrahim Pasha's personal physician. The *pasha,* it seemed, was pleased that the information he had provided a few days before had proven to be accurate, and intended to grant him another audience in order to make whatever petition he desired for himself. But hearing that Rizopoulos had been found ill, he had ordered him to be brought to Doctor Giovanni-*bey,* to be placed under his supervision and nursed back to health.

"*Dere is-a not'ing-a wrong-a wit'* you *dat* a *few-a* days *of-a* rest *and-a some-a food-a cannot-a cure-a,*" said the doctor through the *dragoman.* "I *'ave-a ordered-a some-a food-a* to be *brought-a. It's-a not-a much-a—a little-a soup-a—but-a dat's* about *as-a* much *as-a your-a body-a* will *accept-a right-a now-a.* Eat *it-a all-a and-a sleep-a, and-a* we will *again-a* see *inna de morning-a. Now if-a* you *will-a excuse-a* me, I *'ave udder-a matters-a* to *attend-a.*"

As the two men were quitting the tent, a servant entered carrying a tray with a large bowl of soup, a few pieces of bread and a pot of tea. He set these down before Rizopoulos and also exited, leaving the Paladin lord admiral alone, with only an Egyptian soldier outside to guard the entrance. When the physician and the *dragoman* returned early the next morning to check on the patient, however, they were surprised to find that the tray of food had been left cold and untouched, and that the strange black-robed monk—having disappeared from the tent as mysteriously as he had first appeared—was nowhere to be found.

✜ ✜ ✜

GENEVA, SWITZERLAND—WEDNESDAY, MAY 29, 2075

It had been nine years since Vice Admiral Ephraimoglou was last in Geneva, and on this day in late May of 2075 it was as lovely as ever, bursting with the vibrant colors, scents and sounds of a glorious Swiss spring. After rising early, the Paladin had taken a brisk walk down to the city's famed lake to calm his nerves, and as he heard innumerable birds chirping in the trees along the shoreline and watched dozens of windsurfers and small sail boats tack on the rippling surface of the water, he experienced a current of quiet excitement and inner freedom that he had not felt for a long time.

Breathing in the fresh morning air, it occurred to him that over the last several years as he had ascended the ranks of the Order, the opportunities to venture above ground had become fewer and farther between. Moreover, when they did come, they could hardly be described as relaxing, almost always being connected with some serious threat to the established world order. Enjoying this rare moment of peaceful reflection in the glistening morning sunlight—with the lake's iconic water-jet spraying its towering plume against the background of the distant Alps—was therefore something to be treasured all the more, and he let it linger, trying as much as possible to forget the reason he was there.

At length, as he slowly meandered along the Quai du Mont Blanc by the side of the lake, he began to get the distinct feeling that he was being watched. Turning to look behind him, he saw three men walking along the path straight towards him, and the feeling of inner calm he had so laboriously cultivated instantly vanished. It was almost time.

"Vice Admiral!" called out one of the men as the group approached. "Forgive me, but it's already a quarter past eight. Perhaps we should start heading up?"

It was the three black-robed Paladins who had accompanied him all the way up from Camp Monemvasia to Geneva, and they were walking over to him briskly with anxious expressions on their young faces.

"You boys go on ahead. I'll be along presently," the vice admiral responded laconically, with a nod and a dismissive wave of his regenerated right hand.

Ephraimoglou continued walking for another seven or eight minutes, watching a formation of stately white swans floating majestically by on the wavy surface of Lake Geneva, and trying in vain to recapture his former feeling of tranquility. Unable to do so, he finally took a deep breath and turned back to cross over the busy Rue de Lausanne at its intersection with the Avenue de la Paix.

Passing by the commuters in their matte-toned solar-powered cars—many enjoying the lovely spring weather with their convertible roofs down, and waiting impatiently for the light to change—he reached the other side of the road and then skirted along the edge of the beautifully landscaped botanical gardens he had walked through just an hour before. Walking at a deliberate pace, he at last made his way towards Ariana Park and his final destination—the historied 'Palais du Monde', or 'Palace of the World'.

That monumental fusion of art deco and neo-classical architecture—commissioned in 1926, completed in 1936, and having been originally dubbed the 'Palace of Peace'—had originally been intended as the home of the post-World War I League of Nations. Ironically, it had fulfilled its purpose for less than a decade before the international organization devoted to preventing war was dissolved in April of 1946, having itself become a victim of war.

When the assets of the defunct League were ceded to its successor organization, the newly formed United Nations, after the close of World War II, the complex—rechristened then as the *Palais des Nations*, or the Palace of Nations—had become that institution's administrative hub in Europe. It had continued to function in that capacity for nearly three-quarters of a century, until the organization's headquarters were permanently transferred to Geneva after the tragic loss of New York City in the infamous terrorist attack of September 2021.

Eventually—in the wake of the global civil unrest and governmental collapses caused by the resource wars of the first half of the century, when the bloated and antiquated body of the old UN had finally suffocated under the weight of its own irrelevance—the complex had changed hats and names yet again. This time it had become the so-called 'Palace of the World' and the headquarters of the international political establishment's latest and most ambitious incarnation to date—the World Council.

As he approached the main security entrance to the complex, Vice Admiral Ephraimoglou was alarmed to find himself caught behind a large party of Chinese delegates arriving for a conference of the World Trade Ministry being held in one of the buildings inside. If he had only reached the checkpoint a little sooner, he berated himself, he would have passed on through ahead of them. As it was, now he would surely be delayed for several minutes.

That was certainly one of the disadvantages of being associated with a secretive organization like the Guardians, he observed in silent frustration. Most of the civil servants within the world government, including the security apparatus at World Council headquarters, were not even aware of the organization's existence—let alone that of the Paladin Order. Thus, although he was a high-ranking intelligence officer on official business, he had to enter like any other private citizen, without priority treatment and using the pretext of a routine appointment with someone in the OHCP as the purpose of his visit.

Waiting patiently as the first of the Chinese trade representatives went through the security scanner, the vice admiral was meditating to keep from becoming frustrated, when through the crowd he noticed his three colleagues standing on the other side of the checkpoint near the station's exit door. One of them was talking to a guard, pointing him out and explaining that he was the last member of their party, whom they had evidently mentioned to the security personnel earlier. The Paladin was a dark young man with a sincere and intense face, with whom the vice admiral had spent a great deal of time in the past few months, ever since Lord Admiral Rizopoulos had personally requested that he take him on as his protégé. It was Ensign Rashid Al-Noury.

Much to Ephraimoglou's relief, the guard waved him over and allowed him to skip to the head of the line, where he was able to pass through security and quickly be on his way. Once inside the campus, the Paladins hurried across the manicured lawns dotted with towering beech and plane trees, and adorned with the hundred-thirty-six-year-old Celestial Sphere monument—originally a gift of the United States of America to the League of Nations. In their haste, they took little notice of the occasional peacock spreading its multi-colored feathers in dazzling display and issuing forth its distinct, plaintive cry. It was already almost ten minutes to nine, and Ephraimoglou's nine o'clock appointment was certainly not one for which they wanted to be late.

Rushing along the footpath that led to the antiquated E Building, the perspiring Paladins made it to the security desk just as the clock was striking nine. After being cleared to go upstairs, they took the elevator up to the main offices of the World Council's Organization for Historical and Cultural Preservation—the OHCP.

It was the first time Rashid and the other adjutants with Vice Admiral Ephraimoglou had been to the headquarters of the government agency which served as the public cover for the Guardian directorate. Thus they eagerly indulged their curiosity by looking around at the eclectic collection of artwork and historical memorabilia from all around the world, which was displayed on the walls and in the glass cases of the large waiting room. They did not have to wait long, however, before an attractive young woman in a rather low-cut white blouse with a v-neck and an embroidered lace collar, wearing a close-fitting crimson colored leather skirt, came out from behind a closed office door.

"*S'il vous plaît, messieurs*—right this way," she said in a business-like yet alluring admixture of French and English. "They are expecting you downstairs."

With that, she led them to a door obscured between the stacks of the waiting room's small library. Waving the flat-surfaced gold bracelet she wore around her wrist in front of its electronic lock, she opened the door and went through into a short, narrow corridor whose only exit was an elevator at the opposite end. Waving the bracelet again in front of a featureless panel, she called the lift and stood back against the wall, smiling provocatively as the bearded young monks—flushed and mortified on breathing in her intoxicating perfume—did their best to squeeze by her without making contact.

As soon as the four men were in the elevator, the doors closed and they immediately began a rapid descent, their ears popping from the sudden increase in pressure. After about fifteen seconds, the lift's downward motion began to slow, until the car finally came to rest a hundred meters below ground and the doors automatically opened again. Stepping out of the elevator, the Paladins were met right away by a clean-shaven young man in his mid-thirties, wearing a smart-looking suit with a vaguely military suggestion to it.

He politely welcomed them in American-accented English and escorted them down a long well-lit corridor lined with several doors. As they walked along the passageway, they saw a young lady in a suit similar to their guide's delivering a tray of refreshments to one of the rooms. They passed in front of the open doorway as she entered and, just before the door slid shut behind her, were surprised to observe a group of white-robed female Paladins seated inside.

At last their escort stopped in front of one of the doors. Opening it, he ushered them into a small but comfortable waiting room decorated in a rather minimalistic style, with a long, bench-like sofa along one wall, and a couple of matching armchairs arranged around a low glass table. In one corner was a rough-cut granite pedestal with the ancient-looking marble bust of a curly-haired, bearded man—his shattered nose long worn smooth with time—looking down at an oblique angle; and in another was a large *ficus benjamina* plant, with its glossy sharp-tipped leaves cascading down its lush green branches.

"Here's the remote for the wall screen, if you'd like to watch the news or make any calls," the guide said pleasantly and efficiently. "There's also a call button on it if you need anything." He then inquired: "Can I get you gentlemen any refreshments while you wait? Some coffee or tea?"

The adjutants looked at each other hesitatingly for a moment, and then Vice Admiral Ephraimoglou replied: "Just a glass of water for me, thank you."

"That's fine," said the young man. "Nothing else, are you sure?"

Finally one of the adjutants broke the silence and spoke up, requesting: "Well, maybe some tea if it's not too much trouble."

"Not at all. That's what we're here for. Anything else?" the steward asked, and when the others had finally made their preferences known, he left the room.

Once the Paladins were alone, one of Ephraimoglou's adjutants—a Ugandan who was already in his seventh year at Camp Monemvasia, and who was being groomed for a key STRATCOM role at a soon-to-be-completed Guardian base in Kenya—spoke quietly to the Vice Admiral.

"What do you think the Peers will be looking for, sir?" he asked with a hint of nervousness in his soft and melodic voice.

Ephraimoglou sighed. "I'm not really sure, Elijah," he said. "This is only the fourth time in the last thirty-five years the Council has had to make this kind of decision. But I guess we'll find out soon enough. In the meantime, why don't we review the latest numbers from FINCOM again while we're waiting?"

"Certainly, sir, I have them right here," the young officer replied, and quickly pulled his *FlexTab* computer out of the small briefcase he had brought with him, glad to have something to focus on that would take his mind off the wait. On hearing this, the other adjutant also drew near, and the three men began conferring over various financial reporting and operational issues, while Rashid sat quietly and meditated.

The attendant soon returned with their beverages and an assortment of fresh pastries, and then left the four Paladins alone again to talk over their refreshments. They had been waiting thus for about forty minutes, when the young man finally reappeared at the door.

"Vice Admiral, they're ready for you," he said, holding the door open.

Immediately Ephraimoglou nodded and rose, heading for the door with his colleagues behind him. But the steward stopped them, saying: "Gentlemen, I'm afraid only the Vice Admiral is allowed in the Council chamber. The rest of you will have to wait here."

Looking at his assistants, Ephraimoglou took a *FlexTab* from one of them, as the adjutant quickly tried to show him the locations of the various files they had prepared for his testimony. But his mind was already preoccupied and he only half listened to the young man, saying distractedly as he walked off: "Okay, I think I've got it. Thanks, Jay."

Following the steward out of the waiting room, Vice Admiral Ephraimoglou began to feel a tingling sensation in his gut—the proverbial butterflies in the stomach. It would be his first time ever setting foot in the formal chamber of the Council of Peers, and he had no idea what to expect.

The guide led him down the same hall they had traversed earlier and into an open area with a high-countered hotel-style reception desk, behind which were a couple of doors. As they passed, another steward emerged from one of the portals— apparently the entrance to a kitchen area—carrying a silver serving tray full of refreshments, and headed off down the corridor.

Ahead of them was a large pair of burled-wood double doors with ornate polished-brass handles. As they approached, the steward waved a bracelet, like the one the young woman in the OHCP office upstairs had used earlier, and there was a sudden click as the electronic mechanism unlocked. The automatic doors swung silently inward to reveal a wide corridor leading directly into the council chamber of the Guardian Council of Peers.

"You'll find water and coffee at your station," the steward informed Ephraimoglou in a hushed tone as they walked up the low, upward-sloping hallway, "but if you need anything, there's a call button with a large assortment of preprogrammed requests in the desktop panel. Just press whatever you want and I'll be glad to bring it in."

After several meters, the hallway leveled off and became narrower. When the two men came to the end of the corridor they faced a slightly convex wall with no exit—an apparent *cul-de-sac*. Somewhat taken aback, Ephraimoglou wondered what was happening, until his escort waved the flat gold bracelet once again and what was evidently only a holographic image instantly vanished. Immediately, as the Paladin got his first glimpse of the council chamber, his guide stepped through the now-exposed archway leading inside and announced in a loud heraldic voice:

"My lords and ladies, I present Vice Admiral Alexandros Ephraimoglou!"

Stepping back onto Ephraimoglou's side of the doorway, he bowed his head slightly and, waving him forward, whispered: "Good luck, sir!"

CHAPTER 20

GUARDIAN COUNCIL CHAMBER, GENEVA, SWITZERLAND—WEDNESDAY, MAY 29, 2075

Taking a deep breath and bracing himself for whatever was to come, Ephraimoglou stepped through the doorway and into the council chamber. He was immediately struck with the grandeur and solemnity of the place.

The room was circular and much larger than he had imagined it would be, its diameter stretching about twelve meters across from wall to wall. The interior was constructed from a light-colored material that appeared to be granite block, and which rose up on thirteen great arches into a lofty domed ceiling at least ten meters high. There, placed at intervals in their shadow-enshrouded upper reaches, a series of *Hydrofuse* lamps flickered so as to produce an eerie torch-like effect.

Located deep underground as it was, there were no windows which would have allowed daylight to filter into the room. Nevertheless, the chamber was illuminated by a dim and natural-looking light. The Paladin could not immediately descry its source, but he quickly surmised that it must have been emanating from nano-materials embedded in the very walls themselves.

As he took in everything at a glance, Ephraimoglou noticed that surrounding him on raised daises, elevated about a meter above the floor, were the booths of the individual peers. Numbering twelve in all, these were essentially small office spaces of nearly eight square-meters in area, equipped with an impressive fusion of high-tech functionality and antique beauty.

Each one was fitted out with a large curved table of polished material that resembled mahogany—though Ephraimoglou doubted it could be the genuine article, since the *swietenia* trees from which that wood was produced were all but extinct—with gleaming brass accents. Around the front and sides of these tables were low, contoured smart-glass panels, unobtrusive in their transparency, yet enabling the peers to manage large amounts of information at the touch of a screen.

In the wall behind each of these stations was a doorway communicating with the peer's private lounge, and next to that was a short corridor that led to another door. As the vice admiral would later realize on observing various assistants going in and out during the course of the proceedings, this second entrance apparently provided access to the booth for the peer's personal staff, who worked behind the scenes in a separate office for each Council member.

Ephraimoglou found himself standing behind a wide bowed table which could evidently accommodate three to four people. This station occupied the thirteenth place along the circumference of the circular chamber's outer wall; but in spite of all its beautiful appointments, the entire area somehow made him feel uncomfortable. In fact, more than anything else, it reminded him distinctly of the dock where the accused would have sat in an old Scottish criminal courtroom.

Positioned as it was, each of the peers had a clear view of the dock and its occupants. But in case that was not enough, a transparent column rose up out of the floor in the center of the chamber to a height of about three meters. This apparatus— designed with a precise curvature that allowed each peer to see the images appearing on it in full, independent of where he or she sat in the council chamber—was a screen that could be activated to display magnified holographic or video images directly from the dock, as well as from sources outside the room.

The evident sophistication of the technology with which the chamber was equipped notwithstanding, perhaps the most curious feature of all for Ephraimoglou—who had never before seen the ceremonial garb of the Council's members—was that presented by the occupants themselves.

Sitting impassively in their booths, six of the twelve peers were clothed in the simple black cassock of the Paladin Order. The others, however, wore something rather more ornate. The six peers who represented the Guardian side of the organization were covered in plush dark-crimson robes, reminiscent of academic gowns and accented with ample black velvet cowls and double rows of black velvet bands around their upper arms. In addition, each of them sported a formal white magistrate's wig topped with the common black *petasos* hat worn by all twelve Council members.

There was one characteristic, however, which filled the vice admiral with intense curiosity more than any other. For, from beneath the wide brim of the counselors' hats—evocative of the simple headgear worn in classical Greek mythology by Hermes, the messenger of the gods and guardian of travelers—a thin gauzy veil draped down and concealed each of their faces.

Apart from its rich symbolism—hearkening back to that veil employed by the great Moses to cover the intense luminance of his countenance upon returning from the holy mountain—the vice admiral soon realized that the mysterious accessory had another very practical purpose. It made it difficult, if not impossible, to ascertain which of the veiled peers was speaking at any given moment; and as if to further emphasize the intended secrecy represented by their eccentric attire, the voice of each

Council member was electronically distorted, rendering it personally unidentifiable to those in the dock.

As he entered the Council chamber, Vice Admiral Ephraimoglou was met with one last surprise. He immediately noticed another individual occupying one of the chairs at the dock where he was about to be seated. He too wore the black robes characteristic of the Paladin members of the Council; but the way in which he sat, with his back towards the door and his wide-brimmed *petasos* hat covering his head, made it impossible to tell who he was. The mixture of joy and relief which flooded the vice admiral was therefore all the greater when the man turned to greet him and his familiar face came into view. It was that of the Old Man himself, Lord Lawson.

Bowing formally before the peers and Lord Lawson, Vice Admiral Ephraimoglou moved to take his seat. At the same time, he placed his regenerated right hand over his chest in a gesture of gratitude and whispered to Sir Marcus: "My lord, I didn't realize that you would be here!"

"Well, what could I do?" Lawson replied gruffly in a whisper that was slightly too loud. "It's not every day that a new Paladin Lord Admiral is confirmed, and these characters can't seem to get it through their thick heads that I'm retired. Anyway, it's not really their fault. The Council's canons call for a retired Peer to be present at this kind of a proceeding in case a tie-breaking vote is needed." Then, with an expression that suggested his support for the vice admiral, he concluded: "Hopefully that won't be necessary in this case."

As the two Paladins in the dock were speaking, they heard a gavel being rapped sharply three times, calling the session to order, and Ephraimoglou once again felt a fluttering in the pit of his stomach.

"This plenary session of the Guardian Council of Peers will now come to order," proclaimed an unidentifiable voice, which Ephraimoglou surmised must be that of the first peer, Lord Vasiliádes. "On behalf of the Council, I thank you for your presence here today, Vice Admiral Ephraimoglou. You are already aware of the reason you are here, but before we begin, I will take a moment to explain the process that is prescribed in the canons of the Guardian Council of Peers.

"As you know," the voice continued, "the rank of Lord High Admiral—the leader of all the Paladins worldwide—is one that is bestowed by the Paladin Order itself, not by the Guardians, nor by this Council. However in recognition of the intimate ties and interdependence between the two organizations, the Paladins have traditionally and voluntarily conferred upon this body the high honor and privilege of confirming one of at least three nominees proffered by the former Lord Admiral. Of course, once confirmed, it will be up to the new Lord Admiral to win the loyalty of the Paladins through exemplary leadership. Fortunately, thus far no Lord Admiral has ever been confirmed by the Council of Peers without being accepted by the rank and file of the Paladin Order. We trust that such will remain the case.

"To be clear, the canons also state that the outgoing Lord Admiral shall not indicate—in writing, word or deed—his preference among the candidates he proposes. Therefore, in keeping with this tradition, in his recent letter notifying the Council of his retirement, Lord Admiral Rizopoulos has presented the Council with the names of three nominees, among which you are numbered. It is the task of this body, through this series of confirmation hearings, to deliberate and to select one of the three to be the next Paladin leader.

"I will tell you, Vice Admiral, that the other two nominees have already testified before this Council during the course of our proceedings these last two days, and both are very strong candidates. With your testimony today, we will conclude the hearings and the Council will adjourn to deliberate. And so with that introduction, on behalf of the Council, I wish you good luck and Godspeed. And now, let us begin."

Thus for the next few hours, Vice Admiral Ephraimoglou sat before the Council and answered their detailed questions on a range of matters, starting with his own background and career in the Paladin Order and delving into specific operational, technical and policy issues.

Throughout the course of the hearings, he was impressed with the preparedness of the peers, all of whom demonstrated a surprisingly deep knowledge of Paladin affairs, and who had obviously read many of the reports and strategy documents he had authored over the years. He was also taken aback at times by the pointedness of their questions in trying to assess his leadership abilities and performance. At last, however, as the hour drew near for the Council to adjourn for lunch, the inquest turned to its final subject—and the one which weighed most heavily on Ephraimoglou's heart and mind—the incident from nine months earlier, involving Commodore Ghabry.

"Vice Admiral," Ephraimoglou heard an electronically disguised voice—which he presumed to belong to the peer in charge of the Guardian's Intelligence and Security Committee, Lady Villaréz-Joya—address him in an even but commanding tone, "we have all read the affidavit which you submitted to the Intelligence and Security Committee last September. What I am most concerned about is that, while you have certainly been clear about the role Commodore Ghabry played in this disturbing episode, one could almost conclude that you are not wholly prepared to condemn his actions. In fact, you said, and I quote here from your affidavit—"

As the voice spoke, Ephraimoglou noticed a magnified copy of the relevant text from his affidavit appear on the smart-glass column at the center of the chamber floor. The disguised and genderless voice then proceeded to read.

"'*The incident raises legitimate questions over whether or not the Order is doing enough to monitor and address the emotional and psychological needs of its divers, particularly those involved in undercover operations, who often find themselves in conditions of extreme stress for prolonged periods of time and may suffer from the effects of a form of temporal disorientation.*'"

Referring to another line in the same document, the voice continued speaking.

"Elsewhere, you also stated the following: '*In condemning Commodore Ghabry's actions, which were undeniably an unacceptable lapse of judgment for a Paladin and an officer of his rank, we should nevertheless honor appropriately the many years of distinguished service and the numerous sacrifices he made for the Order and its mission during his lifetime.*'

"Given the danger that such a faction as the one you have described in your affidavit represents, not only to the unity of the Paladin Order but to the security of the entire Guardian organization and mission, I believe we are talking about something more than a simple 'lapse of judgment'. Yet you seem to even go so far as to place some of the blame for what happened on the organization itself. Please explain to this Council if you would, Vice Admiral, your views on this important subject."

Feeling as if he had been pinned down in an expert wrestling move, Ephraimoglou cleared his throat and took a sip of water as he collected his thoughts. He then began to speak deliberately and carefully, saying:

"My lords and ladies, first of all I must thank you for allowing me the opportunity to clarify the remarks I made very shortly after the incident in question. I wish there to be no mistake about it: I wholeheartedly condemn the actions perpetrated by Commodore Ghabry, which not only endangered the life of a fellow Paladin and ended his own, but which also jeopardized the entire mission and flouted the most fundamental principles of our Order.

"Having said that, I do stand by the remarks I made that the Order must do more to monitor and care for the mental health of divers. Commodore Ghabry had a long and distinguished record of service before this terrible incident, and while we must repudiate the unforgivable acts he performed, we should also take responsibility for our own lack of vigilance in this regard. We should look at the role we played in allowing one of our top officers, with years of experience and a massive investment in training and development, to slide undetected into such a destructive path."

"Are you suggesting, Vice Admiral, that there was something that could have been done to prevent this and was not done?" scoffed the voice of one of the peers, seemingly annoyed.

"What I am suggesting, Your Honor, having known Commodore Ghabry for many years, is that with the proper intervention, I believe he could have been helped. I believe we must find a way to distinguish somehow between those cases in which a Paladin has irrevocably adopted an ideology that is incompatible with the Order's principles and has become dangerous to the Guardian mission—or perhaps never truly embraced that mission to begin with—and those cases in which stress and exposure to adverse circumstances over a prolonged period of time has created a kind of breakdown that could be treatable.

"Right now, the Order's mental health capabilities are practically non-existent. It's a matter of the training and background and personal inclination of individual Paladin physicians. But there is very little, if anything, in the way of organized institutional support."

At that point, the digitally disguised voice of another peer—which Ephraimoglou guessed might be that of Lord Hartono, a Guardian from Indonesia and chairman of the Council's Finance Committee—joined the discussion.

"It would seem, Vice Admiral, that what you are suggesting would require a significant expansion of budgetary resources at a time when we are all under pressure to utilize our existing assets more cost-effectively, and even to cut back. And correct me if I am wrong, but might it not also potentially reduce the productivity of the Paladin divers and the frequency of the missions they perform—all at a time when recruitment levels are falling and the mission load is increasing? How would you propose to deal with that?"

For the next several minutes, a detailed policy discussion ensued, with Ephraimoglou arguing the relative merits of increased psychological monitoring and profiling, and referring to a number of proposals on the subject that had been made by various members of the Paladin medical establishment. After a short time, however, the sterile and camouflaged voice of one of the peers—presumably that of Lady Villaréz, whom Ephraimoglou suspected of having originally raised the issue—finally cut off further discussion of the matter by interjecting:

"Vice Admiral, I want to thank you for sharing your interesting views on this matter with us. It is obvious that you have given a great deal of consideration to the subject, and I have no doubt that some of the policies you are advocating would have a beneficial long-term impact. What concerns me, however, is that we have a serious near-term challenge before us, which I'm not sure can be adequately addressed by such a soft policy approach. In any case, I believe my allotted time is almost up. At this time I have no further questions and I yield my remaining time to the First Peer."

The session lasted for a while longer, as a couple of the peers asked for clarification on minor points of Ephraimoglou's earlier testimony; but it was clear from the cross talk beginning to arise that the members were ready to break for lunch.

Once again the gavel rapped loudly and a disguised voice, presumably that of Lord Vasiliádes, called for order. The first peer then accepted a motion for the proceedings to be adjourned, which was quickly seconded. It was over. Ephraimoglou rose and bowed before the peers and Lord Lawson, and then returned to the lounge to wait for the Council's decision in the company of his adjutants, drained and uncertain of the outcome.

A few minutes after his arrival in the waiting room, the steward who had previously attended to them came in and announced that a buffet luncheon had been prepared for the visitors, and guided them to a large dining room. Once inside, Ephraimoglou and his companions saw that a group of their comrades—including the female Paladins they had glimpsed earlier that morning—had already gathered there and were investigating the contents of the numerous chafing dishes arranged about the hall.

As the adjutants headed for the buffet table, Ephraimoglou caught sight of two high-level officers talking to each other and went over to join them. It was the first time any of them had been allowed to see who the other candidates were, and he immediately recognized them both.

As he approached and bowed to the two Paladin admirals, they each greeted him cordially in return.

"Ah, there you are, Alex!" exclaimed Admiral Cheung, a native of Shanghai, who was the senior officer in charge of the Paladins stationed at the four Guardian bases in China. "We've been waiting for you."

"Really? How did you know I was the other candidate?" replied Ephraimoglou in surprise.

"Oh, come on now, Alex!" retorted Admiral Romanyenkova, the tall blonde Russian with beautiful green eyes, who was responsible for the seven female Paladin installations worldwide. "Everyone knows you've been the Lord Admiral's right hand for years."

Then a look of almost amused embarrassment came over her face, which was extraordinarily lovely and still quite youthful in appearance for a woman in her mid-fifties, as the irony of what she had just said hit her. "Speaking of right hands, how is yours? I heard about your unfortunate little accident."

"Oh, it's fine now, thanks," replied Ephraimoglou curtly, as the thought ran through his mind sarcastically: *Just like Olga—as sensitive as ever.*

The three Paladin officers continued chatting as they made the rounds of the room's chafing dishes, each one surreptitiously trying to divine any sign from the others, which might provide them with a clue as to the Council's decision. In the end, however, they were all equally in the dark and concluded their talk with pledges of loyalty to whichever of the three candidates was chosen to be the new lord high admiral. They then each rejoined their respective groups of adjutants and tried their best to enjoy the meal, without agonizing over the decision that was being deliberated at that very moment in the Council's private dining room not far away.

THE BUFFET HAD long since been cleared away, and the Paladins had returned to their waiting-room vigils, when shortly before four o'clock the door opened and the steward entered and advised Ephraimoglou that they were ready for him. Following his escort, he went back in the direction in which he had gone earlier that morning. This time, however, the anxiety he had felt previously was strangely absent, replaced instead by a resolute serenity in the face of whatever the Council's announcement might be.

Arriving at the reception area, he found Cheung and Romanyenkova already standing there with their stewards, one of whom opened the double doors to the corridor leading to the Council chamber. The triumvirate of officers looked at each other in silent curiosity, each wondering which of them was about to be confirmed as lord high admiral, leader of all Paladins worldwide. Then, without saying a word, they bowed slightly to each other, turned and walked in unison to stand before the Guardian Council of Peers.

Chapter 21

When the holographic wall vanished, the three Paladins immediately noticed that the layout of the Council chamber had been rearranged.

The table they had sat at during their respective testimonies was gone, and in its place were only three ornate high-backed chairs, resembling small thrones. The clear smart-glass column at the center of the circle was also no longer there, having been lowered into a recess in the floor. In its place was a circular platform on which a podium and a little table supporting a small wooden chest stood. Presiding at the podium was the first peer, and facing him were twelve chairs, identical to those of the Paladins, arranged in a semicircle.

In one of the center chairs, surrounded by the remaining eleven peers—all of whose faces were now unveiled—sat the former first peer, Lord Lawson. As soon as the three Paladins entered the chamber and took their seats, Lord Vasiliádes rapped his gavel on the podium and called the session to order.

"Lords and ladies, distinguished Paladins," he commenced speaking, his voice clearly recognizable this time, "ours is a solemn duty and a heavy responsibility; one that is carried out daily without fanfare and without recognition. Ours is an army whose quiet victories are not celebrated, but whose failures are often accompanied by great sorrow and disaster. Therefore the opportunities we have to gather in celebration of the accomplishments of our own dedicated people—few as those occasions may be—are important ones.

"They serve to remind us of the honor to which we all strive to attain and they reinforce the unique bond that holds us together—Guardian and Paladin—in our common service to our civilization and our fellow men. Today we come together for only the fourth time in the history of the Council of Peers to confirm our acceptance of a new leader of the Paladin Order, and this transition has never come at a more dangerous time for our world or for our organization.

"Our situation today is dramatically different than it was even a few years ago. Our enemies have become stronger and more numerous; they have made technological advances that threaten to bring them up to parity in the very near future with our own level of development. And, as you all know, we have in recent months been made aware of dangerous factions and even possible traitors operating in the midst of our forces. Indeed, these are critical times, and in such times the Paladin Order needs a strong and decisive leader.

"Fortunately, we have before us three nominees for the rank of Lord High Admiral of the Paladin Order who are all very capable, brave and strong leaders in their own right. Thanks for this is due to our esteemed—and I do not think it out of place to say beloved and sorely missed—Lord Admiral Rizopoulos, who by his example and guidance has brought out the best in all of you. I'm sure he would have wanted to be here with us today if he could, and at this time I ask that we honor him and his long service. Let us pray for his well-being wherever he may be."

"Here, here!" came the resounding affirmation from everyone in the chamber.

Only Ephraimoglou hung his head low at the mention of Rizopoulos's name, his throat tightening with emotion and a deep sorrow momentarily coming over him. But then, as he struggled to maintain his composure, Lord Vasiliádes resumed his speech.

"Before I turn the podium over to our honored former First Peer and the ranking Paladin here, Lord Lawson, who will confer the credentials of office, I would just like to say to all of you that it was a difficult decision for the Council to make. We had to choose from among three excellent candidates, and the process was—what shall I say?—exciting."

As several of the peers smiled or chuckled, he continued: "It was an extremely close vote and we did not have a clear winner until the third round of balloting, which is an indication of the high regard in which we hold you all. We also do not consider that there are any losers here today, because we honor all of you equally for your service. But of course, there can be only one Lord High Admiral. On that note, Lord Lawson, if you please."

The Old Man rose slowly from his chair and took his place at the podium, while the first peer went to join the other counselors. Looking over at the three Paladin officers, Lord Lawson spoke with his characteristic gruff sarcasm, to the approving chuckles of several of the other peers.

"My cousin talks a lot. Always did. In this case, though, I happen to agree with everything he said. Believe me, that doesn't happen too often. In fact, somebody should mark that down. Anyway, before we go ahead with the main part of the ceremony, I have some additional honors to announce."

Vice Admiral Ephraimoglou was surprised when Sir Marcus then turned to him and called him up to the podium. Rising quickly, he bowed to the peers and to Lord Lawson, and stood at attention next to the latter. The nervousness which he thought had subsided suddenly returned, as he began to wonder if indeed he could have been the one chosen by the Council.

"Vice Admiral Alexandros Ephraimoglou, in recognition of your bravery in the line of duty and the serious injuries you sustained as a result thereof, I have the honor of presenting you with the order of the Purple Star. Wear it proudly, but I'm sure I speak for all of us in saying, may you never again qualify for another such medal."

As the assembled audience clapped, a feeling of warm appreciation rose up within Ephraimoglou and he accepted the medal with gratitude. He was about to return to his seat when Sir Marcus stopped him and spoke again.

"Wait, Vice Admiral," he said. "Don't be in such a hurry. I have another honor to present. This was a decision that was already in the works within the Paladin command structure, and it would normally have been made public within the next couple of months anyway. But in his last letter, Lord Admiral Rizopoulos asked that it be expedited in anticipation of today's proceedings, so that it could be formally announced in the presence of the plenary Council."

Puzzled, Ephraimoglou stood in silence and waited as Lawson reached into the wooden chest and pulled out a rolled-up document and a small box. The Old Man then declared:

"Therefore, it is also my distinct honor and pleasure to present you with these insignia and the credentials of your promotion to the rank of Admiral. May God be with you, Admiral Ephraimoglou!"

"Here, here!" the peers and Paladins assembled in the council chamber called out in unison. "Worthy! Worthy!"

Ephraimoglou was immediately hit with a wave of conflicting emotions. Surprised, elated and humbled all at once, he began to feel confused, and he wondered how this unexpected development fit in with the Council's larger deliberations, the result of which they all eagerly awaited.

Had they elevated him to the rank of admiral first, so that he could be made lord high admiral of the fleet without skipping over a grade? Or had someone else been chosen, turning this tremendous honor into a form of consolation prize? As he returned to his seat, greeted warmly and saluted by his Paladin comrades as their new peer in rank, he soon began to feel an odd foreshadowing of disappointment cross over him. It dawned on him that he already knew the Council's decision—and he was not their choice.

As if in answer to his thoughts, at that moment he heard Lord Lawson call another of his colleagues to the podium.

"Lords and ladies, distinguished Paladins," he said solemnly, "it is my great honor and privilege to present to you the new Lord High Admiral of the Paladin Order, Lady Olga Romanyenkova!"

As Romanyenkova gracefully ascended to the podium to be given the credentials of office—her face beaming with a look of serene delight—those present in the room spontaneously stood and clapped, calling out: "Worthy!"

Only Admiral Cheung, the Paladin leader from China, was oddly dour and silent for an instant. Ephraimoglou was surprised to see such a reaction after their earlier pledges of mutual support, and he even thought he detected on the other Paladin's hardened face a fleeting expression of bitterness. The moment lasted for only a second, but it left a chilling impression on the new admiral.

Nevertheless there was little time to consider it further; for at that moment, all eyes—even Cheung's—turned to the new lord admiral in fascinated admiration. With an air of stately solemnity, Sir Marcus Lawson, discoverer of temporal translocation, conferred upon Lady Romanyenkova the insignia of her new rank: the golden pectoral pendant passed on by Lord

Admiral Rizopoulos, representing the *sigillum* of the Order of the Knights Paladin—the double-headed phoenix.

The pendant glistened in the soft light of the room, as if reflecting the golden hue of Dame Olga's hair, and stood out against the flowing white folds of her high-collared robe. As he gazed upon the new lord admiral, radiating power and grace, it seemed to Ephraimoglou that she had always worn it. Despite his personal disappointment, it occurred to him that perhaps the Council had made the right decision after all. She was certainly well qualified, and even if she was the first female lord high admiral ever, she looked every bit the part of a leader of Paladins.

As for what kind of leader she would ultimately prove to be, there was only one way to find out—through the fullness of time. But in the interval, she was owed the honor that went along with her office, and Admiral Ephraimoglou did not hesitate to demonstrate his loyalty by immediately bowing before his new lord admiral. Stiffly and silently, Admiral Cheung followed his example.

Later that evening, at a little before eight o'clock, Admiral Ephraimoglou and his Paladins from Camp Monemvasia, clothed in their official dress uniforms, entered the large reception hall in the main assembly building of the *Palais du Monde*. A secret and tightly-controlled reception had been arranged there for ministers of the World Council and members of the Council of Peers in honor of the new Paladin lord admiral, who—in a small private ceremony shortly before the gala—had been given the title of knight of the World Council.

Feeling overwhelmed and uncomfortable in the glamour of the event—surrounded as they were by a throng of nearly two hundred of the world government's ministers, each a president or prime minister of his or her own home country—the Paladins passed the evening quietly in the company of their own comrades, speaking of the weighty matters that were of particular concern to their Order. As eleven o'clock approached, Admiral Ephraimoglou started to think about making his excuses and retiring for the evening.

He was just getting ready to leave, when he began to feel that someone was looking at him. Sure enough, scanning the reception hall, he soon saw the first-among-peers, Lord Dimitrios Vasiliádes, approaching him through the crowd with two glasses of red wine in his hands.

"Ah, there you are, Admiral!" he exclaimed in Greek, in contrast to the English he had been using throughout the Council's proceedings. "I've been looking all over for you."

Ephraimoglou smiled politely and bowed, at the same time musing that it could not have been very difficult to find him, standing out as he did in this crowd.

"How do you do, my lord?" he replied. "This is quite a reception. I haven't been to an event like this in years. Actually, not since I was one of Lord Admiral Rizopoulos's adjutants when he was confirmed twelve years ago."

"Yes, well, despite the difficult economy these days, there are certain privileges we still try to enjoy when they are called for officially," the older man said, raising his voice over the hubbub of the party. "Oh, here," he said, remembering the second glass of wine in his hand, "this is for you. I wanted to toast your promotion with you. To your good health and long life, and of course to much success in your command as the new leader of the Paladins of Camp Monemvasia!"

As Ephraimoglou thanked Sir Dimitrios and the two men clinked glasses and sipped their wine, the first peer continued speaking: "I understand how difficult this whole proceeding must have been for you, knowing how close you were—I mean, are—to Lord Admiral Rizopoulos."

"Thank you, my lord," the admiral sighed. "I'm fine. I only wish the Lord Admiral himself were here to see the result. I'm sure he would be proud. It just makes it a little difficult not knowing—"

Nearly choking up for a second, Ephraimoglou paused and took a sip of his wine to clear his tightening throat, and then continued: "Not knowing what happened to him—if he's even alive."

"I understand," Vasiliádes sympathized, with an intense look of concern on his face. Then changing the subject, he lowered his voice and said something that stunned the Paladin: "You know, Admiral, I'm not supposed to tell you this, but between you and me, I am sure Lord Admiral Rizopoulos would have wanted you to be his successor."

Ephraimoglou looked at the peer wide-eyed and fished for something to say, but in the end just remained silent as the other man continued speaking.

"Please, don't take me the wrong way. Lady Romanyenkova will make a fine Lord Admiral, I'm quite sure of it. I mean, look at her—beautiful, graceful, intelligent, courageous and fiercely determined. Yes, I'm quite sure she'll do well. But I'm just not sure..."

As he trailed off, Ephraimoglou furrowed his brow and examined the first peer's impassive face, trying to fathom what the older man wanted to convey. Then Vasiliádes looked around, and grabbing Admiral Ephraimoglou by the elbow, said: "Come, walk with me."

Slowly the two men walked through the reception hall and out onto a large stone balcony looking out towards Lake Geneva, with the colored floodlights of the famed water-jet and the illuminated buildings and monuments of the city throwing their sparkling lights into the mild and fragrant night air. Finding a quiet spot, Sir Dimitrios leaned against the parapet and looked thoughtfully into the star-sprinkled heavens and began to confide in the Paladin admiral.

"You know, Alex—you don't mind if I call you that do you?" he said "It really was a close vote this afternoon. The first round was a three-way tie, which is to be expected, and in the second round it was evenly split between you and Lady Romanyenkova. I want you to know that I was supporting you all the way. But Lady Villaréz and Admiral—I should say, Lord Admiral Romanyenkova—are on very friendly terms, and in the end Isabel managed to get one of the Peers who had initially voted for Cheung, and then supported you in the second round, to change his vote in the final ballot. She convinced him that you might be a little too soft."

Ephraimoglou was mortified. Despite Lady Villaréz's professionalism and politeness towards him, he had always known that she did not particularly like him; but hearing that she considered him to be too soft was even more disconcerting. At the same time, the Admiral was extremely uncomfortable about being given information which he knew was meant to be secret. Nevertheless, what could he do? He had not asked the first peer to divulge anything confidential to him, and so he listened without saying a word and tried not to show any reaction.

"Personally, I don't believe you would have been too soft. I do think that, in this organization, we sometimes have a tendency to try and thread a needle with a sledge hammer when a different approach might occasionally produce a better result. You know, it has occurred to me from time to time that the way we're structured often limits our ability to be creative—which brings me to my point."

Pausing for a moment, Vasiliádes took a long sip of his wine and looked intently at Ephraimoglou, who was nodding in agreement at his last point. He then said:

"When I talked about the challenges we face in my little speech this afternoon before the confirmation ceremony, it wasn't just rhetoric. These are very serious problems and there are some of us on the Council who are very concerned that if we only rely on our current methods to deal with them—methods, mind you, that we've been using for the last thirty-five years pretty much unchanged, while the world around us has changed dramatically—well, we're heading for a very rude and painful awakening."

Admiral Ephraimoglou was astounded on hearing the first peer's words, which caught him by surprise and stirred an inchoate excitement within him. It was the first time he had heard ideas coming from such a senior person in the organization which seemed to echo many of the thoughts he had secretly been harboring for a long time—thoughts about change and a different approach to the Guardian mission.

He had hardly dared to articulate such things even to himself, and yet here was no less than the first-among-peers seemingly raising some of the very issues that resonated so strongly within him. Still, uncertain of exactly what Sir Dimitrios had in mind, he remained carefully guarded.

"Well, it's certainly true, my lord, that ours is an institution that doesn't accept change very easily—I think I can speak fairly knowledgeably about that." Then, looking at the first peer circumspectly, he cautiously added: "But I suppose it all depends on what kind of change one is talking about."

Dimitrios smiled. This was not going to be easy, he thought. Then exhaling heavily, he said to Ephraimoglou:

"You're quite right, Admiral, of course. No one is talking about radically changing the mission of the Guardians. But perhaps there might be some room within that mission to consider, shall we say, some different tactics from time to time?"

Then standing up straight and looking out over the dark silhouettes of Ariana Park's towering treetops, he said in a more authoritative voice:

"Look, here's my point. Between the growing threats from outside, and now from inside the organization as well, which the new Lord Admiral is going to have to deal with, I for one am somewhat skeptical that we can continue—what's that the Americans say?—to pitch a no-hitter every time without throwing a curveball once in a while. It has nothing to do with who the Lord Admiral is, or what capabilities she brings with her to the office. The simple fact of the matter is, we cannot be everywhere at all times.

"We've already seen small changes to history on a number of occasions—thankfully nothing major that we've been able to detect so far, but it's only a matter of time. And so there are those of us who feel that, especially now that an increasing part of our attention is going to have to turn inward for a while, we need to have a 'Plan B'—a backup strategy, if you will—for how we're going to deal with the Trustees, while we're also trying to make sure our own house is in order. But that's something which could be a very sensitive matter for a new Lord Admiral to consider, especially when she is going to be spending the next year or two proving herself and cementing the loyalty of the upper echelons of the Order."

Seeing that the new Admiral appeared to be considering his words thoughtfully, Sir Dimitrios decided to play his hand. Looking at him intently, he offered:

"So, Alex, maybe the fact that someone as knowledgeable about the internal workings of the Paladin Order, and as capable as yourself, did not become locked into the rigid demands of the Lord Admiralship at this critical juncture—someone who obviously knows so many of the men as well as you do—is not such a bad thing after all."

Ephraimoglou was taken aback. Even if his interlocutor did happen to be the first peer himself, talking about matters internal to the Paladin Order with a non-Paladin did not sit at all well with him. Still, as uncomfortable as he felt about having such a conversation, he was even more curious about what Lord Vasiliádes was hinting at.

Taking a deep breath and looking up at the starlit sky for a moment, the admiral unconsciously began to reckon how few of the celestial bodies were clearly visible in comparison to the skies of even a hundred years before, which he had seen on so many of his dives. In fact, in this day and age, it seemed that almost everything was murky and the lines blurred.

Finally he looked back at the Council chairman and asked the question that was burning in his mind.

"Is there something specific you have in mind, my lord?"

Immediately he regretted having asked, and was seized by a peculiar sense of creeping guilt. But it was too late. Once he had been given an opening, Lord Vasiliádes did not hesitate to tell the Paladin admiral what he wanted. When the older man left the balcony a few minutes later, Admiral Ephraimoglou stayed there for a long while, alone and highly perturbed, his jaw set and his lips pressed tightly together.

What Vasiliádes had confided to him was so far outside of anything he had expected that at first he could hardly believe his ears. He had sat in stunned silence for a long moment, but then, finally collecting himself, had told the first peer that he would never be able to participate in such an enterprise. Sir Dimitrios had of course understood and graciously accepted his decision; but he also told him to keep what he had said in the back of his mind, in case he had a change of heart.

Now, as the new Paladin admiral stood leaning against the parapet, staring out beyond the park and Lake Geneva, towards the dark outline of the Alps and Mont Blanc in the distance, his mind's eye turned far inward. He gazed back at some of the incredibly difficult decisions he had witnessed being made by Paladins whom he knew to be fundamentally decent and well-intentioned men, and began to have doubts.

Contemplating the choices faced so recently by men like Commodore Ghabry and Lord Admiral Rizopoulos—decisions which in many ways represented two sides of the same coin—Ephraimoglou began to ask himself if perhaps the problem was not which side of the coin one chose, but the very coin itself. Why, he wondered, should men even be put in situations that required such trade-offs to be made between life and death on so grand a scale, especially knowing that none of those choices could ever be completely unbiased? Why should their moral and spiritual integrity be jeopardized if there was indeed another way?

However, as no answers came readily to those questions which weighed upon him so heavily, the questions themselves lingered for a long time. They settled inside of him and eventually took root in the small, invisible cracks of Admiral Alexandros Ephraimoglou's still-wounded and wondering heart.

CHAPTER 22

What a time to forget the wine, the young woman thought disappointedly.

She had been sitting on the sunbaked stone ruins, infused with the accumulated heat of the day, relaxing and allowing the soothing warmth to seep into her. But now it was approaching sunset, and with each passing minute she grew more anxious that he would miss it. Still, looking out over the mirror-like surface of the wide expanse of sea far below her, rimmed all around by the broken remnants of what some believed to have been the ancient continent of Atlantis, it was hard to be too upset. The tranquility and the breathtaking beauty of the view just did not allow for it.

Instead she waited, soaking in the fiery red and golden rays of the solar disc as it drew ever closer to the horizon and spilled out a growing pool of shimmering, scarlet light into the waiting waters. From there, it glistened off the long and rugged crescent of the three-hundred-meter-high Caldera—the rim of the ancient volcano whose annihilating explosion more than three and a half millennia before had wiped out the area's flourishing Minoan culture. In a strange act of reconciliation in the wake of such violent destruction, however, the same eruption had also left behind the dramatically striking island of Thira—otherwise known as Santorini—as an ever-present reminder of the fleeting nature of the civilization of men.

Clearly visible across the bay to the southeast, the whitewashed stone houses, churches and windmills of the capital, Firá, gleamed in the rose-tinted light of the waning day. Clinging to the edge of the Caldera, they gave the appearance of distant snowcapped mountain peaks. Below that, the striated and multicolored cliff face—each layer of which marked the boundary of a long bygone era, punctuated by the volcanic activity that had formed the island in the distant recesses of geological time—glimmered in an earth-toned rainbow of white, black, gray, rust, green and tan hues.

Silently and reverently taking in the marvel of it all, Kyriakí Zisimou leaned back against the weathered dome of a ruined church in the island's once thriving northwestern town of Oía. The area had been largely abandoned for almost a hundred and twenty years, ever since the massive earthquake of 1956, but she imagined that she could still almost hear the strains of an ancient hymn coming from deep within the nave below:

Φως ιλαρόν αγίας δόξις αθανάτου Πατρός, ουρανίου, αγίου μάκαρος, Ίησου Χριστέ...O joyous light of the holy glory of the immortal, heavenly, holy, blessed Father, O Jesus Christ...

She was sitting thus, in peaceful contemplation, and had just closed her eyes for a moment, when she heard a warm and familiar voice next to her.

"Is this seat taken?" said Jean-Luc Pelegris, smiling, having just returned from his mission with a large canvas bag in his hand.

Looking up at him and smiling, Kyriakí moved over a bit to make room and said: "What took you so long? I was starting to worry you weren't going to make it back in time."

"And miss the perfect moment? No way," he said, as he settled down next to her and they kissed tenderly. Opening up the sack he had brought with him, he pulled out a bottle of chilled champagne, two glasses and a bouquet of long-stemmed yellow roses. He then added in a solemn voice: "I just thought these might make the occasion a little more special."

"Wow, what a surprise!" exclaimed Kyriakí with delight. "I believe you have got a romantic streak somewhere in there after all, Mr. Pelegris," she laughed. "What ever happened to that whole 'rebel without a clue' routine?"

Jean-Luc stared back at her in an oddly serious way and said simply: "Oh, that? That all changed about eight months ago when I saw you lying in that hospital bed and..."

His voice broke for a second and he quickly turned away, blinking the moisture from his eyes and exhaling heavily, as he remembered the terrible ordeal that had nearly killed her. Feeling a wave of compassion come over her, Kyriakí leaned her head against his shoulder and gently took his hand in hers.

"Come on now, my love," she said softly. "It's okay. That was months ago, and I'm fine now."

He knew she was right, but it had been such a close call and the memory of it still haunted him. The genetically-engineered virus that had wrought havoc throughout Camp Monemvasia the previous autumn, and which had been responsible for the agonizing deaths of more than three dozen of their colleagues, had almost taken her life as well. Just thinking about the weeks of lockdown and isolation underground, the long desperate nights of vigils kept by her bedside as she clung precariously to life in the installation's intensive care ward, and the months of slow and tenuous recovery, was enough to paralyze him with dread.

It was now early June of 2075, and life in Camp Monemvasia had long since returned to normal; but for Jean-Luc Pelegris, some things would never again be the same. For one thing, as far from his mind as the thought of settling down had been when he and Kyriakí had first become romantically involved nine eventful months earlier, the certainty had been growing within him for quite some time that he never again wanted to risk losing her.

The moment was close now, and the blazing red ball of the sun was enormous as it began its precipitous plunge into the vast and languid pool of liquid fire at the edge of the world. Carefully opening the bottle of champagne, Jean-Luc poured out two glasses and handed one to Kyriakí.

"You know how in ancient times they considered the setting of the sun to be the start of the new day?" he suddenly prompted as the two young lovers clinked their glasses together.

"Yes, what about it?" Kyriakí asked, smiling inquisitively and gazing at him with her deep and soulful brown eyes.

"Well," he said solemnly, raising his glass, "here's to new beginnings."

As they slowly sipped their champagne, quietly basking in the warmth of their love as much as in the glorious light of the setting sun, Jean-Luc held Kyriakí close to him protectively. *No, he thought, some things would never be the same again.*

MONEMVASIA, GREECE—TUESDAY, JUNE 11, 2075

Perhaps it was because of his visit to Geneva of a few weeks before, seeing his cousin in person for the first time in almost a year; or perhaps it was the photos he had seen of Dimitrios's grandchildren, and especially of that nine-year old Dimitraki, who was the spitting image of his grandfather at that age. Lately, however, Sir Marcus Lawson had been overcome by a persistent feeling of nostalgia.

Over the last couple of weeks, he found himself spending more of his free time—which was considerable, now that he was retired—organizing old family photos, video clips and holographic images than he had possibly ever done in his entire life. But somehow, it did not seem to be enough.

Like many people his age, his mind was constantly occupied with memories—people, places, events, and regrets about things said or done and those not said or not done. And of all those memories, the ones that stood out most, and invaded his thoughts daily with a heavy cloud of sentimentality that he could not seem to shake off, were those of his childhood summers in Monemvasia.

Of course, the fact that he was living in his family's old summer house, and could see from the garden the very same places—very little changed over the last sixty-some-odd years—where he and Dimitrios and his other cousins used to play as children, obviously had a great deal to do with it. But it also occurred to him that there was something else. Perhaps the trip he had taken down into the chamber beneath the cistern several months before had jogged memories that had been long dormant, and had made him wonder what else he had forgotten from that sweet time of youthful innocence.

He was not quite sure when the idea had first begun to settle in his mind, but it was a rare overcast morning in mid-June when at last he did something about it. Standing in his living room with a cup of Greek coffee in hand, he looked at the wall screen in front of him and gave a voice command to initiate a video call. After speaking with an administrative assistant, he waited patiently for a moment until the person he wanted finally appeared on the screen.

"Good morning, my lord! And to what do I owe this unexpected pleasure?" Admiral Ephraimoglou greeted him cheerfully.

"Good morning, Admiral! You're looking well. I see the new title suits you. How are they treating you there in the shop now that you're the boss? I dare say, a little different than it was before, eh?" Lawson remarked, sipping his coffee.

"Well, I have to admit, it's certainly interesting. We have a lot going on—a lot to do. And of course this whole process of preparing to move the Paladin Worldwide Headquarters staff functions to Sevastopol doesn't help. It's a huge headache—coordinating the transfer of files and document archives, training the personnel over there, you name it—a real logistical nightmare. But we'll get through it one way or another. There's really no choice."

"Yes, I'm sure you will, Admiral," Lawson sympathized. "Well, Admiral, I know you're very busy, so I really don't want to take up too much of your time—"

"No, not at all, my lord," Ephraimoglou reassured him. "I always have time for your lordship. Tell me, what can I do for you?"

"Well thank you, Admiral, that's very kind of you. What I wanted to talk to you about is...well, it's something rather personal. I have a favor I want to ask you."

"Why of course, my lord, anything," replied Ephraimoglou without hesitation.

The Paladin Admiral gave the Old Man his undivided attention, as the latter explained what he had called about. It did not take long, and when he was finished, Ephraimoglou sat back and let out a sigh.

"My lord, you realize this is something quite irregular," he said thoughtfully, leaning back in his chair. But then quickly sitting upright at his desk, he concluded: "But not to worry—of course we'll get it done. I'll have a word with Master Lao and make the necessary arrangements, and I'll get back to you as soon as possible."

"Thank you, Admiral Ephraimoglou," replied Sir Marcus appreciatively. "And for what it's worth, I think you know what my preference would have been for the outcome in Geneva last month. Unfortunately a tie-breaking ballot wasn't called so—"

"It's all right, my lord," said Ephraimoglou, waving his hand dismissively. "I understand—there's no need to explain. Perhaps it's all for the best. Things have become so...complex lately," he continued with a sigh, "and I sometimes wonder if it wouldn't be best just to keep one's head down and follow orders."

Thanking the Paladin again, Lord Lawson then added: "Oh, one last thing, Admiral—speaking of things being complex. Obviously it goes without saying, but let's keep this little conversation between the two of us and Master Lao. I'm sure the fewer people who know about it, the less complicated it will be."

"Yes, I'm sure you're right," Ephraimoglou agreed. "Well, I'll let you know as soon as everything is ready. Good afternoon, my lord."

The image of the Paladin admiral on the wall screen faded out and was immediately replaced with a slowly swirling, colorful floral pattern. Lord Lawson took the last sip from his *demitasse* and suddenly realized that, for the first time in as long as he could remember, a feeling of genuine excitement was bubbling up within him.

It had been easier than he thought. His plan was now in motion, and he wondered how long it would take before everything would be ready. In any case, he shouldn't be in such a hurry, he thought. After all, he had waited all these years—what was another month or two?

✢ ✢ ✢

SANTORINI, GREECE—MONDAY, JUNE 3, 2075

Like the famed town of Pompeii in southern Italy, visiting the archaeological site at Akrotiri was like stepping into a moment frozen in time. The Bronze Age settlement on the southern horn of Santorini had been captured and preserved intact for thousands of years by the millions of tons of volcanic ash which had rained down upon it during the island's cataclysmic eruption sometime in the middle of the second millennium BC. Unlike the case of Pompeii, however, its inhabitants had been able to evacuate the city long before the catastrophe had hit, leaving behind an empty shell.

Interestingly, some of the residents had apparently expected to be able to return to their homes, as evidenced by the instances of personal treasures found plastered into wall niches or hidden beneath the petrified floorboards of excavated houses. Yet even as an empty shell, the site was nothing short of amazing in its ability to convey a clear picture of an ancient life which was not so different from that of the island's modern occupants.

Its spacious and well-organized buildings—many of which were two- and three-story structures with surprisingly modern features, such as light wells and sophisticated indoor plumbing— were beautifully decorated with well-preserved wall murals and frescoes, depicting various scenes of daily life which gave a picture of a wealthy and advanced civilization. The wooden furniture, transformed into time-enduring plaster casts by the effects of the volcanic ash, showed a delicate artistry and appreciation for fine detail that fascinated the eye. And the various ceramic ware, metal implements and figurines—some clearly domestic and others obviously foreign imports—evinced a high degree of economic integration with neighboring islands and even cultures as far away as ancient Egypt.

As often as Kyriakí had visited the place during her studies in archaeology and history, it had never ceased to amaze her and to draw her into a world of imagination that both intrigued and inspired her. This time, however, she was actually more anxious about the whole excursion than anything else.

Their long weekend together in Santorini had been wonderful, but it had gone by much too quickly, and now unfortunately it was time to head back. She and Jean-Luc had very little time left to get to the airport for their return flight to Athens, and she really did not want to miss it. The next scheduled departure after theirs was late in the evening, and the last thing she wanted was to make the long drive back down to Monemvasia in the middle of the night, having to get up early for work the next morning.

In fact, it would have been better to have arranged things differently, or even to have skipped the side trip to Akrotiri altogether on such a short vacation. But Jean-Luc—who had never before shown the slightest interest in such things—had uncharacteristically insisted that they go.

At the time, she had thought it so very sweet of him to make an effort to do something he thought would please her, even though it must have been incredibly dull for him. But now, tapping her foot impatiently on the raised visitor walkway, she really wished he would hurry back from the restroom he had gone looking for. It was getting late and she was nervous about missing their flight.

After waiting long enough, she decided to go and look for him, and was making her way back along the tour path towards the visitor's facilities when she saw him through the window of the site's only gift shop. He was standing near the counter and talking to a thin blond man with a red face. Wondering who the stranger was, she was about to go in and join them, but at that very moment Jean-Luc abruptly turned away from the man and walked towards the exit.

Coming out of the shop, he seemed startled to see Kyriakí standing there, and with a surprised look on his face said nervously: "Oh, hi! Have you been here long?"

"No, I just got here really," she said taking his hand. Then she continued playfully: "I thought I'd better come and rescue you in case some of those cute shop girls tried to make any sudden moves on you."

"Oh, I see," he replied, playing along. "Well, thanks for watching my back."

"Anytime—besides, it is in that general direction I was looking, but it's not exactly your back I was watching," she added, smiling seductively and patting him playfully on his rear end. "Anyway, I think we really have to be going. I'm starting to get worried about the time."

"Oh, my God, you're right!" he exclaimed, looking at his watch. "We'd better get a move on. We still have to return the car and go through security and everything."

As they walked briskly out of the complex towards the parking lot, Kyriakí casually asked Jean-Luc:

"By the way, who was that man you were talking to back there?"

"What man? Oh, him!" he replied with a strange uneasiness. "Uh, nobody important really."

"Oh—it just looked like maybe you knew him or something," she insisted.

Frowning for a second, Jean-Luc sighed and said: "Well, okay—if you *have* to know. He's an old friend of my father's. Weird running in to him all the way down here in Santorini, isn't it? Well, I guess it's not that strange really—he is an archaeologist, after all."

"That's funny," she said sarcastically, "I somehow never imagined your father as the type to have friends."

They both laughed, and then she added: "But seriously, I'm really glad to see that you and your father seem to be getting along so much better these days, ever since...well, you know, ever since the disaster. I mean, whatever he may have done in the past, you're still family and it's important to stick together."

"Yeah, well," Jean-Luc shrugged uncomfortably. "I guess I just spent so much time when I was growing up being angry with him about what he put my mother and me through that I automatically hated whatever he stood for, you know? I actually think that, deep down, part of the whole reason I joined the Guardians was just to be in his face and, you know, make myself a total pain in his ass. Can you believe it?"

After they had a good laugh together, he then added earnestly:

"But then when I saw what the other side are really all about, and what they're willing to do, I guess I started to realize that, for all his faults—and believe me, he still has a lot of them—there are some realities I wouldn't let myself see before that, well, maybe he was right about all this time. I don't know if I can ever forgive him for a lot of things—but at least I'm trying to forget and move on. There are bigger things to think about than my personal grievances."

They walked the rest of the way in silence, holding hands; but as they approached the rental car, Kyriakí's professional curiosity got the better of her and she suddenly asked: "So what was he doing here in Akrotiri anyway, that archaeologist friend of your father's? Is he involved in the excavations?"

"Oh, I don't know," said Jean-Luc rather curtly, as if beginning to tire of the subject. "I barely spoke to the guy. I was probably about twelve or thirteen the last time I saw him, and he was just telling me how much I'd grown up and all the usual crap. I mean, no kidding, what did he expect? That I was going to stay a geeky teenager forever?"

Then, anxious to change the subject, as soon as they reached the car he pulled something out of his shirt pocket and said: "I almost forgot, these are for you."

"What's this? Oh, thank you!" she said, smiling brightly and putting her long and slender, deeply tanned arms around his neck to kiss him. It was a pair of gold earrings crafted into miniature replicas of one of the site's most precious artifact finds—a solid gold ibex that had been discovered buried under some petrified floorboards almost a century before.

"They're beautiful!" she pronounced, but then suddenly her face fell and she added wistfully: "Oh, but I didn't get anything for you."

"That's okay," he said, smiling reassuringly as he reached over to stroke her dark and wavy hair, "I've already got what I want."

Once they were in the car, he started it and commanded: "Auto-pilot, go to the airport rental car return area—and please check us in on the way."

"Auto-pilot engaged," a gentle computerized voice replied from the car's speaker system. "Next destination: airport car rental Area Beta. Flight check-in in progress. Please buckle up and enjoy your ride."

The couple sat back in their comfortable seats and locked arms, as Kyriakí—already wearing her new earrings—rested her head on her beloved fiancé's shoulder and thought about what a perfect long weekend it had been. Meanwhile, Jean-Luc breathed a sigh of relief. Luckily the well-timed diversion of his gift had succeeded in taking Kyriakí's mind off her previous inquiry.

It had been too close for comfort, and it was unfortunate that she had seen Rivens at all; but there was nothing that could be done about it now. In any case, no harm would come of it. He would just have to be more careful next time—if there was a next time. As much as he wanted to help, he really did not like playing messenger for his father, and he liked keeping secrets from Kyriakí even less. But at the same time, he had also come to appreciate what a dangerous world it was, and he was determined to do whatever it took to ensure those dangers never again came close to the woman he loved.

CHAPTER 23

The short one-hour flight from Athens to the Turkish capital of Ankara had been delayed due to a late arrival of the incoming aircraft, but other than that, the trip had been uneventful. With nothing more than a carry-on bag, Georges Pelegris made it out to the airport's arrivals area quickly and found his driver waiting with a sign that read "Mr. Georges"—his alias for the duration of the trip.

Dressed in khaki shorts and a photographer's vest, and wearing a wide-brimmed safari hat and sunglasses, he looked every bit the tourist as he walked behind the chauffeur. It had been years since he had taken a real vacation, and even though the two weeks he planned to spend in Turkey were anything but a holiday, he was beginning to think that just being away from the office for so many days in a row would be relaxing in itself.

"How long does it take to get to Cappadocia from here?" he asked the driver in English, making an effort to use his best American accent, as they made their way across the bus lane and out to the parking lot in the heat of the midday sun.

"Oh, is long trip," replied the driver between drags on his alpha-wave-stimulating infrasonic cigarette, or *iCig*. "It take maybe two and half, *ts'ree* hours. No problem if *effendi* getting tired. *Dere* is many good places to take rest, eat *somets'ing* on *de vay*. You are maybe first time in *Türkiye*?"

"No," replied Pelegris, looking all around while they walked. "I've been to Istanbul many times, but it's my first trip to Anatolia."

"Forget Istanbul—Ankara *de* best," advised the chauffeur, breathing in deeply through his nose as the smokeless *iCig* hung precariously from his mustached lips. "Fresh air, good *clima*—and girls very nice. Not like Istanbul. Too much rain *dere, clima* not good. Too much...'u...how it is?...'umid. Here, too much sun!"

"Yes, I see that," said Pelegris, already breaking into a sweat from the short distance they had walked to the parking lot.

The two men finally reached the gleaming black limousine, resting on its four horizontal hydrogen-powered fan jets. The driver grinned, apparently proud of his second-hand automobile which appeared to be in mint condition, and which Pelegris soon found out belonged to the Turk himself and not to the travel agency.

"You like?" he said motioning towards the car with his head, as he placed the duffel bag in the trunk and opened the door for Pelegris. "German, not Chinese," he then said, as if no further explanation were necessary. China may indeed have been the world's largest car exporting nation for many decades, but evidently it was still German quality that counted—at least among old Turkish chauffeurs.

Having climbed inside the spotless vehicle, and feeling a bit tired from his trip from Monemvasia, the Guardian operations director put on his seat belt and leaned back to rest against the soft cream-colored upholstery. The driver started the engine, and as the four powerful rotors began to spin with a faint whine, the car slowly lifted up about half a meter off the ground. The driver then took it carefully through the parking lot, paid the fee, and headed out of the airport and onto the ring road in the direction of the Aksaray highway.

As soon as they were out of the airport, he accelerated to about eighty kilometers per hour, making a point to demonstrate his cautious driving; but at that speed, Pelegris knew it would take them all day, and he had a rendezvous at two o'clock.

"It's all right, you can go a little faster," he called up front to the driver.

Tilting his head and checking the side view mirror, the chauffeur instantly jumped out into the passing lane and stepped on the accelerator, quickly hitting a hundred sixty, as Pelegris was pushed into the comfortable seat back. Once they reached Güzelyurt he would be busy enough for the rest of the day, so he pulled his hat down over his eyes, thinking that he might as well try to take a short nap while he had the chance. That, however, proved to be impossible.

After exiting the capital's ring road and heading onto the highway going southeast, they at once entered a narrow two-lane road with plenty of slow-moving trucks and agricultural vehicles, and were once again forced to decelerate to about eighty. As a result, every few minutes the driver would weave around a line of cars and trucks, flooring the accelerator and flying ahead at top speed, only to duck back again into the proper lane at the very last second, just in time to avoid a collision with the oncoming traffic. Thus they drove for about an hour and a half, in hair-raising fits and starts, before finally crossing into Kırşehir province and the western end of the famed ancient region of Cappadocia.

Although he had certainly heard of the natural wonders of the place—formed over millions of years by the seismic and volcanic activity of the Miocene period, and shaped by aeons of wind erosion—Pelegris was nonetheless amazed by what he saw. Sitting upright and practically plastering his face to the window, he observed all around him the rugged and starkly contrasting scenery of the wide plains and river valleys, punctuated by high mesas and colorful buttes and dotted with the most spectacular and peculiar rock formations.

Towering columns topped with large flat boulders, looking like vast stone toadstools, sprouted out of the rocky ground on either side of them; natural archways and strangely shaped figures loomed before them, reminding one of various animals or even human faces; and in numerous locations, protruding from the ground like so many flower beds in a fantasy-laden rock garden, were the exotic white, gray and rust-colored outcroppings of cone-shaped volcanic vents known as 'fairy chimneys'. In many respects, it was a landscape similar to that of the American southwest—which Pelegris knew well from the many years he had spent living in California—except for one important detail: the ancient architecture.

All along the way, one could see the remains of more than a thousand years of Byzantine Greek Christian civilization in the form of beautiful and impressive churches and monasteries—sometimes alone and other times surrounded by the numerous dwellings and structures of entire towns and villages—carved into the very rock walls of canyons and hillsides, and leaving their indelible imprint on the timeless fabric of the richly-woven Cappadocian tapestry. And seemingly around every bend in the road, surrounded by the fields and farmlands of simple rustic villages, there were more tangible remnants of the region's complex and fascinating history—from the ruins of ancient Roman aqueducts, to those of medieval fortresses and bridges dating from the Byzantine, Seljuk and Ottoman empires—some of which still functioned as parts of principal roads and waterways.

Spying his passenger through the rearview mirror as he picked up his camera and began snapping pictures through the lowered window, the Turkish driver sucked on his *iCig*, producing an inaudible wave of mellowing infrasonic vibrations. Then, with an approving smile, he exclaimed over the sound of the buffeting wind: "Beautiful *Kapadokya!*"

'Beautiful Cappadocia' was certainly true, thought Pelegris as he tapped the button to close the window, and settled back into his seat. But he had not come here to appreciate the region's natural wonders or its rich historical heritage. There were other cultural artifacts he was there to investigate, and they would not be visible from the window of a car, or even from the basket of one of the many colorful hot-air sightseeing balloons that floated so serenely and majestically in the skies high above them. In fact, to find the treasures he was looking for, he would have to leave the sun-soaked plains and mountains of central Anatolia far behind—or far above, to be more precise.

The sights he intended to see were nowhere else but deep beneath the surface of the earth. For what Operations Director Georges Pelegris was in Turkey to examine could only be found under the very ground below him, among Cappadocia's ancient and mysterious subterranean cities.

By the time they arrived at the hotel in Güzelyurt—a centuries-old Greek town originally named Karvalí, which had been emptied of its residents and resettled with Turkish families from the cities of Kastoria and Kozani in Greece during the two countries' violent 1923 exchange of populations—it was nearly three o'clock in the afternoon. Except for a ruddy-faced blond man sitting on a sofa as if waiting for someone, the lobby was deserted at that time of day, and Pelegris had no trouble checking in immediately.

He went straight to his room, unpacked his bag and had just taken a quick shower when he heard three sharp raps on the door. Wrapping the thick, white-cotton Turkish bath towel around his waist, he went and opened it without even inquiring who was there. Outside, looking around furtively and rather impatiently, was the red-faced man who had been sitting downstairs in the lobby. Pelegris opened the door wide, stepped to the side without a word, and let him into the room.

"It's about bloody time you showed up. Do you know how long I've been waiting down there?" the man with the Scottish accent said crossly.

"It couldn't be helped," replied Pelegris unapologetically. "Besides, I'm here now. I got your message—what have you got for me?"

"Right, well as I told your son, we've found a very promising location," the man began to report, before pausing and looking anxiously about the room. "You have swept this place to make sure it's clean, haven't you?"

Pelegris snorted in amusement.

"Of course, Rivens, relax. There's nothing to worry about," he said, pointing out a compact but powerful SHIELD device sitting on the coffee table nearby. "Go on now, what about the location?"

"Right. It has everything we'll need. We've already managed to get down to a depth of about forty meters, but that's about as far as we can go without heavy equipment. Clearly, though, there are a number of levels below that. We've taken a series of soundings through a couple of exposed ventilation shafts and we've come up with an estimated minimum depth of eighty-five to ninety-five meters. There's also a nearby inactive volcanic crater with a deep glacial lake in it. It's a wee bit further away than the engineers would like, but with some effort we should be able to pipe into it quite nicely for a water supply."

"That all sounds fine," Pelegris responded in a deadpan voice, "when do we go to see it?"

"I have a car downstairs," the Scot replied. "I suggest that you take a little walk—ask the concierge for a map of the town and for some restaurant tips to cover your tracks. I'll pick you up near the old Greek cathedral—the 'Great Church Mosque' it's called on the map. I'll wait about fifteen minutes before I head down so we're not seen together."

"All right, I'll need five minutes to get dressed and then I'll start out. See you later," said Pelegris, ushering Rivens out of his room. It all seemed a bit too cloak-and-dagger for his taste, but one could never be too careful, he supposed.

THE TWO MEN HAD driven around in the countryside for nearly an hour in what seemed to Pelegris like crazily overlapping circles, when Rivens suddenly veered sharply off the road and headed over a low rise and down an embankment into a rugged glen. Moving slowly over the stony course of a dry streambed, he parked the car in a small clearing obscured from sight by a couple of thick plane trees and assorted brush.

"It's a fifteen minute walk from here," he said, as he grabbed a knapsack and climbed out of the vehicle.

Following behind him, Pelegris picked his way over a narrow rock-strewn footpath that led through the valley, slowly descending and opening into a wider gorge as they progressed. On either side rose up the steep walls of a canyon, in which Pelegris noticed the openings of what appeared to be several small caves. At length his companion stopped before one of them—a low aperture overhung with vegetation and almost indiscernible among the roots and vines clinging to the canyon's rocky sides—and, looking around to be sure no one was watching, waved Pelegris forward and crawled inside.

"This is not the main entrance," he remarked, switching on his *Hydrofuse* lantern, as the two men crawled through a narrow tunnel about a meter and a half high. "You'll soon see where we think it is, though. Lucky us, it must have collapsed at some point, which is what's kept this particular site from being discovered until now. It's possible this tunnel was an emergency escape route or a secret entrance for spies or messengers in the event of a long siege. But it's the only way in for now."

That could be a problem, Pelegris observed silently as they crawled along. If this was the only entrance, there would be no way to get the equipment they needed into the place. But he decided to let it go for the moment, doing his best to keep up with his guide.

After about twenty meters, the passage became large enough for the men to walk upright, and for the first time Pelegris noticed that they were headed down a rather steep slope. He also began to see a dim light in the distance, and soon realized that they were reaching the end of the tunnel. Eventually they arrived at a low entrance and, stooping down, Rivens went through first and beckoned the operations director to follow.

Coming through the other side of the portal, Pelegris was amazed to find himself in a large rectangular chamber carved into the rock. It was roughly ten meters long and six or seven meters wide. There were several hallways branching off from this room and heading in different directions. Three were filled with varying amounts of debris, but two had been cleared and he could even see a dim light glowing from the recesses of one of them, where a work lantern had apparently been hung.

Inside the chamber itself, the surrounding walls were notched with a number of deep niches resembling shelves of various shapes and sizes. There were also what appeared to be stone benches and stools fashioned out of rock protruding from the floor in several spots. From the look of it, the room might long ago have served as some sort of reception area, or perhaps even an underground tavern.

Another remarkable feature that he noticed, just outside one of the larger tunnels and fitted into a narrow groove along the wall, was a massive circular millstone. In ancient times it could apparently be rolled in front of the chamber's entrance to close it off from outside attackers. This was evidently the passage leading to the main entrance, and although it was only a little over two meters in height, it was quite wide as well. It had some potential.

"These underground cities in Cappadocia have been around essentially for thousands of years, since at least the time of the Hittites," Rivens began to explain, as he led Pelegris into the lighted corridor. "They probably started out as simple caves, but each successive civilization that occupied the area adapted and expanded them, using them as refuges in times of political instability and war. And we know from the history of the region that there was plenty of that to go around.

"Some of the sites are absolutely amazing, extending as many as eight or ten levels below ground and capable of housing literally thousands of people and their domestic animals comfortably for long periods of time. In addition to individual residences, several of them have also been found to contain public spaces, wells, storage magazines, shops, churches—even bathhouses. The greatest advantage of this particular site for our purpose—apart from the fact that it hasn't been discovered before, and of course its relative proximity to a significant supply of water—is what you'll see right now."

A moment later, they turned a corner in the passageway and Pelegris could see a vast chamber at least seven meters high, six or seven meters wide and tens of meters long. A couple of structural engineers and a geologist, who were standing near one of the walls discussing some data on the screen of a *FlexTab* computer, came over and joined them. Meanwhile, several workmen trundled through the corridor with mag-lev wheelbarrows carrying bags of dirt, rocks and debris, which they were excavating from another passageway and depositing on the floor of the cavernous hall.

"Unlike some of the region's better known underground cities that were found in the last century, like Derinkuyu or Özkonak," Rivens continued, "from the soundings we've done, this place seems to have an astounding number of very large chambers like this one. It's possible this was some kind of a central storage facility for several of the subterranean cities in the surrounding area. It's known that many of these cities were interconnected by a complex and extensive underground tunnel network, so it's quite possible that this was a place that could be reached from any one of them in order to bring in additional supplies when needed."

"This all looks very promising," Pelegris finally said, nodding his head as his companion spoke and pursing his lips together thoughtfully. "But before we start congratulating ourselves, let's get to the point, shall we? Is it a hot zone or not?"

"Well, we're still taking measurements," replied one of the engineers who had joined them, "but so far the readings show very good potential. If you'd like, I can show you some of the test results—" he started to say as he began unrolling the *FlexTab* computer tucked under his arm.

"That won't be necessary, Carlos," interjected the Scotsman, "I don't think Director Pelegris really wants to study magnetic field line diagrams right now."

"Well, I think that's something we had definitely better answer before we spend too much more time or money here, don't you think?" Pelegris retorted testily.

"Look," Rivens snapped back defensively, "all I'm meant to be doing is scouting out potential sites and making them ready for you to test. We can take as many readings as you'd like, but the final proof of the pudding won't come until we can successfully send a diver out from here and bring him back safely—and we're still a long way from that.

"We still need a willing Paladin and a set of diving bells, which is your responsibility, not mine. Besides, you know as well as I do that we cannot do any testing until we have the proper magnetic field stabilizers and electromagnetic shielding installed. Unless of course you want this little black operation of yours to see the light of day before it even gets off the ground."

Pelegris was silent for a moment. He knew that his colleague was right. Finally he said: "All right, I've seen enough. Tell me what else you need so we can move things along. We have a lot to do and not much time in which to do it."

The men continued talking as they walked back up towards the entrance chamber, rattling off resource requirements and discussing how to progress most efficiently. There were still innumerable issues to be worked out and obstacles to be dealt with, and Pelegris was not taking anything for granted at this stage; but in his gut he had a good feeling about this place. Something told him that everything was going to work out according to plan.

As he thought about it, he wondered for a moment whether or not he should mention anything to Rigas, but then quickly decided against it. Not just yet anyway, he concluded. Not only would he add nothing to the party, but there was also a very good chance that he would inadvertently screw something up. No, for the time being it would be better to keep this to himself—and Lord Vasiliádes, of course. After all, someone was going to have to pay the bills.

Yes, thought Georges Pelegris with a growing sense of satisfaction, he definitely had a good feeling about this. It was turning out not to be a wasted 'vacation' after all.

CHAPTER 24

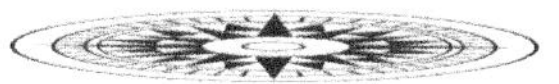

The training was much more rigorous than he had expected, but in many ways it was like riding a bicycle—one never really forgot. The main thing was reacquiring the ability to enter into a state of deep noetic prayer on demand. Unfortunately, that was a skill which had gone soft in Lord Lawson. And after so many years of preoccupation with the worldly managerial and political responsibilities of his position, the required rehabilitation was grueling.

Of course he had never fully abandoned his prayer life. Despite the demands of work, he had continued to attend church services and to say his morning and evening prayer rules with a fair amount of consistency. Nevertheless, over time his efforts had become less and less vigorous. In fact, they often seemed to be not much more than a slavish 'going through the motions', having lost an essential purity of concentration.

What he was attempting to achieve now, however, was something of a totally different nature altogether; and getting it right—or not—would ultimately be a matter of life or death.

'Blessed are the pure in heart', Jesus had said to his disciples, *'for they shall see God'*.

Those had never been easy instructions to follow—not two thousand years ago and not today. It was a gift that often took a lifetime of patient dedication and strenuous effort to acquire, if ever. He had no idea when he started how long it would take to reacquire it, especially now that he had left it unexercised and allowed it to atrophy for so long.

It was extremely difficult at first, and at one point he almost considered giving up; but slowly he managed to stretch and limber up his 'noetic muscles', as he had taken to calling his meditative faculties. After weeks of ascetical practices—fasting, prayer, all-night vigils and deep self-examination in the stillness of his thoughts—he was soon able to block everything out and descend with his mind into his heart, all aflame with deep spiritual prayer. Thus, after a series of rigorous physical examinations and clearance from the medical staff, and two challenging months under the guidance of Master Lao, he had been recertified. Sir Marcus was ready to dive again.

It had been a very long time—twenty-two years to be exact—since he had made his last dive as a Paladin. In those days, things had been different. The Paladin Order was much smaller, much more free-spirited—not at all like the highly regimented, bureaucratic organization it had become today, with its own administration and specialists of every kind, and even its own investment portfolios.

In the old days, it was much more exciting. Every Paladin was a diver and played a major role, no matter what his rank or level of experience. Not only that, but the technology was not yet perfected and each dive was a major risk. There were no gravitational field stabilizers, no EDT tracking, and the geodesic mapping effort was in its infancy. As a result, good divers were occasionally lost, and there was truly a sense of shared danger and responsibility for one another, with everyone considering the other Paladins to be his brothers.

By the same token, their enemies were neither as numerous and organized, nor as technologically advanced as they were today. The demand for Paladin intervention operations was therefore relatively low compared to that of recent years. In any case, despite the significant changes that had occurred since he had been an active Paladin, Sir Marcus felt the thirst of an unbridled excitement and nervous anticipation burning inside of him—and there was only one way to slake it.

It was one evening in late August, a little after ten o'clock, and Sir Marcus was getting ready for bed when the call finally came.

"My lord, forgive me for disturbing you at this hour," apologized Admiral Ephraimoglou, "but tonight's the night—we're ready for you."

"Tonight?" Lawson replied with surprise. "That's wonderful, Admiral. I didn't really expect it to be so soon. Of course I'll be ready. What time should I come?"

"Can you come to Dive Control around 3:00AM? Things will be quiet then. It'll be better if I'm not present, as you can understand, but Dive Master Andrews will be ready and waiting for you."

"Three o'clock it is," said the Old Man, feeling a rush of adrenalin. Then he added: "Oh, and, thank you, Admiral—from the bottom of my heart, thank you for everything."

"Not at all, my lord," Ephraimoglou answered with a smile. "I'm glad we were able to arrange it. Godspeed and smooth sailing!"

After the call, Lawson went to bed, thinking it would be a good idea to get a few hours' rest before the big event; but in the end he only tossed and turned, too excited to sleep. Eventually getting up at around midnight, he got dressed again and made a cup of Greek coffee, and then spent the next couple of hours looking at his collection of old family photos and watching the clock. After so many years, he could hardly believe that he would soon be on his way.

When he finally arrived at the Dive Control Center, it was about a quarter to three, and the place was quiet and dim. Only a few lights flickered on some of the instrument panels and a couple of dive engineers sat quietly at their posts.

"My lord, it's an honor to have you here," said Dive Master Andrews, greeting him with a low bow.

"No, Dive Master," replied Lawson, "the honor is mine." Then looking around the place, he remarked: "My, my! How much things have changed since the last time I was in a Dive Control Center!"

"Really?" said Andrews. "Well, it would be my pleasure to give you a quick tour."

Taking Sir Marcus around the Center, he briefly explained the workings of the various instruments and equipment, and showed him the dive chambers. At last he pointed him towards the locker room, where he was to change into the dive suit that had been prepared for him. A few minutes later, Lawson came out suited up and ready to go. His heart was beating faster than normal, and he tried his best to concentrate as the Dive Master checked his equipment and tested his EDT signal.

With everything appearing to be in order, Dive Master Andrews gave Lord Lawson a few last minute tips.

"I imagine you'll want to be shielded for the duration of the dive, my lord? The technology is much better today than it was in the old d...I mean—," he hesitated, embarrassed.

"It's okay, I know I'm old—go ahead and say it," retorted Lawson good-naturedly.

"Well, it's much better than it was in the old days. I've never seen the old cloaking technology that you had back then, but I've heard that it only worked when you were completely motionless, and you basically became deaf and blind when you used it. Is that right?"

"Yeah—it was a real pain in the butt. None of us liked it, and we seldom used it. It was really only for extreme emergencies. In fact, a lot of the guys used to take their devices off and ditch them as soon as they made depth, because they were so heavy and bulky and it was too much trouble to carry them around."

"Is that so?" asked Andrews, fascinated. "Well, I think you'll find today's SHIELDS a whole different experience. For one thing, the size of the device is no longer an issue."

"Do you have one handy that I can look at?" inquired the Old Man.

"You're already wearing it, my lord," the Dive Master chuckled. "The field generator is now built right into the fabric of the dive suit. There is a limited-function hard control here on the back of your dive-belt buckle, but this just turns the SHIELD on and off, with no other settings. Nowadays, all the advanced settings are accessed through your dive computer—field strength and range, synchronization with other SHIELDS, and a variety of other customizable settings. You can change them manually on the computer if necessary, but most of the divers use mind control—it's much faster and more convenient."

"Mind control?" the Old Man asked uncomfortably. "I know it's been developed much more extensively over the last several years, but isn't it still a little risky?"

Amused at the technology gap between them, Andrews went on to explain.

"Well, my lord, it's not experimental anymore, like it was back in your day. The more recent generations of dive computers from the last five or six years are very reliable and amazingly sensitive in terms of their ability to respond to a diver's brain waves—which are generally rather enhanced in Paladins anyway because of the intensive mental and spiritual training exercises. The wireless optical interfaces you've been given—those little contact lenses—allow a holographic display of infinitely variable focal length to be superimposed directly onto your visual field, but all the work is actually done between your thoughts and the dive computer.

"Another difference you'll appreciate," he continued, "is that you can have it on at all times and you'll still be able to see and hear what's going on around you. It has to do with quantum mechanical tunneling effects. With our advances in quantum computing in the last decade, the dive computers have the ability to interpret the data and transmit it to the diver. You just have to remember that there is a slight delay between what happens outside the SHIELD and the moment you actually see and hear it. It's really quite negligible—on the order of a few hundredths of a second—so for your purposes it shouldn't even be noticeable. It would really only matter if you were performing some action that required extraordinarily precise timing. That's why some Paladins don't like to fight while shielded. But I don't think you'll have to worry about that on this dive."

As a former physicist, Sir Marcus listened to the Dive Master's explanation, fascinated by the developments. Of course, as a Paladin and a peer, he had been given access to every piece of information—from the top secret to the mundane—about what was going on within the organization. However there had always been so much to deal with that he had long ago stopped following all of the technical details.

"The other thing to remember," the Dive Master continued, "is that the faster you move, the less effective the wave displacement becomes and the more likely you are to create some sort of distortion that can penetrate the shielding. Of course, you'd have to be moving quite fast for someone who is not trained to really take notice—but it's just something to keep in mind."

Dive Master Andrews next instructed Sir Marcus in several of the handier functions of his dive computer. At last, when everything was finally ready, he brought out the pair of diving bells that had been prepared for the Old Man.

Holding the luminescent crystalline spheres in the palms of his hands, Lawson felt a surge of excitement coursing through him, unlike anything he had felt in years and making him feel...so young again. He was amazed at how compact and sleek the devices were—especially compared to the clunky diving bells they used to use in the old days—and as he slipped his return bell into the shielded pouch in his dive suit, he marveled at how barely noticeable it was.

"How did you manage it?" he asked the Dive Master, almost whispering, although even he did not know why.

"Oh, it wasn't too difficult," Andrews answered with a smile, already knowing what Sir Marcus was wondering. "If you were to check the log for tonight, you would find that we're scheduled to do routine maintenance testing on one of the dive chambers. The log will record that there was a dive, but we generally don't record who the test diver was on these maintenance runs—just the performance statistics on the chamber."

And so it was time. Sir Marcus nervously stepped into the dive chamber, trying to control his breathing and his pounding heart, and took the safety off the diving bell as he had been instructed. Standing with his arm outstretched, he closed his eyes and used all his concentration to enter into a deep state of mental prayer; and as he began to withdraw from the outside world, he vaguely heard himself calling out:

"Team Snowy Owl armed and ready to go!"

The next thing he experienced after that was the sudden feeling of falling, and the cold, deep impenetrable darkness of the space in between time.

EMERGING FROM HIS DIVE with a hard jolt, Sir Marcus took in a deep breath of musty air. The experience had been just as incredible as it had always been—at least nothing had changed in that—and he felt an inner gratification and peace that could not be explained to anyone who had never dived before. The only difference from what he remembered was that he now felt a little nauseated and his head was spinning, like being slightly sea sick. It was something he never used to experience when diving years before.

You're out of practice, old man, he thought to himself as he manually switched on his night vision and looked around the room.

At least his navigation skills were still good. He had made it, landing exactly where he had planned. The chamber looked just as he remembered it, but he could not help experiencing an odd sense of discomfort, expecting something to be out of place. Indeed, he knew from Dovas's report that it had not always appeared this way.

As he glanced around the room, he saw that several of the shelves had fallen to the floor near the door leading to the caved-in tunnel, and there was a wide crack in the wall. The once concealed door, hanging askew on its hinges from the force of the blast that had occurred inside the tunnel, was now exposed and looked like it would fall at any moment. The wooden beams, broken barrels and loose pieces of rotten wood were all still there as he remembered them, lying carelessly scattered around the place. Overall, the whole situation gave the impression that some great catastrophe had taken place there.

Gazing towards the well shaft, Sir Marcus saw that the iron ladder was where he expected it to be, and he walked over and tested his weight on a couple of the rungs. It seemed that it would hold him, so he slowly began to climb up.

Reaching the top, he was about to try and move the covering, when he suddenly remembered that he was still visible. Activating his SHIELD mentally was harder than he imagined, and in the end he switched it on manually and then tried to slide the cistern cover to the side. It was a little difficult at first, but eventually it moved, and he was gradually able to discern the night sky through the small gap he had opened.

Good, he thought, *it's still night.* That would make things much easier.

Pushing the cistern cover all the way open, he climbed out and stood in the fresh air in the field behind the church of the Panagia Chrysaphitissa in Monemvasia's Lower Town. Except for the distant sound of *bouzouki* music coming from somewhere to the west, the place was still and quiet. The only lights still illuminated were those outside on the verandas of the houses and small hotels, and he could smell the familiar aromatic fragrance of bougainvillea wafting on the light breeze.

Looking around with his night vision, he noticed the faintly luminescent-green silhouette of a young couple some distance away in the shadows. They were leaning against the seawall near the stairs leading to the Portello gate and kissing, two lovers in the flower of their youth, before them myriads of tomorrows waiting to be discovered. For just a few seconds he watched them—moved by a rare sense of poignancy and feeling the briefest twinge of envy of the kind sometimes experienced by those nearer to the end of their lives than they are to the beginning—and then, his heart warmed, he slowly turned away and continued to survey his surroundings.

Still low over the horizon to the east-northeast hung the thin sliver of a waning crescent moon, and the green and red lights of several small fishing boats could be seen out at sea. Pulling out his dive computer to take the standard geodesic readings, Sir Marcus was delighted to find that—unlike in the old days, when he often had to perform a series of complex manual calculations using the positions of celestial bodies—the screen instantly displayed his physical and temporal coordinates. The instrument had obviously picked up the signal of a global-positioning satellite, and although he already knew where he was, now at the touch of a button he also knew exactly *when* he was. It was Monday, August 17, 2009, and the time was 3:12AM.

Having quietly slid the cistern cover back into place and replaced the stones that covered it, Lawson's next task was to find a place to sleep. At first he considered bivouacking on the veranda of his family home, but then he remembered how early he and his cousins used to rise on those seemingly endless summer days. The last thing he wanted was to have one of them run outside and somehow trip over him before he had a chance to wake up. He therefore walked across the field and through the ancient East Gate and found a suitable place along the outside of the city wall to lie down for what little remained of the night.

Fortunately, the weather was fine and sleeping out of doors under the open sky for a few hours—with the soothing smell of wild lavender and rosemary and oregano all around him, and the relaxing crash of the gentle waves against the rocky shoreline nearby—would even be refreshing. Although he was still quite fit for his age, unaccustomed as he was to the snugly-fitting dive suit he wore under his black robes, it was no easy task to lower himself onto the ground. Once he was there, however, he lay back comfortably and gazed up at the starry night sky.

No, he thought, pulling the hood of his long black cassock up over his head and allowing his thoughts to wander as he drifted off to sleep, *it's not too bad at all.*

✦ ✦ ✦

It was already light out, and the sky was a clear cloudless blue, when Sir Marcus woke a little past seven in the morning. It had been many years since he had slept on the ground, and every part of his body was stiff and sore. Several minutes passed before he was finally able to rouse himself and sit up; then he first had to turn over onto his knees in a painful maneuver and lean against the ancient stone wall for support, in order to stand up.

Brushing himself off and combing his still-thick white hair and beard, he made himself as neat as possible under the circumstances, even though he knew that no one would see him. He then went through the East Gate and into the environs of the Lower Town, crossing the field behind the church and walking along the path that led to his family home. It was still early, and as there was no sign of activity yet, he decided to switch off his SHIELD and walk into town to find a café where he could use the restroom and have a coffee.

Having eaten a light breakfast in town, the Old Man returned to the eastern end of the Lower Town at a little before eight thirty, only to find that the scene was different than when he had first awakened. Many houses now had their shutters open, and he could see people beginning to step out onto balconies and verandas—some fully clothed and others in only bathrobes or pajamas—as both tourists and locals started their daily routines.

Finding a secluded corner, he once again switched on his SHIELD and then walked back towards his family's home. He was halfway up the cobblestone path that led to the garden gate, when the front door of the house suddenly flew open and he heard a child's voice loudly proclaiming:

"I'll run you through, you old Turk, or my name isn't Theodoros Kolokotronis!"

Immediately, a young boy with sandy-brown hair, wearing a tee-shirt and camouflage pants that were already too short for him at the ankles, came running out and bounded down the steps towards the gate, while another black-haired boy brandishing a plastic saber followed fast on his heels. It was Mark and Dimitrios.

Lawson froze for an instant, abruptly seized by a powerful mix of emotions—anxiety at the possibility of being discovered, even though he knew he was shielded; a deeply sentimental joy at seeing the children in the fullness of their youthful vigor; and a melancholic feeling at seeing himself again as a boy, a sudden reminder of a youth that had long since faded. He then realized that the boys were coming straight towards him and quickly sidestepped the rush, narrowly avoiding being crashed into by the charging pair as they ran off down the path in the direction of their favorite playground in the field behind the church.

Feeling his eyes becoming misty, Sir Marcus began to wonder if coming back here had been such a good idea; but it was too late to change his mind now. It would not be feasible to get back down to the cistern chamber and resurface without being seen until later that night, and so taking a deep breath, he steadied himself and followed the two children down the walkway.

For a long time, Lawson sat in the morning sun on the edge of a low retaining wall that ran around the courtyard of the church and watched the young Mark and Dimitrios playing in the field. He had given up so much for his calling, he suddenly thought—a family of his own, and grandchildren to comfort him in his old age. Of course at the occasional family gatherings he attended, he was always treated well by his cousins' children and grandchildren as their honored great uncle, but it was not the same as having one's own.

Although he knew that he no longer belonged to this place in time, somehow just being here and seeing the two children for a while gladdened his heart and consoled him. He sat therefore in quiet contemplation, smiling at the sight of the boys running around each other in circles, lunging and dodging with their make-believe weapons, until a sound that he had not heard for decades suddenly seized him by the heart and pulled him out of his carefree reverie.

"Mark! Dimitri!" he heard the sound of a woman's voice calling out, sending a flood of warmth through his chest, which was reflected by the stream of tears that suddenly ran down his cheeks. It was his mother.

His heart flying, Sir Marcus got up and quickly walked back up the path towards the house, and then stopped halfway there. For standing there in colorful summer dresses were his mother, Helen Lawson, his aunt, Maria Vasiliádes, and his two little cousins, Dominique and Jenny. It was the first time he had seen either his mother or aunt in nearly twenty-five years, and his eyes brimmed with tears as his throat became constricted with emotion.

The temptation to run to his mother and embrace her seized him savagely, and he fought it with all his might, knowing how impossible it was to do so. Breathing deeply and regaining his composure, he stared fascinated at the two women who seemed so much younger and more beautiful than ever, and drank in every detail as they chatted gaily with one another. Meanwhile his young cousins skipped around nearby and picked flowers, teasing and playing with one another as innocent children do.

"Mark! Dimitri!" she called again, and eventually the boys came running up, red-cheeked and sweaty, panting for breath.

"Yes, Mama, what do you want?" Mark asked impatiently, eager to get back to their games.

"We're going shopping, do you boys want to come?" she asked, already knowing what their answer would be.

"No, thanks," said Dimitrios, and immediately turned to Mark and added as they ran off again to play: "Come on, Mark, we have to get the message to Karaiskakis to come save Messolonghi!"

"Where do they come up with these things?" Helen asked her sister-in-law, laughing as the two boys disappeared.

"I don't know," replied Maria, shaking her head and smiling. "It's always Kolokotronis-this and Karaiskakis-that with that Dimitrios. Who knows what he's going to grow up to become?"

As they talked, Lawson was deeply touched on noticing his four-year-old cousin, Jenny, clinging to her mother's leg and pulling on her skirt to get her attention. It was she more than any of his cousins who had always gone out of her way to look after him throughout their adult lives, and he marveled at how this tiny little girl was one day to become a feisty grandmother with seven grandchildren of her own.

"What do you want, my love?" Maria asked, bending down to her.

"Isn't Mark coming with us?" she asked, with her fingers in her mouth.

"No, my sweet, he and Dimitrios are going to stay here and play," her mother answered tenderly.

"But I want Mark to come with us!" she whined, and then took a couple of steps in the direction of the church, with a scowl on her little face, and shouted out: "Mark! Dimitri! Come here right NOW! MARK!"

The boys did not come back of course, and after a minute Dominique, who was six at the time, skipped over and took Jenny by the hand to show her a butterfly. Then they slowly headed into town with their mother and their favorite Aunt Ellie, as they were fond of calling Helen. It was hard for Sir Marcus to watch them go, but it was just as well, he thought; for he did not know how much more of his mother's presence he could take without his heart being broken any further.

When the women and girls were finally out of sight, Lawson looked up towards the family house and decided it was time. Taking a deep breath, he went up the path and, seeing that no one was around, quietly went through the green garden gate. Walking up the stairs to the veranda, on which a number of children's toys lay scattered, he listened at the front door and then slowly opened it and went in.

It was strange going into the house in which he now lived and seeing it decorated so differently, as it was so many decades ago in his youth. Of course he had kept a few of the old things for sentimental reasons—the dining room set, a coffee table, various paintings and religious icons—but over the years the place had been renovated two or three times, and much had changed.

Once inside, he immediately heard male voices and stood still, listening. His father and his uncle Andréas were talking heatedly about some issue or another, as he remembered they often did. It was as if he had never left the house, and just hearing them once again caused him to laugh and choke up with emotion at one and the same moment.

Following the sound of their voices, he found them in the kitchen. Uncle Andréas was sitting at the table drinking a Greek coffee, and his father, James, stood at the stove making pancakes. It was a memory from a lifetime ago—one of the many American customs that his father had never been able to do without, even long after they had made their move to Greece permanent—and what he would not have given to be able to taste one of his father's pancakes now, Sir Marcus thought, his eyes welling up with tears.

"Come on, James," his uncle Andréas was insisting, "things are not so bad. The restaurants and hotels are all full! How can you say there's going to be a crisis?"

"I'm telling you," his father replied in his American-accented Greek, "this is no joke. Things are really bad in America, in England, in other parts of Europe. Nobody thinks it can happen here; but it will and, believe me, it's going to get ugly fast—just wait and see."

Lawson knew that his father was right. By the following year, Greece would be in the throes of an economic crisis whose contagion would eventually sow the seeds of instability throughout the then-European Union. Failing to appreciate the severity of the situation, politicians in Greece and in the major European capitals would do too little, too late—looking first to their own electoral interests and to those of foreign bondholders, rather than to the pressing structural and social needs of the country. Ironically, in some ways, little had changed since 1825.

Thus, unable to sustain its debt load and crippled by the so-called austerity measures imposed on it by the international community, Greece would eventually be forced out of the common currency and even pressed to concede some of its sovereign territory to foreign oil interests. Several other peripheral European nations with similar economic problems would follow suit, and the resultant collapse of the *euro* would help tip the balance of the world's fragile economic recovery back into a downward spiral—culminating in a full-scale global depression by the end of the decade.

James Lawson would later admit to his son that even he had never expected anything close to the economic tsunami that was to follow. Neither did he anticipate that the crisis he was so certain about would ultimately set the stage for the resource wars that were to consume an entire decade between the mid-

2020s and the mid-2030s. That unfortunate history, however, was still a long way off, as Sir Marcus observed the two men trading theories in the kitchen of their *Malvasian* summer house over Greek coffee and with the tantalizing smell of hot pancakes and sizzling bacon frying in the pan.

After a long while, his heart full and heavy from seeing his closest relatives again, Lawson decided it would be best to go. But before leaving, he was overwhelmed by a sudden impulse. Without being able to stop himself, he reached out and placed his invisible hand gently on his father's shoulder for just an instant. Immediately, James jumped and looked around.

"What's the matter?" asked Andréas.

"I don't know—I felt like somebody just touched me," he said, a disconcerted look on his face.

"Come on, Lawson!" his uncle laughed. "You've got yourself so worried about everything that now you're seeing ghosts!"

"I didn't say that I saw something, Andréas. I'm telling you," his father insisted, "I felt something. That was so strange." Then with a worried look on his face, he added: "And, you know, maybe I shouldn't tell you this, but it's not the first time I've felt like there was some kind of presence around here."

By that time, however, Lawson had already left the kitchen and was making his way through the house. Without having heard his father's last remark, he stepped back out onto the veranda and into the warmth of a Mediterranean summer morning.

WHEN SIR MARCUS arrived back at the area near the church, the boys were still playing in the field. It was well after nine, and a handful of tourists were already walking around. Some were gazing out from the ancient seawall across the expanse of the dark blue sea, while others contemplated the imposing wall of the Rock, rising up in a sheer vertical climb of almost a hundred meters behind the houses and buildings of the Lower Town.

Deciding to record some holographic images of young Mark and Dimitrios playing, Lawson took out his dive computer and was cycling through the quick menu trying to find the right application, when he accidentally touched the control for the EDT tracking map. He was about to close it when he suddenly noticed something that shocked him. There on the screen, in a spot on the other side of the field from where the boys were playing, he saw what was unmistakably a Paladin EDT signal.

Quickly looking up, Lawson gazed over at the area where the signal must have been coming from and saw a young man in loose fitting clothing, who appeared to be a typical tourist. He was leaning casually against the seawall and surreptitiously observing Mark and Dimitrios as they played not far away. Suddenly everything became clear to him.

Ever since he was a child, he remembered having experienced the peculiar feeling of some sort of presence nearby—as if someone were watching him. He even recalled having told his mother about it on more than one occasion, but her answer had always been that it was his guardian angel. Little had she realized how close she had been to the truth; for all the while, as it now dawned on him, Paladins from the future must have been there watching over him, assigned to protect him.

At first he wanted to approach the Paladin to find out what his mission was; but realizing that the young man was on an undercover operation, he thought better of it. Still, there were so many questions he would have liked to ask him, if only he could. Was he the only one being guarded, or was it his entire family— and for what reason? Was it simply a routine precaution, or had there been some specific threat to his safety? As a Paladin and a peer, why had this information been kept from him?

Immediately he began reviewing his entire life up until his discovery of temporal translocation. There had certainly been a few instances in his youth in which he had been faced with serious danger, and yet had miraculously been saved. In fact, he had always attributed his embrace of a more spiritual way of life to those events. Now, however, he began to speculate that perhaps there was more to it than that. Perhaps those things were not originally part of his personal history, but were instead connected to the invisible war being waged between Guardians and Trustees in the vast and shifting theatre of time.

Mark Lawson's mind reeled with dozens of questions, but he decided that he would have to wait until he resurfaced to look for the answers. He only had a few more hours in which to enjoy his last dive as a Paladin, and he did not want to waste one precious moment. For now it was enough to take in the sights, sounds and smells of his youth—and once again to be in the presence of those whose memory he cherished, and whom he had once supposed to be forever lost to the inevitable judgment of time.

Thus the Old Man spent the remainder of that day quietly watching over his beloved family—the two boys as they played the endless summer games of their youthful imagination; his mother and aunt and the girls when they returned from their morning out; and his father and uncle as they busied themselves around the house and garden. The day was completely unremarkable in and of itself; and yet it would prove to be one of the best and most memorable of his long and eventful life.

Epilogue

Skiáthos, Greece—Monday, April 26, 1826

It was the most difficult journey he could remember ever having made. If not for his years of ascetical experience and rigorous military training, along with the handful of protein pills he still had left, Lord Admiral Rizopoulos might never have survived it.

Moving slowly in his weakened condition and traveling largely by moonlight, he had trekked through rugged and desolate mountain terrain for five nights after leaving the Egyptian camp. Passing scores of the bodies of escapees from Messolonghi who had died along the way, he had finally arrived on Good Friday morning at the Greek-held fortress town of Salona, or ancient Amfissa.

It was there in the garrison that he finally received succor in the form of a little nourishment and rest; and where on the next night, surrounded by several hundred refugees from the catastrophe that had befallen the Sacred City, he celebrated one of the most somber and poignant Easters he could ever have imagined experiencing.

Grateful though he was for the brief respite, Rizopoulos knew however that he could not stay for long. His mind, heavily burdened with guilt over the terrible deed he had so recently been forced to commit, was already set somewhere else—on another far off mountain wilderness, where he would go to do penance for his actions and strive to find some measure of peace for his troubled soul. That goal was the so-called 'Holy Mountain'—the ancient monastic republic of Mount Athos.

Situated far below the city of Thessaloniki on the easternmost of the three long finger-like projections of the Halkidikí peninsula, and insulated from the world by the clear blue waters of the northern Aegean Sea, the rugged wilderness of Mount Athos had already been home to a large monastic community for a thousand years. Its twenty monasteries, each a small town in its own right, along with their innumerable dependent settlements and desert hermitages, were considered by the Ottoman Empire to be an autonomous region under the authority of what the Turks called the '*rum patriği*'—the Greek Orthodox Ecumenical Patriarch in Constantinople.

Men from all over the Eastern Orthodox world—Greeks, Russians, Romanians, Serbs, Bulgarians, Georgians and countless other nationalities—had gathered there for centuries to pursue a life of inner silence, repentance and dedication to prayer. And it was in just such an atmosphere of spiritual renewal that the Paladin lord admiral hoped to live out the remainder of his days.

Of course, the opportunity to retreat to the Holy Mountain had always existed—even in Rizopoulos's own time—and over the last couple of years he had begun to think about it more often as a possible place of retirement for when the time was right. But the many responsibilities of his office, and the distracting forces of a world steeped in instantaneous telecommunication and endless information, had always eclipsed those thoughts.

Having no reason to believe that going to Athos in his own century would be any different for him now that he had retired from active duty, but would instead be full of temptations to return to his professional life, he had refused to accept the diving bell Vice Admiral Ephraimoglou had brought for him. Indeed, he already knew that having a 'return ticket' in his possession would do nothing but weaken his already fragile resolve.

Thus, after remaining in Amfissa for several days to recover his strength, he set out once again on a long and perilous route through the wild mountain passes of Parnassus, the once sacred home to Apollo, the Muses, and the Corycian nymphs. He then traversed the narrow coastal plain of the Thermopylae—that glorious battleground on which his famed namesake, King Leonidas of ancient Sparta, had fallen—and from there traveled northward along the Gulf of Malía. He finally arrived on the evening of the fifth day near the town of Stylída, where he hoped to find a vessel bound for the province of Halkidikí.

Finding a ship sailing for Mount Athos, however, was not as easy as he had hoped. The local fishing boats in the area were not equipped for a long sea voyage, particularly under wartime conditions and with the Ottoman fleet constantly patrolling the nearby North Evian Gulf. Eventually he had to settle for passage on a small bark headed back to its home port in the nearby Sporades Islands. From there, he was advised by the fishermen, he might find transport to his final destination. Thus, under cover of night, he embarked with them on the five-and-a-half-hour voyage through the duplicitous waters of the Straits of Oreoí and around the headlands of North Evia, to make port on the small island of Skiáthos.

When they finally made landfall in a little harbor on the southeast coast of the island, it was shortly before dawn and the men were famished. As the three fishermen secured the boat, stowed their canvases and offloaded their haul, Rizopoulos went off to gather some driftwood and dry brush in the dim morning twilight. By the time the sailors finished their work, the sky was already light and the Paladin had made a cooking fire and was grilling several fresh fish from their catch on the hot coals.

There they sat and partook of a breakfast of fish, bread and homemade *rakí* wine on the beach. As they ate, Rizopoulos was delighted to notice a pack of wild seals, extinct in his own time, playing in the surf about fifty meters down the shore. Although he was certain they had been attracted by the smell of the grilled fish, he decided to take their presence as a good omen, portending the successful outcome of his journey to the Holy Mountain; for they were of the genus and species *Monachus monachus*—Mediterranean monk seals.

When the men had finally finished their meal, the lord admiral wanted to pay them the fare for his voyage and take his leave. But believing him to be a cleric, they refused to take any money from him and instead demanded only that he bless them. Thus he began the long walk into the main town in the bright rays of the morning sun, to look for a vessel that would take him on the rest of his journey.

Strolling up the shoreline, Rizopoulos marveled at the natural beauty of the island's landscape, with its mass of high imposing hills covered with dense green pine forest forming a steep curtain that skirted along the coast. It was because of those same wooded hills that the island had become an important center for shipbuilding in recent decades, and as he came closer to the main coastal port, he could see the devastating toll the industry had taken on the surrounding woodlands.

Huge tracts of forest nearest the town had been chopped down and cleared, and in many of these areas small settlements had sprung up. As the lord admiral reached the outskirts of the municipality, he could see craftsmen beginning to arrive from their homes, taking up their tools to go to work on the frames of ships and boats of different types and sizes, buttressed on pilings and blocks along the shore.

Making his way along the quay, he asked everyone he met for information about transportation to Mount Athos, but they all gave him the same reply. There had been no ships bound for

Halkidikí or even for Thessaloniki for many weeks due to an increase in Ottoman patrols, and no one knew when the next opportunity might arise.

Instead the townspeople suggested that he bide his time at the local monastery, about five kilometers away at the top of the island, and promised to send for him the next time a vessel heading north called at port. Thus it was that, heeding their advice and making the two-hour hike up the rocky and densely wooded hills of Skiáthos, Lord Admiral Rizopoulos found himself before the gates of the monastery of the Annunciation of the Virgin Mary, the *Moní Evangelístria.*

Founded thirty-two years earlier by a group of Athonite monks, the monastery was situated on a hill about two hundred meters above sea level, at the foot of the island's highest peak. Completed in 1806, it had quickly become an integral part of the fabric of life on Skiáthos. Not only did the monastic community contribute greatly to a spiritual revival on the island, but it also played a significant role—lending both moral and material support—in the national struggle for independence.

For one thing, the islanders claimed that it was there, in the year 1807, that the very first flag of the nascent liberation movement had been made, blessed and raised as a standard. For another thing, the *Moní Evangelístria* had become known among the Greeks as a haven for freedom fighters, where every day thousands of food rations were prepared for the needs of those struggling against the Ottomans, and where the monks also maintained a hospital to minister to sick and injured soldiers.

The needs therefore were great, and the community of monks wasted little time in welcoming the newcomer and putting him to work. They immediately asked him to help with whatever chores had to be done, and in Lord Admiral Rizopoulos they found a willing collaborator.

Although he made it clear from the beginning that his was only a temporary stay, he immediately threw himself wholeheartedly into whatever work they gave him—digging and planting in the monastery's fields and gardens; baking bread in the kitchen and serving in the communal dining hall; helping to tend to the sick and wounded in the hospital; and any number of other tasks assigned to him—with an uncommon zeal. For laboring at each so-called 'obedience', he felt that he was somehow offering a small token of recompense for the grievous decision he had made some weeks before on the muddy plain outside of Messolonghi.

Thus, fully immersed in the life of the community, the Paladin participated in the various church services and nocturnal prayer vigils in prayerful silence, and even went to the saintly old superior to confess his thoughts and feelings, as was the habit of the monks. It was on one of those occasions, when he had already been at the monastery for forty days and was beginning to feel that perhaps it was a place he could remain after all, that the old abbot said something unexpected to him during confession.

"Brother," he said, "you have been coming like this for some time now, but I sense that there is something disturbing your soul that you have not yet confessed. Perhaps it is something you are not yet ready to forgive yourself for; but there is something you should consider."

Taken aback by the abbot's words, Rizopoulos bowed his head in silence and listened to what the old man had to say, replying simply: "May it be blessed, Elder."

"Well then, tell me something first," continued the superior, his shoulders stooped and his eyes dimming with the years. "For what reason did the Lord condescend to die on the Cross?"

For a moment, Lord Admiral Rizopoulos, leader of Paladins and knight of the World Council, felt like a Sunday School catechumen again and was perplexed about what the abbot might be trying to tell him. But then it suddenly dawned on him, and he shook his head at his own foolishness. Answering the old man, he said humbly:

"Elder, it was so that our sins could be forgiven, was it not?"

Abruptly the superior looked upward towards the heavens and stretched out his hands as if in prayer, and Rizopoulos saw his lips move as he made the sign of the cross over himself. Then, turning back to Rizopoulos, he said:

"Brother, think about this. The Lord already forgave the sins of as many as he met even before he was crucified for us, saying: *'Your faith has saved you, go in peace'*, and *'go and sin no more'*. How is it, then, that you say he was crucified so that our sins could be forgiven, when he was already willing and able to forgive sins while yet alive? Do you believe that he really had to die on the Cross in order for our sins to be forgiven?"

Rizopoulos was surprised. For his entire life he had gone to church, prayed and read the Holy Scriptures, but somehow he felt as if he were being told something for the first time. Perhaps it was the way the old superior said it; or maybe it was just that he had never before been as ready, or able, to hear and understand the message as he was now. All he could do was to stare at the old abbot with a look of wonder, waiting for his explanation.

"Have you not yet understood?" the elder asked simply. "The Lord said this: *'Unless the grain of wheat should fall into the earth and die, it abides alone; but if it should die, it bears much fruit.'*

"You see, Brother, he condescended to die on the Cross for our sake in order to show the limitlessness of the divine love for us, and at the same time to carry through to its full conclusion the perfect unity of his human will with his divine will. It was only by doing so that he could restore human nature to its original unity with God, trample down death and raise us up to immortal life through his holy and life-giving Resurrection.

"And what do you suppose would have happened if the disciples had tried to stop it from coming to pass? Do you remember what he said to Peter, when he rebuked him for speaking openly about his upcoming death and Resurrection? The Christ told the one who would become chief of all the Apostles: *'Get behind me! You are an affront to me, because you do not pay attention to the things of God, but to the things of men!'*

"Powerful words—powerful words, indeed. So you see, Brother, some sacrifices are necessary, not because they are a punishment from God, but because from them come a much greater good and the seeds of a glorious rebirth," the old abbot concluded.

Rizopoulos was speechless. His mind raced, wondering if the elder had somehow seen into him and already knew what was in his heart. But at the same time, he felt a warmth and fullness inside, like that which he had experienced in the presence of Elder Aetios so many months before. He had also experienced this sensation many times before when in deep noetic prayer, and the fire burning in his heart told him that the elder's words were full of the spirit of truth.

Before he had a chance to respond, the superior had already placed his stole over Rizopoulos's head and said the prayers of forgiveness over him. The confession being over, the lord admiral was rising from his knees to leave, when the elder suddenly said to him one last thing.

"What do you say, Brother? If the Lord forgives us, who are we to refuse to forgive ourselves? But we cannot say that we forgive ourselves unless we first truly repent—for without real repentance, the forgiveness of men is nothing. Go your way in peace, and sin no more—and may God be with you."

Something in the peculiar finality of the elder's words to him disturbed Rizopoulos; but as he walked outside into the mild evening air and smelled the aromatic fragrance of hyssop and basil wafting from the garden on the light breeze, he began to feel more relaxed and peaceful than he had in what seemed like an eternity. He was just crossing the monastery's courtyard to return to his cell, when suddenly one of the younger monks ran up to him hurriedly from the direction of the main gate and called out:

"Father Leonidas, there you are! Quick! They've come for you from the town below!" he said, panting as he ran. "A ship has come—it's headed north to Thasos, and they're willing to take you to Mount Athos!"

The news was so sudden that Rizopoulos did not know how to react. He had finally begun to feel comfortable at the monastery, and although he had been waiting all this time for just such an opportunity to go to the Holy Mountain, he was now torn between his conviction that something important awaited him there and his genuine affection for the place that had given him so much solace during the past forty days. But then thinking about the elder's last words to him—spoken with such tenderness, yet with such conclusiveness—he realized that in fact it had been the old abbot's way of blessing him for his long journey ahead. It was time for him to go.

JUST AFTER SUNSET on the third day of the voyage, Lord Admiral Rizopoulos stood on the deck of the three-masted cargo schooner, *St. Nicholas*, heading northwards toward the island of Thasos, and was sprinkled by a fine spray of refreshing mist.

The seas had been calm and the winds almost non-existent for much of their journey, but earlier that day they had picked up considerably, allowing them to sail at a good clip. As the vessel rocked gently from side to side, he could see a shoal of dolphins leaping in the waves off the starboard bow as if playfully racing with the ship. Low in the eastern sky, a large and just-risen nearly full moon hung over the horizon, bright and orange in the early evening twilight, portending fine weather on the morrow.

In the distance, perhaps only a couple of hours away, he could already make out the majestic peak of a familiar mountain rising up to a height of over two thousand meters and draped in a mantle of clouds, beckoning to him with its silent and mysterious call—Athos, the Holy Mountain. On seeing it, Leonidas Rizopoulos was filled with a rush of joyful anticipation. It had been a long and hard journey that had finally brought him to this place, and he was looking forward with a curious sense of destiny to whatever was to come next.

In a sense, however, it was strangely ironic.

He had spent the better part of his life in the absolute certainty of what was supposed to happen, and had dedicated himself to making sure that everything proceeded along a prescribed and preordained path, with as little change as possible. Thus it was for the first time in as long as he could remember that he felt he was truly stepping into the unknown.

Perhaps that in itself, he pondered, as he felt the gentle swaying of the sea below him being translated through the creaking timbers of the ship, was worth more than he had ever before realized. But just as with everything else in life, whether or not that was true would only be answered by the ebb and the flow of the shifting and unsteady waves of the fathomless ocean of time.

END OF BOOK II

GLOSSARY

This glossary is provided solely for the convenience of those readers who may not be familiar with some of the less common foreign language terms and/or the acronyms employed within the context of this book. Wherever possible, an attempt has been made to highlight at least the first occurrence of these terms with italics, and in certain cases the terms have been italicized throughout the story. Some of the more common foreign terms, or those less common terms which have already been explained explicitly within the text, are not included. The spelling, transliteration and explanation of the words and phrases that follow are solely those of the author, and they should not be relied upon for any other purpose.

Arschloch—(German) Literally "asshole".

bey—(Turkish) An honorific title applied to a man, it is usually appended to the first name, and is roughly the equivalent of 'Mister' or 'Sir'.

bouzouki—(Greek) A type of stringed instrument similar to a mandolin or lute, it also gives its name to the lively Greek popular music that features it. It is usually at its best during the small hours of the morning and accompanied by festive dancing and drinking.

briki—(Greek) A deep and long-handled vessel, traditionally but not necessarily made from copper, brass or ceramic, used to boil coffee.

brûlotier—(French; pl. *brûlotiers*) A term referring to the pilot of a 'fire-boat'—a type of large, usually heavy and slow-moving barge laden with flammable and/or explosive materials, which would be piloted into the midst of an enemy naval fleet's line and set alight. Usually the pilot would attempt to attach the fire-boat to an enemy vessel using grappling hooks and lines so as to sideline any number of additional enemy vessels, which would then be obliged to conduct rescue operations to save the crew of the entangled ship. Once the fire-boat was ignited, the *brûlotiers* would attempt to flee in small, quick escape boats. The use of these types of boats was particularly effective during the earlier stages of the Greek War of Independence against the Ottoman Empire.

chevaux de frise—(Military) Literally 'Frisian horses', they are portable wooden fencing barriers, incorporating sharp spikes, iron pikes or spears into their design. The points project upwards and outwards, creating a formidable barrier against enemy cavalry and infantry charges. *Chevaux de frise* were used extensively in medieval European warfare, generally up until the invention and widespread use of barbed wire at the end of the nineteenth century.

coup de grâce—(French) A blow that finishes off one's opponent; a deathblow.

"crackers and cheese"—Although not a traditional Cockney expression in itself, this phrase is used in the prologue to *The Sacred City* as a literary device that references 'rhyming slang' similar to that used by Cockneys. Its meaning in the story line is "weak in the knees"—i.e. an indication of a saddened or distraught emotional state.

"D'accord"—(French) Literally "Agreed".

demitasse—(French) Literally a "half-cup", it is a small cup, usually made of China porcelain, used for drinking espresso or other forms of strong coffee.

EDT—In the *Guardian Series*, it is an 'electronic dog-tag'—a radio-frequency transponder implanted in a Paladin for identification and location tracking purposes. It is composed of an inert nano-material that is invisible to most types of electromagnetic radiation, but which absorbs and remits certain encrypted Paladin frequencies in a so-called 'friendly challenge and response' procedure.

effendi—(Turkish) A title of respect equivalent to 'Mister' or 'Sir'.

evzonos—(Greek) Deriving from the words for 'well girded', it is a term that has been used since ancient times to describe light infantry units. During the Ottoman period, and in particular during the Greek War of Independence against the Ottoman Empire, the *Evzones* were elite light infantry or cavalry units, comprised of the strongest and bravest fighters. Commonly known as *'tsoliades'* and wearing the characteristic *fustanella* and other traditional nineteenth-century garments, today's *Evzones* are an elite Special Forces corps of the Greek Army, which is deployed as the Presidential Guard.

fascines—(Military) Bundles of wooden sticks or similar materials thrown into trenches or moats and used as temporary (and often disposable) bridges. In modern warfare, *fascines* are often carried on tanks or armored vehicles, with the traditional wooden sticks being replaced by PVC pipe or plastic materials.

first peer (or **first-among-peers**)—In the *Guardian Series*, it is the title held by the ceremonial head of the Guardians' leadership committee, the 'Council of Peers'. See 'peer' below.

florin—The main currency unit of the Austro-Hungarian Empire.

fustanella—(Greek) A white kilt-like tunic worn by men as part of traditional folk costumes in various parts of Greece since antiquity. In more recent centuries, a version of it containing four hundred pleats—said to be one for each year of the Ottoman occupation—was especially worn by partisan fighters.

GPSSI—An acronym for 'Global Positioning Satellite Simulator Interface', it is an application in a Paladin dive computer which uses altimetric, geodesic and astronometric measurements to pinpoint the user's location on a preloaded map. It thus serves as a virtual GPS device for divers operating at depths below that of the earliest functioning GPS satellite networks. In Paladin jargon, it is commonly referred to as a 'gypsy map'.

hara-kiri—(Japanese) Literally "cutting the belly", it is a form of ritual suicide involving disembowelment with a knife, performed in such as way as to strike vital organs.

hookah—A water-filtered pipe with a long flexible hose and mouthpiece, used in the Ottoman Empire for smoking tobacco, or other drugs such as hashish or opium.

iCig—In *The Sacred City* story line, it is a smokeless, nicotine-free infrasonic cigarette. The iCig is designed in such a way that, when air is drawn through it, localized ultra-low-frequency sound waves are produced in a range which is inaudible to the human ear, but which stimulates *alpha*-type brain wave activity. The result is a distinctly mellowing effect on the iCig 'smoker'.

janissary—(Turkish) At one time forming an elite military/imperial-guard division within the Ottoman army, the *Janissaries* were comprised of Christian men who had been taken from their families as small children, forcibly converted to Islam, and raised as soldiers. By the mid- to late-nineteenth century, they had become such a powerful force within the Ottoman military-political establishment that they represented a threat to the *sultan* himself. After an attempted coup, the institution of the *Janissaries* was finally eradicated in a violent purge by Sultan Mahmud II in 1826.

Kapadokya—(Turkish) The Turkish name for the famed ancient region of Cappadocia in Asia Minor.

Karaiskakis—George Karaiskakis (1780-1827) was a famous Greek *klepht*, military commander and hero of the Greek War of Independence against the Ottoman Empire.

__Kathará Deftera__—(Greek) Literally "Clean Monday", it is the first day of the Eastern Orthodox Great Lent, which commences roughly seven weeks of strict fasting before 'Pascha' (Easter).

__kilij__—(Turkish) Literally a "sword" (*kılıç* in Turkish), it is the traditional curved Turkish scimitar.

__klepht__—(Greek) Literally a 'thief' or 'bandit', these were armed brigands who often specialized in attacking and harassing Turkish towns, troops and military outposts during the Ottoman occupation in Greece. After the outbreak of the Greek war of national independence, many *klepht* leaders became officers in the revolutionary militia.

__Kolokotronis__—Theodoros Kolokotronis (1770-1843) was a famous Greek *klepht*, military commander and hero of the Greek War of Independence against the Ottoman Empire.

__mahaira__—(Greek) Literally a "sword" or "knife", it is a type of sword used for close combat in the Graeco-Roman world from antiquity. In the nineteenth-century Greek War of Independence against the Ottoman Empire, the term referred to a short-sword of a length somewhere between that of a *yataghan* and a dagger.

__Malvasian__—An adjective referring to Monemvasia.

__"Mon Dieu!"__—(French) Literally "My God!".

__monoxylon__—(Greek, pl. *monoxyla*) A type of dugout canoe used since antiquity, its name derives from the words for 'single tree'.

__n'shallah__—(Arabic) A common Arabic phrase which means roughly, 'God willing!'.

__nous__—(Greek) In Eastern Orthodox Christian theological tradition, it is the rational or intellectual part of the soul, which is sometimes described as the 'eye of the soul'.

__old-calendar__—Refers to the ancient Julian calendar used in western civilization from the time of the Roman Empire. It was replaced for civic use by the updated Gregorian calendar (still the calendar commonly in international use today), being adopted by most countries at different times between the early nineteenth century and the early part of the twentieth century.

Palais du Monde—Literally "Palace of the World", in the *Guardian Series* it is the global headquarters of the 'World Council', inherited from the defunct United Nations organization. The building complex itself was originally called the '*Palais de la Paix*' (the 'Palace of Peace') and was the headquarters of the League of Nations. It was bequeathed to that organization's successor entity, the United Nations, in 1946.

pallikari—(Greek) Literally a "brave young man", they were revolutionary militiamen and guerilla fighters during the Greek War of Independence against the Ottoman Empire. In modern colloquial Greek, the term is generally used to describe any handsome young man.

Papaflessas—Gregorios Papaflessas (1788-1825) was a Greek Orthodox priest and hero of the Greek War of Independence against the Ottoman Empire. He was also a government official, serving as Minister of Internal Affairs and Chief of Police in the Greek provisional government. He was killed in the Battle of Maniaki in Messina, fighting against the forces of the Ottoman military commander Ibrahim Pasha.

pasha—(Turkish) A title of high rank in the Ottoman Empire, usually denoting a governor of a territory, a general or another high-ranking dignitary. It was roughly equivalent to the English political title 'Lord'.

peer—In the *Guardian Series*, it is a high-ranking title, roughly equivalent to that of a senator, held by members of the Guardians' political leadership committee, the 'Council of Peers'. In the story line, there are twelve active peers at any one time, six of whom are Paladins and six of whom are political appointees representing the Guardian side of the organization. The peers have equal status and voting power within the Council of Peers, although one of the members is designated as the 'first peer' (or 'first-among-peers')—a role roughly equivalent to that of president of the senate—for procedural purposes.

petasos—(Greek) A floppy wide-brimmed hat worn by farmers and travelers in the Graeco-Roman world since antiquity, it was the type of hat also worn by the ancient Greek god *Hermes* (Roman *Mercury*), the guardian of travelers.

philhellene—(Greek) Literally a 'lover of Greece' in general, this term was also specifically applied to the citizens of many foreign countries who came to assist the Greeks in their war of national independence against the Ottoman Empire.

piaster—The main currency unit of the Ottoman Empire.

pinnace—A class of smaller sailing vessels used from the seventeenth through the nineteenth centuries, these craft were light and relatively fast, and often had relatively shallow draughts. For this reason, they were sometimes favored as merchant or pirate ships in their own right, although they were mainly employed as tenders to larger merchant vessels and warships.

Portello—(Italian) Literally 'small door', it is a narrow entrance gate built into the seawall on the southern side of Monemvasia, which opens out onto a small stone jetty.

raki—(Greek) A strong distilled alcoholic beverage consumed as a digestive and produced from the fermented stems and seeds of grapes. It is similar to Italian *grappa*.

roumeli vasely—(Graeco-Turkish) A title given to the *pasha* in charge of the Ottoman province of 'Roumelia', or central Greece. The word *roumeli* refers to the term *romaioi* by which the medieval Greeks described themselves, and the word *vasely* derives from the Greek word for 'king'.

rum patriği—(Turkish) Literally "Roman Patriarch", it is the Turkish language term for the Greek Orthodox Christian

Ecumenical Patriarch. Referring to the Eastern Roman (Byzantine) Empire, the term 'Roman' (*rum* in Turkish) was employed by the Greeks to describe themselves from the early Christian era until modern times, and its use was subsequently inherited by the Turks from the time of the Ottoman conquest.

"S'il vous plaît, messieurs"—(French) "If you please, sirs".

SHIELD—An acronym for 'Stimulated High Intensity Electromagnetic Light Displacement', it is a portable cloaking device which renders users practically invisible and inaudible to anyone outside of the electromagnetic field's range.

sigillum—(Latin) A sign, emblem or seal.

swietenia—A genus of trees in the *Meliaceae* family, which includes the *Swietenia mahagoni*, or 'West Indian Mahogany'. Named after eighteenth-century Dutch-Austrian physician Gerard van Swieten, it is the tree from which mahogany wood was produced.

tsipouro—(Greek) A strong distilled alcoholic beverage produced from the fermented stems and seeds of grapes left over from the wine pressing process. Typically produced in the Thessaly, Epirus, Macedonia, Mani and Crete regions of Greece (though also elsewhere), it is said to have first been made by Greek Orthodox monks on Mount Athos as early as the fourteenth century.

Türkiye—(Turkish) Literally "Turkey".

Wali—(Arabic) An honorific title for a ruler of an Arab territory in the Ottoman imperial political structure. It was roughly equivalent to a governor, and was usually a title conferred upon a *pasha* in charge of a country, e.g. Ottoman Egypt.

yataghan—(Turkish) A type of curved sword of roughly sixty to eighty centimeters in length, commonly used in Turkey, Greece and other areas of the Balkans during the Ottoman Empire. The butt of the hilt was usually flared out in two directions, forming a 'Y-' or a 'T-' shape, and the blade was often 're-curved'.

ACKNOWLEDGMENTS

While a work of fiction, this novel and its prequel depict certain events and personages which are based on historical fact. This is particularly true with respect to the circumstances surrounding the Greek war of national independence against the Ottoman Empire in the first half of the nineteenth century, and certain key actors in that struggle.

In this regard, a debt of thanks is owed to a number of sources that were of invaluable assistance in my research. Among them, none were more instrumental than the riveting firsthand accounts and memoirs of that war, written in the next-to-last century by Messrs. *Thomas Gordon* of Great Britain and *Spyridon Trikoupis* of Greece. Similarly, the works of *George Finlay*, *Sir William Gell*, *Edward Blaquiere* and several others from the same time period, in both English and Greek, were also helpful. For access to many of these sources, I am indebted to *Google* for its *Google Book Search* online digital archive, which offers a treasure trove of material for any researcher or writer delving into historical matters.

As anyone who has undertaken a research project can attest—and nowhere is this truer than in regard to history—not all facts are equal. Therefore it must also be emphasized that, while striving to remain true to a spirit of historical authenticity, the author has taken certain liberties in regard to some of the actual events and characters portrayed in the story, either due to a lack of readily available documentation, or purely for dramatic purposes. In either case, I fully accept that there may be errors or omissions, either in fact or in interpretation, and I beg the reader's indulgence in regard to any that may be found.

In addition to the above, many of the more 'philosophical' elements of the book—i.e. the interpretations and implications of the historical events described, the suggested motives of some of the historical characters, and the theological and ethical arguments—are informed by the various opinions and/or the simple musings of the author. Some of these ideas have been created solely for dramatic purposes within the context of this work, and should be regarded as such. Some have not. I will leave it to the reader to decide which is which.

If the above is true in regard to the historical aspects of the book, it applies even more so to a few key scientific and technological elements incorporated into the novel. They are, generally speaking, a combination of fact and fiction, with a liberal dose of artistic license thrown in for good measure. In a few instances they are the result of an extrapolation or extension of a concept or a technology that is being researched and experimented with at the present time. In other instances they are outright fantasy, or even well-known and oft-repeated science fiction themes, with no known basis in actual technological potential. I trust the reader will overlook these latter inventions, which are mere vehicles for the development of what the author hopes is a grander vision, and enjoy the story nonetheless.

This acknowledgment would in no wise be complete without my wholehearted recognition of, and thanks to, several people who read the manuscript in its various draft stages and provided much needed feedback, criticism, suggestions, research assistance, edits or simple encouragement. They are, first and foremost: Effie Robinson and Nina Robinson; Lauren Ugorji and Scott Brown-Pempeit; Maria Toscas-Zissimos and Peter Toscas. Most probably to the great detriment of this book, not every word of their advice was always heeded—but it was usually carefully considered and always greatly appreciated. The value of a kind word and a thoughtful comment should never be underestimated.

In the digital age in which we live, I do not think it out of place to give mention to certain sources which were of immense help to me in my research on a number of fronts—from elaborating on the descriptions and historical context of places, to understanding military and technological jargon, terminology and principles. Among these sources—although they were by no means the only ones—were *Wikipedia* and *Google Earth*, and I feel it would be remiss of me not to thank the people behind them for the great convenience those services afforded me.

As a final technical note, the reader will notice (in Chapters 13 and Chapter 14) a few actual quotations from historical sources, including the then-widely disseminated letter from Swiss philhellene J.J. Mayer, which are marked by asterisks. While certain of these have been published in recent reprints of historical material, they are widely available from a number of historical sources in both English and Greek, as well as in various editions in several other languages, and may thus be considered to exist in the public domain.

ABOUT THE AUTHOR

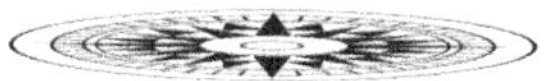

DAMIAN LAWRENCE is a graduate of Harvard University, with a bachelor's degree in Chemistry. He also holds a master's degree from the School of Advanced International Studies of the Johns Hopkins University, where he concentrated in the field of Social Change and Development. Damian has worked in fields as diverse as government, biomedical research and the financial services industry, and has traveled extensively around the world. He currently lives in Greece with his wife and son. *The Sacred City* is his second novel.

Made in the USA
Monee, IL
07 July 2026